The
Invisible
Dead

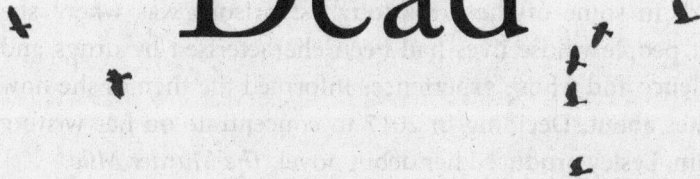

Lesley McEvoy was born and bred in Yorkshire and has had a passion for writing in one form or another all her life. The writing took a backseat as Lesley developed her career as a Behavioural Analyst / Profiler and Psychotherapist – setting up her own consultancy business and therapy practice. She has written and presented extensively around the world for over 25 years specialising in behavioural profiling and training, with a wide variety of organisations. The corporate world provided unexpected sources of writing material when, as Lesley said, she found more psychopaths in business than in prison! Lesley's work in some of the UK's toughest prisons was where she met people whose lives had been characterised by drugs and violence and whose experiences informed the themes she now writes about. Deciding in 2017 to concentrate on her writing again, Lesley produced her debut novel, *The Murder Mile*.

These days she lives in Cheshire with her partner but still manages to lure her two grown-up sons across the Pennines with her other passion – cooking family dinners.

Also by Lesley McEvoy

The Murder Mile
The Killing Song
A Deadly Likeness

Lesley McEvoy

The Invisible Dead

ZAFFRE

First published in the UK in 2024 by
ZAFFRE
An imprint of Zaffre Publishing Group
A Bonnier Books UK Company
4th Floor, Victoria House, Bloomsbury Square, London, WC1B 4DA
Owned by Bonnier Books
Sveavägen 56, Stockholm, Sweden

A CIP catalogue record for this book is
available from the British Library.

ISBN: 9-781-80418-478-3

Also available as an ebook and an audiobook

1 3 5 7 9 10 8 6 4 2

Typeset by IDSUK (Data Connection) Ltd
Printed and bound in Great Britain by Clays Ltd, Elcograf S.p.A.

MIX
Paper | Supporting
responsible forestry
FSC® C018072

Zaffre is an imprint of Zaffre Publishing Group
A Bonnier Books UK company
www.bonnierbooks.co.uk

For Leah, who lights up my world.

Prologue

I'm dying.

Oh God – this is how it's going to end.

The wind whips long hair around my face as I fall backwards. Fatal gravity pulling me down.

Alex – my son. I'm so sorry.

Why did I do it?

I know why, as I look at the shocked face staring over the edge of the roof parapet. The expression of utter horror. Watching me fall. Helpless to stop it. Mouth open, screaming something. Last words I can't hear through the wind whistling past my ears. The thundering of my heartbeat.

I see them reaching out towards me. Futile now as I'm dropping fast.

I did it for them.

So much to say.

Too late now.

I brace myself for the ground.

The last time I'll touch the earth.

Chapter One

Fordley, West Yorkshire – Monday morning

The insistent scream of an alarm was coming from somewhere inside the Fordley DAAT.

The community Drug and Alcohol Action Team building, was situated in a converted warehouse on the edge of town. Far enough from Nimbys, who'd paid eye-watering prices to enjoy a trendy urban lifestyle and objected to drug users on their doorstep, but close enough to be accessible to the DAAT client base.

Arriving early for my meeting, the car park was empty as I locked my Roadster and ran through the double doors into reception.

The siren was louder in here – pulsing against my ribcage.

I dumped my briefcase on the counter as Tess Bailey, the receptionist, bolted out of the office.

'Jo. Am I glad to see you,' she shouted above the din.

'What's going on?' I yelled.

'Client,' she yelled back, pushing her dark fringe out of her eyes. 'Up on the bloody roof . . . threatening to jump!'

'Who?'

'Pip Holden.' She was already pulling the case file from that day's appointments. 'One of Rina's.'

Rina Graham was a newly qualified counsellor, my mentee and the person I was here to meet.

'Rina's on her way in.' Tess pre-empted my next question.

'Where is everyone?' The log was on the counter. I turned it around so I could see today's entries.

'I got here first. Pip was waiting outside. I let her in, then went to make us a brew. That's when she must have gone up there.' I could hear the guilt in her voice.

'And the alarm?'

Tess looked on the edge of panic – unusual for her. Working in the third sector with the addicted and homeless, there wasn't much she hadn't seen in her twenty-nine years.

'Went through the fire door to the roof – set the security alarm off.'

'Anyone with her?'

'Pat Rodgers.'

That's when I understood the panic in those pale blue eyes.

'Shit!'

I ran to the stairs, sensing Tess at my shoulder as she tried to keep up.

Tess was the first person I'd met when the DAAT opened its doors several years before. I'd been Clinical Director at Fordley Psychiatric Hospital back then, before I'd become a freelance consultant. Tess had a no-nonsense competence, blended with empathy and compassion for the clients, which meant we'd hit it off straight away. And she was amused by my legendary direct-ness, rather than offended by it – which was a happy bonus.

'Talk to me.'

'Pip Holden,' She panted behind me. 'Twenty years old. Single mum to four-year-old Maisie.'

A little girl with blonde pigtails. I'd seen her playing in the day room a few weeks before.

'Previous cocaine and alcohol use,' Tess was saying. 'Referred under a multi-agency care plan.'

'How long's she been with us?'

'Eight months.' Tess's voice was ragged as she slowed down. I waited as she came up the last flight.

'Family?'

3

'None. Been clean for over a year. Responded well to therapy sessions . . . attendance at parenting classes. Social services happy with her. Doug was going to sign her off today.'

'So why this?'

'No idea – she hasn't said anything, apart from that she's going to jump.'

Doug was a senior therapist and Rina's supervisor. He'd handed the file to Rina for the final few sessions – let her fly solo on what should have been an easy case.

At the top of the flight, magnolia paint gave way to cinder block walls and overhead ducting.

A breath of cool air touched my face. Pat Rodgers, the charity's office manager was standing with her back to us at a half-open steel door that led onto the roof.

She was petite with short blonde hair, shaved at the neck with an absurd purple-tinted fringe. She probably hoped it looked trendy, but missed the mark, looking ridiculous instead. Dressed in her usual businesslike grey skirt suit, her sensible shoe propped the door open as she spoke around its edge.

'Come on now, Phillipa.' She had the tone of a headmistress in a girls' school. 'This silliness has gone on long enough . . .'

A muffled voice came from beyond the door – too distant for me to make out the words. 'I've called the police, Phillipa.' Pat's tone became firmer.

'*Fuck off*!' The words, screamed this time – loud and clear.

My boots scraped against the concrete steps as I cleared the distance.

'Who let you up here, McCready?' Pat hissed over her shoulder.

I put my arm out to hold the door – not quite edging her out of the way – but close enough.

She glared at me. 'I've called the police—'

'I heard.' I nodded towards the roof. 'Hasn't persuaded her to come inside though, has it? Why don't I give it a try?'

4

She slipped her foot further into the doorway – her expression fixed.

'*I'm* office manager.' She flashed the words like a badge. 'I'll take care of it.'

She turned to call out again but I put my shoulder in the way – wedging myself between her and the opening.

'Why don't you go do something you're *actually* qualified for?' I indicated downstairs with a nod of my head. 'Like turning that bloody alarm off – it's making my ears bleed.'

I glanced through the gap, trying to see Pip, but she was just out of sight. 'It can't be doing much for *her* stress levels either.'

'Now look here, McCready—' The use of my surname compounded as she put her hand on my arm.

I flashed her a look – she pulled her hand away as if she'd been scalded.

'Get the alarm,' I said quietly – my eyes conveying a silent warning.

Her mouth opened, then clammed shut. She turned on her heel. 'You—' she snapped at Tess. 'Come with me.'

'Tess stays,' I said. 'I need her here.'

Blotchy red patches stained the woman's cheeks. She made a strangled noise as she pushed past Tess.

We listened to the footsteps echoing down the stairwell.

'I'll pay for that one,' Tess said quietly.

'Trust me, you won't.'

I peered around the edge of the door.

A small figure was sitting on the raised parapet. Like an Antony Gormley sculpture staring blindly across her own private horizon – lost to inner torment only she could see.

I reached for the file Tess was holding, clutched to her chest. 'Got a pen?'

Tess knew the girl – I didn't. Better for Pip to speak to someone she trusted, but I needed to get her agreement to speak to *me*. I wasn't about to wade in to this without a 'soft' introduction.

I scribbled a hasty note on the inside cover of the file and held it up, watching Tess as she quickly scanned it.

'You OK with that?' Her eyes met mine and she gave me a quick nod, her teeth catching her bottom lip.

I put my hand on her shoulder and squeezed it reassuringly, using my other hand to pull the door open a little more and moved her into the gap.

She glanced again at my note, then taking a shaky breath, read what I'd written.

'Pip . . . it's Tess. I want to help, love.'

'I'm not talking to that stuck-up bitch!' Pip shouted back.

'It's OK, Pip . . . Rodgers is gone.'

'She called the police, Tess. If they come up here . . . I swear I'll jump.'

'Please don't . . .' Instinctively Tess tried to step forward. I put a gently restraining hand on her shoulder. 'I . . . I've got to go downstairs for a minute, Pip . . . but I've got my friend, Jo McCready, here. Will you just let her stay with you while I'm gone?'

No response.

'I won't be long. Jo's just going to sit with you . . . OK?'

'OK.' The words were quiet – almost snatched away by the breeze.

Good enough.

That's what success looked like in these situations. Incremental agreements to the smallest things – hard won and easily lost.

'Keep Rodgers occupied,' I whispered. 'Ordering paperclips or something. Then make us that brew.'

'What?'

'Two cups please, love,' I smiled.

She stared at me for a minute, then simply nodded.

I listened to the receding footsteps.

The alarm suddenly snapped off – the residual echo, ringing in my ears for a moment, until silence reclaimed the space.

Taking a long, steadying breath I stepped out onto the roof.

Chapter Two

I stood by the door, careful not to make any sudden movements.

Pip sat, shoulders hunched, her feet dangling over the edge like a kid at the side of a swimming pool, gazing down into unfathomably deep water. Her shoulder-length brown hair hanging like a curtain, obscuring her face.

The white gravel on the roof reflected the thin warmth of early morning sunshine and I took a lungful of the air – clean up here above the city.

I could almost have enjoyed the moment, if it wasn't for the circumstances.

I hunkered down – resting my back against the wall by the door, concentrating on the almost imperceptible rise and fall of Pip's shoulders. Calibrating her breathing. It was erratic. Hardly surprising.

'Peaceful up here, isn't it?' I said quietly.

No response.

'At least that bloody alarm's stopped.' My eyes never left her. Looking for any tension in her body. Any telltale signs that she was going to lean forward and roll out into the void.

'Tess is really worried about you.'

Nothing.

I was looking for a hook into her psyche. A foothold that I could leverage to get her to engage with me, about anything. The view . . . the weather . . . better still – what had brought her up here onto this ledge?

We all know this precipice. The perilous confluence of physical and emotional exhaustion. A place where relationships are broken and trust is illusive. That place where we feel alone and in despair. I'd been there myself – knew it all too well.

Unfortunately, some people are driven beyond that figurative ledge and onto a real one.

This was all about keeping the dialogue going. Saying something – anything to get her to speak.

But sometimes people didn't speak. Not for hours.

Sometimes never.

Instead, they took their pain and their reasons with them. Depriving those who cared about them of answers.

For some, there was a point at which no amount of logic or reason could penetrate the pain, or scream loud enough for them to hear. The aim was getting to them before they reached that point.

Soft white clouds drifted through a pale blue sky – pushed along on the warm air. It was shaping up to be a beautiful July day.

A seagull glided close, hovering over us for just a moment. Then, as if sensing the tension, he tipped his wings and drifted below the edge of the roof and out of sight.

I watched the young girl, wondering what she was thinking – what was playing out inside her head. Whatever it was, I needed to see it too. Get inside that achingly painful space between hope and hopelessness. Catch hold of the frail thread, that is sometimes all that separates the living from the dead.

The distance between us was about ten paces to where she sat – ahead and just to my right.

How long to clear that distance?

Too long.

I shifted my position slightly.

'Mind if I move?'

No answer.

'I have a bad leg – can't stay crouched down for very long.'

That wasn't a lie.

A stab wound to my left thigh, years before, had severed the femoral artery. If it hadn't been for the quick thinking of DCI Callum Ferguson – the senior investigating officer I'd been working with at the time, I could have lost my life – or the leg. As it was, I kept both – along with a constant ache and an occasional limp if I overworked my leg.

'Just stretching . . . going to walk over here a bit, OK?'

Her head tilted imperceptibly – glancing at me through the curtain of hair.

'Don't come near me,' she said.

I walked slowly to the parapet, about fifteen feet to her left and put one foot on the edge – leaning to peer over.

A broken window cleaner's cradle hung at a drunken angle three floors below – tethered to the building by just one high-tension cable, which creaked softly as the platform rocked in the breeze.

I could sense her watching me.

I rested my arms on my bent knee and leaned over a bit more. 'Long way down.'

She shifted slightly – her full attention on me now.

'Tess said she was making you a brew, when you came up here. That's always my first stop . . . kitchen – make a cuppa.' I glanced across to her and smiled. 'Sets me up for the morning . . . not today though.'

'Sorry,' she said quietly.

In one movement, I dropped down – sitting on the ledge – my legs swinging out into empty air.

She gasped and her hand instinctively shot out towards me.

Good sign. Concern for someone else.

I pretended not to have noticed. Keeping my eyes straight ahead – fixed on the city skyline.

I was trying to decide on my next line, when she shifted, tilting her head as she studied me. Hooking the hair behind her ear.

9

'You don't work here, do you?'

I shook my head, but said nothing – still taking in the view. I'd learned long ago, that the most powerful prompt was often a silent one.

'You don't look like a therapist,' she said finally.

'What *do* I look like?'

Her eyes did a quick scan. Taking in the blue jeans – high-heeled boots and leather jacket.

'A cop?'

'No. Forensic Psychologist, as it goes.'

Pip glanced quickly over her shoulder, towards the door.

'Did that cow send you up here?' she snapped – the friendly tone evaporating.

'No,' I said quickly, to reassure her. 'I have as little to do with Pat Rodgers as possible.'

Common ground. Find rapport.

Pip sucked through her teeth. 'Hate that bloody woman. Treats me like shit on her shoes.'

I shifted on the parapet – moving imperceptibly closer.

'Don't take it personally, she's like that with everyone. Has a bowl of bitchiness for breakfast every morning.'

I turned to see her studying me, like a wounded bird warily watching a cat.

'So, can I ask, what you're doing up here, Pip?'

The million-dollar question that headlined this unwritten contract between us. The one that would let me know where her head really was.

She raised her eyebrows. 'What the fuck d'you *think*?'

I shrugged. 'Can't assume this is what it looks like. I mean . . . you *might* just be here to admire the view . . . or clear your head.' I shrugged again. 'Lots of reasons.'

Surprisingly, people could come this far without thinking too deeply about the actual act of dying.

10

I looked into her eyes and asked again – with no ambiguity this time. That's how it had to be. Asked and answered – twice, so that we both knew exactly what this was.

No euphemisms like, 'hurting yourself', or even worse, 'doing anything silly'. Just plain, straight out, calling it what it was.

'Are you thinking of killing yourself, Pip?' My tone was gentle, non-judgemental – the words floating across the space between us.

She turned her face away from me and looked out over the abyss.

The silence strained between us like a fine wire – taut – resonant.

It was a silence I had to sit with. Painfully long and achingly heavy. A necessary silence.

I waited.

When her words finally came, they were so quiet – breathed rather than whispered, that I had to strain to hear. 'Is it a sin?'

I took a long breath. 'Do you believe in God?' Not an answer, but a safe reply.

She shrugged lightly. 'They say it's a sin – don't they?'

'Do *you* think that?'

'My mum took me to church when I was little. So, you know . . .'

'Me too. Irish Catholics my lot.'

'Went to church this morning, after I dropped Maisie at nursery. First time for years. Thought it might help.'

'Did it . . . ? Help?'

Another shrug. 'Wanted to ask if I'd go to hell. But didn't want anyone to stop me. So, just confessed it all. Did an act of contrition . . . so if I do . . . you know, go there . . .'

'Confessed what?'

'How I've messed everything up. Let everyone down. Maisie . . . Rina, Doug. Everyone.' Her head dropped.

'Want to tell me about it? Maybe I can help.'

'No one can help – it's over.'

11

I looked out across Fordley, starting an everyday morning. People going about their business, blissfully unaware of the drama unfolding above their heads.

The commute was building up on the black ribbon of the M62, visible in the distance. The low hum of traffic carried to us on the warming air.

'Everything can be fixed, Pip. But sometimes, when you're in the middle of it, it's hard to see. Sharing it with someone can help find a way through. And there is always a way through.'

She sniffed, her hand lifting to rub her nose – coming away wet with tears.

'Problems are never forever. They feel it, sometimes. But they're not . . . trust me.'

In peripheral vision, I saw the door from the stairwell being nudged open. Tess appeared, clutching two mugs of tea. She stood awkwardly, unsure what to do.

'Tess has brought our tea. Fancy it?'

'You can, but I'm not moving.'

I stood up, stepping back onto the roof. 'I'll get them.' I smiled. 'Just don't go anywhere . . . OK?'

The crunching of gravel under my boots sounded deafening as I went over to Tess. Her eyes looked warily over to Pip.

'Police are here . . . so's the ambulance. They've cordoned off the street,' she whispered as I took the cups. 'There's a cop on the landing back there. What do you want me to do?'

'Stay by the door with him – but make sure she can't see you.' I spoke under my breath. 'If this looks like it's going tits up, I'll need him ready to move.'

I carried the mugs back. Sitting down, slightly closer than before . . . but far enough away that it didn't spook her.

'What were you whispering about.' Pip asked.

'I was telling Tess not to panic . . . she's worried because she cares about you.'

I reached over – putting her cup as close to her as I could stretch.

Two arm's lengths away. Still not close enough.

'No one cares . . .' she said quietly.

'I do . . .'

'You don't know me.'

'I know enough.' I watched as she gazed into the empty space beneath her feet. 'I know you've been through a lot and survived it – that you've got yourself clean. That Doug and Rina are really proud of everything you've achieved. That you're building a new life—'

'Some life,' she snorted. 'Not worth living.'

Time to throw that hook.

'What about Maisie?'

Her shoulders lifted as she took a heavy breath.

'They're going to take her away – so what's the point?' She looked at me, tears streaming down her face.

'Who's taking her away?'

If there'd been anything in the file about Pip losing custody, Tess would have told me.

No reply.

'You're an amazing mum. Maisie is well looked after and *so* loved.'

'She's better off without me.'

'That's *not* true. She adores you. You're her mum. No one could replace you in her life.'

'I want it to end,' was all she said.

I made a show of leaning out to look down.

'Going over the edge is permanent . . . but the problem isn't. Whatever it is, we can work it out.' I looked at her. 'Is it *really* your life you want to end? Or just the pain?'

'The pain . . .' A whisper I could barely hear. 'Of watching it all go to rat-shit. Losing what I've worked so hard for . . . everything.'

'I can only imagine how you must be feeling right now, but you're not alone. There are lots of people who care about you. Who will help with whatever this is. It won't always feel like this, Pip. It'll pass . . . things *will* change . . . but not if you go off the roof.'

'If they take Maisie . . . I might as well.'

'Who's taking her away?'

'The social.'

'I don't think so.' I shifted again, as if to ease my leg – inching slightly closer. 'Doug was arranging to sign you off today.'

'They *will* take her.' She dragged her sleeve across her nose and sniffed back more tears. 'Once they know.' She shook her head. 'I can't face it . . .'

'Once they know what?' I prompted, gently.

'That he's back.' As if that explained everything.

'Who?'

'Bri . . . Brian Curtis, Maisie's dad.'

I took a sip of tea and stared out over the city.

'And he's bad news?' I hazarded a not-so-wild guess.

Pip nodded.

'Drugs?' Another educated guess.

Another nod.

I rode the silence – waiting for the story I'd heard all too often. The almost predictable litany of events that had brought Pip into the DAAT. An unhealthy relationship with a man who was an addict and had probably introduced his girlfriend to drugs.

'Was fifteen when I met him.' She spoke quietly. 'He was twenty-two. My dad went mad – but the more he tried to stop it, the more I wanted to be with Bri.'

'And your mum?'

'She died. Just me and dad.' More tears dripped onto her jeans. 'He's passed away now. Just as well . . . he'd kill Bri if he was here.'

14

'I'm listening.' Was all I had to say, for it to pour out of her, like a torrent she couldn't stop. The pent-up pain and fear that until now, had nowhere to go. Bursting like a breached dam. A silent weight, too heavy for her to hold on her own any longer.

How she'd never smoked a cigarette or tasted alcohol until she met Bri. How he'd introduced her to the drugs he dealt on the streets of the estate where she lived. A teenager struggling with hormonal adolescence, no mum, and a father whose strict discipline was the only way he knew to keep her safe.

When she told Bri she was pregnant at sixteen, he left. Breaking her into a million pieces because she naively thought he was the love of her life.

'My dad was great,' her voice trembled. 'Hated Bri and what he'd done . . . but took me and Maisie on.'

'And Bri?'

'Moved off the estate. I never heard from him again until this weekend . . .' She took a sip of tea. Gazing out at the brightening horizon – almost talking to herself. 'Turned up, late Friday night. Said he wanted to see Maisie. But that was just so I'd let him in . . .'

'What did he really want?' Although I could guess.

'Not me . . .' She snorted. 'The flat . . . a clean address.'

'To deal drugs from?'

She nodded.

'That's "Cuckooing", Pip.'

'What?' She frowned.

'When a drugs gang takes over someone's home and uses it to deal drugs, without their permission. It's named after the cuckoo bird.'

Her brows drew together as she stared at me. 'The bird . . . does drugs?'

'No.' I stifled a laugh. 'It steals other bird's nests – moves in.'

The 'cuckooing' drug dealers targeted the vulnerable. Usually someone with an addiction themselves, or learning disabilities,

15

who didn't realise what's going on. Pip was neither, but I suspected, Bri, the charmer he was, would know she was someone he could manipulate.

'It's a crime, Pip. That makes you a victim in all this. You've done nothing wrong.' Her silence prompted me to ask. 'Did he offer you anything? Money . . . drugs?'

She nodded to both.

'Did you accept?'

'No.'

'That's good.'

She turned to look at me then. The agony in her eyes, almost unbearable to see.

'It's a condition . . . no drugs.' Her voice went up an octave. 'Dealing from the flat . . . Christ!'

'But you said no.'

She slowly lifted the side of her shirt so I could see the livid black bruises across her ribs and back.

'He leaves the face alone,' she said quietly. 'So it's not obvious.'

I took a long breath. 'Did he do . . . anything else to you?'

Her eyes held mine. She nodded slowly, then lowered her head.

'And Maisie?' I almost daren't ask.

She shook her head. 'I would never let him hurt her. But he . . .' Her eyes filled with more tears – her words a hoarse whisper. 'He locked her in the bathroom, while he . . .' She couldn't say it.

'Where is he now?' It was a struggle not to grind my teeth. My voice sounded calmer than I felt.

'At the flat. He moved his girlfriend in over the weekend. Put me in Maisie's room. I'm sleeping on the floor.'

My mind was racing to compute the options.

'He said if I tell anyone, he'd kill me.' What she said next made my blood run cold. 'He's got a gun.'

That raises the stakes.

16

'Have you seen it for yourself . . . the gun?'

She nodded. 'He showed me when he . . . to make me . . .'

'It's OK. You don't have to spell it out.' I didn't want her reliving that trauma – not while we were on the edge of a precipice – literally.

'If he deals from the flat,' she was saying, 'it won't stay secret. Not on that estate. And then I've got my caseworker coming round. How can I hide it? I can't.'

'The best chance for Maisie not to go into care, is for you to let me help you.'

She stared straight ahead.

'Too late, he's already started. Put new, heavy locks and chains on the door and brought all the gear in. People were coming to the flat all weekend. I can't live like that – not again. I don't want this for my daughter. If I'm not here, she'd be away from him . . . from that life and I wouldn't have the pain of losing her – of seeing her go to another family.'

'It's not too late. We can sort this. I promise. Nothing is bad enough that killing yourself is the answer.' She stared at me in silence. 'In fact, jumping off this roof, solves nothing. But staying here . . . working with me to get this sorted . . . is the only way to look after you and Maisie.'

Her eyes locked onto mine, probing the sincerity of what I was saying.

'Can you really help . . . keep us safe?'

'Yes.' Said with as much conviction as I could put into one word.

She caught her bottom lip in her teeth. 'He'll kill me . . . and Maisie.'

'He won't.'

'You don't know him . . .'

'I've dealt with a lot like him.' My tone was grim. 'You're not the first person to be in this situation. It's sortable . . . honestly.'

17

I could feel a slight shift in her energy. Hardly noticeable . . . but seismic in its significance.

'How do you feel about coming away from the ledge?' I said. 'Just a bit . . . make us more comfortable while we talk?'

I almost held my breath as I watched and waited.

Then, an imperceptible nod of the head.

I stood carefully, stepping backwards off the parapet and extending my hand.

Slowly, she reached out.

Out of the corner of my eye, I could see the edge of the fire door open just a fraction, as the police officer prepared to rush if things turned bad.

Pip's skin felt ice cold against mine, as our palms touched. I closed my fingers tightly around hers – determined to hold on to her now, no matter what.

Chapter Three

Fordley DAAT – Later Monday morning

Doug was sitting in a therapy room talking quietly to Pip.

Rina arrived before we'd come back into reception. I'd heard the distinctive growl of her motorbike engine as I'd walked down the stairs, with my arm firmly around Pip's shoulders.

We were standing in the corridor outside the consultation rooms.

'Jesus.' Rina ran a hand across her purple buzz cut hair. 'Poor lass. What's she been going through, to get to this?'

The police sergeant who'd been upstairs with us, slipped the notepad back into his pocket.

'I've got everything I need for now. If you're sure you don't need us to take her to the psychiatric unit?'

'No need,' I said. 'She understands what's happening and she's consented to treatment.'

'OK. We'll take down the cordon and get traffic moving again.'

We both watched him go, then Rina turned to me. 'Is that it? They don't do anything else?'

I watched Tess going into the kitchen to make everyone a much-needed brew. She was followed by Pat Rodgers, whose expression resembled a bulldog sucking a nettle.

'What do you want him to do? Pip's not broken any laws and she's not so ill that she needs sectioning under the mental health act.'

'But what about this bastard, Brian Curtis?' she asked, with her customary bluntness. 'Surely he's a matter for the police?'

I was still watching the kitchen door over her shoulder. Imagining what was going on in there.

'He is, and I'll talk to Callum about it. But for now, Pip's our main concern.'

'Well, she can't go back to the flat – to that bastard.' Rina blew out a hard breath. 'I'd like to throw *him* off the fucking roof!'

'Me too. Unfortunately, it's not a treatment option.'

To watch a client in a toxic situation, being damaged, despite our best efforts, was the most painful part of the job. Especially for someone like Rina. Drawn to the profession because she was a 'fixer'. Someone who desperately wanted to make people's lives better.

'I'll speak to Callum about the drug dealing from the flat,' I said. 'I'm sure Doug's already arranging to get them to a place of safety. She won't have to go back there. Your job is to help her navigate her way through the process.'

'I know.' Rina scuffed the carpet with the steel toecap of her biker boot.

I squeezed her shoulder. 'You go sit with Doug. He'll be agreeing a safety plan with Pip. That's something you should be part of.'

She glanced towards the therapy room door. 'Do you think she'll try again? I mean . . . to take her own life?'

My eyes followed hers. 'The thing with suicidal thoughts, is once you've allowed your mind to go there, the route is open. It's always a consideration. The mind gets drawn back there during dark times,' I said. 'A deadly path, trodden down that makes going there all the easier the next time.'

'Why would she even think about it?'

'For some people, it's a way of taking back control. After what Curtis did to her, it probably felt like a last attempt to be free of the pain, on her own terms.'

Her eyes were moist when she looked at me. 'So, you're saying she might . . . try again?'

I gave her a smile, squeezing her arm. 'I'm saying, that with support and understanding, Pip can learn that there are other ways of dealing with her pain.' I nodded towards Doug's room. 'That's why the work you do with her now is so important.'

* * *

In the kitchen, Tess was leaning back against the sink, looking every inch the cornered animal, as Pat Rodgers, stretching to her full five foot five, was giving her both barrels.

Tess saw me over the manager's shoulder.

'Jo.' She sounded relieved.

Rodgers spun to face me. 'This is a private conversation, McCready.'

'Then you should be having it in a private place.' I reached between them to get mugs out of the cupboard.

Tess took the chance, to move aside and get Rodgers out of her face.

I turned, cups in hand – now standing between them.

'So, where were you this morning, when Pip arrived?' I asked the manager.

'What?'

'You're the keyholder. You're supposed to be the one to open up.'

'I . . . well . . .' she blustered, before regaining her composure. 'I don't have to answer to you,' she spat.

'No.' I agreed, flipping on the kettle. 'But you *do* have to answer to the Board of Trustees and I'm sure they'll be interested to know that, since Christmas, you've given Tess the keys and told her to do your job for you—'

'I don't—'

'Because you've moved in with your new boyfriend, on his houseboat and the commute from the sticks in North Yorkshire

21

is a complete bitch. Meaning, you can't get here in time, without crawling out of a nice warm bed at sparrow's fart.' The thin smile, didn't reach my eyes. 'How am I doing so far?'

'How did you—?'

I waved a hand to cut her off as the kettle boiled. 'And to make matters worse, to cover it up – you cheat your time sheets. This morning's log says you were here thirty minutes before Tess. Interesting to see how you explain that one.'

'You can't—'

'If you *had* done your job,' I pressed on, 'Tess wouldn't have been alone with a vulnerable client and Pip may not have gone on to the roof.'

'I don't have to listen to this.' Rodgers turned on her highly polished heel and made for the door.

'You're welcome,' I called after her retreating back.

Tess looked worried. 'She'll blame me.'

I handed her a mug. 'She can try.'

The chief executive of the board was a good friend, who'd confided in me about problems at the DAAT.

'The board have been investigating Rodgers on the QT,' I explained. 'They've known for a while she's been stealing time – not to mention her expenses.'

'Oh – I didn't know.'

'No reason you should. But trust me – she's on thin ice after today.'

Chapter Four

Fordley Police Station – Monday afternoon

DCI Callum Ferguson was sitting at his desk in the CID office, as I brought him up to speed.

'And this is Pip Holden's address?' He glanced at the notes I'd made before leaving the DAAT.

'Yes.'

As he bent over the papers I looked down at the head of thick silver hair. An unusual feature for a man in his forties, but one that enhanced his good looks and earned him the 'Silver Fox' tag he hated so much.

I rested my briefcase on the edge of his desk, not comfortable enough to take the seat opposite as I once would have done.

'Doug's managed to get her and Maisie into a refuge, until we can do something about this ex-boyfriend.'

Callum sat back and stretched knotted shoulders. 'Brian Curtis. Remember him when he first started running drugs for the gangs. Nasty little shit at fourteen. He obviously hasn't mellowed with age.'

He got up and went to the coffee percolator that lived on the bookshelf in his office, gesturing to me with the pot. I shook my head. He knew I only drank tea, but he was being polite. We both were.

Stepping around each other with cringeworthy courtesy ever since our fledgling relationship had ground to a shuddering halt a few months before, when I'd discovered he'd been seeing another woman.

Any anger I felt at the betrayal quickly evaporated when the woman in question – another police officer, had been killed during a police operation. Callum had been in charge and felt responsible for her death.

The combination of guilt and grief – shredded his usual professional detachment, leading to several weeks of sick leave. Probably more than he'd taken in his entire policing career.

He'd returned to duty a few months ago and there had never seemed to be a good time to autopsy what had happened between us. Although the pain of losing him had ripped a hole deep inside me that I felt may never heal. But it wasn't fair to lay that one at his feet right now. Maybe never.

The whole complicated mess, compounded by the fact, that, since our 'break-up', I'd been seeing someone too. Eduardo Mazzarelli. The owner of a tech company, occasionally called in to advise the police on cyber-crime issues.

If I was being brutally honest, Ed was just a distraction. A sticking plaster to cover a gaping emotional wound. Attention that made me feel a little less raw. Affection that went some way to ease the pain of rejection by the only man I had ever allowed myself to love, since my husband had died over two decades before. Not that I'd ever told Callum that.

But Ed was in far deeper than I was. Another complication I would have to unravel. But not today.

Callum stuck his head out of the office door. 'Tony,' he called to a DS on his team.

DS Tony Morgan looked up from his desk. 'Boss?'

Callum gestured for him to come into the office, pushing his notes across the desk.

'Phillipa Holden. Lives on the Butterfield estate. Being cuckooed by Brian Curtis and his crew.'

'Curtis.' Tony looked surprised. 'Hasn't been on our patch for years.'

'Well, looks like he's back.' Callum nodded to me. 'Jo can give you the intel she's picked up. But it needs corroborating. Phillipa says Curtis has a gun. We need more on that. Get someone out to interview her. Jo can give you the refuge address.'

Tony scooped up the notes. 'On it, boss.'

'So, what now?' I asked once he'd left.

'We'll do some digging. If it pans out, it's enough to justify getting a drugs warrant for the address.'

'And how long will that take?'

Pip was fragile and vulnerable. The longer this dragged on, the worse it would be for her. Being away from home – keeping Maisie out of nursery. The repercussions were endless.

He shrugged, already picking another file from the toppling pile on his in-tray.

'Three, four days. Depends how quickly we can verify the intel. If there's enough to suspect there's a gun on the premises, we'll need a firearms team to execute the warrant.' He glanced up at me, raking fingers through his hair – something he did when he was frustrated or tired. 'You know how slow it can be, Jo.'

Unfortunately, I did.

I got up to leave.

'By the way.' His voice made me pause. 'Thanks for putting me on to Geoff, when I . . . needed to see someone.'

Professor Geoff Perrett was my old college lecturer and mentor and the sharpest psychologist I'd ever met. Now long retired, he'd remained a close friend and the only person I trusted with my own psyche, if ever I needed a mental shakedown.

After the incident, Callum had refused to see West Yorkshire police's own psychologist and had asked for my help. His message had come just as I was about to board a flight with Ed.

For a fleeting moment, I had considered missing the flight and going to him. But as I was so closely involved, I couldn't deal with it – so I'd referred him to Geoff.

25

'Did he help?' I already knew the answer, but didn't want Callum to know we'd spoken about him.

'Said he was too close to you to be objective.' Given the sub-text, he couldn't meet my eyes – scanning some paperwork instead. 'He gave me a list of therapists he'd recommend.'

'Did you find one?'

He nodded, but didn't elaborate – subject closed.

I went to the door.

'Jo . . . ?'

I turned – my hand on the door handle.

'I'm sorry,' he said quietly. 'About . . .' He was struggling to find the words.

'I know. It's OK,' I said, even though it wasn't.

He simply nodded.

I left his office and went to find Tony.

Chapter Five

McNamara's, Fordley – Monday evening

Finn McNamara, the eponymous owner of the Irish bar in the centre of Fordley, was conspicuous by his absence, when I arrived to meet my friend for dinner.

The place didn't seem quite as vibrant without his booming voice and jovial anecdotes.

A long-time friend of my father's, back in the old country, they'd made the move from Ireland together and Finn had quickly become a larger-than-life character, in an already colourful city.

My father enjoyed embarrassing his friend as he retold how Finn filled up when he'd asked him to be my godfather. An uncharacteristic show of emotion from a bear of a man, renowned for his tough disposition.

Since my father's death, he'd worked hard to fill his shoes. Not that anyone could. But having his solid presence in my life was something I was eternally grateful for.

I spotted Elle as soon as I went through the door. The striking red hair, falling in lustrous curls to her shoulders, was hard to miss. Along with her stunning looks, which inevitably drew the attention of most men in the bar.

She sat, delicately sipping a cocktail. Her legs elegantly crossed at the ankle, looking as if she'd just stepped off a catwalk. Most people would imagine she was a model, or a fashion designer – which was about as far away from the truth as you could get.

Dr Eleanor Richardson was the Home Office Pathologist, who spent her days wearing scrubs and wellies in the mortuary behind Fordley Royal Infirmary and was more comfortable holding a scalpel than a Gucci handbag.

'Darling,' she purred, putting her glass on the table to give me a tight hug and a kiss on both cheeks.

'Am I late – or are you early?' I shrugged off my coat, feeling dishevelled beside such effortless glamour.

'I'm early, sweet pea. Had a bitch of a day and took an early dart.' She took another sip of the espresso Martini. 'Thought I'd get a freshener before dinner. Want one?'

'Can't.' I ran fingers through my tangled hair, in a vain attempt to look less tousled. 'I'm driving.'

'Oh, how boring.' She smiled mischievously over the rim of the glass. 'I've arranged for Rina to pick me up later.'

Rina Graham, the counsellor I'd gone to meet at the DAAT, was Elle's partner. Fifteen years her junior and with an altogether different taste in just about everything, she'd lived with Elle in her beautiful farmhouse, in a remote part of the dales, for the past five years. Although seemingly diametric opposites, their relationship was an enduring one, that I knew made Elle happier than she'd ever been.

I raised my eyebrows. 'On the back of her bike?'

Elle's laugh was like the tinkling of ice in a glass. 'In *these* heels? Don't be ridiculous, darling. I've asked her to bring the car. Though you're right – she'd rather have me as pillion on that beast of a thing.'

That image made me laugh. 'She might be in need of a freshener herself after this morning.'

Elle's expression was suddenly serious. 'Yes, she told me about the girl on the roof. How is she?'

I spoke as I scanned the menu. 'Doug's managed to get her emergency accommodation in a refuge. I'll go over in the morning, see how she's settling in.'

'The sooner they sort out that bastard ex of hers, the better.' Elle curled her lip in contempt. 'Have you spoken to the Boy Scout about it?'

Elle's pejorative term for Callum.

'Why do you insist on calling him that?' I was surprised by my protective tone.

An almost Gallic shrug of indifference. 'So bloody anal about procedure – he probably swallowed the rule book.'

'No bad thing in a cop.'

'If he wasn't so damned righteous, he might not have taken it so personally when his girlfriend died.'

'Bit harsh.'

'You know what I mean . . .' She drained the last of her Martini. 'Grieve, yes of course. But what unravelled him so badly, was the fact he felt responsible for her being there . . . doing her job.'

'He *was* the senior investigating officer, in charge of the operation,' I said – still not sure why I felt the need to defend him.

'But it wasn't any failure on *his* part that got her killed, was it?' She waved her hand, dismissively. 'He took it too personally, because he was *already* feeling guilty about cheating on you. Probably believed it was karma, delivering justice on them both. Fate paying him back for being a two-timing bastard, or some such Boy Scout bollocks.'

'Don't ever switch disciplines, Elle,' I said as the waitress approached. 'Your brand of psychotherapy is too brutal – even by my standards.'

'Well, I haven't forgiven him for what he did to you,' she muttered.

'No shit. I'd never have guessed.'

* * *

An hour was spent in companionable small talk as we ate, finally pausing in conversation as the waitress collected our plates. Considering I hadn't felt hungry, I'd almost licked the dish clean.

'So how *is* Rina – after this morning?'

'Upset, as you can imagine. I've told her she needs to develop a thicker skin.'

'It'll come.'

'She can't afford to get too attached to her clients,' Elle persisted. 'In our line of work, we all see chaos, hurt and death. If she gets emotionally involved, she won't last two minutes.'

'Not wanting to state the obvious,' I said, about to do just that, 'but in your line of work *all* you see is death.'

'True.'

'Not as easy to stay dispassionate, when you get to hear their life stories . . . meet their families, or in Pip's case, their children. It hits home sometimes.'

I spoke from bitter personal experience. Even after all my years in clinical practice, I wasn't above getting involved. Caring for some of the people I dealt with – living *and* dead.

In the past, that's what had driven me to take certain cases. The feeling that I owed it to victims and their families to find out what had happened to them. Give them a voice.

'She's incensed by this ex-boyfriend,' Elle was saying. 'Wants to go and beat the evil scrote with a baseball bat.'

I couldn't help laughing. 'Don't sugar it up.'

'Well . . . you must feel it too? After all, you deal with the worst of the worst – serial killers and rapists.'

'Careful . . . you're starting to sound like Mamma.'

My mother had never approved of my job. Even though police work was only a small part of what I did. Called in to consult on serial offences, when they needed an insight into how an offender's mind worked. What their drives and motivations might be. Anything that could help catch them before they could commit further atrocities.

As a Forensic Psychologist, my usual day-to-day involved carrying out psychiatric assessments for the courts or offender profiling for solicitors' clients and parole boards.

In recent years, I'd also written a couple of books – based on the work I'd done profiling some of the most dangerous offenders in the criminal justice system.

The fact that they had become bestsellers had been a welcome surprise. Opening up a whole new career, as I was invited to make TV documentaries and appear as a 'talking head' whenever the media wanted an 'expert' to comment on the latest trial of an offender who'd made the news.

My mother had always felt it was no job for a woman and, in her opinion, it was the reason I was still single, after almost twenty years as a widow. A flawed logic, but one she refused to relinquish.

I suspected she just enjoyed using it as a topic to beat me with, and one I couldn't defend. My career *had* brought me into contact with some of the most dangerous people in the criminal world. Which was, coincidentally how Elle and I had met – being called as expert witnesses on various high-profile cases.

'Rina's good at what she does . . . she'll soon grow a professional skin.'

'*You* haven't always managed it,' Elle said, without malice.

'True.' I carried the physical scars of too many close encounters to argue.

'Anyway – what happened with Pip couldn't have come at a worse time for Rina – it's all been a bit much recently.' Elle took a sip of wine.

'Oh?'

'Another service user died a couple of weeks ago – hit her hard.'

'I know all the clients on her list,' I said, puzzled. 'Don't recall any of them dying.'

'It wasn't one of Rina's,' Elle said. 'Steve Lowry. She'd taken an interest in how his rehab was going. So, it was a blow to find out he'd died. To make matters worse – he ended up on my examination table.'

'How come?'

As the senior pathologist, a straightforward post-mortem would usually go to one of Elle's team.

'It was escalated when his family raised concerns,' Elle explained.

'About what?'

'Cause of death – an overdose.'

'Not so unusual for a drug addict.'

'That's just it. He'd been clean for nearly two years. Got his life back together. Rina had only been telling me about him the month before he died. He'd just got an apprenticeship with a construction company.'

'So, what happened?'

'No one really knows. Looked like a heroin overdose. The family insisted he wasn't using again.'

'Suicide?' I suggested.

'The family wouldn't accept that. He had some legal hassle with an ex-girlfriend. Police suspected that might have driven him to do it. But the family insisted he was in a good place in his life.'

'And after you'd examined him?'

'Heroin certainly caused his death – but, taking everything else into consideration – especially what his family said, I concluded it wasn't suicide.'

'What then?'

'The amount he'd taken that night wouldn't have killed an addict. Certainly, would have been the usual amount for him to take when he was injecting regularly. But, after so long, his body no longer had the tolerance for it.'

'You mean, he'd injected what he always had, without thinking – but for his clean system, it was an overdose?'

'Exactly. And a massive one at that. A shock to his system that he couldn't survive,' she sighed, leaning back in her chair. 'The coroner ruled it was "foolish and incautious behaviour" an accident, but not suicide. It's unusual for an ex-addict to get it wrong . . . but not uncommon. This is the second one I've seen in the last few months. The family still couldn't accept that he'd gone back to using heroin. We'll never know why he did.'

'And Rina?'

'Upset and still in shock. Then today happened – one of *her* clients this time.' She shook her head. 'Just worry about how she's going to cope in the job if she can't get used to unexpected deaths.'

'Not sure anyone becomes immune to death,' I said quietly. 'Expected or otherwise. If I ever do – you can tell me it's time to quit.'

Elle's perfect brows drew together in a frown. She looked as though she was about to say something, then thought better of it.

'What?' I prompted.

'I don't know . . . something – maybe nothing . . .'

'What? I pressed again.

'Just a feeling – nothing concrete, really.'

I knew that instinct. My gut often told me more than I could prove sometimes – but I'd learned to trust it.

'Coming from you – that's good enough for me,' I smiled.

'Lately, I've had more awkward conversations with police and the coroner than I'd like,' she said, watching her elegant fingernail run around the rim of her glass – her lips pursed thoughtfully. 'It's starting to feel like a pattern – but too random.'

It was my turn to frown. 'A random pattern? Bit of an oxymoron . . . but go on.'

'You're probably going to tell me there's a psychological term for seeing patterns where none exist?'

'Two actually – "apophenia and pareidolia". But knowing you as I do – I wouldn't say you suffered from either.'

'Had one or two cases, which just felt "off" somehow. Nothing I could point to as hard evidence – if there was anything, it was tenuous and could be explained away. Do you know what I mean?'

I nodded. 'Pathologists equivalent of a "copper's nose".'

'Something like that.'

'Want to tell me?'

She took a breath and leaned back in her chair.

'Not here,' she said. 'Come down to my office later this week and I'll explain.'

Chapter Six

Fordley Women's Aid Refuge – Tuesday morning

Pip's room was south-facing and the early morning sun, streaming through large sash windows, warmed the small space and gave it a cheerful feel.

I sat in the only armchair. Pip perched on the edge of the single bed – we both nursed mugs of tea.

'Maisie's happy enough,' she said, blowing the steam off her cup. 'She's in the play area with the other kids at the moment.'

'And how are you?' I asked.

She certainly looked better than when I'd last seen her – though that wasn't a high bar to reach.

'OK.' She rewarded me with a small smile. 'Didn't sleep much last night, though. Turning everything over . . . you know?'

'Have you heard from Brian?' I knew when Pip didn't return home the previous day, he would have been desperate to track her down.

'Phone was pinging all night. I said I'd gone to stay with a friend for a few days. That I didn't want to be at the flat, with . . . everything going on.' She pulled a face. 'He kept messaging, so I turned it off in the end. Staff here advised me not to answer if he tried to call, so I didn't.'

She handed me her phone. I glanced down the stream of messages that had started mid-morning the day before and gone on until the early hours. The content went from demanding, to irritated, to downright abusive and threatening.

'Anything since 2 a.m.?' I asked.

'No, but he'll be asleep now.'

Drug dealers were a nocturnal species.

'I know it might be tempting to reply – but don't,' I cautioned. 'Don't give him any way to track you both down.'

'My caseworker's been really good. Showed me how to turn the location thing off on my phone. I'll probably change my number, eventually.'

'Good idea.'

I told her about my conversation with Callum and the wheels that had been set in motion.

'The police sent someone yesterday,' she said, tucking her legs underneath herself. 'Showed me pictures of different guns, so I could show them which type he's got. They asked what other weapons he keeps in the flat. I told them about some of the things I'd seen. Think I did OK.'

I gave her a reassuring smile. 'I'm sure you did. The main thing is to keep your head down and stay out of the way, until the police can serve a warrant on him.'

She nodded. 'The refuge said we can stay here as long as we need. Then there's a resettlement service – so we can find somewhere else.' Her eyes looked haunted. 'Can't go back there.'

I waited, knowing she had more to say – giving her the space.

Her words came quietly. 'I told them what he did to me.' She looked down, talking to hands which twisted in her lap. 'They've done tests . . . to make sure he didn't give me any infections . . . or make me pregnant. Took pictures of the bruises.' Then she looked up – taking a long breath. 'The policeman who came yesterday asked if I wanted to make a report . . . of the . . . rape.'

'And do you?'

She shook her head vehemently – long brown hair swishing around her shoulders. 'Can't face him. Just want him gone, so me and Maisie can get our lives back – go back to normal.'

'You don't have to decide now. Take time to think about it.'

'I know.' She distracted herself with another sip of tea. 'Sooner the police arrest him, sooner this is all over.'

I watched her – this mother, who wasn't much more than a girl herself – and hoped Callum could get the result we all wanted.

Chapter Seven

Kingsberry Farm – Wednesday morning

I glanced across my office to the woman sitting at the other desk. The light from the computer screen illuminated her face.

Jen, my closest friend and PA. The person who'd organised my life since I'd met her when I was a junior psychologist on my first placement. Ten years my senior, she'd been the unit administrator. She took me under her wing then and we'd stayed together ever since.

With encyclopaedic knowledge of the cases we'd tackled together and the offenders who committed them – she had a mind to rival the best internet search engine and a heart as wide as the ocean.

'I've got an appointment tomorrow with Elle,' I said. 'If we can block some time out in the diary?'

'At the mortuary?' She didn't look away from the screen as she shuddered. 'Rather you than me.'

'Hmm, not my favourite place either.'

She looked up, absently scratching her grey curls with the end of a pencil. 'Let's just be thankful the only prone body we have to work around is Harvey.'

I looked at my brindle Boxer dog – sprawled in his favourite spot, on the Chinese rug in front of my desk.

'Think I'll let him out. He's been lazy today.' I smiled, watching his ears prick up, even though he looked sound asleep.

Jen got up and collected our empty cups. 'Right – time for a brew then.'

Endless cups of Yorkshire Tea was my fuel. It had to be made in a teapot and preferably served in a mug. I was a purist when it came to the type of tea and how it was brewed. My mother called it my 'foible', shaking her head and lamenting that I'd inherited my father's Irish gene, rather than the coffee-drinking Italian one.

I followed Jen and Harvey down the glass corridor that connected my barn conversion office to the original farmhouse.

The kitchen was my favourite place in the house and the room I spent most time, after the office. Constantly warm from the Aga, it always felt cosy and reassuring as I came through the door.

Jen lifted the lid on the Aga, and put a heavy-bottomed kettle onto the hotplate. I let Harvey out through the porch door. His huge paws skittered on the gravel drive before he plunged through the gap in the hedge, into the field.

I leaned against the door, breathing in the warm summer air and the delicate scent of wild flowers – listening as Harvey thundered around, chasing trails of rabbits long gone.

There were six acres, including a small wood marking the boundary of my land. A freedom that allowed us to roam, often without seeing another soul, up here on the Yorkshire moors.

I looked over the landscape of wild moorland and tufted heather. A raw and ragged beauty that always left me with a feeling of tranquil isolation.

My mother hated the remoteness of where I lived. But for me, it was a peaceful balm against the brutal nature of the work I did and the things I dealt with.

The shrill of my mobile shattered the serenity. I pulled the phone from my jeans pocket.

'McCready.'

'Just calling to give you an update.' The familiarity of Callum's voice, with its soft Scottish accent, caused a tug somewhere deep inside my chest. 'Seeing as you brought us the intel,' he was saying.

'Brian Curtis?' I went into the kitchen, where Jen had left a teapot freshly brewing on the counter.

'Looks like he's supplying.' I could hear the shuffling of papers. 'Using younger kids on bikes as runners. Most look to be about twelve or thirteen years old. Delivering drugs to dealers in the area.'

'He really is a piece of work.' I poured myself a mug of tea.

'Standard practice for gangs like this.' He sounded distracted. 'Kids that age are less conspicuous riding bikes on the estates. And if they're caught, they don't get heavy sentences. Plus, he doesn't have customers coming to the flat day and night, making the neighbours curious.'

'So, what now?'

'Pip identified the gun. He always carries a handgun and has another hidden in the flat. Other weapons too. Knives, a machete. So, firearms team will execute the warrant.'

'When?'

'Probably early hours of Saturday morning. Keep that to yourself though.'

'Who am I going to tell?' I couldn't keep the indignation out of my voice.

'Pip, for starters . . . or her counsellor – that mate of yours at the DAAT . . .'

'Credit me with *some* sense, Cal,' I said, irritated.

'Sorry.' His tone gentled.

I noticed him doing that a lot lately. Softening the edges. Treating me with the sensitivity he used to. A result of him feeling sorry for what had happened between us? Or something else?

'Will you let me know how it goes?' I asked.

'Of course.' A long pause, and then, 'Maybe we could go for a drink over the weekend? I'll bring you up to speed with everything?'

After months of tension and distance between us, hearing the tenderness in his voice again was more than I could take.

'Can't,' I said, far too quickly. 'Got plans,' I lied.

Eduardo had suggested we do something, as he had a rare weekend free and I'd fobbed him off too.

Lately, I felt like I was tiptoeing though an emotional minefield, where one misstep could prove fatal to my feelings and, right now, I couldn't deal with either of the men in my life.

Better to be alone.

'Maybe another time,' was all he said as we ended our call.

Chapter Eight

Fordley Mortuary – Thursday

The morgue, as I insisted on calling it, was in a low-level building, at the back of Fordley Royal Infirmary. Surrounded by manicured grass verges and shielded by trees, it had a discreet entrance and a small staff car park.

I looked up at the security camera above the steel door and pressed the buzzer, rewarded by the metallic click that unlocked the door.

The familiar route took me through an entrance hall, past an office where the deceased were booked in, and into an echoing white-tiled corridor that led down to the autopsy rooms.

Gus, Elle's mortuary assistant, was pushing a trolley towards me. Thankfully, it wasn't occupied.

'Hi, Jo,' he beamed. 'Here to see the boss?'

'Is she free?'

'Yep.' He parked the trolley in front of the bank of stainless steel fridges that lined one wall. 'Just picking up her next customer,' he said cheerily, nodding in the direction of her office. 'She's catching up with paperwork until we're ready for her.'

The whine of a Stryker saw came from somewhere down the corridor, sending an involuntary shiver down my spine as I pictured what it was being used for.

I walked quickly into Elle's office before Gus could open the fridge and present me with another sight I knew I didn't want before lunch.

'Hello, sweet pea.' Elle smiled and pushed an office chair towards me with her foot. 'Is Gus sorting out a brew for you?'

I thought about what Gus was doing at that very moment. 'Err, it's fine. I'll pass.'

'*You* refusing tea?' She feigned shock. 'Should I call a priest?'

'Very funny.'

'Well, if you're sure.' She pulled some files from a precarious stack.

'These your random patterns?' I asked.

She pursed her lips. 'I've worked this patch for more years than I care to count and I can tell you, there's a rhythm to this city.'

'A rhythm?'

'People think death is random and, to a degree, it is. But in any given geographical area there's a "norm". Taking into account the demographic of the population, time of year, the weather, etcetera.'

'Like flu season?'

'Exactly. You get a *feel* for what's usual.'

'And something feels unusual?'

'We keep detailed records of every case we deal with, as you can imagine. The datasets are broken down by age, sex and region.' She tapped the keys on her computer and pulled up rows of graphs.

'These are our figures for 2020 and 2021. You can see here, an unusual spike in deaths.'

'Covid?'

She nodded. 'If there's an anomaly, such as the pandemic, then it's explicable.'

'And you're seeing something inexplicable?'

Her sculpted eyebrows pulled together again in that frown. 'They're all "explicable", that's the problem.'

'Sorry – I'm being a bit slow.' I was beginning to wish I'd accepted that brew. My brain always worked better with tea.

'I know this city. And I can tell you that in Fordley . . .' She counted the points off on her fingers, 'the highest percentage of people die in hospital, followed by nursing homes. The top two causes of naturally occurring deaths are heart disease and cancer – in that order and when it comes to accidental deaths, top in our particular hit parade, are road accidents on country lanes and falls. When we look at the data, straightforward accidents don't really raise any flags. If there are no suspicious circumstances – there's no need for concern. They happen in any busy city. They're almost the "invisible dead".

She took a long breath and sat back, stretching her arms above her head. 'But in the last year, I seem to be seeing more "accidents",' she drew quotation marks in the air, 'that feel "off" to me. I raised my concerns with the police and the coroner, but in the absence of hard evidence – they've been recorded as accidental deaths.'

'Such as what?'

She pushed a file across to me. 'Remember I told you about Steve Lowry?'

'The ex-addict Rina knew – accidental overdose?'

She nodded. 'I wasn't happy with the fact that no one suspected he'd gone back to using again and had no clue why he would. The way he'd injected himself, didn't look right to me either . . .'

'In what way?'

'Addicts veins eventually collapse, due to the amount of injecting. It becomes harder for them to find a good injection site – so they move around the body. Groin, between the toes or fingers . . .'

She was making me cringe. 'OK, I get the idea.'

'When I examined Lowry, there'd been a couple of failed attempts to get the needle into the inside of his elbow – but with no luck. The fatal injection was into his groin.'

'So?'

'He'd know which sites to go for. Why would he even try to get a vein where he knew he wouldn't succeed?' She ran her fingers through her hair in frustration. 'It didn't look right to me. But there was nothing else I could find, to show it was anything other than an accident.'

'Except your gut feeling?'

'And that's not sufficient evidence for the police to take another look.'

Her long fingers moved over the keyboard and other graphs filled the screen.

I studied the images.

'We have more than our fair share of drugs overdoses in this city, but these have deviations my instincts don't like.' She pushed another file across the desk, to join Lowry's. 'This one – three weeks ago.'

I read the label on the front.

'Peter Wearman.'

'He was a first-time user.' She flipped open the file. The photo of a good-looking young man with a floppy fringe and dark brown eyes looked back at me.

I scanned the file notes. 'Says he injected heroin for the first time and got the dose wrong. You said yourself – a clean system doesn't have the same tolerance as an addict. Would it be so unusual for him to overdose?'

'That's what the police said. And I agree. That seems quite plausible . . .'

'But?'

'He had no history of drug use. Nothing on his medical records. Came from an affluent family. Good education, great job . . .'

'Plenty of city boys and high flyers use class A drugs recreationally.' I was playing devil's advocate.

'Cocaine or ecstasy usually, although I couldn't find any evidence of him having used either. Unusual to start your drugs journey by injecting heroin right off the bat. Especially as it appears to be his first time, and it seems he was alone when it happened. The location too . . . a back alley in the town centre. Not a club or wine bar – or even the privacy of his home.' She shook her head. 'Why would someone like Wearman go down a sleazy back alley to shoot up? To be found lying among the rubbish in a puddle of his own urine.'

'He'd wet himself?'

'Not unusual in these circumstances.' She shook her head sadly. 'But an ignominious end for a slick city boy like him.'

I knew what she was getting at. Most intravenous drug users are usually introduced to it by a friend or partner who shows them how to do it and is familiar with the paraphernalia and the process.

She passed another manila folder across the desk.

'Andi Kilpin,' she said. 'Just last month. The strangest of the lot.'

I read the cause of death. 'Autoerotic asphyxiation?'

She rested her chin on interlaced fingers. 'That's so rare, I've only seen one case in my entire career. Autoerotic fatalities account for less than 0.5 per million of the population.'

'How can you have half a person?'

She pulled a face. 'Equates to maybe one or two cases in the whole of the UK in any given year.'

'Asphyxiophilia, if you want to give it its psychological name.' I looked at the photo of an overweight man with thinning hair and bad skin, though those were the least of his problems now. 'Increasing sexual excitement by restricting the oxygen supply to the brain. More commonly called "breath play".'

Elle pursed her lips. 'Practiced by consenting couples, it's risky – but when it's a solo activity, it's downright stupid and often fatal.'

Given the things I'd seen in my time, nothing surprised me.

'To be fair, we don't really know how many deaths a year are actually down to it.' She nodded towards the graphs on her screen. 'Unlike most other causes, there are no reliable statistics.'

'How come?'

'Majority of autoerotic experimenters are young males – early teens to mid-twenties. If it goes wrong – which it invariably does, it's usually family members who discover the body and clear up the scene. Removing items like pornography or sex toys, because of the embarrassment of it – or to preserve the dignity of their loved ones. So, it often gets recorded as suicide.'

'What's so unusual about . . .' I checked the name on the file again. 'Andi Kilpin's case – apart from the fact that you don't see many instances of it?'

'He was found kneeling behind his bathroom door – naked, with a rope around his neck, tied to the door handle. Gay porn magazines on the floor around him. The ligature was a piece of washing line. Door was locked and the key was on the floor on his side. He appeared to have been sitting on the key.'

'Alone, in a room locked from the inside? I'll bet Poirot never got one like this.'

She smiled. 'From his phone; internet history and eye witnesses who saw him at an auction, we know he was alive eight days before his body was discovered. That fits with the level of decomposition when he was found.'

'No one missed him for over a week?'

'He was an antique dealer. High end – not the kind who sells tat in a junk shop. Worked from home. His wife and daughter were abroad on holiday, so no one was visiting the house.'

'Who found him?'

'Courier delivering the antique he'd purchased at auction. Couldn't get an answer from the door. Opened the letterbox and was almost knocked over by the smell. He called the police.'

'Wouldn't have thought the smell would have drifted through the whole house in a week.'

'It was hot outside that week. But the bathroom had underfloor heating, which was set at twenty-five degrees. Because he

47

was kneeling on the tiled floor, the additional heat hastened decomposition. It also made it more complicated to estimate time of death – which can be a bitch at the best of times.

'At post-mortem, I couldn't find any defence wounds or signs of a struggle. No evidence of lethal trauma or unusual bruising. The ligature mark around his neck matched the washing line, the remains of which were found in his garden shed. Though he actually died of a heart attack.'

'Not asphyxiation?'

She shook her head. 'Pressure on the neck affects the carotid artery and the jugular, but also the vagus nerve. When the vagus is compressed, instantaneous death can occur, which is often what happens when chokeholds prove fatal in restraining people. The sudden increase in pressure sends a message to the heart to shut down – a vagus reflex. Death was almost instant. My examination, showed no sign of sexual climax before death.'

'Poor sod got the pain without the pleasure,' I said without humour.

'Police took the path of least resistance. In the absence of any physical evidence to the contrary, they decided that it was exactly what it looked like. Autoerotic asphyxiation.'

I watched her across the desk. 'But you don't think so?'

The auburn tresses flashed in the light as she shook her head. 'Why not?'

She took a long breath and blew out her cheeks. 'I might only ever have seen one other case, but I know how these things typically present. People, experimenting with this know the risks and usually build in a safety mechanism to release the pressure on the neck. Young boys, experimenting in their bedroom, are often the ones who get it wrong. If Kilpin had reached the ripe old age of fifty-eight, I doubt this was his first time – so he would know to build in some kind of release mechanism – a slip knot, typically, with a ligature.'

'But he didn't?' I said, looking at the crime scene photographs taken when his body was discovered.

Elle shook her head. 'Also, he didn't put any padding around his neck, to cover up telltale marks of his secret hobby. Welts across the throat, could lead to awkward questions from friends and family. Forensics say the length of rope was cut from the washing line found in his garage. The cut was fresh. If Kilpin had this as a regular hobby, he would have all the kit pre-prepared. Most people into this kind of stuff use tried and trusted paraphernalia. Why would he have to go to the garage to cut a fresh piece for this particular session? The magazines were closed – usually the person opens up the pornography – looking at it for a while before they begin the asphyxiation.'

I studied the photographs. Kilpin's body lay on one side, in almost a foetal position, where first responders had moved him out of the way to open the bathroom door.

'From the way he was found,' Elle continued, 'it looks as though he laid the magazines out in a neat row, slipped the noose round his neck, leaned forward to apply the pressure and died.' She shook her head again. 'It just doesn't *feel* right to me.'

'Is it possible that he intended it?'

'Suicide?' She shook her head. 'I don't think so.'

'Why not?'

'Why bother with the porn?'

'To go out with a bang?'

She pulled a face. 'No note, either.'

'That's a myth. You know as well as I do, most suicides don't leave a note.'

'The only thing I *could* find, was a small trace of gamma-hydroxybutyrate in his blood.'

'GHB,' I said. 'The date rape drug?'

'Yes. But people use it in very small doses to get high. It's only in larger doses that it renders the victim unconscious, or dead.

49

The margin for overdosing on it is slim – which is why it's so dangerous for recreational use.'

'Seems like Andi Kilpin did a lot of risky things for recreation,' I said thoughtfully.

'The problem is,' Elle went on, 'Hydroxybutyric acid occurs naturally during decomposition. The amount I found was so low, it *could* be a result of post-mortem changes.'

'You think he took the drug, though?'

'But I can't prove it. GHB leaves the system pretty quickly. I estimated that if he had taken it, the dose was borderline between a recreational high and enough to render him unconscious.'

'How borderline?'

She ran her hand through her hair in frustration. 'Too close to call.'

'So, he could have been getting high, before settling down to a fun evening of asphyxiophilia?'

'Like I said – it's all explicable. But the behaviours seem wrong. That's why I wanted your take on it. You're the behavioural analyst.'

I moved the photos around with my index finger – considering everything my friend had said.

'Sequence of events does seem a bit off,' I agreed. 'What have his family said?'

'His wife says she wasn't aware of his kink, but seems to have accepted the cause of death.'

'Well, given the secretive nature of this kind of paraphilia, it's not surprising that she wouldn't know.'

'It's not the family who are having their doubts – it's me.'

Elle wasn't given to wild speculation. Her discipline was grounded in hard facts and science. If her instincts felt something wasn't right, then I was inclined to believe her.

'In all these cases, it's the uncharacteristic behaviours, rather than the pathology, that points to something not quite right,'

Elle was saying. 'And that's your department. If we can come up with something new, we might be able to get the police to take another look.'

I considered the files on the desk between us. Steve Lowry; Peter Wearman and Andi Kilpin.

'Just so we're clear,' I chose my words carefully. 'You're saying these cases have been ruled as accidents, and you think they're not?'

She nodded – her eyes locked on to mine.

'And if not suicide,' I said. 'Then what?'

'Murder.'

Chapter Nine

Kingsberry Farm – Friday

I sat at my desk, absorbed in the notes I'd made after meeting with Elle. The last thing she'd said rattled around my brain like the earworm of an annoying song you hear on the radio and can't get out of your head for the rest of the day.

Murder.

I had to be sure, so I'd pressed her again.

'You're saying there have been *three* separate murders, here in Fordley, in the past . . . how long?'

'Fifteen months.'

'And they've slipped past the police to be recorded as accidents?' I couldn't hide my incredulity.

I wasn't naive enough to believe that murderers never got away with it. I knew beyond doubt they did. I could even believe that, occasionally, an offender might be sufficiently forensically aware to make it look like an accident, convincingly enough to get past the scrutiny of expert crime scene investigators – although that would be a rarity.

But to think that a convergence of such exceptional circumstances could occur on *three* occasions, for *three* different offenders, was defying the laws of chance.

Elle was quick to put me right.

'Not three *different* killers.' She was almost matter-of-fact. 'Just one.'

* * *

'A serial killer?' Jen said, regarding me over the top of her computer screen, with the same incredulous tone I'd probably used on Elle.

'That what she said.'

'Is that likely? Or even possible?'

'Nothing's impossible, Jen. You of all people should know that, after some of the cases we've had over the years.'

'But still . . . a serial murderer who makes his kills look like accidents . . . really? Has there ever been a case like that?'

'Not in the UK, that I can think of.' I pushed my notes away and stretched aching shoulders. 'Samuel Little, in America, is thought to have killed ninety-three people between 1970 and 2005. Reason he got away with it for so long is because the deaths were originally ruled overdoses, accidents or undetermined causes. But fifty-three years ago, forensics weren't what they are now.'

'Is there anything linking these three victims?' Jen's organised mind was already sifting the possibilities. 'Or the way they were killed? If they *were* killed.'

I shook my head. 'The deceased didn't know each other, and the causes of death all have different elements.'

We were interrupted when the office phone rang.

'McCready.'

'Jo?' Callum said. 'Just wanted to give you an update on Pip Holden. We're ready to execute the warrant at her address in the early hours of tomorrow morning.'

'That's good.' She'd be relieved when this was over – not that I could tell her about it.

'Surveillance identified some of Curtis's suppliers. We're going to hit their addresses across West Yorkshire in a coordinated strike, before they can tip each other off.'

'In for a rude awakening then.' That thought cheered me up.

'That's the plan.' He sounded distracted and I could hear the shuffling of papers. 'It was good intel, Jo . . . thanks.'

'Accidental really.'

'Want to meet up after? I can fill you in on the details.'

My reflection in the computer screen chewed my bottom lip. I'd already lied to him once about having plans this weekend.

53

'Sorry, I . . .'

'Jo,' that coaxing tone that I always found hard to resist. 'Please . . . we need to talk.'

'Not sure we do.'

I heard him take a steadying breath. 'OK, then *I* do.'

I swivelled my chair to face the arched window that looked out over the moors. 'I can't,' I murmured, more to the view than to him.

His breath came down the phone in a gust of frustration. 'If you're being like this to punish me – then it's working.'

'I'm not,' I said, honestly. 'That's the last thing I want. It's just . . . difficult for me. Not sure raking over it is going to make things any easier.'

'That's exactly why we need to talk.' His tone was persuasive. 'Clear the air . . . for both our sakes.'

I turned back to the desk, covered in my notes. 'OK – but only if you agree to look at something for me.'

'Great . . . I mean – yes. What?'

'I'll explain when I see you.'

If he knew it was about the closed cases, he wouldn't agree.'

'When?'

'Err – I'll let you know.'

Chapter Ten

Kingsberry Farm – Late Friday

If I was going to help get Elle's cases reinvestigated, I had to come up with something new and compelling.

I'd taken each scene in turn, collating crime scene photographs, which Elle had given me – totally against protocol – and the notes I'd made when I was in her office.

The most complex was the most recent.

Andi Kilpin.

I spread out the photographs taken during his post-mortem. All the elements Elle had mentioned were there . . . or *not* there.

The mark of the key, clearly visible on Kilpin's buttock, where blood had settled to the lowest part of the body, after death – a process called 'hypostasis' – creating a red-wine pattern on his skin.

The absence of padding under the ligature, leading to marks across his throat, which matched the pattern on the rope he'd used.

Then other photographs taken at the scene. Pictures from all the other rooms in the sprawling Edwardian house.

I flicked through a bundle of pictures, showing each room and its contents – but nothing jumped out as significant.

On a low coffee table in the lounge there was an empty wine bottle, and a single glass. The notes said that only Kilpin's fingerprints had been found on both items.

The bathroom, with its checkerboard-tiled floor and impressive rolltop bath, looked like the ideal place to indulge in a relaxing bubble bath, had it not been for the naked corpse of an overweight bloke curled up behind the door.

Forensic officers had opened the bathroom cabinet and photographed the contents, as they had for the bedside cabinets and dressing table.

I looked again at the unopened pornographic magazines – originally laid out around him – then scattered, as first responders had pushed the body aside as they forced their way in.

'Very old school,' I muttered out loud, causing Harvey to look up from his spot on the rug. He tilted his head in a silent question. 'Magazines, boy ... old school. Most people watch porn on their phone these days. Not that you'd know.' He put his chin back on his paws, with a 'huffing' sound.

I tapped my teeth with a pen. A habit when I was thinking and one that drove Jen nuts. I added a note to my growing list.

I was so deep in thought, I jumped when my mobile rang. It was a landline number I didn't recognise.

'McCready.'

'Jo? It's Pip.'

'Hi – where are you calling from?'

'Landline at the refuge.' Her voice carried a tension that immediately put me on high alert. 'I've turned my mobile off.'

'Why? What's wrong?'

'It's Bri ... do you know ... I mean what's happening?' Her words were stilted and disjointed, as if she was on the edge of panic.

'Like what?' I had to be cautious. The raid was just a few hours away and no one outside Callum's team should know anything about it.

'I'm scared that he knows where I am ... that he might be coming for me and Maisie.' A sob caught in her throat.

'What makes you think that?'

'He's gone quiet ... I don't trust it.'

'What do you mean?' I pulled my notebook towards me and grabbed a pen. This could be trouble.

'He's been messaging ever since I left the flat on Monday . . .
I showed you . . .'

'Go on.'

'They got worse . . . more threats . . . demanding to know
where we were. Saying if I went to the police, I was dead . . .' She
started to cry.

'It's OK,' I said gently. 'Take a breath . . .'

'He . . . he said, it didn't matter where I was hiding, he'd find
us. He stopped messaging and started calling.'

'You didn't answer, did you?'

'No!' she almost shouted. 'I'm not stupid . . . you told me . . .
everyone told me. So, he started leaving voice notes – loads.' She
sniffed and I heard the rustling of a tissue. 'Then it just stopped.
He *knows*, Jo. He knows where we are and he's coming for us.'

'Because he stopped calling?'

'Yes!' She screamed down the phone. 'Why else?'

'Pip.' I had to raise my own voice to cut through her panic.
'Calm down. I need you to think for me.'

'OK . . . OK . . .'

'When did you last hear from him?'

'Thursday . . . yesterday.'

'When yesterday.'

'About half seven at night. Then it all stopped. No calls, no
messages . . . nothing.'

'But he didn't *say* he knew where you were?'

'No! He's not going to warn me, is he?'

'What was the last thing he *did* say?'

'Err . . . a WhatsApp – "*Snitches get stitches*". Then a voice
message – "*If you've grassed me up, you're dead, bitch*".'

'Nothing since last night?'

'No . . . that's why, isn't it? He's coming here.'

'Have you told anyone where you are, Pip? I mean . . . anyone
at all?'

'Of course not. I wouldn't put Maisie at risk.'

'Have you been outside the refuge ... even to just walk in the garden?'

'No.'

I took a long breath, my mind turning over the possible scenarios.

'I don't think he knows about the refuge and I don't think he's coming for you.'

More likely, he knows about the raid. I thought.

'Sit tight and hold your nerve.' I sounded far more certain than I actually felt. 'I'll call the refuge manager and the police. They'll make sure you're safe, but you have to promise me not to do anything stupid, like making a run for it – OK?'

'Yes.' Her voice sounded small – as though she'd shrivelled inside.

'You did the right thing, turning your phone off. Keep it off.'

'I will.'

'OK. Stay around people – in the lounge or somewhere and keep Maisie with you.'

Her tearful promises were echoing in my mind as I hung up and dialled Callum's number.

It was answered on the third ring, by a woman.

'DCI Ferguson's phone.'

'Hi, this is Dr McCready.'

'Jo, it's Beth.'

Beth Hastings. A DC on Callum's team. She was only a few years older than my son, but had become a firm friend since we'd met a few years before, when I'd begun working with West Yorkshire Police.

'The boss is briefing the team for tonight's warrant,' she said. 'It's like a zoo round here.'

'That's why I'm calling,' I said hurriedly. 'There might be a problem.'

I told her about my call with Pip.

'I doubt he's got wind of the raid.' Beth sounded confident. 'More likely he's planning to move out. If he thinks she's grassed him up.'

'Or he's gone already.' I was thinking out loud.

'I'll pass this on to the boss. We can get uniform to keep an eye on the refuge until we've got Curtis in custody. Could mean the boss moves the raid forward, though. I'll keep you posted.'

Chapter Eleven

Kingsberry Farm – early hours of Saturday morning

It was just after midnight when I called the duty manager at the refuge and told her about Pip's concerns. Having given Callum's team a heads-up, there was nothing else I could do.

Sleep didn't come easily. I tossed and turned for most of the night. My jumbled thoughts twisting from Pip and Curtis to Elle's suspicious deaths.

Finally, as the slivers of bright sunlight crept around my blinds, I gave up and crawled out of bed.

Harvey was waiting when I went into the kitchen. He uncurled from his bed by the Aga and padded across to me as I knelt to hug his huge sides.

In winter my Aga kept the house cosy, but in the summer, it could make the kitchen far too hot.

I pulled my dressing gown around me and opened the porch door to let a welcome breeze of fresh air inside and let Harvey out.

I'd just flipped the lid on the Aga and put the kettle on the hotplate, when my mobile rang. Automatically, I glanced at the clock. 6.10 a.m.

A call this early, could only mean trouble.

My heart thudded just a little harder as I plucked the phone out of my dressing gown pocket.

Caller ID – 'Callum'.

'Sorry for the early call, but I guessed you'd want to know how the raid went, especially after your call with Beth?'

I cradled the phone under my chin as I prepared the teapot. 'Was Curtis still there?' I asked.

'Oh, he was there.'

I breathed a sigh of relief. 'You've got him in custody, then?'

'No.'

'What?! Why not?'

'He's dead.'

My hand froze over the whistling kettle. 'You had to *shoot* him?'

'We never fired a shot.'

'Then—?'

'He was already dead when the entry team went in . . . along with his girlfriend.'

'How?'

'Not clear.'

'I don't understand.' I frowned, knowing I was probably sounding completely dim.

'It's complicated.' He exhaled down the phone and I knew he was dragging frustrated fingers through his hair. 'I can't go into it over the phone. Come down and I'll explain. Your input wouldn't go amiss on this one, either.'

'OK. Give me an hour.'

Chapter Twelve

Fordley Police Station – Saturday morning

The incident room was buzzing with activity. Familiar faces, nodded and gave me tired smiles as I walked in.

The room was already filling up. Some new faces I didn't recognise, still in body armour, I guessed were from the warrant team.

Beth came over and handed me a mug of tea. 'What a shit-show,' she murmured, rolling her eyes. We both grabbed a seat as Callum came in with his DI, Frank Heslopp.

Callum didn't waste any time. 'Right. You've all heard – when the entry team went into the flat on the Butterfield estate this morning, Brian Curtis and his girlfriend Stephanie Parks, were found dead.'

He nodded to the sergeant in charge of the entry team. 'Tom?'

All eyes were on the burly officer as he addressed the room.

'Team went in at four thirty this morning. Immediately on entry, we saw a male lying face down in the living room. Established the male was dead. On clearing the rest of the flat, we found a female, in the main bedroom. She'd suffered gun-shot wounds to the head and body. No one else present. Male matches description of Brian Curtis. Awaiting formal ID on both victims. A quantity of drugs was found on the premises. Scene secured and forensics are processing it now. No shots fired by our officers.'

'How did Curtis die?' asked Tony Morgan, a DS on Callum's team.

'Looked like he'd shot himself,' the sergeant said.

'If he *didn't* shoot himself,' Callum said to no one in particular, 'then we're looking at a double murder. Any sign of forced entry to the flat?'

'Bit difficult to know, boss.'

'Why?'

'We put a buzz saw through the door.'

'Buzz saw!' Frank Heslopp, the gnarled DI, snorted. 'Bloody hell – why not just use dynamite?'

There was a ripple of laughter round the room.

The sergeant shrugged. 'Intel said Curtis had installed heavy-duty locks and chains. Couldn't risk the "Enforcer" not breaking through.'

The Enforcer. A heavy red-metal battering ram, carried by the entry team to smash in a lock.

'OK.' Callum raked fingers through his hair. 'Forensics are processing the scene. Hopefully they can shed some light on things.'

'Good luck with that,' Heslopp said. 'After a load of hairy-arsed cops have trampled over everything it'll look like a rampaging rhino's gone through the place.'

'I resemble that remark,' Tom grinned.

I half-listened as actions were allocated and the team sorted out the initial lines of enquiry. My attention pulled back when I heard my name.

'. . . after Jo called,' Beth was saying. All eyes turned on me.

'Err, yes. Pip thought Curtis had found out where she was staying. His calls stopped on Thursday evening. It spooked her.'

'What time?' Callum asked.

'Around seven thirty.'

He turned back to the team. 'That gives us an initial timeline to work from, then. Pathologist will tell us more after the post-mortem, but he could have stopped calling, because he was already dead by then.' He turned to the sergeant. 'Was his phone recovered, Tom?'

'Several phones in the flat – not sure whose is whose yet.'

'OK. Let's get the phones analysed. There's also likely to be some valuable intel on those phones about his drug's business. Make that a priority.'

Notes were made and papers scooped up as everyone started to leave the briefing.

Callum hung back. 'Jo – you wanted me to take a look at something?'

'It's OK. You've got enough on.'

'Can spare a minute – come on.'

I followed him to his office, knowing he was giving me the time as a courtesy, rather than because he actually had it to spare.

He went to the coffee pot and poured himself a mug then gestured me to a seat.

I didn't waste time.

'Elle Richardson spoke to me about some cases she's concerned about.'

He raised a curious eyebrow. 'Oh?'

I'd already prepared notes the night before. I slipped a printed sheet out of my briefcase and pushed it across his desk. He skimmed down the page as he took a sip of coffee.

'Kilpin was one of mine,' he said. 'Lowry and Wearman were originally referred to CID, but their deaths were recorded as accidental.'

'Elle doesn't think so.'

'Which one?'

'All of them.' Even as I said it, I knew how outlandish it sounded.

He quirked an eyebrow. 'Really?'

I just nodded.

He planted his mug on the crowded desk. 'She raised her concerns with me about Kilpin, at the time. But there was nothing to point to anything other than misadventure.'

'She's still not convinced – neither am I.'

'Why?'

'In all three cases, it was the behaviours that seemed wrong to her.'

'Which is where you come in?'

I nodded – sending another sheet of notes to join the first.

He read it silently.

'We took all this into consideration at the time,' he said finally. 'No one knowing why Steve Lowry went back to using drugs. Unusual for a first-time user like Peter Wearman to inject alone. Andi Kilpin's family denying he used GHB or was into the kinky stuff.' He took another mouthful of coffee. 'But then, the family never want to know that good old Uncle Andi gets off on half strangling himself, with a satsuma up his arse, do they?'

'He didn't have a satsuma up h—'

'Figure of speech.' He took a long breath. 'Look, Jo – HMET were as thorough as we would be with any sudden death. But they are what they seem.'

West Yorkshire Police's Homicide and Major Enquiry Team. I knew they were good and I hated questioning their decision.

'I thought so too. But the more I look, the more uneasy I get.'

'Then stop looking.'

'Cal, you can't expect . . .'

'Without more compelling evidence, we can't just reopen them.' He cut across me.

'What kind of evidence would you need?'

He shrugged. 'Forensic. Physical. A confession from someone would be nice.'

I pulled my notes back across the desk.

'I've studied the photos taken in Kilpin's home—'

'How did you get—?'

'The porn bothers me.'

'Should hope so – not my cup of tea either.'

I rolled my eyes as he grinned at me. 'Magazines though?'

'So?'

'Why not phone or computer?'

'If he didn't want his family to know what he was into, he wouldn't want any evidence of it on his search history. Magazines don't leave a digital footprint.'

'He didn't put padding round his neck to hide ligature marks.'

'Wife and daughter were away – maybe he felt he didn't need to be so cautious.'

I wasn't giving up. 'No traces of GHB found in the house.'

'He wouldn't leave class A drugs in the bathroom cabinet, would he?'

'But if he took GHB that night, where's the bottle?'

'Put it back in his hiding place before going into the bathroom?'

'Doubtful. If he used it to get high, he would use it in the bathroom where he laid out all the other paraphernalia. He was alone in the house, so would have been expecting to tidy up later, he wasn't planning to die. And you never found a hiding place, did you? Despite a thorough search?'

'No. But it was never conclusive that he took the drug. Your pathologist friend admitted that GHB can occur naturally as a body decomposes. The amount found at post-mortem was so low the coroner agreed that it was most likely natural.'

'Speaking of decomposition – that's another thing . . .'

'He was dead for over a week before his body was discovered.'

'In a room where the temperature had been cranked up to twenty-five degrees,' I persisted.

Callum wasn't so easily persuaded. 'Lots of people have the bathroom temperature set higher . . .'

'The average temperature that week was twenty-three degrees. Hardly glacial.'

'So, what are you saying?'

'That if someone wanted to speed up decomposition, to make establishing time and manner of death difficult – turning up the heat in a closed bathroom would be one way to do it.'

He studied me across the desk for what seemed like an age, before taking a long breath. 'You think he was murdered?'

'It's a possibility.'

'The bathroom was locked from the inside. It's three floors up and no sign of a ladder or footprints beneath the window, which was also locked. No forced entry to the house either, until uniform kicked the door in.'

I washed a hand across my face. 'Look, I'm not saying I have all the answers, Cal. But the more I study the behaviours, the more I think Elle might be right.'

'And the others?'

'It's a stretch, I know, but Elle thinks they might have been killed too.'

He raised his eyebrows. 'You want to add three more murders to our caseload – even though there's no evidence for it?'

'Maybe not Lowry and Wearman – I agree they're thin. But Kilpin? Maybe.'

'We don't have the time or the resources to go chasing shadows, Jo.' He stood up and gathered his notes. 'And after this morning's raid – which was good intel from you, by the way – we might have a double murder to add to our workload.' He pulled open the office door. 'So, if that's all you've got?'

I put my notes back in the briefcase. 'Well, can I at least look into them myself?'

'As long as it doesn't come out of my budget – knock yourself out. Beth can get you whatever you need.'

He stopped in the corridor outside his office. 'Sorry we couldn't get that drink, Jo. But we'll be putting in all the hours on this lot now.'

'That's OK.' I gave him a half-smile, secretly relieved.

Chapter Thirteen

Savile Park, Halifax – Sunday morning

I pulled my Roadster into an available space in front of the imposing Edwardian mansion Andi Kilpin had called home.

Despite only being 10 a.m., the temperature was already over twenty degrees. A rare occasion, to be able to drive the twenty minutes from my farmhouse, with the roof down on the car.

The house was on the edge of Savile Park. A large expanse of open green fields where kids played football and people walked their dogs.

Even this peaceful neighbourhood belied a grim history, as the place where, forty-five years earlier, the Yorkshire Ripper had murdered his tenth victim. A pretty, teenage girl walking home across the green after visiting her grandparents.

I looked at the spot where Josephine Whitaker's body had been discovered. She had been just 300 yards away from home.

Most people living here now were probably unaware of those events. Houses around the edge of Savile Park green were some of the most exclusive in the area.

Jen had already called to arrange my visit with Andi Kilpin's widow, who was now standing at the top of the stone steps, waiting for me in the open doorway.

'Dr McCready?' She smiled, extending a slim hand as I reached her.

'Yes, thank you for agreeing to see me, Mrs Kilpin.'

'Please, call me Marion.'

She walked ahead of me, past a gallery of family photos, all in matching black frames, arranged artistically along the cream walls.

The kitchen was huge, with bifold glass doors that opened onto a large, well-kept garden. Pretty watercolours adorned the walls, and a large cork board by the door held reminders and notices, stabbed with coloured pins.

'I've taken the liberty of making a pot of tea – does that suit?'

'Absolutely. Thank you.'

I stood at the long dining table, watching her put the tea things on a tray. 'Thought we might sit in the garden.'

I followed her outside, onto dark-stained decking and took a wicker armchair opposite hers as she sorted out cups and saucers. 'We can talk while the tea brews.'

She was a woman who prided herself on doing things the 'right way'. Someone who observed the niceties. The manners of an almost bygone era. My mother would have approved.

'It's good of you to see me, so soon after your husband's death.'

She slowly stirred the delicate china teapot. 'I was curious,' she said. 'About why a forensic psychologist would want to speak with me.'

'I work with the police, sometimes. When circumstances around an unexpected death aren't clear.'

The teaspoon stopped mid-stir, as she regarded me over the teapot. 'The police were happy that my husband's death was an accident. He didn't intend to kill himself that night, I can assure you of that.'

My smile was as reassuring as I could make it. 'I'm not here on behalf of the police, Marion.'

'Then who?' She poured tea into small china cups.

'The pathologist who carried out the post-mortem said there were one or two things that puzzled her about the way your husband died.'

'Is that why his body hasn't been released yet?'

'Possibly.'

Elle hadn't told me that. But if she had doubts, I could understand why she would hold on to the body until she was satisfied. 'The pathologist thought I might be able to shed some light on things. Once she's happy, I'm sure she'll release your husband's body.'

'What things?'

There was something about Marion's demeanour that didn't chime. Her 'emotional energy' – that element that I could never quite describe to others, but something I'd sensed in people, ever since I was a child. A 'vibration' around them, like a magnetic field. Marion Kilpin's, 'vibrations' were jarring to me. It was a sensation I'd learned to trust.

'Behavioural analysis is my field,' I said. 'Not pathology. I'm interested in what your husband did in the days and hours leading up to his death. His behaviours . . . routines, that kind of thing.'

She took a sip of tea, her eyes never leaving mine. 'I'm told autoerotic asphyxiation is the term used to describe what my husband did to himself.' She seemed far more matter-of-fact than most widows would be under the circumstances. 'I wouldn't have thought many behaviours would be regarded as "normal" in such a situation?'

Her cup went back on its saucer with a clack.

'I'm not part of the official inquiry, Marion. I can only do this with your consent. If you're not happy, of course I'll leave.'

She nodded slowly, pursing her lips as she considered it. 'I don't want things to drag on,' she said finally. 'If I can help expedite matters, then of course I will.'

There was a silence as we both drank our tea. The sun warmed the atmosphere around us, which had threatened to become decidedly chilly.

She sat back against the soft cushions. 'Initially, the police suggested that my husband might have taken his own life. But because of the . . . magazines and so on, they dismissed that possibility.'

70

That was the second time she'd mentioned suicide, without being prompted.

And then I understood why Marion Kilpin was so accepting of the way her husband died, when most wives certainly wouldn't have been.

'Does that thought upset you?'

'Of course. What wife wouldn't be upset that her husband took his own life?'

About as many as would be upset at the thought of asphyxiophilia and gay porn. I thought.

'Do you have a religious faith?' Is what I actually said.

'I like to think of myself as a Christian.' She smiled. 'If you're asking whether I have strong beliefs about suicide . . . yes, I suppose so.'

But I knew, even as she said it – that wasn't the reason she was so against the suggestion he might have taken his own life.

'And your husband. Did he have strong beliefs?'

She gave a short laugh. 'Not at all. He used to tease me about volunteering at the local church. He wouldn't come with me – even to help carry my boxes. Said if he set foot in a church, he'd probably be struck down by a lightning bolt. I had to take Jordan with me.'

'Jordan?'

'My nephew. Andi's brother's son. He spent a lot of time with us when his parents passed away.'

'I'm sorry.'

She waved a hand as if to brush away the sentiment. 'Oh, it was a long time ago. Jordan was only a toddler when they died. Car accident.'

'And you looked after him since then?'

'He went to his grandmother originally. Lives with us now. But after the accident, Andi took him under his wing. Like the son we never had. Lately, Andi was involving him in the business. To give him work experience. He wants a job, but he's only fifteen. It's difficult at that age. Most places don't employ until they're sixteen. Andi took him along to auctions, then got him to photograph the pieces and put them on the website. Andi's not ... wasn't good with computers.'

'Me neither.' My levels of technophobia were a standing joke among my friends. 'Jordan must have taken your husband's death quite hard?'

Marion busied herself rearranging things on the tea tray.

Displacement activity.

'He's been very good. Helping me arrange things. Sorting out stock and so on.' She wasn't answering the question. I decided to try another tack.

'Still, after losing both parents – it's quite a blow.'

'He'll be all right.' She still didn't meet my eyes. 'I'll look after him.' Something in her tone jarred. I made a mental note of it.

'And his grandmother?'

'She was in her late eighties. Last year, she had to go into a home. Died a few months later – so Jordan came to live with us.'

'And how's that been for you all?' I watched her hands, fidgeting with the teapot. 'I mean, a teenage boy is a lot to take on.'

'He's no trouble. And when Leanne's home, she helps – takes him on days out in the holidays and so on.

'She's your daughter?'

'Yes. She's away at university. Well, not at the minute. We took a last break together when Andi ... when he ...'

'You were abroad at the time?'

'We actually left the day police think he ... died. That's why no one found him at first. Jordan would normally have been back, but he wasn't – which is why no one found Andi until a few days later.'

'Back?'

72

'Oh, he'd been away on holiday with a school friend and his parents. A camping trip in the lakes. He should have come back the day Leanne and I left, but they decided to stay on another week. He rang and left a voice message for my husband, to explain.' Marion took a sip of tea. 'The police found Jordan's message on my husband's phone. He hadn't had chance to listen to it.'

'Was he usually good at staying on top of messages – replying to texts, that kind of thing?'

'Yes.' She dropped her gaze – not meeting my eyes as she said quietly. 'Andi was quite fastidious about most things.'

There was that jarring energy again.

I let the silence stretch between us, until it was obvious Marion wasn't going to offer any more.

'If it's OK, I'd like to just take a look at one or two things, and then I'll leave you in peace?'

Marion put her cup down. 'Of course. What can I show you?'

'The bathroom – if that's OK?'

She nodded, silently leading the way.

Chapter Fourteen

Kilpin's bathroom – Sunday morning

'Walking the scene.' A process I used to map events as another person had experienced them.

In recent years, it was something I'd done to get into the mind of offenders. To walk through a crime scene and see the same things they had seen. Hear the same sounds; breathe the same air, in an attempt to map their thinking and understand what had driven them to commit whatever atrocity we were dealing with.

Today, I was trying to get into the mind of a victim. But the procedure was the same.

What had Andi Kilpin done before he died? I needed to rec-reate events, that would fit with the evidence the police had. Fill in the gaps if I could and answer some of the questions Elle had posed.

Marion led me through the elegant Edwardian mansion, along high-ceilinged corridors and staircases to the master bedroom.

As I stood in the open door to the en suite bathroom, a cool breeze coming from the open sash window ruffled the blind.

'Do you always keep the window open?' I asked.

She hesitated for just a moment. 'In the summer, and only during the day. My husband is . . . was, very security conscious. He made sure all the windows were closed and locked at night.'

'The heating was on when they found your husband. Is it usual for you to have it so warm in here?'

A look crossed her face. A 'micro expression', that happen in a fraction of a second.

Marion didn't know the answer.

'Err . . . not really. I don't know . . . I mean I wasn't here, so I have no idea why he would.' She lifted her shoulders in a slight shrug. 'Perhaps it was just chilly that night.'

'Yes,' I smiled. 'That must be it.'

As she turned to go, another thought occurred to me. 'When police photographed your house, they found a wine bottle and glass downstairs?'

She nodded. 'Yes, Andi would have a glass of red most evenings. Is it important?'

'Probably not,' I lied. 'I just want to get the sequence of events clear in my mind.'

'Right,' she said. 'I'll leave you to it. If you need anything, I'll be in the kitchen.'

I listened to her soft footfalls going down the stairs, then opened my files to the photographs taken by forensic officers at the scene.

I went to stand with my back to the bath which faced the door and held up a photo, taken from the same spot. Comparing it to the room as it was now.

Gone was the naked body of Andi Kilpin, curled in a foetal position behind the door, which had been pushed open just enough for first responders to get inside.

I preferred working from photographs. I could only imagine the actual scene on the day. The overpowering smell as people came into this cramped space. The heat – the sight of a partially decomposing body.

I wrinkled my nose at the very thought of it.

In the photo, Kilpin still had the noose round his neck – the other end tied to the brass door knob.

The door jamb was splintered where police had used force to break in.

I walked over and examined the door. It looked like an original feature. Heavy panelled wood with an ornate brass mortice lock.

75

I ran my fingers down the door frame, where someone had done an almost invisible repair and repainted the new wood.

The elaborate brass key was still in the lock on my side. I slipped it out and examined it – weighing it in my palm.

Still holding the key, I walked into the master bedroom and knew instantly why Marion Kilpin had been unable to answer my question about the temperature of her bathroom.

* * *

Andi Kilpin's bedroom was exactly that.

His room.

More minimalistic than the rest of the house, which bore all the hallmarks of a feminine touch.

Here things were functional. The bedding was plain dark grey. On one bedside table, there was a lamp and a coaster. The other table was empty. I pulled open the drawer on the 'occupied' side. There was a book on antiques and a pair of men's reading glasses.

A wooden clock ticked loudly on the marble mantlepiece of the large open fireplace, which unlike the others in the house, wasn't filled with a display of pretty dried flowers and candles. Just a plain, wrought-iron grate.

I stepped outside the room, onto the landing.

Below, I could hear sounds coming from the kitchen as Marion did the washing-up.

Quietly I walked to the next door along the corridor and pushed it open.

A large bed with pretty floral throws and pillows. On the bedside table, a pile of books and a vase filled with freshly cut flowers. Women's clothes folded over the back of an armchair set in the bay of a window overlooking the garden.

Marion's room.

76

I went back to Kilpin's room and looked at the photos from my file. The room wasn't much different to the way it looked now, with the exception of his clothes on a chair in the corner, and his shoes on the floor in front of the wardrobe.

I opened the wardrobe. Empty hangers jangled on the rail. A thick towelling bath robe hung on the back of the bedroom door.

Walking back into the bathroom, I studied the picture of Kilpin's body. Then flicked to the post-mortem images.

There were several photos of the mark left on his right buttock by the key I still held in my hand. I carefully turned it over – looking from it, to the place on the floor where it had lain.

Why would you take the key out of the lock and then sit on it?

I put the key back in the lock, then closed the door and knelt down – grimacing as pain shot through my left thigh.

I faced the bath, with my back against the solid wooden door, presumably as Kilpin had done.

Putting my photographs on the floor in front of me, I studied the image of his corpse and the magazines scattered in front of him. I reached behind my head with my left hand, grasping the door knob, to mimic the ligature tied to it, then leaned forward, as he must have done, to put pressure on his neck. I put the key behind me on the floor.

I was too far away to sit on the key.

I held the contorted position, until my arm ached too much, then sat back on my heels, studying the key, as though it might suddenly speak and give me all the answers.

What would I have to do, to sit on the key – post-mortem . . . long enough for blood to settle and leave that telltale mark on my skin?

I shuffled back a few centimetres, then slipped off my knee, to half-sit on my right buttock.

The key was underneath me now.

My knees were still bent – feet together. It wasn't the most comfortable position and I wouldn't have been able to hold it for long.

But, by then, that wouldn't have been a consideration for Kilpin.

I struggled to my feet. Pain shot through my leg and I stood for a second, massaging, through my jeans, the ridge of scar tissue that ran from my thigh into my groin.

When the pain passed, I stooped to pick up the key and walked into the bedroom, closing the bathroom door behind me.

The bedroom floor was polished wooden floorboards – waxed to a dark patina. Along the bottom of the bathroom door there was a gap of about an inch. I pushed the key under it, listening to it slide easily on the checkerboard tiles on the other side.

I returned the key to its home in the lock and stood, looking at the bathroom again. My senses jangling, with that same, unmistakeable instinct that had alerted Elle.

This scene just wasn't *right*.

Now that I was here – in the space where Kilpin had died – walking the scene, I could see a flickering image. Like a shadow at the edge of my emotional eye. Fugacious, but unmistakeable to me, because I'd experienced it before.

The faint silhouette of a killer.

I went downstairs to find Marion still in the kitchen.

'Just one last question,' I said as she walked me to the front door. 'Your husband's clothes . . . the ones in his wardrobe?'

'I cleared them out,' she said without emotion. 'Gave them to charity to distribute to the homeless.'

Chapter Fifteen

Kingsberry Farm – Sunday evening

I sat back from my computer and rubbed tired eyes. I'd been writing my notes on the Andi Kilpin scene.

The grandfather clock in the corner of my office said 8 p.m. I was weary and hungry. Time to call it a day.

Just as I turned off the desk lamp and closed my computer, the office phone rang.

'McCready.'

'Jo?' Ed's familiar voice. 'Thought I'd find you still working.'

'Hey.' Trying to sound cheerful. 'I did say I had work to do this weekend.'

'I know . . . missing you, though,' he said softly.

I prepared myself for a conversation I knew was long overdue.

'Can I come over?' There was a heaviness in his voice – a sadness I felt responsible for.

I looked at my computer – shut down for the night. 'I'd love you to, but I'm up to my eyes in it, Ed. Probably be pulling a late one.'

Frustrated breath gusted down the phone. 'Haven't seen you all week . . . come on, Jo. All work and no play.'

I perched on the edge of my desk. 'I know . . . sorry.'

'I wanted to tell you face to face – but as I can't see you . . .'

'What?'

'I have to go away on business in the next day or so. California.'

I suddenly felt relieved.

'Lovely for some,' I smiled.

'You could come along?' I could hear the hope in his voice and I hated myself for swerving him.'

'That's a lovely offer, Ed – but I can't . . . not at such short notice.'

'Jen would look after Harvey and—'

'Ed.' That sounded more abrupt than I'd intended. 'I'm sorry, but I can't do this anymore.'

I heard his intake of breath and knew he'd been expecting this – dreading what was coming.

'Jo, please don't . . .'

'I'm sorry Ed.' I meant it. 'You're really lovely and it's been good, but—'

'Don't.' His anguish tore at me – but not enough to stop what I'd started.

'We met too soon . . . bad timing—'

'No.' He sounded more angry than upset now. 'It's him, isn't it? Ferguson?'

'No.'

'You haven't had time to get over what he did – how you felt. I get that. But you will, if you give it time.'

I squeezed my eyes shut – listening to his pain was unbearable.

'Give us a chance, Jo . . . please. If you need more time, that's fine – I'll give you all the space you need – but don't do this . . . please.'

'Ed . . .' I felt hopeless.

'Look – I'll be away a couple of weeks. When I get back, we can talk again . . . please?'

I couldn't give him false hope. 'It won't change anything, but if that's what you want . . .'

'What I want is to come over there right now and see you . . . not do this over the phone . . .'

'I know – I'm sorry, but I can't.'

'OK – well, at least say you'll think about it while I'm away? Don't make any final decisions until I get back . . . promise me?'

'I promise,' I murmured, knowing I owed him at least that much.

* * *

Harvey followed me down the glass corridor to the kitchen.

My stomach was churning after the conversation with Ed.

I knew I was hurting him and he didn't deserve that. But he didn't deserve being in a one-sided relationship either and my emotions were shredded ever since I'd discovered Callum's affair. The mess, compounded by the fact that his lover had died, leaving my anger and hurt with nowhere to go.

There was no way to 'have it out' with Callum to get the answers I so desperately needed. What was fashionably called 'closure'.

Instead, the pain festered inside me like an open wound. Raw and untreated. Leaving no room for anyone else, despite Ed's best efforts to exorcise my emotional ghosts.

I'd been unfair to begin a relationship with Ed, knowing the way I still felt about Callum. But then – I knew better than most, that when our hearts are hurting, we'll grab any sticking plaster of affection.

I stood in front of the open fridge, but my appetite had gone. Instead, I reached for a bottle of Chablis and poured a large glass, sipping the cold wine as I stood in the doorway, watching Harvey run round the garden.

The soft evening air was still warm.

I stepped outside, footsteps crunching on the gravel drive, as I followed Harvey, taking in the scent of lavender and fresh moorland heather. My garden was deliberately low-maintenance, as I rarely had time to work in it. Gravel paths edged with perennial and hardy plants that thrived on neglect.

I sat on a wooden bench and took another sip of wine just as my mobile rang.

'Callum.' I was surprised.

'Just calling about the Curtis scene. You got a minute?'

'Of course.' The disparity between the way I felt about this call and the last, wasn't lost on me.

'Could you come out to the scene and take a look?'

I looked at the glass in my hand. 'What – now?'

'No – the morning's fine.'

'OK – what's up?'

His breath left him in frustration and I could imagine him raking fingers through his hair, in that way he had when he was tired.

'Looks pretty straightforward, but just want you to walk through it . . . get your take on it.'

My hesitation was momentary, but he immediately read the silence – understanding my concerns before I could verbalise them.

'It's OK,' he said. 'The bodies have been removed.'

I exhaled slowly. 'Good. No problem then.'

'Great – I'll meet you there at ten.'

Chapter Sixteen

Butterfield Estate, Fordley – Monday morning

My Roadster looked incongruous parked outside Ridings House – a block of flats in the middle of the Butterfield Estate. One of the toughest housing estates in Fordley, with a reputation for crime and violence that made it one of the most dangerous areas in West Yorkshire.

Ordinarily, I wouldn't have parked here, but the reassuring sight of police officers and marked support vehicles nearby gave me a sense of security.

Crime scene investigators were still working the scene, and forensic officers were in and out of the block, dressed in their white scene suits.

A uniformed officer, stood guarding the outer cordon – checking the ID of those residents who needed to get into their homes, whilst steering the morbidly curious away.

A familiar figure ducked under the blue and white police tape and walked towards me. Despite the anonymising white coverall, he was unmistakeable. Even with the hood covering his distinctive silver hair and the mask over his face, I could have picked Callum out of any crowd.

He pulled the mask down, leaving it dangling round his neck.

'Thanks for coming out, Jo.' His smile tugged something deep in my stomach. He handed me my scene suit, mask, shoe covers and gloves. 'I know you don't like seeing fresh crime scenes.'

I leaned against a forensic van as I pulled on the overalls. 'Does anyone actually *like* them?'

He laughed. 'Your mate Elle, for one.'

'Hmm – but she's not "normal people".'

I signed the scene log and ducked under the tape, following Callum to the glass doors.

The stairwell entrance stank of urine and stale cooking smells coming from the flats. The walls were covered in graffiti. A young boy kicked a football against the doors to the lift with a loud clang.

'You shouldn't be in here.' Callum caught the football.

The kid pulled a face. 'I live here.'

Callum gave an exaggerated look around the stairwell. 'What . . . in here?'

'Very funny . . . give us the ball back.'

Callum tossed the football from one hand to the other. 'What's your name?'

'Billy.'

'Billy what?'

'Wilson.'

'And how old are you, Billy Wilson?'

'Eight. You're a copper . . . you shouldn't steal a kid's ball.'

I stifled a grin.

'I shouldn't clip a kid round the ear either.' Callum said, half seriously.

'I'd have you up for assault.'

'Which flat do you live in Billy?'

'Forty-one.'

'Then, that's where you should be.' He tossed the ball back. 'While police are in and out, you should stay in the flat – or play outside.'

Billy headed for the stairs. 'Pig!' he shouted over his shoulder.

'Make a note, constable,' Callum said loudly. 'Flat forty-one. Armed response, to go burst Billy Wilson's football.'

We listened to Billy clattering up the concrete stairs, making oinking noises as he went.

'Community policing at its best,' I laughed. 'And since when did I become a constable?'

'Improv.' Callum pressed the button for the lift. 'Used to get a clip round the ear from the community cop when I was a kid. Shame we can't do it now.'

'You should put it in the suggestions box.'

The doors slid open and we stepped into an even more putrid-smelling space. I pulled the mask over my nose, but it didn't make much difference.

He hit the button for the third floor. 'Didn't think you'd fancy climbing six flights,' he said, nodding to my leg.

'Thanks.' I appreciated the consideration.

* * *

The doors from the lift and stairwell led onto a concrete balcony, with the open side overlooking the estate. The flat we'd come to see was halfway along. A uniformed officer stood guarding the entrance.

Neighbours further along were leaning against the balcony edge, smoking and chatting – some even nursed mugs of coffee while craning to get a glimpse of the unfolding drama.

It never ceased to amaze me how sudden death had become a spectator sport.

'Don't think Curtis is going to be missed by many round here,' Callum said quietly. 'They've probably come out to make sure he's really dead.'

Callum showed his ID to the scene guard.

A thin piece of what had evidently been the front door hung by two hinges. The rest – just splinters and sawdust. I paused to look at the remains of heavy chains and locks Curtis had fitted – clinging loosely to the fractured framework.

We went inside, careful to walk on the stepping plates put down by forensic officers, to prevent potential evidence being trampled underfoot.

Despite the buzz of activity, the house was quiet. Scene of crime officers worked silently in each room, photographing, collecting and bagging evidence.

I let Callum lead the way – never comfortable visiting a scene that had once been someone's home.

Even if this wasn't Curtis's home – it had once been a happy place for Pip and Maisie – but not anymore. I understood why Pip wouldn't want to come back here. How could her safe space ever feel the same again?

As soon as we went through the remains of the front entrance, we were faced with the open door to the living room across the narrow hallway.

Callum spoke quietly to the crime scene manager, who nodded, then stepped out to let us have the space.

I stood by the front door – my eyes fixed on the large dark-brown bloodstain that had spread on the living room carpet.

Callum stood beside the stain – watching me silently, in that way he had that made me feel I was the complete focus of his attention.

He was waiting for me to say something. When I didn't, he indicated the stain with a latex clad finger.

'This is where Curtis's head was. Face down – inside the room.'

'How tall was he?'

'Six two.'

I looked at the stain, then tracked a line back towards the door. 'Entry team said they thought he'd shot himself?'

Callum pulled images from his iPad and handed it to me.

The first one showed Brian Curtis lying, as Callum had said, face down in the living-room. His left arm down by his side. His right arm, bent at the elbow, holding a pistol. His feet were just inside the living room door.

'He didn't,' I murmured to myself.

Callum's forehead furrowed above his mask. 'What?'

Shoot himself.

'Nothing.'

There was an intense dissonance of a domestic setting, contrasted with the horror of the crime that happened there.

Maisie's doll's house and toys were scattered around the room with a dead body lying in the middle of it all.

'It's the handgun Pip Holden identified from photographs as the one Curtis always carried.' Callum leaned in to look at the iPad. His familiar cologne a sudden reminder of the intimacy we'd once shared. Instinctively, I moved my head away.

The involuntary gesture wasn't lost on him. Out of the corner of my eye, I saw him shoot me a look, but he didn't remark on it.

'A 9mm Baikal – smuggled in from Lithuania. Weapon of choice for street gangs here.' He continued. 'We found ten rounds of ammunition to go with it. Only Curtis's fingerprints are on the gun. Post-mortem will confirm whether the bullet that killed him came from this weapon.'

'It will have,' I said quietly.

I could see why a 'murder-suicide' was the logical conclusion. But I already knew it wasn't what had happened here.

A subliminal perception had alerted me to the fine details that told a very different scenario. One that, for now, I couldn't put into words. But one that I would have to prove, if it was to explain what had really taken place.

He pointed out more stains, dotted across the carpet towards the TV. Each one indicated by a yellow evidence marker. 'Brain and skull fragments.'

A brightly coloured unicorn toy, splattered with blood, looked over the gruesome scene. An unwilling and silent witness to whatever had happened here.

Tearing my gaze away, I took in the rest of the room. A glass-topped coffee table, strewn with drugs paraphernalia. Weighing scales and small plastic bags. Residue of white powder staining the surface. A beer can beside the couch – TV remote on the cushion.

'He was relaxed just before he died,' I said. 'Unconcerned.'

'About what?' Callum asked.

'Anything,' I said simply. 'There isn't a feeling of anxiety here. Rage . . . torment, anything like that.' I scanned the room again. 'Looks as though he simply stopped whatever he was doing . . . here on the couch . . . stood up and shot himself.'

Callum said nothing. Just continued to watch me – as though he was trying to read my very thoughts.

I went into the room – on the stepping plates – glad I didn't have to tread on the stained carpet. There was a TV on a glass stand facing the couch.

'Was the TV on when they found him?'

Callum glanced at his iPad and nodded. 'Does it matter?' He frowned. His impatience, almost as legendary as mine.

'Maybe.'

'The girlfriend was found in the bedroom.' Callum left the room and went down the corridor. With one last glance at the living room, I followed.

Two forensics officers were just coming out, carrying armfuls of equipment. 'We're not finished in there yet,' one said.

'We won't be long.' Callum stood aside and gestured for me to go in.

I looked past him and froze.

88

Chapter Seventeen

Crime scene, Fordley – Monday morning

The bedroom was a scene of utter horror.

The mattress on the double bed was marred by a large brown stain in the centre. Further up, another dark stain at the top of the mattress near the wooden headboard – which was splattered with solid matter.

My mind shied away from thinking too much about what part of Stephanie Parks's body they'd come from – but I could guess.

'They moved the body with the duvet and bedding, to preserve evidence,' Callum said, watching me as I remained outside the room.

He scrolled through images on his iPad and held it out – as if to coax me closer – like holding out a tasty titbit to tempt a timid animal.

I took a breath and stepped inside. The room was unbearably hot and the metallic smell of blood still hung in the air, mingling incongruously with the soft scent of a woman's perfume. It crept round the edges of my mask, making me press my lips together to stop it getting into my mouth.

'If this is too much . . . ?' he said gently.

'No,' I said too quickly. 'It's fine.'

This was why I hated visiting fresh murder scenes. When the smells and sights brought home the harsh reality of brutal death. The component parts of a once vital, living human being, spread out like so much detritus. Reducing a sentient being to biological material and body fluids.

Maybe because behaviour and emotional responses were the elements I dealt with. Seeing those things, that makes us uniquely human, suddenly and violently stripped away – affected me more than most. Or maybe I'd been working too long with the brutal side of human nature and it was beginning to get to me.

I cleared my throat – pulling myself back to the task at hand – trying to see the room as it was before a tornado of destruction had crashed through here and ended Stephanie Parks's life.

'How old was she?' I asked, staring at the stain on the bed.

'Twenty.'

I held out my hand and he passed me the iPad. Reluctantly, I gazed past the devastating injuries to what had once been a pretty girl. She was dressed in shorts and a cropped T-shirt, her long blonde hair matted around her shoulders.

The photo showed her in a semi-reclined position. Her head against the headboard – the pillows scrunched up behind her, arms flung out by her sides – legs sprawled at an awkward angle.

'Entry team said she'd been shot in the head,' I said quietly. 'But it looks like she suffered more injuries than that?'

'Looks like a shot to the torso too. There might be more once they've done a post-mortem.'

I thought about Elle and didn't envy her the job.

Empty takeaway cartons and beer cans strewn around the bed. Clothes flung across a chair and belongings scattered across the dressing table.

Not the way I imagined Pip had kept the room when it had been hers. Chaos painted over a pristine canvas.

'Is there anything else?'

Callum shook his head. 'Rest of the flat pretty much as you'd expect.'

He led me on the short tour through the remaining rooms, most heartbreaking of which was Maisie's. A sleeping bag on the floor beside a single bed with a My Little Pony quilt, bore out Pip's statement that she had been sleeping next to her daughter.

This room, in contrast to the others, was neat and tidy. Filled with the trappings of childhood innocence.

'Photographs of how it all looked are on the file,' Callum said. 'I'll send it through to you.'

I nodded distractedly. Already wanting to get out of this depressing place that smelled of death.

* * *

'What do you think?' Callum asked as he watched me strip off the scene suit.

I leaned against the forensic van and took in mercifully fresh breaths of warm air – trying to get the stench of the flat out of my nose.

'You'll have a working hypothesis?' Wasn't an answer, but I wanted to know where his thinking was before I put in my two pennies' worth.

He was looking across the green in the middle of the estate, where a group of kids were playing football – using the NO BALL GAMES sign as one of the goal posts.

'Typically, on this estate, people aren't saying too much. Initial enquiries got some residents reporting a loud argument on Thursday afternoon but apparently Curtis and his girlfriend rowed all the time.'

'What's your guesstimate on time of death?' I knew Elle wouldn't have given her evidence on that yet – not until both post-mortems had been done. Even then, time of death was always difficult to pinpoint with any great accuracy.

'Neighbour in the flat below said she heard a woman scream, then a couple of loud bangs. Assumed they were fighting again and the bangs were doors being slammed or things being thrown – happened a lot since Curtis moved in.'

91

'What time?'

'She couldn't be exact – but thinks it was just before eight in the evening.'

'A couple of bangs?' I asked. 'Not three?'

He nodded. 'Which doesn't fit with the injuries, but maybe it wasn't gunshots she heard. Could have been doors banging, like she said. So, it's not conclusive.'

'It would fit with Pip saying he stopped communicating with her about 7.30 p.m.'

'We'll get a better idea when we've had the phones analysed.' Callum leaned his shoulder against the van. 'Got that young DS, Charlie Thompson, on it. Kid's mustard when it comes to communications intelligence.'

I remembered the young DS from the previous year, when he'd cracked a communications code in a previous case.

'Nothing else?'

He shook his head. 'Like I said – even though no one on the estate is going to shed a tear for Curtis – they're too scared to talk.'

'And your working theory?' I pressed again.

'Curtis and the girl argue. He shoots her . . . then himself.'

'You believe that?' I said, straightening up and handing him the kit I'd just taken off.

'Until I have evidence to the contrary . . .'

'I can believe Curtis was quite capable of killing his girlfriend,' I said, fishing car keys out of my bag. 'But to kill himself?' I shook my head. 'That's about as likely as Harvey becoming a vegan.'

He fell in step beside me as we walked to my car.

'We need hard evidence, Jo.'

'I'll have to look into Brian Curtis's background before I can give you a profile.'

'But . . . ?'

'From the little I know already; he doesn't strike me as the kind of character who would kill himself.'

'Hmm.'

'And over what?'

We'd reached my car. Callum leaned on the soft-top as I threw my case on to the passenger seat.

'Presumably whatever he and his girlfriend had argued about?' he ventured. 'Or because he'd just killed her?'

I quirked a sceptical eyebrow. 'Killers' remorse? I don't think so.'

He shrugged. 'It's all we've got so far. And you *did* say, you'd need to look at his background in more detail. I'll get Beth to send you what we have. Think there's some psych reports from a previous court case.'

'Great.' I went to get in the car, but he put his arm across the door. 'Jo . . . I still want to talk.' I had to look at him then and the pain in his eyes stopped my refusal in its tracks.

'Meet me for a drink?'

I hesitated for just a second – then let out a breath. 'When?'

'Tonight? Shibden Mill Inn.'

'OK.' Even as I agreed, I knew it wasn't a good idea.

Chapter Eighteen

Ferndean House – Monday evening

Rina bustled around the spacious farmhouse kitchen, preparing the evening meal as I nursed a mug of tea.

She took a sip of Malbec as she chopped vegetables. 'Sure you won't have a glass?'

'Can't,' I said, regretfully. 'I'm driving.'

'One won't hurt,' she persisted. 'Especially if you're eating.'

Elle had invited me to dinner, saying she might have more from the post-mortem that she could share with me.

'Tempting,' I sighed. 'But I'm meeting Callum later. Think I might need my permitted glass of wine then.'

'Oh.' Rina paused in her chopping. 'That bad?'

'Put it this way, he's angling for a conversation I really don't want to have.'

'Not like you to swerve a difficult convo,' she said, wiping her hands on a tea towel.

I shrugged. 'I can't see that raking over what happened is going to do either of us much good.'

She sat opposite and took another sip of wine, running a hand over her buzz cut hair. 'He must see a point.' She was using her counselling voice. I stifled a smile. 'What do you think he wants out of it?'

'For me to tell him it doesn't matter.' I took a sip of tea. 'That he didn't hurt me as badly as he thinks. That I forgive him.'

She pursed her lips thoughtfully. 'Hmm – absolution'

'Well, I'm not a priest.' That sounded harsh. But among friends, I didn't need to pretend. 'And I'm not going to lie, just to make him feel better.'

'Which is why you've tried to avoid the conversation,' she concluded.

Whatever I was about to say was interrupted as Elle walked in, dropping into a chair with an exaggerated sigh.

'I love the boys,' she said, referring to her horses, Butch and Sundance. 'But having to muck out, after a long day at work, is something I could do without.'

Rina poured a second glass of Malbec and pushed it across the table. 'Get yourself on the outside of that.' She got up to carry on the food prep.

'Come on, Jo.' Elle gestured to the patio doors that opened on to an outside dining area. 'I've got some preliminary results back from the PM on Curtis and his girlfriend.'

Elle's farmhouse sat on the stunningly beautiful border between Yorkshire and Lancashire, nestled into the hillside and surrounded by trees on three sides. The open side looked out over the moor.

I sank onto a comfortable wicker sofa and took in the view, which stretched to Pendle Hill in the far distance. Made infamous by the Pendle witch trials when ten unfortunates, found guilty of witchcraft, had been executed on the moors. It was a wild landscape, full of myth and mystery, but also stunningly beautiful.

We sat for a moment, both breathing in the tranquillity. The silence only broken by the distant bleating of sheep and the cry of a buzzard, wheeling high above us, as he tracked some unsuspecting prey on the moor.

'So,' Elle brought us back to more unsavoury topics. 'Preliminary examination confirms Brian Curtis's cause of death was a gunshot wound to the right side of his skull. Apparently, he was right-handed and the gun was still in his hand as he lay dead on the living room floor.' She sat back and took a sip of wine, savouring it with her eyes half shut before continuing. 'The bullet entered his right temple. Death would have been instant.'

She opened her eyes to look at me. 'I swabbed his hands and found firearms residue, consistent with him firing the gun.' She sat back and began twirling the fine stem of her wine glass between her elegantly long fingers. 'There was evidence of bruising on the right temple, which I believe could have been pre-mortem. It was difficult to see because of the damage caused by the bullet.'

'Could he have hit his head on something as he fell?' I was grasping at straws, but I had to test the theories before I dare present them as anything compelling to Callum. If I didn't punch holes in them, he would.

'There was nothing to hit his head on that would cause such an injury,' she said thoughtfully. 'The arm of the sofa and the coffee table were the hardest objects and they were too far away.'

'What about his girlfriend? Could she have hit him when they were arguing?'

'Possibly,' she conceded. 'I can't give you anything conclusive yet. But if it's there – I'll find it.'

'What did you find when you examined her?'

'No firearms residue on her hands or body. A gunshot wound to the stomach, which would have been fatal, but not instantly. Death was caused by the bullet to her head. Entered just above her right eyebrow. Bullet was recovered from the headboard. I've sent it to the ballistics testing centre for analysis.'

I took a long breath. 'Two sudden deaths then.'

'Three, actually.'

'What?'

'Stephanie Parks was pregnant when she died.'

Chapter Nineteen

Shibden Valley – Monday night

The Shibden Mill Inn has been a part of the valley since the seventeenth century. The mullioned windows and whitewashed exterior covered in creeping ivy, probably changed little since horse-drawn coaches made it a regular stop.

Not that we were there to admire the scenery or sample the award-winning food.

Callum had arrived before me and bagged an outside table in a relatively quiet corner of the garden. He nursed an orange juice as he watched me cross the car park, and waved me over.

The sun still managed to produce some heat and I was grateful for the umbrella over the table.

My Celtic skin could burn in front of a lightbulb. When I went abroad, it took me a week to turn from blue to white. The only way I could tan would be if my freckles all joined up.

Apart from shade, the umbrella gave us a bit more privacy. Whether the conversation he had in mind was going to be about dead bodies, or our dead relationship, I'd rather it wasn't broadcast to the whole pub.

'Have you eaten?' he asked as soon as I'd sat down.

'Yes – before I left.'

'Drink?'

'Malbec, please.' An easy choice, since Rina had offered one earlier. Felt like I might need it.

He went to the bar and came back with a larger glass than I might have ordered, setting it down in front of me like the spoils of war.

As he sat opposite, his expression was serious. Not the usual banter or small talk that used to happen so naturally between us. The silence was strained, but I didn't feel inclined to break it.

I wanted him to open this. I waited, taking a sip wine.

'Glad you came, Jo.' His head was down, speaking to the tabletop.

I could tell he was struggling to find the words – hoping I'd pre-empt what I knew he was thinking and carry some of the weight. When I didn't, he took a long breath, still not looking up. 'Before we talk business . . . I just wanted to tell you again how sorry I am.'

'For what?'

'Everything.' He looked at me then – blue eyes trying to reach into my thoughts. 'Hurting you . . . betraying your trust.'

'So why did you?' The million-dollar question. The one I'd wanted to ask for over half a year.

'I've gone over it a thousand times since Abbie died—'

'You weren't responsible for that, Cal,' I cut him off. 'Don't play the blame game. It serves no purpose. It'll keep you on a hook of guilt that you don't deserve.'

'My therapist said the same thing.'

'Your therapist is right.'

He took a sip of juice, but his eyes were looking over my shoulder – recalling events neither of us wanted to revisit.

'I know,' he said quietly. 'The guilt I feel is more about using her, than about the way she died.'

'Using her?'

'I'm shit at this self-analysis stuff.' He looked at me and the regret was genuine and obvious. 'But in the months I was on leave, I had to go there. Be honest with myself.'

I took another sip of wine, knowing silence was the best response . . . the only response I could give for now.

'You and me . . . were getting close.'

I nodded, watching him over the rim of my glass.

He was speaking so quietly, I had to strain to hear over the din coming from the other tables. He sat back in his chair, tipping his head back to look up at the cloudless sky. 'I couldn't handle it. I had never felt about anyone, the way I felt about you.'

I could sense what was coming, but I had to hear him say it. I knew too, how difficult this was for him. This man, who never really spoke about his deepest feelings.

'I used her . . . to distract myself. To create a distance between us, because I didn't know what to do with the way you were making me feel.'

That was coming perilously close to putting the blame for his cheating, squarely on me . . . but I let it slide.

He moved his glass around the table. 'I tried to look for fault with us – with you. Anything that could validate what I was doing and get me off the hook . . .'

That's counsellors speak, if ever I'd heard it. His therapist talking.

He stopped and I knew he'd run out of steam. His eyes, when they met mine were imploring me to help him out.

'And then, Abbie died,' I provided, seeing the emotional flinch behind his eyes.

He nodded. 'I was going to end it with her after the enquiry. I *was* fond of her,' he said quickly. 'But not in the way she wanted.'

'You never got to put things right with her,' I said, without judgment.

He reached over and put his hand over mine. 'But I need to put it right with you.'

I slid my hand from beneath his and took another sip of wine – a bigger one. 'I know,' was all I could say.

'I realise how difficult it was for you to let someone in . . . under your defences. I hurt you and I'll carry the guilt of that forever.'

'Absolution,' I said, more to myself than to him.

'What?'

'Something Rina said. Let yourself off the hook, Cal. It's not doing either of us any good.'

He nodded and a silence stretched between us. The chatter from the beer garden seemed to offer some semblance of normality. Life carrying on for other people, as we picked at a raw emotional wound in our own, private bubble.

One of us had to break the silence. I decided it was me.

'So, what have you got on the Curtis case?'

If he was bothered by my changing the subject, he didn't let it show.

'His girlfriend was pregnant – three months.'

'I've spoken to Elle.'

He nodded. 'Just as I was leaving to come here, I got a call from the lab.'

'And?'

'The baby wasn't Curtis's.'

'Elle didn't mention that.'

'Results just in. She probably hadn't seen them when she spoke to you.'

'You think Curtis knew?' I asked.

'If he did, it might be what they were rowing about. Maybe even a motivation for killing her?'

'Men have killed women over less' I had to admit. 'No other prints on the gun but his?'

He shook his head. 'Pip Holden gave us intelligence about other weapons in the flat. Apart from the gun he always carried on his person, she said she'd seen another handgun at the property. But we can't find it. Having another gun out on the streets is something we could do without.'

'Was Pip certain there was a second gun?'

He stretched aching shoulders. 'Yep. While she was at the flat, one of Curtis's associates came to visit. Said he needed to buy a gun. Curtis showed him a handgun. Apparently, Pip says they argued about the price and, in the end, Curtis refused to sell. It got heated. The visitor grabbed Curtis and threatened him. Saying he'd be back and Curtis would be sorry.'

'So, he could have come back and bought it later – which is why it's missing?'

'Possibly.' Callum pursed his lips thoughtfully. 'Or, our mystery man could have used it to kill Curtis and his girlfriend, rather than pay for it.'

'But why would he leave cash and drugs behind. Why not take everything of value?'

'Maybe he was disturbed – or robbery wasn't the motive and it was a professional hit to take out a rival.' He drained the last of his drink. 'Just one working theory – early days yet.'

'Any CCTV around the flats to help identify the mystery man?'

'Plenty of cameras,' he said. 'But none that work. The gangs damage them faster than the council can repair them. Don't think they even bother anymore.' He ran long fingers through his hair. 'Got initial phone analysis from the mobiles recovered from the scene.'

'Anything useful?'

'Lots of intel on the drugs business. Dealers and runners. Importantly for our crime scene though, last calls to and from Curtis's phone between 19.30 and 19.55. No activity after that.'

'Which fits with Pip saying he stopped harassing her then.'

'Plenty of people tried calling and messaging him, but he didn't read or reply to anything, or accept any calls. Not conclusive, but could indicate he was dead by then.' He stood up. 'Going to get another drink. You?'

'Can't,' I said for the second time that night. 'Driving.'

He nodded and left for the bar. He came back with a soda and lime for me. Knowing, without having to ask, what I wanted. That was how it was between us.

101

We know each other so well. It could have been perfect. What a bloody waste.

Any chance of dwelling on that thought was lost as he sat down, saying, 'Meant to ask . . . did you go visit Andi Kilpin's place?'

'Hmm. Met Marion.'

'What did you think of her?'

'She's adamant that her husband didn't kill himself. But then, she has a strong Christian faith.'

'Wouldn't want to entertain the thought of suicide, then.'

'Most wives wouldn't entertain the thought of their husbands being into gay porn and autoerotic asphyxiation, either.'

'Your point?'

'Did Kilpin have life insurance?'

'They both did . . . don't recall the details though. Why?'

'I'll bet you all the pension I don't have, there's a clause in the policy that says it doesn't pay out on suicides.'

'So, you think Kilpin took his own life, and to protect the insurance payout, his wife made it look like a sex fetish gone wrong?'

'Either Marion, or someone close to her. It's one of two possible scenarios I came up with. Have you met Jordan – the nephew?'

'Not personally. Beth interviewed him. Why?'

'If the scene was altered to cover up a suicide, it would be someone close to the family. There was no sign of forced entry – so either Kilpin let the person into the house, or they had legitimate access – a key?'

Callum nodded. 'Jordan was away at the time. Camping with a friend and his family. Beth checked – it's confirmed.'

'What time did Jordan leave the voice message that Kilpin never picked up?'

'Ten a.m. We know the uncle had a call the previous evening at 8 p.m. So Kilpin could have died anytime between those hours.'

'Would you mind if I spoke to Jordan?'

'No – help yourself. You'll have to get permission from his aunt though and make it clear it's not part of a police enquiry.'

'OK.'

'You said you'd come up with two possible scenarios ... What's the other?'

'That Kilpin was murdered.'

Chapter Twenty

Kingsberry Farm – Tuesday afternoon

Callum nearly choked on his drink when I'd said I thought Kilpin had been murdered.

'By his wife?'

'Not sure about the "who",' I'd said. 'But possibly, the "how".'

Whatever he'd been about to say was cut short when his phone rang. I listened to one half of a conversation with the incident room – enough to know he was needed back at the station.

'Sorry,' he'd said, grabbing his jacket from the back of his chair. 'Got to go.' I fell in step with him as we crossed the car park. 'But you can't drop a bomb like that and then leave it,' he'd said.

'Didn't intend to.' We'd reached our cars. 'It's not me who's being called away.'

'OK.' He'd yanked open the car door, throwing his jacket onto the passenger seat. 'Come down to the station, or call me when you can and tell me the rest.'

* * *

That was the previous night and we'd not had chance to speak since.

As I shut down my computer, Jen looked up from her desk across the room. 'You off?'

'Yes. Be gone most of the day.'

'OK. I'll take Harvey out for a walk before I go, in case you're late. Don't want him leaving you any nasty surprises.'

* * *

Jen had arranged for me to meet with Jordan Kilpin, back at the house in Savile Park.

When I arrived, I was surprised to find him on his own.

'Your aunt not in?'

He shook his head, leading me into the kitchen.

'She's at church,' he said over his shoulder. 'Helping set up for the summer fete, but she should be back any minute. Can I get you a brew?'

'Tea would be lovely – thanks.'

I watched as he busied himself around the kitchen. He looked older than his fifteen years. Tall and slim, with a shock of blond hair that continually fell over his eyes. He swept it back as he poured boiling water onto a teabag in a large mug. No fine bone china tea service this time.

He sat opposite me at the breakfast island. 'Not sure what you want to see me about,' he started cautiously. 'I told the police everything I could. But I wasn't even here when they found my uncle.'

I suddenly heard Callum's voice – *'Good old Uncle Andi, with a satsuma up his . . .'*

'Just need to get a bit of background, really.' I kept my tone light. The less important it seemed, the easier it would be for him to talk to me.

'We can wait until your aunt gets back.'

'No, it's OK.' His smile seemed nervous. 'Don't need her to hold my hand.'

'Your aunt said you came to live with them last year, after your grandmother passed away.'

'That's right.'

'I'm sorry.'

He gave a slight shrug. 'It's OK.' He attempted a wry smile, but missed the mark – just looking sad. 'I'm used to losing people.'

'I know about your parents. That's tough.'

Another shrug. 'Don't really remember them. I was only two when they died.' He pushed his fringe to one side, and began fidgeting. Twisting his fingers. 'Grandma though – that was the worst.'

I took a sip of tea. 'That's when you came to live here?'

He nodded. But his body was beginning to leak pressure signals. I watched the rise and fall of his chest as his breathing became a little faster and when I looked at his face, he wasn't looking at me. Concentrating intently on the granite countertop.

'How do you get on with your aunt and uncle . . . your cousin Leanne?'

'OK . . . yeah . . . good, I suppose.'

'Your uncle gave you a job?'

He nodded, avoiding my eyes, and his cheeks began to flush. I let the silence drag out – letting whatever pressure he was feeling build. Eventually, he blew out his cheeks.

'I . . . err, did the computer stuff for my uncle. He . . . isn't – I mean, wasn't – any good with that sort of stuff.'

I took another sip of tea, but my eyes never left his. 'You said losing your grandmother was the worst.'

'Well, yes . . . because she'd brought me up. I mean, I was too young to remember when I lost my parents, but when she died . . . well . . . everything changed.' The twisting began again.

A 'tell'. The leaking of emotions. Body language indicators of the way we're feeling that everyone has, and no one can control all of the time.

Jordan's cheeks flushed a deeper red and his breathing rate increased as his pulse rate began to climb.

This conversation was touching close to something he really didn't want to talk about. He was more than nervous now – he was scared.

'Everything changed, because you came to live here?'

'I . . . err, yes – of course.'

'Did you get on well with your uncle?'

'Uh huh . . .' His gaze dropped away again.

'How did you feel about the way he died?'

'What do you mean?' A micro expression flitted across his face – gone in a second, but not before I could read it.

Fear.

If this had been a therapy session and Jordan had been a patient of mine – I would steer away from whatever topic was causing this reaction. Give him space. Back away and circumnavigate whatever trauma was triggering him.

But he wasn't a patient and this wasn't therapy.

I knew Jordan was about to take us to the heart of what I suspected had happened in this house.

'The way he died, Jordan. I mean . . . were you surprised he was found the way he was?'

'I suppose.' His words said one thing, but his body language said another.

'You spent a lot of time with him – did you ever get a hint that he was into gay porn or asphyxiophilia?'

'Err – no, I mean . . . not the breath stuff – no.'

What about the gay porn?

I'd read the case notes Beth had sent me. I quoted from them now.

'People who worked with your uncle said you seemed very close. When he took you to the auctions, they said he was very protective. Kept you with him. Always wanted to know where you were.'

His knee began to bounce – nervous energy that had nowhere else to go.

'Was he being protective, Jordan . . . or something else?'

He sat up straighter and cleared his throat. 'I don't know.' He stood up suddenly. 'I should . . . perhaps I should call Aunt Marion.' He fished his mobile out of his jeans pocket. 'She should be here by now.'

He held the phone, but wasn't dialling. He was staring at me, waiting for something.

'Yes, call her. I think maybe she should be here for the rest of this conversation . . . don't you?'

He stood still. Holding the phone, but looking at me. 'No . . . I. Not in front of her.' He suddenly seemed less tense. As if he'd made a decision.

'Did she know, Jordan?' I asked quietly. The question deliberately ambiguous, so he could interpret it anyway he chose.

He nodded slowly.

'Is that why you feel you need to protect her? Because you're frightened she might have something to do with the way your uncle died?'

His whole body seemed to slump as he fell back onto the chair. Dropping his head in his hands as his shoulders heaved with silent sobs.

'I couldn't tell her.' His voice was muffled.

Slipping off my chair, I stood beside him, putting an arm across his shoulders. Shivers were running through his body.

'None of this is your fault,' I said gently.

He lifted his head – red eyes imploring as tears ran down his face and dripped from his chin, to plop onto the counter.

'He said if I told anyone I'd be taken into care.'

With his head on my shoulder, he couldn't see my gritted teeth, as I thought about my own son, when he was just fifteen years old.

If 'good old Uncle Andi' hadn't already been dead, I'd have wanted to kill him myself.

His words were barely a whisper. 'I didn't tell anyone – but she saw . . . she came home early one day and saw . . .'

I squeezed his shoulders. 'It's OK, Jordan . . . it's going to be OK.'

'I wasn't here when he died.' The words were tumbling out, as if they'd gone past a tipping point and he couldn't stop. 'She never said anything – just arranged for me to go on holiday for a while . . . when I got back, they told me he was dead.'

'After she saw,' I said carefully, 'she didn't discuss it with you?'
He shook his head – sniffing and wiping his nose on his sleeve.
'Did your uncle know she'd seen what he'd done?'

Another shake of the head. 'He had his back to the door . . .
I saw her over his shoulder. I thought I was going to be taken
away, like he said – but nothing happened.' When his eyes met
mine – the anguish and pain were unbearable to see.

'If she did it . . . she'll go to prison. I don't want that . . . not
Auntie Marion – or Leanne. I'd lose everyone again . . . everyone.'

Chapter Twenty-One

Fordley Police Station – Wednesday afternoon

Callum's office was quiet. Most of the team were out chasing lines of enquiry and the incident room wasn't as busy as usual.

We were watching a recording of Marion Kilpin's interview from the day before.

I'd called Callum after my conversation with Jordan and detectives had been waiting for her when she got back to the house.

He paused the recording. 'What do you think?'

I tapped my teeth with a pencil as I thought about the interview.

'Her body language is tense – but it would be for most people, if they're being formally interviewed in a police station. But she wasn't leaking massive stress signals and when she denied having anything to do with her husband's death, I didn't see any obvious signs of deception or evasion.'

He perched on the corner of his desk. 'But that doesn't mean she's *not* lying.'

'No,' I conceded. 'I'm not infallible. But taking into account that she's an ordinary member of the public and not a professional criminal, who's used to being interviewed, she'd find it hard to cover her feelings and unconscious body language to that extent, if she was lying.'

He went to the eternal coffee percolator on his bookshelf and poured himself a mug, then sat behind his desk, reading from the notes Beth had made after she and DC Shah Akhtar had concluded the interview.

'Marion and Leanne were booked on a flight from Manchester airport at 6 a.m. on Tuesday. They booked into the airport hotel the night before – Monday – and Marion's car was parked in the airport multi-storey. We know Kilpin was alive at one o'clock, on Monday because he took a call from the auction house.' He scanned down Beth's notes. 'Marion and Leanne left while Kilpin was at the auction that morning.'

'Airtight, then.'

'Not quite.' He restarted the video – skipping to a particular point.

Beth was mid-question. '. . . what did you do when you got to the airport?'

'We didn't go straight there. We did some shopping in Manchester during the day. Then, around five-ish, I left Leanne in town. She was meeting some university friends for dinner. She was going to get the train back to the airport when she left them. There's a train from Manchester Piccadilly straight to the airport.'

'What did you do after you'd left her in town?'

'Drove to the airport. Parked my car in the multi-storey. Went to the hotel and checked us in.'

'Then what?'

'Watched TV in the room and did a bit of reading, then fell asleep on the bed.'

'Did you go to the restaurant or the bar?' Beth asked.

'No. I'd bought some sandwiches while we were shopping earlier. I had those.'

'Did you see or speak to anyone in the hotel while you were there and before Leanne got back at . . .' Beth checked her notes. '11p.m.?'

'No.'

Callum paused the video.

'Plenty of time for her to leave the hotel and take a taxi back home to kill her husband. If that's what you're suggesting,' I said.

'You told me you thought Kilpin had been murdered. More your suggestion than mine.'

I nodded. 'There are a few things that make me think so – but if it *was* murder, I don't think it's likely that Marion did it.'

'Go on.'

'If Kilpin had taken his own life – then it's entirely possible Marion staged the scene to remove evidence of suicide and point to something else. I think she's more than capable of that.'

'For the insurance?'

I nodded. 'They wouldn't pay out on suicide. I believe their marriage had been in trouble for a while. There was no love lost there – especially once she knew Kilpin had been abusing their nephew. Staging the scene was one of two scenarios I told you I'd considered.'

'And the other was murder?'

'Yes. But if that's the case – it's unlikely Marion could have done it alone. For a start, how would a woman of her height and build, force her husband into the position we found him in?'

'GHB . . . maybe in the wine he was drinking?' Callum was playing devil's advocate.

I played along, to explore the possibilities. 'She'd have to spike the bottle beforehand – which is possible. But if she goes back to the house later, finds him drugged – how would she manhandle him into the bathroom and set up the scene?'

'Not likely, I agree.'

'I don't think Marion would have a clue about where to source GHB either.'

It was one thing constructing possible scenarios, but we also had to consider the mechanics of the act. The individual elements that the offender would have to go through to pull off such a thing. Marion scoring an illegal date rape drug just didn't seem plausible to me. Even if she knew people who could – I couldn't see her entering into that kind of collaboration.

'She's definitely not a grieving widow – that much is clear.' I went on. 'It's one thing to manipulate an event that presents itself – I could see her taking an opportunity like that – but murder? No.'

We both sat in silence for a moment, thinking over the possibilities, before Callum restarted the recording.

'You knew about your husband abusing Jordan?' Beth was asking.

Marion's head dropped and her hands twisted in her lap. When she looked up, her eyes were moist.

'Yes . . . I'd caught them . . . him.'

'Did you confront your husband at the time?'

A vigorous shake of the head.

'Why not?'

'Jordan,' she said simply.

'But Jordan was aware that you knew?' Beth prompted.

'Yes. I told him I wouldn't let it happen again. I kept him away from my husband – got him running errands for me at the church. There's a lot to do in the summer – church fete, garden parties . . . various things. He didn't work for my husband for several weeks. Then his friend's parents invited him away with them at the start of the school holidays. The day after he left, I told my husband I knew what he'd done.' She curled her lip, 'What he was.'

'How did he react?' Beth asked gently.

Marion lifted her chin. 'He denied it, of course. Said Jordan was lying. Pretended to be furious. Until I told him I'd seen it with my own eyes.'

'Go on.' Beth encouraged.

'I said I wanted him to move out, but he refused. Said I should leave. I threatened to tell the police if he didn't make arrangements to move.'

'How did he react to that?'

'I don't think he believed I'd do it. He knew Jordan wouldn't want that kind of drama. My nephew just wanted it to stop.

113

When Jordan's friend invited him to stay for longer, I decided to book a last-minute trip with Leanne. I couldn't bear the atmosphere in the house. The arguments ... recriminations.' She dabbed her nose with a tissue.

'How long had you and your husband been sleeping in separate rooms?' Beth asked.

'Over a year.'

'And whose idea was that?'

She fiddled with the hem of her skirt. 'My husband's.' She looked back up and her jaw was set – eyes hard. 'Looking back on it, I realise it was just after Jordan came to live with us. I didn't make the connection at the time, but now ... I suppose it's obvious that he wanted his own room, so he could ... they ...' She dabbed her eyes again.

Beth and Shah walked Marion through the events of the day she and Leanne had gone to Manchester airport. Taking her back and forth – checking for inconsistencies. There were none.

They asked whether she'd returned to the house, while Leanne was out with her friends. She denied it, but agreed that she'd had the time and the opportunity and no witnesses who could confirm that she'd been asleep in her room.

Finally, Beth cut to the chase.

'How did you feel when you were told about your husband's death?'

Marion paused for a moment, as though considering the best way to answer the question.

'Relieved,' she finally said, honestly.

'Anything else?' Beth's tone was deliberately non-judgemental.

'Angry.'

'Why angry?'

'At his lack of consideration,' she said simply. 'He couldn't wait until we were out of the house to indulge in his sick fetish. Selfish – self-centred. The fact that I knew what he was – what

114

he'd done, didn't make him feel ashamed – or change his behaviour one little bit. On the first night we were away he wasn't sitting there, worried about what would happen when we got back. Wasn't reflecting on the damage or upset he'd caused – or ashamed that I might tell Leanne while we were away.' She put her tissue in her lap. 'No. He just drank a bottle of wine – looked at his dirty magazines and indulged in his disgusting fetish – as if nothing had happened.'

'Were you glad he was dead?' Beth again.

Marion's chin jutted defiantly. 'Yes. I was. It solved everything.'

'Solved what?'

'No need to sell the house. No more pain or police for Jordan. Peace for us all.'

A moment's silence – then Beth leaned forward, her elbows on the table.

'I have to ask you this, Mrs Kilpin . . . did you kill your husband?'

I leaned into the screen, studying Marion's face and body language intently.

Her eyes widened momentarily as she processed the question.

'*Killed*?' Her surprise was impossible to fake. 'He died, playing his stupid game . . . didn't he?'

'That's not an answer.' Beth pushed.

'No,' she said firmly, 'I did not. But I wish I'd been brave enough to . . . years ago.'

Chapter Twenty-Two

Kingsberry Farm – Thursday afternoon

'Marion Kilpin's back home.' Callum's voice sounded weary. I cradled my mobile under my chin, as I continued to type notes on my laptop.

'I'm glad she's back with Jordan. Poor lad doesn't need any more upheaval in his life,' I said.

'Changing the subject – I asked Beth to send you Brian Curtis's psych report.'

'Got it.' I opened the file on my laptop. 'That was the next job on my to-do list.'

'Good. Can you put something in writing for me and email it over?'

'Will do.'

'With regard to Kilpin,' he went on, 'Beth and Shah did some digging, in light of what you said. I got them to check Kilpin's life insurance.'

'And?'

'A policy was taken out on both of them, ten years ago.'

'Hmm, would have been nice and tidy if the wife had recently insured her husband, wouldn't it?' I murmured.

'Only in an episode of *Murder She Wrote*,' he said. 'Before you ask – it *was* a substantial amount . . . five million, to be exact.'

'Wow! I never thought it was wise, to be worth more dead than alive.'

'You're right, it's not. And you're right about something else . . .'

'What?'

'It doesn't pay out on suicide.'

'Moot point, seeing as I'm pretty certain Kilpin didn't take his own life.'

'As we haven't got the resources to throw at this, I almost daren't ask . . . but, in the absence of this being exactly what it looks like, why have you eliminated the possibility of suicide?'

I read from my notes.

'In a hanging, most people automatically choose a high ligature point – he didn't. They don't all leave a note – but for what that's worth, he didn't do that either. By his wife's own admission, he was meticulous about planning everything in his life. His personality wouldn't have changed when it came to planning an ending for himself. But I don't see that here. For a start, he would have waited until he knew his wife and Leanne were safely abroad before carrying it out . . .'

'To avoid them returning unexpectedly, or phone calls, raising the alarm?'

'Exactly. His reaction when he was confronted about Jordan wasn't that of a man so bereft by what he'd done – *or* worried about the repercussions, that he would resort to taking his life, to avoid the fallout. So, I'm not seeing sufficient reason. Kilpin was arrogant enough and sure enough of his wife being too dominated by him, to worry about what might happen when they got back. He'd be confident in his manipulation of everyone around him, that he could talk his way out of it at best—'

'And at worst?'

'Paint such a dark picture of what the fallout would be, that Marion and certainly Jordan, wouldn't want to pursue it. As a fallback he would probably have suggested a discreet divorce. But take his own life . . . ?' My reflection in the computer screen, shook her head. 'Doesn't fit.'

'And if his death is exactly what it looks like?' Callum asked.

Again, my reflection shook her head, even though Callum couldn't see it.

'I read the forensic report, Beth sent over. No traces of GHB found in the empty wine bottle—'

'It could have occurred naturally, post-mortem,' Callum reminded me.

'Then why was the wine glass rinsed clean?' I said. 'Only Kilpin's fingerprints on the outside of the glass. Why would he rinse the glass but not leave it by the sink – or throw the empty bottle out?' I ploughed on. 'Why did he lock the bathroom door and take the key out of the lock? Putting it on the floor on his side of the door? Why not leave the door unlocked? He was alone in the house.'

'I'm sure you've got a theory,' he said without sarcasm.

'I think, whoever spiked his drink cut a fresh piece of washing line from the garage, strangled him with it, then posed him behind the bathroom door, while it was ajar. Turned up the thermostat in the bathroom, making sure the window was shut. Placed the magazines – which they'd brought with them, on the floor – slipped through the gap in the door, back into the bedroom and carefully pulled the door closed. Locked it from their side, then slipped the key under the gap at the bottom of the door, so it slides to Kilpin's side. Making it look like he's locked it from inside.'

'So, we've gone from a family cover-up, to an organised killer who brings everything they need with them, to commit the act? Including porn magazines . . . Really?'

'I looked at the evidence log. The magazines were old – 1990s. Where did they come from?'

'Kilpin's hidden stash?' he supplied helpfully.

'Porn that he'd had for three decades? He would have seen them hundreds – thousands of times and become familiar with them. They wouldn't have fuelled his fantasies – most people get addicted and add to their collection.'

'Maybe he wasn't easily bored? But even if we leave that aside for now – go back to the key. How did he end up sitting on it?'

'He didn't. The key was beside his body. But, after they'd shut the door, his body slipped from its posed position, so his right buttock was on top of the key. Hypostasis forms as the blood settles to the lower part of the body after death.'

'Which accounts for the imprint of the key on his buttock.'

'Yes. The scene was staged Cal. I knew it as soon as I walked through it and reconstructed events. But at first I thought it might have been Marion – finding him on returning home and covering up a possible suicide to look like paraphilia, because of the insurance. But the more I learned about Kilpin's character, the more unlikely it seemed that he would take his own life.'

'Bit of a leap to murder, though.'

'Hmm.' I chewed my pencil.

'And even if I was to go along with that – who's our suspect, if not Marion . . . Jordan?'

'No,' I said quickly. 'Besides, you've checked out his alibi – and Leanne's.'

'Like I said when you first brought this to me – I think you're chasing shadows, Jo.'

'That's what scares me,' I said quietly.

'Scared? Of what?'

'That there's a killer out there, who's so clever at what he does . . . that no one believes he exists.'

'He doesn't.'

His certainty terrified me.

'Then no one is looking for him . . . and while he's a ghost . . . he can keep on killing.'

* * *

The more I looked at Callum's 'shadows', the more I knew they were being cast by a killer.

The fact that Elle had her own doubts only strengthened my conviction. I trusted her gut, almost more than I trusted my own. Good enough reason to keep going until I could find something that Callum would regard as 'compelling'.

In the meantime, I busied myself going through the records Beth had sent over.

Brian Curtis's file made grim reading.

I scrolled through the typical police record of a kid who'd become involved with street gangs from an early age. First as a lookout, when he was still in primary school – to running drugs in his early teens.

The depressing litany of early drug use, funded by petty crime, and arrests which escalated as he climbed the ranks. Resulting in spells in young offenders institutions, to adult prison by the time he was eighteen.

Unlike many of his peers, Curtis had ambition beyond an easy supply of drugs and a wad of cash to throw around. He aspired to bigger things and didn't intend to lose many more years inside the prison system.

By his early twenties, when he met Pip, he was running a drugs gang of his own. Staying at arm's length from the business on the streets – preferring instead to get his minions to take all the risks. Particularly younger boys. Giving them the same kind of apprenticeship, he'd had.

I read through the psych report that a judge at his last trial had requested, prior to sentencing.

The conclusion of the forensic psychologist was that Curtis displayed all the signs of being a malignant narcissist.

I made my own notes as I read through the file. Adding information I'd gleaned from Pip.

When I finished, I sat back and stretched – contemplating the whole picture.

Brian Curtis had never been arrested for murder – although he'd been implicated in gang attacks that resulted in life-changing injuries for several rivals. Only sheer luck meant he hadn't faced a murder charge.

On one occasion there had been rumours that he'd ordered a rival killed – but there was insufficient evidence for the Crown Prosecution Service to proceed.

Was Curtis capable of murder? Undoubtedly.

Had he killed his pregnant girlfriend? That wasn't for me to decide – though I was sure he wouldn't have any moral qualms about it, if he'd felt compelled.

Did I think it likely that Brian Curtis had taken his own life? Absolutely not.

Chapter Twenty-Three

Butterfield Estate, Fordley – Thursday evening

All the evidence the team had pointed to the fact that Brian Curtis and his girlfriend had died between seven thirty and eight the previous Thursday.

I checked my watch. Seven thirty.

It had always been crucial for me, to 'walk the scene' at the same time an offence took place. It wasn't always possible, for lots of reasons, but whenever I could, I'd replicate it.

People were habitual. They had set routines, especially when it came to their environment. If you simply stand and watch an area for long enough, patterns begin to emerge. The areas people frequented the most and those they seemed to avoid. The street corners favoured by groups of youths. The shortcuts carved by locals as they navigated their neighbourhood.

At certain times, and on specific days, different things happened. Delivery rounds, bin collections, scheduled visits. All of those could be insignificant – or crucial pieces of a jigsaw.

I leaned against the corner of a row of shops and watched the block of flats – Ridings House – where Curtis had operated his drugs business.

There was an area of greenery in the middle of the estate, where kids were kicking a football.

Behind me, older youths gathered around a heavily fortified newsagent, its windows protected by thick wire mesh, and a Perspex partition at the counter – the kind you'd get in a post office or a bank.

A local shop that sold everything. Newspapers; cigarettes; sweets; bread and alcohol. Serving locals, who might run out of something, but charging top price for the convenience.

A steady flow of youths came and went. Leaving the shop with recharged vapes and bottles of vodka. The underage trade that fuelled this estate and many more like it. Happening in plain sight, in an area where the moral code was far different to more affluent areas, like Savile Park.

The scene guard at the door to Ridings House had gone and a few residents were going in and out. I knew the flat itself would still be cordoned off, as forensics hadn't released the scene, but things were being scaled down.

I pushed away from the wall and walked over to the flats, skirting round the green. Even before I reached the double glass doors to the foyer I could hear the rhythmic thud of a ball being kicked against the wall.

Billy Wilson, the cocky eight-year-old, we'd met on Monday, was alone, kicking his football against the lift doors. He glanced over his shoulder as he heard the doors open – catching the ball and hugging it to his chest as he recognised me.

'There's no copper on the door now,' he said defensively, 'so I can be here if I want.'

I smiled, leaning back against the wall, arms folded as I watched him square up to me. All four feet of him.

'It's all right,' I said with a grin. 'I'm not here to check up on you.'

He jerked his head towards the stairs. 'Your lot are up there.'

'They're not "my lot",' I said, still with a smile.

He sat on his football, a frown wrinkling his forehead. 'That other copper said you were a constable.'

'That other copper was pulling your leg.' I went to sit on the bottom step as he twisted round on the ball to face me. 'I'm a doctor.'

He raised his eyebrows. 'What kind of doctor?'

I stifled a smile. Most people didn't bother to ask and I usually didn't elaborate – letting them draw their own conclusions. But not Billy. With the typical directness of youth, he pressed. 'Forensics like that lot upstairs?'

'Kind of,' I hedged. 'In any case – I don't work for the police and I'm not a cop – OK?'

'What were you doing here with him, then?' He refused to let it go.

'Just helping out at the scene – that's all.' I needed to shift gears, before he painted me into a corner – this miniature inquisitor. 'Bet you know everything that goes on round here, don't you, Billy?'

He shrugged, getting up and kicking the ball against the lifts again, the metallic clang almost deafening in the small space.

'Are you here every night?' I tried to make it sound completely inconsequential.

'Most.' His eyes never left the ball.

'So, you'd know who came and went last Thursday?'

'Cops broke Bri's door down on Saturday morning . . . not Thursday.'

'Did you hear that?'

'Hard not to,' he snorted. 'Woke me up with the bloody chainsaw.' He spoke like an old man – not a child and I thought about myself at eight years old and the innocent and sheltered life I'd led, by comparison.

'You're on the floor above, aren't you?'

He nodded, slamming the ball noisily against the doors.

'Must have wondered what was going on, hearing all that commotion in the early hours.'

He shrugged. 'Never quiet round here.'

'One of your neighbours said they heard Brian and his girlfriend arguing on Thursday . . . doors slamming, that kind of thing.'

He paused, catching the ball on rebound this time. 'What's it with you and Thursday? What's special about that day?'

No flies on this kid.

'Like I said, I'm a doctor. I'm interested in Brian and his girlfriend . . . about how they got on? Whether they argued a lot, or were good neighbours? That kind of thing. Other people have said there was a bad row on Thursday – just want to know a bit more,' I shrugged, making light of it, in an attempt to breach his innate mistrust.'Just background on the people involved.'

'What, like a social worker?'

'Something like that.'

He nodded, launching the ball again – seemingly satisfied. Social workers were something he could relate to.

We both looked up as the outside doors opened and a short, stocky man, carrying a large black briefcase, walked in, bringing a blast of warm air with him.

'Hello, Billy.' He smiled cheerfully as he went to the lift and pressed the button.

'Out of order,' Billy said.

The man pulled a face, rolling his eyes. I got up and moved aside so he could pass.

Billy paused in his game until the man disappeared round the bend on the first landing.

'So, who's that?' I asked.

'Doctor,' he said simply, launching the ball against the lift doors again. 'Goes to see the old biddy on the fifth floor – she's dying. Got cancer.'

'Like I said – you know everything that goes on round here.' He carried on kicking.

I sat with the silence – knowing I'd get more if he was the one to break it.

Finally, he caught the ball and sat on it again – regarding me with shrewd eyes, far older than the rest of him.

'What's in it for me?' he said, finally.

125

'What do you want?'

'Twenty quid.'

I raised my eyebrows. 'Blimey, that's steep'

He shrugged. 'Take it or leave it.'

'Paying minors hard cash,' I tried to look serious, 'goes against my professional code, Billy. I could get struck off. Besides, how do I know your info is worth it?'

Just then the unmistakeable chimes of an ice cream van echoed. Billy's head snapped round to look outside.

'Tell you what?' I said. 'How about I buy you whatever you want from the ice cream van, as a deposit?'

'What?'

'A down payment on what you tell me. Then we'll see?'

He stood up, sending the ball skittering into the corner. 'OK.' He held out his hand. I dug a fiver out of my bag. He snatched it and ran for the door.

I stood and watched through the grimy glass as Billy ran across the green and joined the small queue at the van.

He hopped excitedly from one foot to the other as he waited his turn – this tough lad from an inner-city estate. Trying to be so grown up – but, thankfully, still just a kid at heart.

Eventually he walked back, licking the edge of the cone that dripped melting ice cream down his hand. I held the door open for him, then took my seat on the bottom step again.

He came to sit beside me – still licking the cone.

'So, tell me about Brian and his girlfriend.'

He slurped the strawberry sauce from his fingers. 'Yeah – they argued a lot. And it'll be nosey Mrs Russell who told the police about the noise . . . she's always complaining about summat.'

'And last Thursday?'

'When I came down the stairwell, past their flat, they were shouting. The telly was on loud too.'

'What time was that?'

126

He shrugged, biting the top of the ice cream. 'In the afternoon sometime. I'd been home for my dinner . . . was coming back down here.'

'Why didn't you use the lift?'

He pulled a face. 'Cos it stinks . . . prefer the stairs.'

'Then what?'

'Nothing special. Went back to mine to use the loo later and it was all quiet then.'

'Were you here playing at about this time in the evening?'

He nodded, biting some of the crispy cone as ice cream ran down his chin. I resisted the temptation to get a tissue out of my pocket and wipe it for him.

'Ice cream van came and I ran upstairs to ask Brit for some money, so I could get a lolly.'

'Brit?'

'Britney. My sister.'

'Did you see anyone go into Curtis's flat then? Anyone coming and going that you didn't recognise?'

'There're always people going to his flat that don't live round here. I don't know them all.' He was being cagey.

'Did you see anyone that Thursday night?'

He shook his head. 'When I went past, it was all quiet and there was no one hanging about. I'd have told Brit if there was.'

I frowned. 'Why would you tell your sister?'

He paused then – mid-lick. An expression flitted across his young face. He'd been so absorbed in his ice cream, he'd obviously said more than he should.

'No reason.'

I let it slide – not wanting him to clam up completely.

'If Thursday wasn't a special day – how come you remember it so well?'

'It was special . . .'

'Why?'

'Cos Brit, who's usually a tight cow, gave me a tenner – to get stuff from the van for her and her mates. They were watching telly in the flat. They were so pissed on voddy and stuff, she forgot to ask for the change back.'

'OK'

'When I got to Bri's floor, that's when I heard the scream and stuff.'

'Scream?'

'Yeah. A door banged and a girl screamed. Then a bit more banging about.'

'What did you do?'

'Didn't do nothing – just came down here.'

'And there was no one around?'

'Old Mrs Russell. She was standing outside her flat, complaining about the noise.'

'Which flat is she in?'

'The one underneath Bri's. When I got to her landing, she was shouting up . . . telling them to calm it down. That's what she does . . . stands on the landing, screaming at people.'

The neighbour Callum mentioned, who'd said she heard a scream and two loud bangs.

'This is important, Billy.' I half turned on the step, so I could look directly at him. 'I need you to think carefully . . .' He'd finished his cornet and was licking sticky fingers. 'How many bangs did you hear?'

He paused, with a finger in his mouth – his eyes looking up as he retrieved the memory.' Three,' he said finally.

'Are you sure?'

A nod. 'Certain . . . three.'

'In what order did it happen?'

'What?'

'The screaming and the bangs. Which came first? What order?'

He sucked the remaining juice from his thumb, then wiped his hands on his jeans. 'A bang . . . then the scream . . . then two bangs.' That's when Mrs Russell started yelling.'

'Can you do it for me?'

'Huh?'

'Make the sounds . . . with the gaps in between. That's the really important bit, Billy. The time between the bangs. Were they in quick succession . . . one straight after the other? Or a gap in between?'

He stared at me for a second, as if I was totally mad. 'It'll cost you a lolly, from the van.'

'Deal.'

He clapped his hands. 'First bang,' he said. 'Scream straight after, then . . .' He paused, nodding his head as he silently counted, then clapped his hands twice more . . . one after the other.

'There was quite a long gap between the first bang and the last two, Billy.'

He nodded. 'Yeah . . . that's about how long it was.' Then he held out his hand. 'Come on, then.'

I stood up. 'I'm walking that way,' I said. 'I'll come to the van with you.'

He opened his mouth to argue, then thought better of it and made for the door. Obviously not happy that he wouldn't get to keep the change this time.

* * *

The queue had gone by the time we got to the van. The vendor stuck his head out of the hatch, grinning at Billy.

'You finished that ice cream already, lad? Blimey . . . you must have hollow legs.'

Billy pointed to the picture of the ice lolly he wanted. 'Two of them, mister.'

The man looked at me and I nodded. Hard not to smile at the cheek of it.

'That's three quid, love,' he said to me, waiting for the cash before handing the goods over to Billy.

'There you go, son.'

Billy ran back to the block without so much as a thanks or a backward glance.

'There's gratitude for you.' The man grinned, wiping his hands on a towel.

I leaned my elbow on the edge of the serving hatch.

'Is this a regular stop for you?'

'Yeah . . . considering most of 'em round here can't afford much – it's one of my best pitches. Specially if you're around.' He nodded towards the retreating Billy and laughed.

'What nights are you here?'

'This time of year, every evening . . . bar Monday. Rain or shine.'

'About the same time?'

'Near as dammit. Any later and a lot of kids are inside.' His eyes narrowed and the smile faded.' Why you askin'? You a cop?'

I smiled, shaking my head. 'Social scientist . . .'

'Eh?'

'Doing a research paper on the social habits of residents on inner city estates.'

'Oh.' He looked like he wished he'd never asked.

'Were you here last Thursday?'

He began packing up. 'Will have been . . .'bout this time . . . yeah. Half-seven, then leave when the queue dies down.'

I looked at my watch. It was ten past eight.

'About this time, then?'

I moved my elbow to let him wipe the counter. 'Was it raining . . . last Thursday?' he asked, distracted.

'No.'

'Then it would be about now . . . yeah.'

I began walking across the green as he started the engine and pulled away. The estate was becoming quieter. The footballers had gone. A group of teenage girls were gathered outside the newsagents, smoking and laughing.

I crossed the street, giving them a wide berth, hugging the line of the buildings opposite.

Preferring my Roadster unscratched and with all four wheels, I'd parked away from the estate, on the main road, about a fifteen-minute walk away.

Chapter Twenty-Four

Butterfield Estate, Fordley – Thursday evening

It soon became obvious I was being followed and not subtly.

The clatter of running feet bounced off the wall beside me and the sound of voices grew louder.

Ahead, the warren of maisonettes and flats stretched out to the edge of the estate, punctuated by graffiti-stained underpasses and metal footbridges that criss-crossed the neighbourhood.

My left thigh began to ache and I knew couldn't walk much faster. These days, because of my leg, I couldn't run far or for long. Besides, I'd always been a big believer in facing trouble head on – whether it was a problem or a person.

Sticking my head in the lion's mouth had become a specialty of mine. Sometimes, the lion just gave me a big sloppy lick, sometimes I came off worst. My philosophy was that if the worst happened, it was going to anyway – might as well be facing it.

My hand closed around the car fob in my jacket pocket. The key ring, with its large, shiny metal heart charm. A present from Eduardo. It fitted neatly into my palm, reassuringly solid and heavy.

As I neared the end of the block to my right, I took the decision to stop and see who exactly was coming up behind me.

Maybe whoever was there had no interest in me at all and I was just being paranoid?

As soon as I turned to look – that hope disappeared faster than a rabbit on a promise.

* * *

The girls I'd seen earlier, outside the newsagents, slowed to a walk as I turned.

Five in total, all looking slightly worse for wear, after sharing various bottles of alcohol from the shop.

The eldest, who looked about nineteen, walked slightly in front of the others. She flicked her long blonde hair over her shoulder, tossing her head as she pinned me with what she hoped was an intimidating look.

'Well, well,' she sneered. 'If it isn't the doctor-cop.'

'Think she must be lost, Brit,' a tall girl with long brunette hair said, hooking thumbs into the top of her jeans.

With my back to the wall – literally, I scanned our surroundings.

This part of the estate, was quiet. Few passing cars to disturb proceedings. High walls on either side, closing us in. No over-looking windows and no cameras.

This obviously wasn't their first rodeo.

'Britney,' I said. 'Billy's sister.' It wasn't a question – just a statement of fact. Letting her know I wasn't completely ignorant.

'Ten out of ten, doctor-cop.'

I pushed away from the wall, turning to face them, so I could keep them all in sight.

A memory flashed through my mind, to when I was head prefect at secondary school. The tough girls deciding to try their luck when they caught me on my own in the girl's loo.

Afterwards, their blood dripping from the edge of the sink, to leave red star-burst patterns on the white-tiled floor and my sense of exhilaration at being able to deliver.

Later, my husband, Pete. Special Forces soldier, worried about the job his young wife did and the institutions I had to work in. Insisting I work out with him in the gym and learn a few choice techniques, if ever I found myself in the kind of trouble he lost sleep over.

'Have we got a problem?' My tone was icy calm.

'You're the one with the problem, lady.' Britney took a step closer as the others fanned out on either side of her in a well-choreographed move.

I stared at her, keeping the rest in my peripheral vision.

'And what would that be, Brit?' I said quietly.

A light flickered behind her eyes, as she recognised some-thing we both shared. The absence of fear and a confidence in this situation, that she hadn't expected.

Our eyes locked together in unspoken communication and then she seemed to remember that her little girl gang were watching.

'You've been asking too many questions.'

'Really? I said.'And why should that matter to you?'

'Buying my little brother ice cream, to make him talk to you, like some nonce.'

The thin smile didn't reach my eyes. 'Is that what you think, Britney? That I'm a nonce?' I raised my eyebrows. 'Seriously?'

The other girls shot her uncertain looks. This wasn't how it was supposed to play out.

My arms were by my sides – the heavy steel fob nestled in my left palm, hidden against my thigh.

'If you're not a cop,' Britney went on, 'then what?'

'Other people talk to kids,' I said evenly. 'Not just cops or nonces.'

'So, what are you, then?'

'Drug dealers talk to kids too, don't they?' I ignored her ques-tion. 'When they get lads like Billy to act as lookouts at the flats.'

The brunette's head snapped sideways to look at Britney. 'Fucking 'ell Brit?'

'Shut up.' Britney barked at her, without taking her eyes off me.

'That's why Billy's always in the hallway, isn't it?' I said, conversationally – as if we were discussing the weather. 'Why he never takes the lift . . . because he has to know what's going on in the block. Who's coming and going. And reports everything back to you.'

'You're full of shit,' Britney sneered, but didn't seem so cocky now.

'Were you one of Brian Curtis's runners? Or just his eyes and ears?'

One of the girls, the youngest, swayed a little, as she grinned. 'His link.'

Street slang for casual sexual partner.

Britney rounded on her. 'Fucking shut it, you stupid cow.'

I raised a curious eyebrow. 'Is that right? Did his girlfriend, know about that?'

'You're stickin' your nose in where it don't belong, bitch. That gets you all kinds of trouble you don't want.'

I gave an exaggerated sigh. 'You're right, Britney. I don't want any trouble. So why don't we just go our separate ways and call it a night?'

She took another step closer, fists clenching and unclenching. Her whole body starting to tense – unconsciously telegraphing her intentions.

'Look,' I said calmly, 'Curtis and his girlfriend are both dead. You don't have to keep watch . . . nor does Billy – not for a while anyway.' I could see a slight hesitation in her. I pressed the advantage, before the cocktail of alcohol and adrenalin in her system blocked out any remaining reason.

Her eyes narrowed a fraction as she processed what I was saying.

'Why buy into more trouble with the police?' I reasoned. 'Just turn round and go back – no harm done.'

The brunette curled her lip. 'Show her, Brit . . . no posh bitch tellin' us what to do on our own turf.'

135

The goading tipped her ego just enough.

She slipped her right hand into her pocket, her fingers closing around some kind of weapon. Then the muscles tensed in her thighs, giving me a split-second's notice, before she launched.

Her right hand appeared, holding a short-bladed lock knife, which she held straight out in front of her.

I let her come, never taking my eyes from the knife – her expression confused in those last few feet as to why I hadn't moved.

At the last second, with the knife inches away, I twisted my upper body to the left. The knife sliced empty air. I tangled my right hand in the hair on top of her head, pushing her face down onto my left hand as I brought it up, with the heavy fob in my open palm crashing into the bridge off her nose.

I heard the bone crack. Her scream echoed off the walls, amplifying the sound to an ear-splitting pitch.

Stepping back, I released her hair and let her crumple onto the concrete.

The knife clattered across the pavement, out of reach.

She instinctively curled into a protective foetal position, hands over her face as she writhed, screaming and cursing.

The others stared, as if frozen to the spot, as blood seeped between her fingers.

I kicked the knife even further away as I stepped over her, planting my feet slightly apart, to face the others.

'Any more, for any more?' I asked calmly.

Whatever they might have done, was interrupted by a shout from the end of the street.

'Oi . . . !'

The group turned, as if activated by a collective breath and started running – scattering in all directions.

'You OK?'

The doctor I'd seen at Billy's block of flats, ran up to me, panting heavily – his face flushed with the exertion.

'Can you take a look at her?' I indicated Britney as he crouched beside her.

'I saw what happened,' he said, already rolling the teenager onto her back, attempting to pry her hands away from her broken nose. 'Unfortunately, I don't move as fast as I used to.' He glanced up at me. 'Don't feel bad about this. You really had no choice.'

'I didn't,' I said honestly.

'I'm Dr Stanton, by the way ... Colin,' he said, pulling a gauze dressing out of his bag.

'I'm going to do you for this.' Britney's words – muffled in her cupped hands until the doctor pulled them away from her face.

The damage looked satisfyingly bad as he pressed the dressing over the bridge of her nose and began to sit her up.

Just then, headlights swept across the wall, illuminating us in a pool of light, as a familiar black BMW pulled up to the kerb.

Chapter Twenty-Five

'Accusing *me* of assault!' I said, incredulous. 'You've got to be kidding?'

'That's what she said, when they arrested her,' Callum said, as he drove to where I'd parked my car on the edge of the estate.'

He'd radioed for uniform to attend the scene and I'd sat in the car while he waited with the doctor and his cursing patient.

'She can say what she likes. Her and her little girl gang were intent on giving me a good kicking,' I fumed. 'Where does it say I'm not allowed to defend myself?'

I watched his profile in the blue glow of the dashboard lights. He nodded. 'Five on one . . . odds would bear out your version of events.'

'And Dr Stanton,' I reminded him. 'He saw what happened. Britney made the first move,' I said, like a kid caught fighting in the playground.

'And you made the last one.' He shot me a quick look. 'You almost seemed to be enjoying it . . . from what I could see.'

'Take my fun where I can find it these days.' I was only half-joking.

'Not funny. Better not say that if it comes to a charge.'

'Can't say I'll lose any sleep over breaking her nose.'

'Evidently.' He was trying to sound disapproving, but couldn't hide the half-smile. 'Anyway, I doubt she'll bring charges, once she's calmed down. You'll have to make a statement, if we're going to charge her with assault.'

'No problem.'

'But I wouldn't come on to this estate again, anytime soon. Especially on your own.'

'I've no need to now.'

'What were you doing here anyway?' He pulled up behind my car and cut the engine, twisting in his seat to look at me.

I shrugged. 'Wanted to see the area – same day and time. You know how I work, Cal. Need to see who's around – the comings and goings.'

'You should have told me.' He sounded disapproving. 'I was here to see the crime scene manager at the flat. I'd have come with you.'

I wasn't about to admit that, even had I known, I'd still have come alone. People weren't as easy to open up if there was a cop there. And despite not being in uniform, Callum's very demeanour screamed 'cop' at a hundred yards.

'Talked to Billy Wilson,' I said instead. 'Britney's his sister.'

'That explains a few things.'

'Sounds like Britney was involved with Curtis on the side. His girlfriend probably didn't know about it. But Billy's been used as a lookout at their block. Reported back to his big sister and I suspect Britney, and maybe her little cohort, were runners for Curtis.'

He nodded, staring straight ahead as he thought through the implications. 'Her name didn't come up in the original intel before we served the warrant on his flat. We'll round them up for questioning, see what falls out.'

His hand rested across the back of my seat. I could feel the warmth of him against my neck. It was stirring up long-buried feelings. The chemical reaction to being near him that we'd always had.

I pushed those feelings deeper down, so that I could concentrate. 'Last Thursday, Billy heard a woman scream inside Curtis's flat. Three loud bangs – which could have been shots, between seven thirty and eight-ten.'

'How can you be so sure of the time?'

'He'd been to get ice cream. I spoke to the vendor. This is a regular stop, between those times.'

Callum nodded slowly.' Three bangs – not two. That fits with Stephanie's injuries. But not the neighbour's account.'

'I know he's only a kid,' I said. 'But my money's on Billy being a more reliable witness. He's got street smarts . . . using his eyes and ears is what he's rewarded for. The gangs wouldn't use him if he was inaccurate. There's something else . . .'

'What?'

'The sequence.'

'What of it?'

'One shot . . . then a scream. Then a long pause, before two more.'

I stared straight ahead as I pictured the events unfolding across the darkened windscreen – like a movie playing in my mind.

Threading together all the elements that made both me and Elle uneasy. But which fitted in a certain, chilling order.

'Stephanie Parks was probably dead after she suffered the first gunshot wound. Or at least unable to scream . . .'

'Go on.' He was watching me intently.

'So, that first shot couldn't have been Curtis shooting her. I think the first bullet fired was for Curtis. Stephanie hears it and screams. There's a pause, while the gunman moves to the bedroom to find her – and the last two shots were for her.'

'Gunman?'

I turned slowly to look at him. 'I can't give you the solid evidence you need, yet. But I can tell you this . . . You've got a killer out there, Cal. A cold, calculating killer. He murdered Brian Curtis and his girlfriend . . . and the unborn baby.'

Chapter Twenty-Six

Fordley Police Station – Friday

'Ey up!' DS Tony Morgan shouted as I walked into the incident room. 'Here she is . . . Tyson McCready.'

I rolled my eyes, dumping my briefcase on his desk. 'Very funny.'

'Not a mark on you,' Beth laughed.

'No.' Tony pushed a chair towards me with his foot. 'But you should see the other guy.'

A ripple of laughter went through the team – quickly cut off as Callum came out of his office.

Everyone settled, some coming in at the back, cradling mugs of coffee. Beth handed me a cup of tea.

'I asked Jo to come in for this briefing, as she's the one who got the information from Billy Wilson . . .' Callum started.

'And beat the living crap out of his sister,' Tony chipped in, as everyone laughed.

'Not ideal,' Callum said, shooting me a disapproving look, 'But, Britney Wilson's been charged with assault and possession of a bladed weapon, in a public place. Released on bail.'

'Nice one, Jo,' Beth muttered to me, under her breath.

Callum told the team about Billy being a lookout, and his sister and her girl gang acting as runners for Curtis.

'We've brought the other girls in for questioning,' he said. 'Just waiting for an appropriate adult for Billy.'

'What about his mother?' someone asked.

'A heroin addict. Don't think she's been off the piss-soaked couch in that flat, since 2016.'

'Poor Billy,' I said, more to myself than anyone else.

'Is there much more the kid can tell us?' Beth asked.

'His account of hearing a scream and loud bangs, which could have been gunshots – pins the time of the killings to between 7.30 and 8 p.m.' Callum said. 'Plus, the sequence of what he heard.' He indicated the notes everyone had been issued with. 'If they *were* shots, then that doesn't fit with Curtis shooting his girlfriend twice and then himself, once.'

'Which leads us back to a potential third party,' Tony chipped in.

Callum indicated me with a nod of his head. 'Jo walked the scene and came up with a possible sequence of events. Jo?'

I walked over to the whiteboard, with its grim gallery of crime scene photographs and tapped the one of Curtis, lying face down, with his torso in the living room and his feet out in the hallway.

'This scene was staged,' I opened. 'It was meant to look as though Curtis shot himself in the head.'

'But you don't think so?' Heslopp said.

I shook my head. 'Even if we leave the forensic and post-mortem findings aside, the behaviours don't fit.

'Explain that a bit more.' Callum said.

'If we go with the original hypothesis,' I spoke to the photograph on the whiteboard, 'we're meant to believe that Curtis shot his girlfriend, after a row. And then, in a fit of remorse, or despair – took his own life.' I turned to face my audience. 'Brian Curtis was about as likely to suffer killer's remorse, as my dog is, to refuse a sausage.

'He was totally capable of killing Stephanie Parks,' I continued, 'but wouldn't take his own life – absolutely not in his make-up. But even if we stretch our disbelief that far – if he *did* shoot himself – his body wouldn't have been in this position.

'Why not?' Tony asked.

'People make themselves comfortable before the final act. Counter-intuitive, I know. But that's the typical behaviour. People sitting on a sofa, their favourite armchair or lying on the bed. Not doing it as they walk from one room to another. For Curtis to end up lying here, he'd have to shoot himself while standing in the living-room doorway.'

'Which brings us back to a third party,' Callum said. 'Any thoughts on that?'

'Having walked the scene, a few things jump out,' I continued. 'We can't tell whether there was forced entry to the flat—'

'Because Ronnie the Rhino's entry team, went in with a buzz saw,' quipped Heslopp.

'Forensics have gone over the door frame and locks,' Callum read from his notes. 'Looks like the drop latch was on, but the chain and security bars were off before the door was cut through.'

'So, I believe Curtis let the killer in,' I said. 'Which fits with the sequence of events I saw, when I walked the scene.'

'Which was?' Callum asked.

'Curtis opens the door to his killer. Given his line of work – it would have to be someone he knows, for him to let them into the flat. Then turns his back and begins to walk into the lounge. The killer delivers a blow to Curtis's right temple – consistent with the bruising Elle Richardson found at post-mortem. She said it was delivered with enough force to render Curtis unconscious.'

'That puts him face down in the lounge.' Beth followed my thread.

I nodded. 'The killer then takes Curtis's own gun out of his jeans' waistband – where he carried it – puts it into Curtis's hand and fires the fatal shot, to leave gunshot residue on Curtis. That's consistent with Billy saying he heard a bang – and then a scream.'

'Stephanie Parks?' Shah said.

'Stephanie was in the bedroom – probably lying on the bed, when she heard the shot and screamed. Maybe the killer didn't know she was in the flat until that moment—'

'Even if he did.' Callum cut in. 'He would have to neutralise Curtis before taking care of his girlfriend.'

'True,' I agreed. 'In any case, the killer then goes to the bedroom to find Stephanie.' I pointed to the picture of her, as she was found on the bed.

'The pillows are bunched up behind her back – quilt tangled round her feet – consistent with her pedalling up the bed – scrambling to get away from the gunman as he appeared in the doorway. She ends up in a half-sitting position, pressed up against the headboard – when the killer delivers the fatal shots.'

'The final two bangs Billy said he heard,' Callum concluded.

'The gap between the scream and the final two shots – is about the time it would take for the killer to register the scream,' I said, 'realise there was someone in the bedroom – walk down the short corridor and kill Stephanie. He then has as much time as he needs to go back to Curtis and finish staging the scene.'

Callum took up the narrative.

'Gunshot residue was found on Curtis's hand, arm and the right side of his head and face.'

'But not enough,' I said.

All eyes turned to me.

'What do you mean?' Callum asked.

'That residue is made up of fine particles, invisible to the naked eye. They spread everywhere. In this case, it was present on the right side of his head and face and his hand – none on the left.'

'Is that so unusual?' Beth asked, chewing her pencil.

'Frankly – yes. It would have been in his hair, clothes ... everywhere. The barrel of the pistol was pressed up against his head – the killer hoping it would destroy evidence of the blow to the temple. There was no gunshot residue on the left side of his face, or body,' I said. 'Because he was already lying on the floor when the shot was fired.'

Beth concluded,' Not standing or sitting, which he would have been, if he'd shot himself?'

I glanced back at the crime scene photos – almost talking to myself. 'Whoever this killer is . . . he knows what he's doing.' An involuntary shiver trickled across my shoulders.

Callum nodded. 'The concentration of deposits on the carpet, is consistent with the shot being fired, while Curtis was on the floor. The science doesn't lie.' He glanced round his team. 'If this had been a rival drugs gang eliminating the competition, they wouldn't have bothered staging the scene. They would have shot Curtis as soon as he answered the door. Drugs and cash, all left behind, so we know robbery wasn't the motive. Even a customer, coming to buy, would have cleaned the place out before legging it, if things had gone tits up with Curtis during a deal. So, what's the motive?'

All eyes turned to me.

'Find the motive and you find your killer,' I agreed.

I looked again at the crime scene photographs on the board, reading the scene as a whole. Both bodies . . . both rooms where the shootings took place.

'This is personal' I said. 'I think it's all about Curtis and Stephanie. Or, maybe she just happened to be in the flat and had to be killed to tidy up loose ends, but it suited the killer. He could stage the scene to make this look like a domestic.'

'That's cold . . . and quick thinking,' Beth said.

'It's got the hallmarks of a professional hit,' I said, still looking at the board. 'But a professional wouldn't go to the trouble of trying to make it look like Curtis shot himself.' I tapped my teeth with my pencil. 'Unless they wanted to make it obvious, that this wasn't about money or Curtis's drugs business.'

'What then?' Heslopp asked.

'Relationships,' I said simply. 'We were supposed to think this was between Curtis and his girlfriend. Murder-suicide.'

'But if not that . . .?' Beth asked. 'And not drugs related – then what?'

'A grudge. Revenge maybe, or a payback that had to end in murder.'

Chapter Twenty-Seven

Briefing room, Fordley Police Station – Friday

'What can you tell us about our offender, Jo?' Callum asked, over the rim of his mug.

I'd already drawn up a preliminary profile.

'Beth was spot on – cold and quick-thinking for a start.' I went to stand in front of the board, looking again at Curtis's body, face down in the lounge.

'This one image tells us, not just about the offender, but about Curtis's attitude . . . or even his relationship with his killer.'

'How so?' Heslopp asked.

'Curtis opens the door and lets him in – so it's someone he knows. He either trusts them enough to turn his back on them, or doesn't feel threatened by them.'

I indicated the pictures of the lounge. The drugs and cash on the coffee table. 'Curtis would have checked who was at the door, before opening it. Whoever it was, he didn't feel the need to clear away any of the incriminating evidence on the table. So, it's safe to assume it wasn't anyone posing as a cop or an official to gain entry.'

I sat on the edge of the table. 'For those who like statistics, the killer is probably white, male and aged between thirty and fifty-five – maybe older, but certainly not younger. Familiar with handguns – or at least knowledgeable enough to understand how to fire one and stage the scene. Forensically aware – enough to ensure Curtis has gunshot residue on his hand and arm. He's also familiar with the neighbourhood, but I don't think he lives on the estate.'

'Why not?' Callum asked.

'Because he made sure no one saw him leave the block after the killings. If he lived there, it wouldn't have mattered. Whoever this was – might have stuck in someone's memory, once the police started asking questions about who was around at the time of the shooting.'

'Picking up on that . . .' Tony cut in. 'How did he get past Billy?'

'Timed it for when the ice cream van was there,' I said simply. 'That Thursday night, the van arrived at 19.30 on the dot. As usual, Billy went to ask his sister for money to get an ice cream. I think the killer watched until Billy left his post – then probably took the lift to avoid meeting anyone on the stairs. As Billy's coming back down, he hears the first bang and the scream outside Curtis's flat. The killer can wait as long as he wants, before he leaves. As it happens, Billy goes back up to deliver the ice cream to Britney and her mates – while he's doing that, the killer could slip back out of the block without being seen.'

'Or he could have waited until later that night and then left.' Tony surmised. 'No working CCTV around there to check.'

I nodded. 'Either way, the ice cream van is a big distraction for the kids around those blocks. Ideal time to get in and out.'

'As you say,' Callum pursed his lips as he thought about it, 'obviously knows the neighbourhood well enough to predict that.'

'My money's on Curtis's associate, who came to the flat the week before, to buy a gun.' Heslopp said. 'The gun's missing, and he fits everything the doc just said.'

Callum nodded, scanning his notes. 'Pip Holden gave a description, which was circulated. Where are we on that?'

Beth said, 'Arranged for Pip to take a look at some mugshots, see if she can pick him out, and forensics are running fingerprints found at the scene.'

'OK. DS Charlie Thompson is checking the phones. There's a lot more to do, but so far it's led us to some of Curtis's associates – so they'll be rounded up. If we're lucky – Beth's ID search for the visitor to the flat, will cross reference with some phone data.' He scanned the notes Charlie had already sent. 'Curtis's phone shows he was messaging and calling Pip constantly that day. All communication stopped at 19.36. Burner phones at the scene, used to communicate with his runners, show them contacting him about drops and pickups, but he doesn't reply after that time.'

'Looks like that's when he was hit,' Tony concluded, to nods around the room.

I made my exit as soon as the briefing ended – not wanting to be collared by Callum for any more awkward conversations. But not before I'd spoken to Beth about getting access to the files for Steve Lowry and Peter Wearman – the two drugs deaths that Elle wasn't happy about.

Looking into those deaths was my next priority.

Chapter Twenty-Eight

Kingsberry Farm – Saturday morning

Callum said he was happy for me to look into the other cases, as long as I did it in my own time – and made it clear to anyone connected to them, that my involvement wasn't part of an official police enquiry.

At my desk, at the farm, I found myself going back to Peter Wearman's file. Of the two drug-related deaths, his had more unusual elements than Steve Lowry's.

Elle was right. It was highly unusual for a first-time intravenous user to try injecting heroin alone. They are usually educated into the intricacies of cooking up the heroin and using the paraphernalia by a more seasoned addict, or by their dealer. With no history or record of any 'gateway' drugs to start his journey, his death didn't feel right to me either.

I looked again at his photograph as I read the notes.

Thirty-two-year-old entrepreneur business man. Running a successful IT consultancy in Fordley. Jen had done a fact-find on all the cases we were looking at.

For Wearman, she'd found newspaper articles in IT trade journals and the *Yorkshire Post* business section, cataloguing the company's successes and listing awards they'd won in the three years since he'd founded the business.

I scanned through the journals before finally coming to the obituary in the *Fordley Express*. I glanced at the date and time of the funeral.

Today – two o'clock.

Grabbing my mobile, I dialled a familiar number.

Eduardo answered on the second ring. 'Hi.' He sounded overly happy to hear from me. 'You changed your mind about coming to California?'

'Unfortunately, not.' I could almost hear him deflate.

'Shame.' I could hear announcements in the background. 'Though you'd be cutting it close – I'm in departures at Manchester.'

'Sorry, Ed.' I meant it.

'You OK?'

'I was just ringing to pick your brains – but if the timing's bad . . . ?'

'No,' he said quickly. 'It's fine – what do you need to know?'

Ed's IT consultancy was one of the biggest in the country, but he was still based locally and had his finger on the pulse – so this didn't feel like too much of a long shot.

'Does the name Peter Wearman mean anything to you?'

He didn't even pause. 'Wearman's IT? He's just died, hasn't he?'

'Hmm. What do you know about him?'

'Never worked with him – but apparently, he was technically pretty good—'

'I can sense a "but".'

'I was brought up never to speak ill of the dead.'

'I won't tell.'

'Some of my team knew him. Had a reputation for being arrogant – difficult to work with. His staff turnover speaks for itself. The brightest and the best were drawn to the glittering press he was getting and the big money he was offering. But he couldn't hold on to talent for very long. Once they had him on their CV, the best people left – we scooped most of them up.

'Interesting.'

I heard an announcement in the background.

'That's my flight.' Ed said. I could hear him gathering up his bags. 'In a nutshell, he wasn't liked. Usual story – good at the job, but a shit person. One of those who felt he had to destroy the competition to be successful. Not that it matters now, I suppose.'

'No,' I said thoughtfully. 'Suppose not.'

'Why are you interested in Wearman? He died of a drug overdose, didn't he?'

'Supposedly.'

'Why does hearing you say that make me nervous?' But I could hear the smile in his voice.

'No idea.' I smiled back – even though he couldn't see it.

'Well – whatever it is – try not to get yourself into too much trouble while I'm away.'

'As if.'

Chapter Twenty-Nine

Fordley – Saturday afternoon

The offices of Wearman's IT were based in the centre of Fordley. They occupied the first two floors of a shiny block of glass and steel that was part of the new business quarter.

Peter Wearman – according to the press release, had been one of the first to secure his company's place in the new development, on an old brownfield site, that had once been a seventies shopping centre.

Now, the building presided over a multi-storey car park, cinema complex and a variety of restaurant chains, designed to breathe new life into a regenerated city centre.

My heels echoed back to me as I clicked my way across the large expanse of grey-coloured marble flooring, towards the backlit, glass reception desk.

'Can I help you?' The young receptionist, flashed a brilliantly enhanced, white smile.

'I wonder if you could tell me who Mr Peter Wearman's PA is please?' I handed her my card.

'Oh – err, well, that would have been Ainsley McKenzie,' she said. 'But she's been off sick for a while – they've been getting temps to fill in – but no one permanent.' She glanced up at me. 'Dr McCready?'

I nodded, but didn't explain – letting her make her own assumptions about what a doctor might want.

'But Mr Wearman passed away two weeks ago.'

'Yes, I know. I'm working with the pathologist who handled his case.' *Not a lie.* 'Is there anyone in the office I can speak to?'

She glanced at the register in front of her. 'Usually there would be. They have rostered staff in most Saturdays.' She glanced up at me and smiled. 'Tech never sleeps, does it?'

I smiled back, but said nothing.

'The best person is Karl Ronson. He's the sales director. But the offices are closed today – for the funeral.'

'Are all the staff going?'

'Not sure.' She dropped my card onto her notepad. 'I work for everyone in the building – not just Wearman's. But I know they were all given the afternoon off, so anyone who wanted to go, could. Most of them went over the road to The Bull for drinks.' She glanced at the clock on the wall. 'It's early yet – they'll probably still be in there.'

* * *

The Black Bull was typical of the city centre. Not a traditional pub that had been there for years, but a chain, trying to look as if it had character – and failing.

The place was full as I walked in and glanced around. Most tables were taken, and young waiters hurried from the kitchen carrying trays of pub food.

There was a crowd of young people at the bar wearing Wearman's lanyards. I found a place to stand at the mahogany counter and attracted the barman's attention.

While I waited for a soda and lime, I tried to see the names on the Wearman's badges.

This group were as far away from the mood of a funeral party as you could get. Laughing and joking – obviously enjoying having an afternoon off, even if it was for a memorial service.

The young man in front of me, stepped back to let one of his colleagues get to the bar, treading on my foot.

He turned, as I yelped. 'Oh, God – sorry. You OK?'

154

I tried not to grimace too much as I rubbed my foot. 'I'll never dance again, but otherwise I'm fine.'

I read his ID badge. 'Karl Ronson. You're actually the person I came to see.'

'Really?' He handed me my drink from the bar.

'I wanted to talk to someone who knew Peter Wearman.'

His eyes narrowed a fraction. 'You're not press, are you?'

'No.' I smiled. 'Doctor, actually.'

'Oh – right.' He sounded surprised, but didn't pursue it. 'Not sure what I can tell you. He died of an overdose – stupid bugger.'

A couple moved from the table next to us and I gestured to it. 'Can we sit?'

'Sure.' We sat and he took a sip of his pint. 'What's Peter's doctor doing here then?' He was smiling as he spoke, but his eyes held a caution that hadn't been there before.

'I'm actually working with the pathologist on the case.' The line came so easily. It had worked before, so I used it again.

He nodded, taking another sip, wiping the froth from his top lip. 'Case is over, surely. I mean, it's his funeral today.' He glanced at his watch, to remind himself of the time.

'I'm just interested in tying up a few loose ends.'

'Like what?'

'The drugs, for a start. You sounded as surprised as everyone else that he died that way.'

It wasn't a question – but he took the opening. 'Didn't know he did shit like that.'

'Have you known him long?'

'Few years. Met him when I was backpacking round Asia. Before he started this business. We travelled together on the last leg. Only ever saw him drink – maybe take a bit of hash, but then we all did that. But not the heavy stuff—'

He was interrupted as one of the lads from the bar came over and slapped his shoulder. 'Come on, Kaz – your round, mate.'

He leaned back and smiled. 'You get them in. I've left my card behind the bar – tab's open.'

His colleague winked at me. 'He's a good 'un, this lad.'

I watched him rejoin the group, who were getting louder.

'They all seem pretty happy – considering.'

He sat back, regarding me for a silent moment, before saying. 'Look, it's no secret . . . Peter wasn't popular. In fact, that's putting it mildly.'

'Oh?'

'I've known him longer than anyone else at the company – but I wouldn't call myself a friend.'

'Why not?'

'Apart from some Hooray Henrys that hung round with him from his university days, I don't think he had any friends. But it didn't bother him. He wasn't like that.'

'Like what?'

'The kind of person who likes to be liked. I mean, technically, he was genius. The business is a good one and people in our industry wanted to work for him. Until they did.'

I took a sip of my drink. 'Meaning what?'

'The hype in the press made him look like a great guy. All smiles and donations to charity – but he was a total bastard to work for. Chewed up talent, then spat it out. Squeezed people dry, until he burnt them out and when they had nothing left, he dropped them. Worse than that . . . he was a bully.' He glanced over his shoulder to his colleagues, who seemed oblivious to our conversation. 'Only a matter of time before it's going to be public knowledge anyway.'

'How's that?'

'Ainsley . . .'

'His PA?'

He nodded. 'She's been with him since the beginning – like me. But man . . .' He shook his head. 'He treated her like shit.

156

She put up with it because he paid so well and she always got invited onto the jollies – you know, Caribbean, Hawaii. He was generous with bonuses and gifts – but that only compensates for so long.' He pushed his glass around on the table. 'She went off sick a few months ago. Stress.'

'Caused by Wearman?'

He nodded. 'Sometimes, I used to think the way he treated people – Ainsley in particular – bordered on the sadistic, you know? The shouting and bawling were par for the course. If something went wrong, he'd come out of his office, chewing some poor bastard out in front of everyone. Not acceptable, but . . . you know.' He shrugged again. 'But he would humiliate Ainsley in front of the office – just for the hell of it, it seemed to me.'

'In what way?'

'Throwing paperwork at her, then making her get down and pick it up . . . calling her a dimwit, barking at her every five minutes.'

'Surprised she stayed as long as she did,' I said. 'Bonuses or not.'

He sat back, seemingly thoughtful. 'I asked her about that once, but she told me that often, when everyone else had gone – and believe me, she was always the last to leave – no matter how late – he'd come out of his office and sit at her desk and chat to her about the day. As if nothing had happened. Often bring out a bottle of red and a couple of glasses, and apologise to her. Ask her opinion about how things were going – get her view on other members of the team – or clients we were dealing with. He made her feel valued then.'

'But only when they were alone?' I asked.

He nodded. 'If she hadn't confided that to me, you'd never have known. Don't think anyone else *did* know.'

'And you never spoke to him about the way he was treating people . . . Ainsley?'

'Tried, once. Told him it was bad for morale and we were losing good people.'

'How'd he take that?' I asked, though I could guess.

'Bout as well as you'd imagine. Let's just say, I never mentioned it again. Just did my best to run interference between him and the team – protect them from some of the flak.'

'You said it was all about to go public?'

'Ainsley was bringing a tribunal against him. Allegations of bullying. It would have been all over the press. That's why I thought maybe you were a journalist.' He glanced again at his watch.

'Sorry. I don't want to keep you.' I looked at the group at the bar. 'They won't want to be late for the funeral.'

His eyes followed mine. 'Oh, they're not going – just me.' He downed his pint. 'And I'm only going because I have to. His parents have asked me to do a reading. Bloody farce, really.' He nodded to the other staff. 'They're having a party – to celebrate the fact that he's dead.'

Chapter Thirty

Wilsden – Monday morning

Jen had called Ainsley McKenzie ahead of time and arranged for us to meet. Though, according to my PA, it had been with a great deal of reluctance.

'Nervous as a cat,' Jen had said as she'd passed me Ainsley's address. 'She only agreed because I said you'd go to the house. No way was she going to travel to see you. Not even when I said you'd pay for lunch.'

I slowed my car, scanning the house numbers on the quiet lane, in this rural village, six miles west of Fordley, finally finding what I was looking for and turning down a long driveway to a stylish barn conversion.

The door opened, even before I got out of the car and the woman I took to be Ainsley, waited in the doorway.

Her smile was thin and didn't reach her eyes, which darted around suspiciously, as if she expected me to have accomplices hiding in the bushes, ready to leap out at any minute.

I offered my hand as I reached her.

'Ainsley' I smiled. 'Thanks for seeing me.

She nodded, and stepped aside to let me in. 'Your secretary said you were working with the pathologist ... into Peter's death.' She spoke quietly – almost sounding apologetic as she led us into a large, sunlit kitchen.

'That's right.' I took the offered seat at a huge centre island.

She busied herself with boiling a kettle – without bothering to ask if I wanted a brew.

Her whole demeanour was one of tension and anxiety. Jen's description was spot on – like a highly-strung cat.

'I'm surprised,' she said as she poured boiling water into a cafetière. 'I mean – it's his funeral today . . . so it's all over, isn't it?'

Now was probably not a good time to say I didn't drink coffee.

'There isn't an ongoing investigation.' I chose my words carefully. 'But we still have some unanswered questions – things I'd like to understand about what happened.' I didn't specify who 'we' were – and she didn't ask.

'Like what?' was all she said.

'You and Karl Ronson knew Peter longer than anyone else at Wearman's.'

She nodded, putting the coffee pot on the counter, along with two china mugs. 'You've spoken to Karl?'

'Yes. I saw him earlier . . . before he went to the funeral.' She perched on the stool opposite me, concentrating intensely on the marble countertop. Unable to meet my eyes. 'He was surprised at the way Peter died,' I said. She nodded, still not looking at me – pursing her lips in thought and obviously uncomfortable with the way the conversation was going. 'Did you know about his drug use?'

She shook her head slowly, looking up only to depress the plunger on the cafetière.

'Was it something you *would* have been aware of – having known Peter for so long?'

She took a long breath, hooking her hair behind her ears, before resting her elbows on the counter. 'There was probably a lot I didn't know about that man,' she said quietly. 'He only showed people what he wanted them to see – so if he was into that . . . maybe I wouldn't have known.'

'Do you think it likely?'

She shook her head. 'He had a thing about drugs . . . even smoking. Wouldn't allow fag breaks for anyone who smoked in the office. Said they should give it up. If they didn't, that was

160

their lookout and they'd have to do it in their own time. But it wouldn't surprise me to find out he was a total, bloody hypocrite. That it was just a front, to cover up the fact that he took drugs himself. Anything was possible with that bastard.'

'Did he ever say anything about friends who were into drugs?'

She began pouring the coffee – more as a distraction than anything else. 'No.' I thought she was going to leave it at that – to make me work for anything more. Until she added, 'Like I said, he had a thing about it. Saw addiction as a sign of a weak character.'

'But he drank?'

'Yes. But never to excess . . . at least, not that I saw.'

'Did he have a girlfriend?'

She snorted. 'You've got to be joking. Can't imagine any woman putting up with him . . . unless he had a personality transplant.'

'Good-looking guy.' I was playing devil's advocate. 'Wealthy – successful business. Unusual for him to not have anyone in his life.' I took a sip of coffee – wishing it was tea.

'Oh, don't get me wrong,' she swept her long hair back, almost angrily, 'he had women in his life. Plenty. Just no one in particular and never for very long.' She topped up her cup from the cafetière.' He flashed the cash. Got VIP access to the best clubs in town – lots of women are attracted to that. But it soon wore thin, when they realised what a misogynistic bastard he was.'

She wasn't even trying to cover the depth of her contempt. No need to tiptoe around the issues – so I didn't.

'Karl said you were bringing a tribunal against Peter?'

'I struggled with that for a long time.' She let out a long breath. 'There were times he would be nice to me . . . when there was no one else in the office. Like Jekyll and Hyde. It threw me. I never knew which of his faces were real . . . what to believe . . .'

'So, what changed?'

She shrugged. 'It was a strain. Tiptoeing around his moods. His unpredictable behaviour. Exhausting. When my mental health began to suffer and I was signed off on sick leave – I decided it was time. The bad behaviour simply outweighed the good. I realised those nice interludes were just his way of keeping me off balance. I saw him do it to others . . . it was a tactic used to manipulate people. Leaving the company wouldn't be enough. Plenty of people told me I needed to call him out and they were right. Make sure he couldn't do it to anyone else. He offered to pay me off, to make it go away.'

'You weren't tempted?'

She shook her head – long hair swishing around her shoulders. 'As usual, he overdid it.'

'What do you mean?'

'I mean, if he'd made the offer through the solicitors – called it an "out of court settlement", then I might have thought about it. Instead, he phoned me – night and day. Made my life a bloody misery. More threatening than persuasive. Typical bully-boy tactics. Just made me more determined to have my day in court. I needed closure – to have a voice and give other women a voice too.'

Something she said chimed – somewhere in the distance. Something I needed to pay attention to.

'Which people?' I asked.

'What?'

'You said, *people* encouraged you to make your complaint official?'

'Oh yes. Well, friends and family certainly did. But it was the doctor, actually.'

'Really? In my experience, GPs don't usually prescribe industrial tribunals.'

'He offered me six sessions of CBT – Cognitive Behavioural Therapy – on the NHS. Gave me a list of therapists attached to the surgery. He said getting closure might help. Then a counsellor told me the same. Encouraged me to "take control of the narrative".'

'This was the counsellor that gave you the CBT?'

'No. I had to wait to see him and I was really struggling.' She got up and went to a kitchen drawer, rummaging round until she found what she was looking for. She turned and dropped a leaflet on the counter.

Sanctuary. Community helpline.

'Leaflet came through the letterbox with the rest of the junk mail. Luckily, I didn't throw it away. They're all qualified counsellors. I could call anytime and no waiting list. It's a local charity. Helpline is free. If you want a face-to-face, you have to pay, but it's cheaper than a private therapist. Everyone volunteers their time.' She collected our empty mugs and put them in the sink. 'I still haven't got the appointment for the CBT . . . don't need it now, though.'

I watched as she washed up. 'And it was someone you spoke to on this helpline, that suggested the tribunal?'

'Well, not in so many words. But they said I might feel more empowered if I took control.'

When she turned back to me, she was smiling. 'They were right.' She dried her hands on a tea towel. 'It *did* feel good.'

There was a name written on the front of the leaflet. 'Lexi Royle – was this who you saw?'

'Didn't see her – just spoke on the phone. But she was good. Got me through a dark time, I can tell you. You can keep the leaflet. Don't need it now.'

We talked some more, about therapy, her mental health and how taking control of a bad situation helps stress and anxiety. Finally, she walked me out, holding the door open. 'Today's a good day,' she said.

'Because you don't have to go to court?'

She shook her head. 'Because they're burying the bastard.'

Chapter Thirty-One

Kingsberry Farm – Monday afternoon

'We couldn't find anything to connect our supposed "victims".' Jen drew quotation marks in the air with her fingers. 'Nor could the police.'

'The police weren't looking for a connection,' I pointed out, as I poured boiling water into the teapot.

We were taking a break from the office as Harvey sniffed around outside, enjoying the heat of the afternoon.

'They didn't know each other and had nothing obvious in common,' Jen went on. 'Unless this killer, Elle supposes is out there, chooses his victims completely at random?'

I was silent for a moment as I thought about that.

'What?' Jen prompted.

I shrugged. 'That's what bothers me,' I said quietly.

'The randomness of it?'

I took a long breath. 'If we're right . . . there's a killer out there who's so bloody clever, he's gone under the radar for . . . God knows how long.' I ran frustrated fingers through my hair. 'Elle started smelling a rat about fifteen month ago . . . but he could have been prowling for longer than that.'

'And if he picks his victims entirely at random . . . that makes him harder to catch.'

I looked at Jen. 'Worse than that . . . no one *is* trying to catch him.'

'Except you . . . and Elle.' Jen was trying to sound optimistic – but somehow, it just deepened my sense of dread. She reached out and covered my hand with one of her own, giving it a reassuring squeeze. 'Hey . . . come on. This isn't like you. You've dealt with worse than this.'

I shot her a look. 'That's just it, Jen. I'm not sure I have. Because if these three cases *are* the work of a killer . . . he's just about the most calculating . . . malevolent person I've ever come across.'

She finally looked as concerned as I felt. 'You sound unnerved.'

'That's because I am,' I confessed. 'Because without the police . . . we're on our own with this one. How the hell can you catch a killer that no one believes even exists?'

She sighed, taking a sip of tea. 'We've got to find out how he chooses his victims . . . there has to be a link . . . somewhere.'

'There is something that connects at least two of them,' I said, helping myself to one of the digestive biscuits Jen had put on a plate.

'Which two?'

'Andi Kilpin and Peter Wearman.'

'I've gone through everything.' Jen frowned, trying not to sound defensive. 'Work, schools, friends, membership of clubs . . . nothing I can find.'

'You wouldn't. Unless you'd spoken to people around them.'

'Come on, then – what do they have in common?'

'Everyone's happy they're dead,' I said bluntly.

'Bit harsh.' She sounded shocked.

'But true. Kilpin's wife is hardly the grieving widow. His nephew, Jordan, has plenty of reasons to be glad his pervy uncle is pushing up daisies – and when I went to Wearman's workplace – the staff were having a party to celebrate his funeral.'

'And Ainsley McKenzie?'

'Happiest of all, I'd say.'

'What about the other one on Elle's list?' Jen scratched her grey curls. 'Steve Lowry?'

I took a sip of tea. 'Don't know. Haven't spoken to anyone about him, yet.'

'That's the next job, then.'

Before I could answer, my mobile rang. Caller ID said it was Callum.

'Jo.' He launched straight into business. 'Something interesting came out of the interview with Britney Wilson and her charming crew.'

'Hello to you too.'

'Oh, sorry.' I could almost see him raking fingers through his hair. 'Just busy. The girls said that Stephanie Parks was worried about the pregnancy.'

'Oh?' I sipped my tea. 'Can't imagine Curtis's girlfriend confiding in that lot.'

'She didn't – but Curtis apparently told Britney. He was pissed off that Stephanie couldn't run errands over the weekend for him. She had stomach pain and was worried something was wrong. He got Britney to do the deliveries instead.'

'Did Stephanie go to hospital?'

'No. She rang the surgery for advice and got a call back from the GP. He said he was going to another house call nearby and would call in and see her on Thursday night.'

'The night she and Curtis died.'

'Want to guess who the GP was?'

I thought back to my run-in with Britney and her mates. The doctor who had suddenly appeared out of nowhere.

'Colin Stanton?'

'The very same.'

'Was he questioned during the door knocks?'

'His name never came up – but it should have done. More to the point, after the bodies were found, he didn't come forward to volunteer the information either.' I could hear the shuffling of papers. 'Wouldn't slip your mind that you made a house call to a patient who was shot dead the same night, would it?'

'You wouldn't think so.'

'I'm sending Beth to question him – informally, for now. I'd like you to go with her.'

'Really?' I didn't hide my surprise. It wasn't usual practice.

'Need you to read him.'

'He's not a cup of tea leaves.'

'You know what I mean. Get your take on how he is, when it's not a formal interview. See if you think he's got something to hide.'

Chapter Thirty-Two

Butterfield Estate – Monday evening

Parkfield Medical Practice was on a main road that ran along the edge of the Butterfield estate. It straddled two distinct areas with very different demographics.

The council estate was regarded as a 'poor socio-economic area'. People who lived there generally had a lower standard of living than those from the other side of Butterfield Road. An area which was more affluent – where the majority of houses were privately owned.

The low income and standard of living of residents on the estate, also correlated to a poorer state of health. Which meant the medical centre was always busy. Understaffed and under-resourced – reflected in the expression of the receptionist, who barely glanced at the warrant card DC Beth Hastings pressed against the glass.

'Dr Stanton is expecting us.' Beth smiled at a woman who looked as though this was the last thing she needed. 'He said to come at the end of surgery.' Beth looked back at the crowded waiting room. 'When it wouldn't be so busy.'

The waiting room was like every other. Modular chairs against the wall, which was covered in posters advocating better diets, regular blood pressure checks and screening programmes for bowel cancer. A cork board by the door had various leaflets and advertisements for local services.

'Yes, well, we're running late.' The harassed receptionist pushed a pencil behind her ear – tapping the keys of her computer. 'I've told him you're here, but you might have to wait.'

'That's all right, Sandra.' The cheerful voice came from behind her as a door opened and the man I recognised appeared, holding the elbow of an elderly female patient.

He guided the lady to a chair. 'Sorry it's all a bit chaotic,' he beamed, ignoring Sandra's glare. 'I've got a few minutes before my next patient.'

He led us into his office, closing the door on the hubbub outside as he gestured us to chairs.

He smiled at me as he tucked his large stomach behind his desk. 'Is this about your run-in with Britney Wilson? I gave a statement to the officer at the time.'

'No.' I returned the smile, glancing at Beth, in a silent cue.

Beth made a show of looking at her iPad, but she didn't need her notes.

'We understand that Stephanie Parks was a patient of yours?'

He shifted slightly in his chair – his brow creasing in a frown. 'Err, well, she was a patient at this surgery. We don't have allocated GPs any more. Patients see whoever has available appointments.'

'She called the surgery on Thursday the sixth and spoke to the receptionist, who arranged a callback with a GP.' Beth looked up from her notes – raising her eyebrow in a silent question.

'I'd have to check the date . . . but if you say it was the sixth, then it probably was.' He smiled, but the expression was thinner – more cautious. It was obvious from his body language that he didn't like the way this was going.

Was it because he had something to hide? Or just the innate caution of a medical professional, worried that some kind of malpractice or negligence charge was about to be laid at his door?

My sensory acuity was good at picking up the signals people gave off – but interpreting them was a whole different matter. Knowing *how* someone was thinking or feeling was one thing – knowing *why* they felt like that, was another matter altogether.

'I would have thought you'd remember that date.' Beth's tone was measured – but it was obvious she was leading him somewhere.

Dr Stanton sat back in his chair, picking an imaginary piece of lint from his trousers. 'Yes, well ... obviously in light of recent events, it's significant now.' He wasn't smiling anymore.

'You were the GP who called her back?' Beth posed the question. 'Yes.'

'We understand, Stephanie was worried about her pregnancy.' Glancing at her notes. 'She was in the early stages – but she'd been having stomach pains during the night and wanted some advice?'

Another uncomfortable shift in his chair. The leather creaking under the bulk of his weight. Stanton cleared his throat. 'I can't disclose information in a patient's medical records,' he said, choosing his words carefully. 'Confidentiality you under—'

'Your patient's dead, Doctor.' Beth cut across him. 'I really don't think she would mind you sharing.'

'But her family – there are still protocols to follow.'

Now it was Beth's turn to give an insincere smile. 'We are getting the relevant releases signed, Doctor. You can make us wait until we have those, or you can make things easier and tell us now – this *is* a murder enquiry and time is of the essence.'

'Yes, err, of course.' He sat forward, resting his elbows on the desktop. 'I spoke to Miss Parks over the phone and said that I would try to visit her that evening.'

'Did she mention the baby's father, at all?'

His expression of surprise wasn't faked. 'I assumed the father was the boyfriend she lived with? Brian, is it? No, she didn't, not when we spoke on the phone.'

Beth switched gears. 'In view of the fact that she was found dead on Saturday morning – didn't it occur to you to tell the police that you'd seen her less than forty-eight hours earlier?'

'Well – I didn't come forward, because I didn't, you see.'

It was Beth's turn to frown. 'Didn't what?'

'See her on Thursday.'

'You said you were visiting another patient in the area.'

'I was. In the same block of flats, actually. I have an elderly patient on the fifth floor. Mrs Cantor – she's got terminal cancer.' He picked up a pen and began twiddling with it. Displacement activity for nervous energy that had nowhere to go. 'I went there earlier, but my patient was in a lot of pain and I called the family. We had to make a decision about whether to admit her to hospital. Mrs Cantor wanted to stay in her own home – so I was waiting for the family to arrive, to decide the outcome.' He smiled ruefully 'Contrary to popular belief, we can't force patients to go into hospital and have treatment, if they refuse it.'

'I didn't think doctors made house calls these days,' I chipped in.

He glanced at me. 'Most don't,' he agreed. 'We try, where we can, and usually with elderly patients who struggle to come to the surgery. We're a community service, after all.'

'What time did you arrive at the flats?' Beth was adding to her notes.

'About six thirty. After surgery finished.'

'And what time did you leave her?'

'It was late. Family arrived sometime before eight. Mrs Cantor's friends had been there during the day, to comfort her, some left when the family took over. I'd already called paramedics and they'd administered morphine to settle her pain and were ready to transport her to Fordley Royal Infirmary.'

'What time did they leave?'

'The morphine alleviated the pain a bit, but she refused to go. In the end, her daughter said she'd stay with her that night – so we all left. It would have been about nine-ish.'

'So, you didn't call on Stephanie, because it was late?'

171

'Oh, no, I *did*. I walked down to her landing and knocked on the door. I could hear the TV on inside the flat – it was quite loud. I knocked a few times, and waited, but no one answered. So, I left without seeing her.'

'Did you pass anyone else on the stairs – or see anyone else near her flat?'

'I don't think so . . . no.'

'And no one hanging about as you left the block, or on your walk back to your car?'

He thought for a moment. 'I . . . well – Billy, the young lad, was kicking his football in the entrance to the flats. I was chatting to the paramedics as they left – so I wasn't really paying much attention.'

'It still didn't occur to you to tell the police about your call to Stephanie's flat?' Beth pushed the point. 'Once you learned she'd died?'

'I know how that looks.' He was getting flustered. 'But I didn't actually know she was dead until my receptionist told me, on Monday morning, about the shootings over the weekend. It didn't occur to me to report what had happened, because nothing did – really. I mean, I hadn't seen her. It didn't seem relevant.'

In fact, if the times were correct, both Brian Curtis and his girlfriend would have been lying dead behind that door, as he was knocking on it.

Chapter Thirty-Three

Parkland Medical Practice – Monday evening

I fell in step beside Beth as we walked across the medical centre car park.

'What do you think?' she asked.

'I don't think he's lying – if that's what you mean?'

'Easy enough to check with the ambulance service . . . about the paramedics being called out. I'll contact the family too, to corroborate the times he's given us.' She fished around in her handbag for her car keys. 'I don't think he knew about them already being dead on Thursday.'

I leaned against the side of my car. 'I agree. He was nervous – but not about seeing Stephanie.'

'What then?'

'Not sure – but it could have been because he was being questioned by a cop.' I grinned. 'Makes everyone feel guilty, even when they've done nothing wrong.'

She laughed. 'Suppose so.'

'Think he's uncomfortable that one of his patients is a murder victim,' I said. 'Enough to bring any medical professional out in a cold sweat.'

'And when he said he believed Curtis was the baby's father?'

I thought about the reaction I'd seen. 'I think he's telling the truth about that, too. Seems genuine enough.'

As we were about to get into our separate cars, Beth's phone rang. She glanced at the screen.

'It's the boss.'

I listened to one half of the conversation, unlocking my car and getting ready to go.

'I'm with Jo now, boss.' Beth was saying. 'We've just left Dr Stanton. Yeah – OK, I'll let her know.'

Beth ended the call. 'We've got an ID for the guy who visited Curtis's flat to buy the gun.' She unlocked her car. 'Dean Gavney. He's in the system – predictably.'

'Good news.' I threw my briefcase onto the passenger seat.

'They've also got the owner of the newsagents on the estate, saying Gavney was in the shop at around seven o'clock on Thursday – buying cigarettes.'

'Why so memorable?' I asked.

'He didn't have the right money – tried to get the fags on tick. There was an argument and he left empty-handed. He'd been drinking – it got a bit ugly and he kicked a stack of tins over on his way out of the shop, just for good measure. They're bringing him in tonight – if we can find him. The boss wants you to observe the interview – that OK?'

'Sure.'

'I'll let you know the time.'

* * *

As Beth pulled away, I dialled Pip from the car. Sitting with the engine idling, I lowered the soft top to get some air.

'Hi, Jo.' She sounded more upbeat than when we'd last talked.

'How are you?'

'Great.' I could hear the smile in her voice. 'Looking at some flats for me and Maisie.' I could hear a child laughing in the background. It made me smile. 'The resettlement service has been really helpful. Might have to go somewhere temporary – but it's a start.' She distractedly spoke to Maisie, then came back to me. 'Liaison officer told me about Bri . . .'

174

'I'm sorry,' I said – not sure whether that was the right response – but he *was* Maisie's father after all.

'Don't be.'

'Still, a shock though?'

'Not really.' Her tone was harder. 'When they said an armed unit was going to serve the warrant, I almost expected him to get shot. Result's what I expected – just not the *way* I expected it.'

I ran a hand through my hair, lifting the length of it off my neck, as the heat began to rise. 'You *could* go back to the flat – once it's released by forensics. They'll arrange to have all traces of what happened cleaned away.'

'No.' She was adamant. 'Can't go back there.'

'Understandable.'

'I was sorry to hear about Stephanie, though,' Pip said quietly. 'She didn't deserve that.'

'Did you know she was pregnant?'

'Not until the police told me. They asked if Bri and Steph had argued about it – but when I was there, I didn't even know. That makes it sadder, really . . . I mean, a baby being a victim as well.'

'Yes. Yes, it does,'

Chapter Thirty-Four

Fordley Police Station – Tuesday morning

Dean Gavney slouched in the uncomfortable chair in the interview room. The young duty solicitor appointed for him flicked through the notes in her file.

Maybe it was sign I was getting older, but she looked about twelve to me.

Callum was sitting next to me in the observation room, watching what was taking place in real time, across the corridor.

'I've got jumpers older than her,' I said, to no one in particular.

Opposite them sat DS Tony Morgan, who was leading the interview, along with DC Shah Akhtar – observing and taking notes.

'We brought him in in the early hours of this morning,' Callum said, his eyes never leaving the screen. 'Predictably, his solicitor advised him to go "No Comment" on us.'

I regarded the man in the interview room. He looked like a bedraggled hippy, with a straggly, dirty-blond beard that matched his unkempt hair, wearing the grey Fruit of the Loom sweatshirt and jogging bottoms he'd been given when his clothes had been taken for testing by forensics.

His long legs stretched out under the table, in an exaggerated display of nonchalance.

'And is he sticking to that?' I asked.

'So far,' Callum murmured. 'But, as he was being put in the cell for the night, we told him a little bedtime story. Just to give him something to think about for a few hours.'

'Oh, what was that?'

'Tony happened to mention that we had a witness who saw him visiting Curtis's flat to buy a handgun.' Callum stretched his legs and folded his arms as he continued to listen to the monotonous litany of 'no comment', coming from the interview room.

'Maybe when we get to that, having stewed on it all night, he might have more to say.'

I turned my attention back to the screen. Reading the body language and demeanour of the man being questioned.

That 'emotional energy' – the illusive vibration I could see – was resonating in a way that told me Dean Gavney wasn't as laid-back about this interview as he wanted to appear.

'You live on the Butterfield estate, Dean. Just a few minutes' walk from Curtis's flat?' Tony was saying.

'No comment.'

'And you can't corroborate your whereabouts on Thursday the sixth.'

'My client has already said he was in his flat, watching TV all night,' the solicitor supplied helpfully.

'But he claims he was alone that night ... and he can't remember what programmes he watched?' Tony frowned as he checked his notes.

'He didn't know he was going to be questioned about it, weeks later,' the solicitor said tightly.' No doubt you're going to check his phone data. That will confirm my client was at home all night.'

'It proves his phone was at home,' Tony said with a thin smile. 'Not that he was there with it.'

'Did you go out at all that evening, Dean?' Tony's attitude was intentionally disarming.

'No comment.'

'Where were you around 7 p.m.?'

'No comment.'

'You see, we have several witnesses that put you within two hundred yards of the flats on the night of the sixth – at around seven o'clock?'

'No comment.'

'You went to the newsagents, to buy cigarettes?'

The solicitor leaned in and whispered something in Dean's ear. He listened, then took a breath. 'Yeah. I went to get some fags. Then straight back home.'

'What time would you have been back at your flat then?'

He looked at his solicitor, who gave him a slight nod. 'About quarter past seven.'

'So, you didn't leave the shop and then go into Curtis's block?'

'No.'

'But you left your phone at home when you went to the shops?' Tony pressed. 'Why would you do that, Dean?'

The solicitor urged no comment – but Gavney ignored her. 'I just forgot it. OK? Just went out and left it on the table.'

'You didn't leave it because you knew we'd check and you wanted it to look like you were home the whole time?'

This time he did as he was told.

'No comment.'

'We found your DNA and fingerprints in Curtis's flat, Dean.' Tony was saying.

The solicitor's breath left her in an exaggerated sigh.

'My client doesn't deny that he was a visitor to the flat. He was a friend of Brian Curtis. There are legitimate reasons for his DNA to be there. Unless you're telling us that his fingerprints were found on the murder weapon?'

Tony ignored her question. 'And we have a witness who identified you as the person who visited Brian Curtis to purchase a handgun just a few days before he and Stephanie Parks were found dead.'

'No comment.'

'The same make and model of the gun Curtis always carried.' Tony made a show of checking his notes – though he didn't need to. 'A 9mm Baikal.'

'No comment.'

The solicitor leaned over her notes. 'Forensics confirm that the bullets that killed Stephanie Parks and Brian Curtis came from Curtis's own gun,' she said. 'Not this second weapon. Which you can't produce anyway.'

Tony directed his remarks to Gavney. 'That Baikal . . . the one the witness states you came to buy, was missing from the flat when we searched the scene. Where did it go, Dean?'

'No comment.'

Gavney's knee was beginning to bounce nervously beneath the table. His fingers started fiddling with the seam of his sweatshirt.

'Leaking stress signals,' I said quietly.

'Our witness says that things got heated when you went to Curtis's flat. You said you needed a gun, to do a job. But he was asking too much money for it.'

'No comment.'

'The witness said you got into a fight with Curtis. You grabbed him by the throat and threatened him.'

'No comment.'

Tony made a show of reading from his notes. 'Apparently you said, "I'll be back . . . and you'll be sorry." What did you mean by that, Dean?'

'No comment.'

'Did you go back for that gun, Dean?' Tony pressed. 'And did things get out of hand?'

'No comment.' His voice was the same monotone, but his breathing had changed – becoming more rapid. I watched the rise and fall of his chest.

'You'd already told Curtis he'd "be sorry",' Tony went on. 'Is that why you killed him, Dean?'

179

Finally, he'd had enough. His head dropped and he leaned forward, blowing his cheeks out in a gust of frustration.

'I *didn't* go back for the gun.' He raised his voice despite his solicitor's restraining hand on his arm. He shook her hand away. 'I didn't buy no gun . . . not from Curtis . . . not from anyone.' He washed a hand over his face, glaring at Tony Morgan.

'I. Don't. Own. A. Fucking. Gun.' Each word emphasised by a chopping motion of his hand – slicing his sentence into bite-sized pieces.

'Can you explain why the gun's gone missing?' Tony asked calmly.

Again, the solicitor leaned in to advise caution. Gavney ignored her.

'How the fuck should I know?' he shouted. 'Maybe he sold it to someone else.' He suddenly pushed away from the table, standing up – his fists clenching and unclenching by his sides.

Shah was on his feet – between Gavney and Tony Morgan. 'Sit down, Dean,' he said firmly.

The young solicitor stood, her chair scraping back as she put her hand on Gavney's shoulder. 'Please, Dean,' she said, showing surprising calm in the face of a man at least a foot taller than her and two feet wider. 'You're not helping yourself, here.'

Gavney paused for just a moment before slumping back down in his chair.

'I think we should take a break,' the solicitor said. 'I need to speak to my client.'

'Good idea.' Tony smiled, as if the explosion hadn't happened. 'I think we all need a brew.'

* * *

Tony and Shah were standing behind our chairs in the small observation room, nursing plastic cups of disgusting vending machine coffee as they discussed strategy with Callum.

180

There was a light knock on the door, and Beth stuck her head in.

'Boss.' She was frowning. 'You need to take a look at this.' She handed Callum a slip of paper.

I watched his expression as he read the note. Finally, he looked up – his face serious and handed the paper to his DS.

Tony scanned the contents. 'Bloody hell,' he breathed.

'Forensics . . . and results from Stephanie Parks's post-mortem.' Callum said. 'Dean Gavney's DNA is a match for the unborn baby.'

'"The CPI – Combined Paternity Index,"' Tony quoted directly from the lab results, '"is greater than 1000 – meaning this result provides extremely strong support, in favour of paternity".' He handed me the paper. 'Elle Richardson has written on the bottom – 99% probability. Just in case we were in any doubt.'

'Question is,' I said what everyone else was thinking, 'did he know she was pregnant?'

'Or,' Tony added, 'that it was his?'

'Only one way to find out,' Callum murmured.

* * *

Given the gravity of the information about the baby's paternity, and in the interest of disclosure, Callum had to speak to Gavney's solicitor about it in private.

Unsurprisingly, the solicitor insisted on breaking the news to her client, prior to the team resuming their interview.

Considering the kind of news Gavney had just been given – I was surprised at how quickly the detectives were asked back in to the room.

Callum and I leaned towards the monitors – keen to read every nuance on Dean Gavney's face as the interview resumed.

Chapter Thirty-Five

Fordley Police Station – Tuesday morning

For a frozen moment, Dean's face was expressionless. It was hard to decide how the information had landed.

Then, as if in slow motion, his features crumpled – along with the rest of his body, which seemed to deflate.

He leaned forward, hands covering his face, and doubled up in a paroxysm of physical pain, a low moan escaping from behind his hands.

His solicitor put a hand on his shoulder, leaning in to speak to him. 'Dean,' she said gently. 'Are you OK ... Dean?' She looked up at Tony and Shah. 'I've just told my client he's the father of a baby that's tragically died. We need another break.'

'No.' Gavney's voice was muffled behind his cupped hands. 'Let's get this over with.'

Tony wasn't about to lose the leverage this moment might provide. Callous as it seemed – it was a pivotal moment in Dean Gavney's interview.

'I'm sorry, Dean,' Tony said quietly. 'It's obviously come as a shock.' He leaned his elbows on the table. 'Did you know Stephanie was pregnant?' Tony's voice was calm, but firm. 'I know this is upsetting, but we have to ask.'

Finally – slowly, Gavney let his hands drop down. He lifted his head and even in that short space of time, his face had changed. His cheekbones seemed sharper, as if his face had been hollowed out by an instantaneous blow of grief and shock.

'I thought ...' His voice trembled in a way that could never be faked. 'I suspected it was mine.'

'You knew Stephanie was pregnant?' Tony asked again.

He simply nodded, washing a hand across his face. 'She told me a few weeks ago. But she couldn't be sure whose it was. I *knew* it was mine.'

'You'd been having a relationship with Stephanie?' Tony was treading carefully, but there was no delicate way to put it. 'While she was with Brian Curtis?'

Another nod. He squeezed his eyes shut, as if trying to block out the images that were obviously running in his head. He sniffed, dragging his sleeve across his nose.

'She wanted it to be Bri's.' His voice was so quiet, I had to lean in to the screen to hear. 'Said, it could easily be his. Said if he found out about us . . . he'd kill us both.' He looked up then, his eyes filled with a visceral pain. 'She was passing it off as Bri's.'

'Were you two still seeing each other?' Tony asked.

He shook his head, drawing his hand down his beard, to smooth out the straggled hair. 'After she told me she was pregnant – she finished it.'

'How did you feel about her ending the relationship?' Tony asked.

The big man shrugged. 'Didn't think I'd be that bothered. Probably wouldn't have been . . . if it hadn't been for . . .' His voice tailed away and he closed his eyes again. Struggling to hold on to his emotions.

'The baby?' Tony.

Gavney nodded. 'I was cool with it at first – I mean, who wants the hassle, right? But then . . . the more I thought about being a dad.' He sniffed heavily, tilting his head up to look at a spot on the ceiling. 'I'd never known my dad. Always said I'd make a better job of it.' He took a long breath. 'I wanted to know . . . for sure, if it was mine. But she wouldn't go there. Kept saying it was Bri's and I just had to get over it.'

'Did you tell Brian Curtis? About you and Stephanie?' Tony asked the million-dollar question. 'Tell him that the baby might not be his?'

Gavney's expression hardened. 'Not then . . .'

'But you were going to?'

His head dropped – chin on his chest. His fingers twisting together. 'Maybe . . . prob . . . I don't know.'

'That Thursday – after you went to the newsagents . . . you'd been drinking. You went to Curtis's flat, didn't you Dean?' Tony's voice was calm – steady. 'Were you going to confront them both . . . tell Brian about you and Stephanie?'

Dean's head was down – he couldn't look at Tony.

'You went there, didn't you, Dean? To the flat?'

Dean nodded his head slightly – an imperceptible movement, but enough. Both detectives had seen it.

The solicitor squeezed Gavney's arm – leaning in to urgently whisper in his ear. Gavney lifted his head – his eyes had a sudden clarity. The old, familiar hardness. 'No comment.'

Chapter Thirty-Six

Fordley Police Station – Tuesday afternoon

The incident room was full. Every seat taken by members of HMET. Callum was at the front of the room, bringing everyone up to speed.

'Search teams have turned over Gavney's flat,' he was saying. 'Drugs; scales; cash; all seized. Gavney's been charged with possession with intent to supply. He's already on bail for a previous drugs offence, so this is enough for us to seek a remand in custody. He'll be moved to Armley prison later today. Bad news is, no sign of the gun . . . *any* gun.'

'Any other weapons?' Shah asked.

'Knives, machete and a vintage-style knuckleduster.' Callum read from his notes.

'Probably a family heirloom,' someone at the back said. 'Always good to have something to pass down to the kids.' Greeted by a ripple of laughter around the room.

'Phones seized and passed on for analysis,' Callum continued. He flipped to a sheet and read through it. 'Interestingly, although we didn't find the gun, we *did* find ten rounds of ammunition, 9mm. Which would fit either Baikal – Curtis's or the missing one. He's been charged with being in possession of a firearm – as bullets count.'

'Why would he have ammunition and no gun for it?' I asked.

Tony shrugged. 'It's not uncommon. Could have been holding it for Curtis . . . or someone else.'

'Or, he *is* in possession of the missing weapon – we just haven't found it yet' Callum summarised. He took a mouthful of coffee.

'Further on from our interview this morning with Gavney – I'm arranging for Billy Wilson to be questioned again. We have to wait for a specialist officer from the Child Protection Unit.' He scanned the details on his iPad. 'Social services have placed Billy with foster carers who will provide a responsible adult to accompany him. We're getting someone over there, hopefully this afternoon, to find out if he *did* see Gavney entering the block on Thursday, after his visit to the newsagents.'

'Billy was Curtis's lookout.' Beth was almost thinking out loud. 'Unlikely he's going to tell us about drug couriers, like Gavney, coming and going from the block – or visiting Curtis.'

'Worth a shot,' Callum said. 'Especially now most of the people he was loyal to are either dead or in custody. Once kids are away from the environment, they often open up more.'

I thought about young Billy and the carefree life an eight-year-old boy should be having. Playing out; scuffing his knees and worrying about whether he'd be allowed sweets at the weekend. Not maintaining the twisted honour code of drug dealers, or the consequences of betraying his street gang.

I was glad he was with foster parents – experiencing what a 'normal', caring family was like.

My attention was pulled back to the room by Tony.

'Working hypothesis,' he was saying. 'If Gavney *did* go to the flat on Thursday, he could walk past Billy with impunity. Go up to Curtis's flat and confront Stephanie about the baby.'

'It gets ugly,' Shah picked up the narrative, 'and Curtis kills Stephanie . . . then Gavney kills Curtis?'

'That sequence of events doesn't fit the order of gunshots and screams Billy said he heard.' All eyes turned to me as I spoke for the first time.

'With all due respect,' Callum trotted out a phrase I hated – because it usually meant that whatever came next, wouldn't be in the least respectful.

186

'We only have the statement of an eight-year-old boy that that was the order and timing of those bangs. If they were shots at all. It doesn't square with the neighbour who heard bangs and a scream afterwards. And even she said she thought the noise was banging doors – not shots.'

'So that sequence isn't conclusive?' Beth said, frustrated.

'Nothing a newly qualified defence counsel couldn't drive a coach and horses through,' Callum said. 'Not something we can rely on in court.'

DI Frank Heslopp, who'd been uncharacteristically quiet up to now, put his cup on the desk and stretched. 'If we discount the order of "bangs" or "shots" or whatever for a minute – Tony's working hypothesis fits the facts we *do* know.'

'Go on, Frank,' Callum said.

'We know Gavney was at the newsagents around the time we suspect the killings happened. Thursday between 7 p.m. and 8 p.m. We know he left his phone at home when he went out – presumably so we couldn't pin his location. We know now Stephanie was pregnant by him . . . and that Curtis didn't know they'd been seeing each other behind his back.' He leaned back and stretched – the buttons on his shirt, straining over his belly. 'Doesn't take much imagination to picture the scene in that flat when Curtis finds out.'

'And, in whatever order it happens,' Callum finished, 'Curtis and Stephanie Parks end up dead.' He looked to me. 'Jo's pretty certain the scene was staged.'

I nodded. 'Absolutely. Not a murder-suicide.'

Callum turned back to his DI. 'What about the clothes Gavney was wearing on Thursday, Frank?'

'CCTV in the newsagents wasn't working, so we can't check on that and as we know, there's no functioning CCTV around the flats. Curtis and his crew made sure they're all damaged. All the clothes he was wearing are with forensics to test for gunshot residue. As for the rest of his clothes – he says he can't remember what he was wearing that Thursday. Search teams have brought everything we can find from his flat.'

'Suppose he could have washed the clothes he was wearing, by now,' Beth said.

Frank snorted. 'More likely to burn clothes than wash 'em. State of his flat – don't think the washing machine's ever been used.'

'Right,' Callum said. 'See if the newsagent remembers what Gavney was wearing that night and we get all the clothes we've got, tested. If he fired a gun there'll be traces and if they exist we'll find them.' He turned to me. 'Anything to add, Jo?'

I tapped my teeth with a pencil. 'We can all agree that the scene was staged to look like murder-suicide.' I glanced around to see heads bobbing in silent agreement. 'So, if we go with this scenario – you're saying Dean Gavney is the likely killer of either Curtis or Stephanie—'

'Or both,' Heslopp added helpfully.

'He's not the kind of character to stage this scene afterwards.' I hated doing profiles on the fly. 'He doesn't have the imagination to make this look like murder-suicide. I just don't see that.'

'How does anyone react when they've just killed two people?' Heslopp said.

'Three,' Beth reminded everyone.

'In Gavney's case,' I said. 'He'd be more likely to stuff his pockets with the drugs and cash lying around and make a fast exit. I don't see the self-regulation and cold rationality to clear the scene and then stage an elaborate scenario like the one we found. Even though we saw through it – it takes a certain kind of person to stay in the flat after killing two people and manipulate the evidence in the way they did.'

Callum stared at me for a moment – then shrugged. 'Take your point. But this can't hang on a profile. We have to go where the evidence takes us. And right now, the evidence points to Gavney being a murderer.'

Chapter Thirty-Seven

Fordley DAAT – Wednesday

Tess had made us both a brew and we'd found an empty therapy room to have a chat in private.

The waiting room was quiet and the trainee receptionist was holding the fort.

'Things moved pretty fast,' Tess was saying. 'One minute, Pat Rodgers was in her office and the next, she was being escorted off the premises, with all her stuff in a cardboard box.'

'The board of trustees wouldn't want to waste any time. It was fraud after all,' I said, blowing the steam from my cup. 'Once they had firm evidence of her cheating on her expenses and time sheets. That incident with Pip . . . last straw, I guess.'

She nodded, taking a sip of tea. 'Still, I didn't expect them to offer *me* her job.'

'You'll make a great manager,' I smiled. 'Been doing the job long enough. Think you've forgotten more about running this place, than Rodgers ever knew.'

She looked uncomfortable. 'Feels like dead man's shoes.'

'Don't be daft.' I put my cup down. 'Someone's got to take over. Makes perfect sense for it to be you. No point in bringing in a total outsider. You know all the clientele as well as the staff.'

'Which brings us to why you wanted to see me.' Tess brought us to the point. 'You wanted to know about Steve Lowry? The client who died of a drugs overdose?'

'He was close to Rina, but Elle said his death hit her quite hard. Didn't want to rake over it with her. Thought you might be able to fill in some gaps for me?'

'Like what?'

I shrugged. 'Whatever you can tell me. Rina said he was a nice guy. Got his life back together. Everything seemed rosy.' I regarded her over the coffee table. 'But maybe it wasn't all it seemed to be? Figured if there *was* anything else going on in his life, you might know?'

She hesitated for just a moment, pursing her lips thoughtfully and I knew I was right.

'I knew him when he first came to us – years before Rina. So, she didn't see the whole picture. She saw the best version of him, I suppose. Not the violent addict he was before.'

'Violent?'

She nodded, sitting back against the sofa cushions. 'Had a history in his youth – especially during the years he was a heavy user. Had offences for domestic violence. First his mother – he was stealing from her to fund his habit and would knock her about. Then, when he left home, he took his temper out on his girlfriends. Was arrested for assaulting a police officer. Did time for that one. Came to us as part of his probation conditions. We put him on anger management courses as well as drug rehab.'

'I take it he improved?'

'He responded well to all the interventions. Got clean. Went back to college . . .'

'I sense a "but" coming.'

She shrugged. 'He'd been signed off. Used to come back to visit us. Volunteered in the peer support group – that's how Rina met him. One day his girlfriend, Vicky, turned up here looking for him. They'd had a blazing row. She was in a mess – emotionally and physically. It was obvious she'd taken a beating.'

'From Lowry?'

'She said so.'

Something shifted in Tess's demeanour. An almost imperceptible change in her energy, that told me she didn't believe Lowry had done it.

'Vicky said the abuse had been going on for months,' she went on, 'wanted us to call the police. Lowry wasn't here. I calmed her down. Took her in the medical room and cleaned her up.'

'Anything come of it?'

'Vicky pressed charges and Steve got arrested. I had to give a statement to what happened here. It was going to court, which she was dreading.'

'Did Rina know about this?'

Tess nodded. 'But Lowry always maintained he didn't do it. Said Vicky had been beaten up by an ex-boyfriend. I suppose Rina gave him the benefit of the doubt.' Tess shrugged. 'She liked him. We all did.'

'Do you think the legal case hanging over him was enough to make him start using again?'

She shook her head. 'He seemed pretty solid to me. Plus, his family said he wasn't that cut up about it. They didn't think it was enough to push him over the edge. Anyway, it never came to anything, because he died before it got to court.'

'And Vicky?'

'She was a total wreck on the run up to the court case, poor lass. I managed to get her some free counselling and made her see her doctor. He put her on antidepressants, which helped. But to be fair, once Lowry died, the stress seemed to lift – although she did grieve.' Tess finished her brew. 'Funny isn't it,' she finally said, in a quiet voice. 'Despite the emotional torment some people put us through, it can still be hard to stop loving them . . . or at least caring about them.'

Ain't that the truth.

'Do you know how I could contact Vicky?' was what I said aloud.

'She moved abroad. Took a job in Ibiza, working at a friend's club. Said if I ever went over, I could have drinks on the house.' Tess laughed. 'Don't think I'll be taking her up on that anytime soon.'

'Any chance I could take a look at Steve Lowry's records?' I knew the service had to keep them for a period of time, which varied – but most would archive old client files for at least a year after discharge. The DAAT kept all their archives in the basement,

Tess hesitated for just a second. 'You know how it works, Jo. Usually, confidential. But seeing as you're a psychologist, and on the books here as a mentor . . .'

I smiled my appreciation.

'I've got to get back,' she said. 'But I'll ask the new receptionist to get the file and bring it to you.' She gave an exaggerated shiver. 'She can go down to the basement – I hate it . . . full of spiders.'

I smiled. 'See . . . being the manager has its perks. You can delegate the "spidery" jobs to someone else now.' I collected our mugs. 'I'll get us another brew.'

* * *

Everything in Steve Lowry's records confirmed what Tess had already told me.

If I was expecting a flash of inspiration, then I was disappointed. The clinical notes from various institutions, since childhood, reflected the kind of life and experiences I was, unfortunately, all too familiar with.

Abandonment, neglect and emotional abuse. The kind of start in life no child should have. Serving, in Lowry's case, as a grim apprenticeship for an adolescence of drug use and petty crime to fund it.

Predictably, after ploughing through police reports and juvenile offenders' notes, I was feeling decidedly jaded. Knowing how this young man's life had ended only added to the dark cloud hanging over my shoulders.

I stretched and eased my aching neck, draining the last of my tea.

At the back of the file notes was a list of medication Lowry had been prescribed. Not just while he was in rehab at the DAAT, but by the various doctors he had seen over the years.

By tracing it from a few years previously, it could give me an overview of where he was medically and, maybe, psychologically.

I debated making another brew, to help get me through the last wedge of paperwork but decided against it, preferring to get this done.

Tess poked her head round the door, just as I was finishing up.

'How you getting on?'

'Done.' I jotted down some final notes on medications he'd been taking and closed the file. 'Thanks for letting me take a look.'

'No probs.' She held the door open as I followed her out. 'You OK to sign the file back in at reception?' she asked as we parted in the corridor. 'I've got another meeting.' She rolled her eyes.

'Get used to it,' I laughed. 'Managers spend their lives in meetings . . . occasionally you even get something done.'

The new receptionist smiled in a frazzled kind of way as I took the logbook from her. As I scrawled my signature against the file number, something suddenly occurred to me – as if my 'third eye' had noticed something my conscious brain had failed to register and was giving me a mental dig in the ribs.

The receptionist held her hand out for the file, looking puzzled when I didn't hand it over.

'Hang on a minute,' I said, opening Lowry's file again and flicking to the medication lists at the back. I scanned the pages, running my finger along the list of pharmacies, until I saw, what I'd half-seen on the first pass.

'Bloody hell,' I breathed.

'What?' The receptionist frowned.

'Nothing,' I said, distracted now. 'Or maybe . . . everything.'

Chapter Thirty-Eight

Kingsberry Farm – Thursday

Back in my office, I looked again at the postcard from Ibiza that Tess had given me. Scrawled, in an untidy hand at the bottom, Vicky's signature included a mobile number.

I wasn't sure what I expected to hear – or even what I was exactly looking for. At best, I was on a fishing expedition. Hoping Vicky would be able to confirm my half-baked suspicions. That she would be able to add that one piece of the jigsaw that would confirm I was on to something.

At worst, I was fumbling in the dark, towards a dead end.

There was only one way to know.

I picked up the phone and dialled the number.

* * *

Jen looked over at me from her own desk. 'Vicky confirmed she was a patient at Parkfield Medical Practice?'

I nodded, tapping the notes I'd made when I'd spoken to Steve Lowry's ex-girlfriend early that morning.

'Registered with them when she moved into Lowry's flat on the Butterfield estate. I realised when I saw the prescription list in the back of Lowry's file. He used the pharmacy next door to the medical practice. Vicky used to pick his prescriptions up for him when she went to the doctors.'

'Was Lowry a patient at Parkfield too?'

'That would be nice and neat, wouldn't it? But, no. He'd stayed with the GP he'd had since he was a kid, at the medical centre in Fordley.'

'Did Vicky say she'd been a patient of Dr Stanton ... specifically?' Jen's laser-like reasoning was doing what I always wanted it to do – probing my initial hypothesis for holes.

Jen had spent her working life assisting some of the best forensic psychologists in the country, long before she decided to 'adopt' me. A fact for which I was eternally grateful. She had an encyclopaedic memory for cases she'd been involved with and I was constantly amazed at the number of contacts and sources she brought to the table.

Her input and opinion were priceless, which is why I ran my ideas and theories past her. She knew me better than anyone and I could trust her to be totally – and sometimes brutally – honest with me. If she thought I was barking up the wrong tree, she'd say so.

'She confirmed what Stanton told us. Patients don't have an assigned GP. They see whoever has available appointments. She couldn't remember the name, but said it was a male GP she saw when she went about her depression. The description she gave sounds a lot like Stanton.'

Jen was already tapping keys on her keyboard. She turned the screen round so I could see the web page of Parkfield Medical Practice. A gallery of photographs of the staff.

'Only two male doctors registered there.' She peeked round the edge of the screen. 'One looks younger than your Alex ... the other is Colin Stanton.'

We both sat in silence for a moment – considering what options this new piece of information gave us.

'What exactly are you ... we, saying here?' Jen was choosing her words carefully.

'Only that the medical practice *could* be a common denominator between our victims ... or at least people in their lives.'

'Dangerous ground to tread, Jo.' The volume dropped – as if she suspected we might be overheard – here in my remote farmhouse, on top of the Yorkshire moors.

'I'm saying the *place*, Jen . . . not any person in particular – not yet.'

'Pointing the finger at a medical professional . . . not something to be done lightly.'

'Did my last sentence not reach across the room?'

'You know what I mean?'

'Yes, I do and that's why I'm stressing, the only link, so far is to the medical centre. The connection could be anyone who works there. Cleaner, receptionist —'

'Doctor,' she said quietly.

'Which is why we need more . . . a lot more, before we even think that thought outside of this room.'

She nodded, pulling a notepad towards her and fishing the pencil from the curls behind her ear. 'So, a deep dive into all the others – see if Kilpin, Wearman or anyone they were involved with at the time they died, has a connection to Parkfield?'

I nodded, but already could see the obstacles. 'We can't get access to medical records. But to be fair – there's no harm in just contacting them and asking the question.'

'Right.' Jen was scribbling notes. 'I'll get on with that. What are you going to do next?'

I reached for my phone. 'Callum said if we came up with anything else he might be able to allocate some resources. We're going to need access to information we won't be able to get on our own.'

'You giving him a call?'

'No, he's got enough on his plate– but he said Beth was my go-to if I needed anything.'

My call was picked up on the fourth ring.

'Beth, it's Jo.'

She listened as I told her what I'd found so far, and what I needed.

'Sorry Jo – I'm up against it at the minute with the Curtis case. We all are. Technically, Kilpin and the others aren't on our

196

caseload anymore. They were signed off as accidental deaths. Can't spare the time.'

'OK. I understand.'

'But,' there was a shuffling of papers, 'we've had a couple of people seconded to the team, to help out. Got Charlie Thompson with us. He's been analysing the phones we've collected in the Curtis raids. Might be able to spare him for a couple of hours.'

'That would be great – thanks.'

'Right, I'll—'

In the background, I heard Callum calling from his office. Beth's voice was muffled as I imagined her holding the phone under her chin.

'I'm on the phone to Jo now, boss,' I heard her say. 'Want to speak to her?'

Then she came back to me. 'The boss wants a word – I'll pass you over.'

'Jo?' He sounded hassled.

'What's up?'

'We arranged for a specialist officer to interview Billy Wilson again . . .'

'I know, he's been looked after by the Child Protection Unit, isn't he?'

'Yep. Joint investigation between them and social services. We had an officer good to go with the interview.'

'So, what's the problem?'

'Billy says he'll only speak to you.'

Chapter Thirty-Nine

Fordley – Friday morning

The Children and Young Persons Social Care Unit was in a large, modern building on the outskirts of town.

The police officer from the Child Protection Unit, Jane, was specially trained in ABE Interviewing. Achieving Best Evidence, in the interviewing of children – which I wasn't.

She'd built up a good relationship with Billy, but when it came to this – the thorny issue of giving explicit information about the gang he felt so loyal to, he wasn't being so forthcoming.

Jane had briefed me on how to put the questions to our young witness. She would be in the room – but unless it looked like I was going to compromise the interview, she would sit discreetly in the background.

The room we were in was flooded with sunlight from high windows on two sides. It was set out more like the living room in a family home than an interview suite. Comfortable sofas and armchairs around a central coffee table, scattered with children's books and comics.

It reminded me of playrooms in nurseries or day centres, with boxes of toys and kids' drawings stuck on the walls. The only difference was the recording equipment in the corner, which would capture everything on video and audio.

Billy looked strangely out of place in such a cosy domestic setting. He was sitting on the floor, looking at a comic and it took a me a minute to realise why he looked so different.

His hair – usually an unruly mop of blond, looke two shades lighter – presumably because it had been washed and was neatly combed down.

Instead of his well-worn shorts, torn above dirty knees, he was wearing jeans and a pressed T-shirt and what looked like new trainers.

His whole face lit up in a bright smile as he recognised me. 'Jo.' He grinned. 'You came.'

I dropped my bag on the floor and sat opposite him on the rug. 'Of course, I did.' My beaming smile matched his. I was surprised at the genuine emotion I felt at seeing him again.

Putting my hands on his shoulders, I made a show of checking out his new clothes. 'Looking good, buddy.'

He pulled a face. 'Feel like a right ponce.'

I couldn't stifle a laugh.

'Anyway, how are you getting on with your foster carers?'

'Yeah . . . they're nice.'

'Good.' I ruffled his hair playfully and he laughed, ducking from under my hand. 'I'm here because they said you would only talk to me.' I sat back on my haunches, gesturing to the room with open arms. 'So here I am . . . at your command.'

He grinned and I got a glimpse of the innocent eight-year-old. Then he seemed to catch himself and the serious expression returned. Still trying to be the hardman. To emulate the behaviours he saw in the older members of the street-gang. Feeling that, to be accepted, he had to lose youthful exuberance – to be replaced by the serious business of drug dealing and playing cat and mouse with the cops.

'So,' I said, trying to hold on to the light-hearted mood. Not wanting him to revert to his default caution. 'Let's talk.'

His eyes flicked over my shoulder.

I followed his gaze. 'It's OK. Jane's here for you . . . to make sure you're all right.' I playfully punched his arm. 'Make sure I don't beat you up or anything.'

He laughed, sitting cross-legged – seeming to settle himself.

'Is Brit OK?' he asked – his eyes never leaving Jane.

'Yes. She's fine.'

'Is she in prison?'

'No. She's back home.'

For now – I thought. Knowing that carrying a knife could result in a custodial sentence for her.

I waited for him to ask why he couldn't go back too. Braced myself to start explaining safeguarding in a way an eight-year-old might understand. But he surprised me, by simply nodding – his brow furrowed in thought.

He was far more streetwise than he ever should have been. I knew, from his demeanour, that he understood perfectly what was going on.

'We're here to talk about that Thursday night, Billy.'

'What, the one when Brit gave me the money to get ice cream for her and her mates?'

'Yes, that's the one.'

Another nod. Good enough.

'You don't need to protect anyone now, Billy,' I said gently. 'Bri and his girlfriend are gone. The gang's been split up now.'

'I know.'

'Who went in and out of the block, while you were ...' I had to stop myself from saying 'on lookout'. 'Playing in the entrance?'

He shrugged, looking intently at the carpet. 'Just the usual. No strangers.'

'Who were the "usual" people you saw, Billy?'

He started to count them off on his fingers. 'Amazon delivery man for nosey Mrs Russell. Then friends that come to see Mrs Cantor on five who's got cancer. She had visitors on and off all day. I thought she must've been about to cark it.'

I tried not to smile. 'Who were they then?'

'God botherers.'

'What?'

'People she used to go to out with on Sundays, to choir or summat. Before she got sick. Old ladies mainly. Like I say, usual lot.'

'Who else?'

'Britney's mates who went to our flat. Then the doctor ... going up to see Mrs Cantor. Then later, ambulance came and two of their lot went up to hers.'

'Don't know how they all fitted into her little flat,' I smiled.

'Well, by the time the ambulance and doctor and stuff came – her friends had left. Then her family came.'

'Busy night. Then what?'

He suddenly couldn't meet my eyes and started fiddling with the laces on his trainers.

'Billy.' A gentle prompt. 'I came to see you because you said you'd talk to me. Please, don't leave anything out.' I couldn't ask him directly, or give him a name, so instead I said. 'Who else did you see that night?'

More fidgeting. 'Well ... Err'

'Who?'

A shrug.

'Come on Billy. You're doing really well. You've come this far ... don't stop now.'

'Will he know I said?' He spoke so quietly; I almost missed the words.

'You'll be looked after, Billy. No one will be able to hurt you for helping us.'

I waited. The silence seemed to stretch out interminably. And then – finally – he said it.

'Dean.'

Chapter Forty

Fordley Police Station – Friday afternoon

Callum was perched on the corner of a desk in the open-plan incident room.

'We've got the video interview with Billy,' he was saying to the team. 'He confirms Dean Gavney *did* enter the block of flats after leaving the newsagents. He went past Billy and took the stairs.'

'But he wouldn't be able to confirm which flat Gavney was going to,' Heslopp pointed out helpfully.

'No – but it puts our man in the block at the right time – which is significant.'

'Especially as he denied ever going into the flats when he was interviewed the first time,' Beth added.

'Question is,' Tony picked up the thread, 'we don't know how long he spent up there.'

There was a crucial gap in Billy's evidence. He'd told us he'd been upstairs to get money for ice cream and while he was at the van he saw the commotion at the newsagents.

'Gavney and Billy walk back into the block at the same time and Billy watched Gavney take the stairs up to the flats,' I picked up the narrative. 'But because Billy was carrying so much stuff, he took the lift back to his own floor and delivered the ice cream to his sister. When he goes back down to the entrance there's no sign of Gavney and he never sees him come back down.'

'He could have been inside Curtis's flat by then,' Callum said.

'Or,' Tony added, 'he could have stayed in Curtis's flat until later that night – when things outside had calmed down – then left.'

'Okay,' Callum concluded. 'We'll have Gavney produced from Armley Prison and brought back here for interview. See what he has to say in light of the new evidence.'

* * *

As I was leaving the incident room, DS Charlie Thompson collared me.

'Got a minute, Jo?'

'Always.'

I followed the young sergeant into one of the offices next to the incident room. 'Beth told me what you needed,' he said as he sat behind his desk. 'I gave it a couple of hours last night.'

He gestured me to the seat opposite.

'You wanted to know about Wearman's GP?'

'Jen called his ex-PA but she didn't know and I didn't want to call his mother. Apparently, the poor woman's in pieces. They've only just had his funeral.'

He tapped some keys, then read from the screen. 'He's registered with a practice near his apartment in Leeds and his PA, Ainsley McKenzie's, registered with the medical centre in Wilsden. Neither of them connected to Parkfield Medical Practice that I can find.'

'That would be convenient, wouldn't it?' But I couldn't keep the disappointment out of my voice. 'Never mind.'

I was getting up to leave when he stopped me by saying, 'But I did find something else you might be interested in.'

I sat back down. 'Oh?'

'His PA was bringing a tribunal against him.'

I felt my hope deflate. 'I already knew that.' I frowned as a thought struck me. 'But how did *you* know?'

'Because, *this* came up on the police records.' He turned the screen to show me.

'What exactly am I looking at?'

'Ainsley McKenzie filed a complaint with us about Wearman harassing her after he found out she was bringing the tribunal.'

'Really? She didn't tell me about that.'

Charlie began scrolling through the record. 'Wearman was calling her constantly, trying to get her to drop the case. She said at first he was offering her money – trying to pay her off – settle out of court. But she was adamant she wanted it to go the distance.'

'He'd know the press would be all over that.' I was thinking out loud as I watched the notes scrolling. 'Given his high profile, once it was listed for court, it would be in the public domain.' I thought about my conversation with Ainsley. 'But then that's what she wanted. For people to know what he was really like – behind that charming exterior. She was never going to let him buy his way out of it.'

'Eventually, she said, his calls became abusive and then threatening,' Charlie said. 'That's when she got the police involved. Accused him of ringing her at all hours. He denied it, of course.'

'Of course.'

'So, we downloaded the phone data for her mobile and home phone.' He traced his finger across the screen. 'These numbers were the ones.'

I could see the time log on the calls. 'One and two in the morning,' I murmured as I leaned into the screen. 'Were these numbers listed to him?'

'Nah – he was too clever for that,' Charlie said. 'Burners mostly. Until he slipped up with this one.' He pointed to a mobile number that had called Ainsley at four o'clock one Saturday morning. 'His own mobile number,' he said. 'Ainsley reported it as an abusive call. Said he sounded slightly drunk and was really aggressive. She thought he'd been out to a club with his mates that night – or so she'd been told by someone in the office.'

'Presumably that's why he slipped up,' I guessed. 'Out on the lash . . . egged on by his friends . . . used his own phone without thinking about it.'

'Ainsley's solicitor got us to apply for his call data. Was going to use it to prove the abusive nature of his association with his PA. But they never got to use it.'

'Because he ended up dead and the case never happened.'

'Yep.' Charlie pushed a memory stick across the desk. 'Call logs for both of them are on there. Don't know if they'll prove useful . . . but thought you might take a look.'

'Thanks.'

'Goes without saying – confidential police info. But Beth said the boss has approved it – long as it doesn't go anywhere else.'

Chapter Forty-One

Kingsberry Farm – Friday night

The lamps in my office cast the room in a soft-honey glow. The gently soporific effect making me feel even more like calling it a day.

I'd spent the hours since I'd come back from the police station looking over the call lists that Charlie had provided. A pretty fruitless exercise, since I had no idea what I was looking for.

Scrolling through endless rows of seemingly meaningless numbers, was made worse by the fact that I found it difficult to organise information into any kind of logical sense when it was on a screen.

Eventually, I'd printed off a hard copy. One bundle for Ainsley's phone log and another for Peter Wearman's.

And now I was doing what I always did when I had to find any kind of pattern in a jumble of disconnected information. Sitting on the floor, surrounded by sheets of paper, with different – coloured marker pens – highlighting and sorting the data.

Harvey, as usual, was lying on his side, snoring loudly. His long tail, occasionally twitching, sending nearby papers fluttering across the rug.

My notebook was underneath his front paw. I lifted it and retrieved my notes, then dropped his leg like a dead weight. He never flickered an eyelid and his snoring didn't miss a beat.

'You're so helpful, mate. Don't know how I'd manage without you.'

I made a note about a number that had come up on Ainsley's call list. She'd called from both her mobile and her landline and the calls had lasted between one and two hours each time.

The thing that made it stand out was that I'd found the same number on Peter Wearman's list. In his case, the calls were just a few minutes long. If I hadn't laid the lists out old-school, on paper, I'd have missed it.

I did a quick Google search, but apart from saying it was a Fordley number, it didn't list who it belonged to. I could ask Ainsley in the morning. A glance at the clock in the corner said 11 p.m. Too late to call now.

'In fact,' I said to Harvey, who continued to snore, 'it's too late to be still doing this on a Friday night.'

I left everything as it was on the floor and began switching off the lamps. Harvey finally raised his head and gave me a disgusted look as I packed up for the night.

Reluctantly, he left his warm spot and followed me down to the kitchen.

My brain was buzzing too much for me to go to bed yet. I knew I wouldn't sleep.

I opened the fridge and took out the bottle of Pinot Grigio that had been calling to me for the past hour.

Pouring a large glass, I took it back into the lounge and settled in my favourite, overstuffed armchair, with Harvey curled at my feet.

It felt as though I had too many hares running.

Something about all three supposedly 'accidental' deaths, was niggling at the back of my mind, but I couldn't get hold of it. An element they all had in common.

Was it something someone had said – that I'd heard? Whatever it was, it was 'jarring' and my unconscious mind was nudging me to find it.

I closed my eyes, recalling conversations with Marion Kilpin . . . Ainsley McKenzie . . . Callum. Somewhere, was a thread that connected things together. If I could find it and give it a tug, it would begin to unravel this seemingly unconnected weave of events, that was driving me nuts.

Since childhood, I'd been able to recall dialogue, almost verbatim. The audio equivalent of a photographic memory. Both a gift and a curse. The reason words and discourse had always chimed with me.

Invaluable for a therapist – as words are usually the only way a person can describe their inner world. The route map to what is going on inside someone's head.

But, this time, my auditory recall was coming up empty.

I took a long breath, over a count of four. Box breathing. In for four . . . hold for four . . . breathe out for four . . . Hold for four.

Useful for reducing stress or anxiety – but in this case, a way to recentre myself. Still the chatter of the endless conversations I'd begun replaying and let my unconscious mind roam.

Somewhere in that vast database of the subconscious, that records everything and deletes nothing from the moment we become sentient would be the piece I was looking for.

I let myself drift. Relaxing deeply. A state of self-hypnosis that the mind enjoys. Like a spa for the brain. A break from the busy madness of modern life.

Harvey's snoring was almost lulling – like a nasal metronome.

My thoughts drifted over the past couple of weeks. Floating above my timeline, like an all-seeing eye hovering above events, skimming past the insignificant, to look for something relevant.

I was back in the GP surgery. Standing beside Beth as she chatted to the receptionist. I was looking round the room. At the people . . . the walls . . . the furniture.

In Marion Kilpin's garden drinking tea . . . then drifting back to Ainsley McKenzie's stylish kitchen.

In the incident room – replaying the briefing with the team and my conversation with DS Charlie Thompson.

The call lists . . . the numbers . . .

My eyes flew open and I took a second to refocus. Then, putting my glass on the table, I ran out of the room and down the dark corridor to my office.

Harvey seemed to spring up on all fours while he was still half-asleep, only coming fully awake as he lolloped behind me, barking in anticipation at this new game.

I switched on the lamp and scattered papers across my desk until I found what I was looking for. I took it over to the sheets on the floor as Harvey danced around excitedly.

I was on my knees, holding the paper in my hand as I checked it against the number I'd written in my notes. The number both Ainsley and Wearman had called.

It matched.

I also made another connection to this number. To something I'd seen before. On the noticeboard in Parkfield Medical Practice.

Chapter Forty-Two

Kingsberry Farm – Saturday morning

Ainsley McKenzie answered the phone almost immediately.

'Ainsley, It's Jo McCready.'

'Hi.' She sounded out of breath.

'Is now a good time to talk?'

'Yes – no problem. I'm just out for a run.'

Being able to run and speak at the same time – blimey.

'When we spoke, you never mentioned reporting Wearman to the police for harassment?'

'I told you he'd made my life a misery – trying to get me to drop the case.'

'But not about the police report.'

I could hear the pounding of her feet as she ran. 'Didn't omit it intentionally,' she said finally. 'Didn't seem important – well, not now, anyway. Why?'

I told her about the number I'd found on Wearman's call history. 'It was Lexi Royle's number . . . from the leaflet you gave me when I came to see you.'

There was a pause, and I could hear heavy breathing and the bleating of sheep somewhere in the background.

When she answered, her confusion was evident.

'Well, yes. Obviously, I called it. Sometimes from my landline at home and sometimes from my mobile. They would last an hour or more . . . I mean, they were therapy sessions. But I don't understand why Peter called them.'

'I don't either.'

'How long were his calls to them?'

'Just a few minutes. Looks like he only called twice over a period of a week. Around the time you reported him to the police for the harassment.' I circled the questions I'd made on the call log the night before. 'Did you tell Peter Wearman that you were having therapy sessions with Sanctuary?'

'No,' she panted. 'Of course not . . . why would I?'

'Then how would he have their number?'

'Suppose it could be a coincidence?'

My instincts didn't like coincidences like that and I didn't think for one minute this was one.

'Though I can't imagine *him* ever needing therapy,' she was saying. 'That bastard didn't suffer from stress – he was just a carrier.'

'Did you tell *anyone* about your sessions?'

I listened to the pounding of feet and the gusting of Ainsley's breath as she ran in silence for a moment.

'Come to think of it . . . I *did* tell one person . . . apart from my mother.'

'Who?'

'Kaz . . . I mean, Karl Ronson.'

'The sales director at Wearman's?'

'Yes. He's a friend.' As soon as she mentioned Karl, her tone changed. Something I'd noticed before, in both of them, whenever they spoke about one another. Maybe nothing – maybe something? I filed it away for later.

'He came to see me, when I was signed off sick. He was really worried, especially when I was put on antidepressants. He used to come round after work, or weekends sometimes and we'd have a coffee. Still does.'

'Do you think he could have told Peter Wearman about the Sanctuary therapy?'

I could almost hear her shrug. 'Maybe. You'd have to ask him.'

'Are you happy for me to speak to the crisis line too? Tell them you gave me Lexi Royle's number?'

'Yeah – no problem, if it helps.'

* * *

Karl Ronson didn't have to think too hard.

'Yeah, I told him.' He was out of breath too, because he was at the gym.

What is it with all these fit people?

'I was that bloody angry after I'd visited Ainsley. Shocked when I saw her. I'd been round to her place and she looked like a shadow of herself. She told me the doctor had put her on anti-depressants – just short term to help her while things were so raw. I'd never seen her so wrung out.'

'So, you told Wearman?'

'Not at first.' I heard him taking a drink. 'Used to visit her after work. Didn't say I was seeing her, because Peter wouldn't have liked it. But when he found out she was taking a tribunal against him – that's when the shit really hit the fan. Ainsley told me about his calls, about the harassment and how bad it was getting.'

'That's when it came out?'

'I saw him at the office. Told him I'd gone round to see Ainsley. That she'd told me what he was up to and what effect it was having on her. Think I said something like, "She's even having to talk to a therapist because of you".'

'And he'd asked which therapist?'

'Not so directly. He was a total prick. Laughed and said his calls were obviously having the desired affect and if she wanted it to stop, all she had to do was drop the legal case. At some point, I think he said something like, "who's the crazy cow seeing anyway"?'

'That's when you told him?'

'Don't think I said the name – because I couldn't remember it. Just said she'd been put on to a local charity that used qualified therapists – because there was such a long waiting list, even for private ones. That he'd made her so desperate, she couldn't wait that long.'

There it was again – that softening of his voice when he spoke about Ainsley.

There was the clanging of metal in the background and a male voice saying something to Karl.

'Sorry,' he said. 'Got to go. My turn on the weights. Have you got what you need?'

'Yes, thanks for taking the time.'

* * *

It was obviously my day for making phone calls. After getting a fresh brew and taking it down to the office, my next call was to Vicky in Ibiza.

I had a question that couldn't wait. I could have asked Tess at the DAAT, but it was closed at weekends and I didn't have her personal number.

As I listened to the international dialling tone, I glanced at the clock – 10 a.m. UK time. Ibiza was one hour ahead – so I reckoned it wasn't too early to be calling.

I reckoned wrong.

'What the fuck?' Was the way she answered the phone.

'It's Dr Jo McCready. Sorry – I didn't mean to wake you.'

'Didn't get in from work till after six this morning.' Her voice was thick with sleep . . . and possibly something else, less natural.

'I'll make it quick. Tess at the DAAT said that she'd managed to get you some free therapy?'

'Hmm.'

'Was it with a therapist at the centre?'

'No. She tried. Doug, the counsellor, offered his time pro-something . . . ?'

213

'Pro Bono.'

'That's it . . . but that cow Rodgers said no, because I wasn't a client. So, Tess organised some phone therapy.'

'Can you remember who with?' The silence went on that long, I thought she'd fallen back to sleep. 'Hello?'

'Yeah . . . I'm still here. Err . . . "Sanction" . . . something.'

'Sanctuary?'

'Yeah . . . that's it,' she mumbled. 'Can you piss off now, please?'

'Sorry. Night.'

* * *

Jen was the person I always told first, if we had a breakthrough. On Saturday she'd be at home with her husband Henry, who was fiercely protective of their family time.

I knew, though that if I didn't tell her what I'd discovered and where I was going, I'd get it in the neck from her on Monday morning.

Instead of calling the house and risking Henry answering, I chanced her mobile.

'Hi, Jo. You OK?'

I could hear the shrieking of children in the background. 'Is this a bad time?'

'No. I've brought the grandkids to the park. Henry's watching football.'

I quickly brought her up to speed with developments.

'The Sanctuary helpline,' she repeated. 'That's what connects them all?'

'Not all,' I had to confess. 'But certainly Wearman and Lowry, through Vicky, his girlfriend.'

'Well, that's a start.'

'And I saw the Sanctuary leaflet on the noticeboard at Parkfield Medical Practice, which is another link. I'm on my way to the helpline offices now, to see what I can find out.'

'OK. By the way – Henry asked me to remind you that I'm on holiday next week. He's been to the caravan and got everything ready.' She didn't sound ecstatic at the thought. I had to smile.

'I'm sure you'll have a blast.'

She snorted. 'Only if the weather holds. Being cooped up in a caravan, with Henry, in the rain, playing Scrabble for a week, doesn't exactly fill me with joy.'

'I'll miss you.'

'Not half as much as I'll miss you. Murderers are much easier to deal with than Henry if he loses at Scrabble, let me tell you.'

Chapter Forty-Three

Fordley – Saturday afternoon

Parkfield Community Centre was in a small precinct of run-down shops. It occupied most of a two-storey block, sandwiched between a fish and chip shop at one end and a second-hand furniture shop at the other.

There was already a queue for In Cod's Name. The smell was making my mouth water. Couldn't remember the last time I'd had fish and chips.

Resisting the temptation to grab an early lunch, I headed for the community centre, whose mesh-covered double glass doors were welcomingly propped open.

Just inside I found myself at the back of another queue. As my eyes adjusted to the dim interior, I could see we were in a line for food – set up on two trestle tables at the end of the hall.

A man was serving soup from two large urns – passing the polystyrene cups to a young girl next to him, who added a bread bun and then directed people to baskets of sandwiches and cakes.

I stepped out of the line and walked to the front, standing at the edge of the table, until the guy serving noticed me and handed the ladle to his assistant.

'Can I help you?' he smiled.

'I'm looking for the Sanctuary helpline office?'

He wiped his hands on a tea towel and extended his hand. 'I'm Father Bassett.'

'Please, tell me your first name is Bertie?'

He laughed. 'No. Luke, actually.'

I shook his hand. 'Dr Jo McCready. Sorry, I couldn't resist.'

He beamed good – naturedly. 'Not the first time I've heard it, as you can imagine.'

I looked down the line of customers. Now that I could see them properly, it was obvious that this was a soup kitchen, set up to feed the less fortunate. No money was changing hands. Just food, smiles and comforting words.

'You're busy today.'

His eyes followed mine. 'Unfortunately, we're busy every day. My aim is to put ourselves out of business. But I doubt we'll be redundant in my lifetime.'

I studied his profile, guessing him to be in his early sixties, but he was one of those older men who kept himself in good shape and whose age was hard to determine. His skin was tanned, with the leathery look of someone who spent most of his life outdoors, his dark hair, salt – and – peppered now, but still full. A man, I thought, who had been even more handsome in his youth.

'You won't get much competition from the chippy next door, I'm guessing?'

He shook his head. 'Sadly, my customers can't afford that. For most of them, we're the only hot meal they get in a week. If we weren't here . . .' He splayed his hands in a gesture of resignation.

'Are you here permanently?' Somehow, I felt guilty, that I hadn't even known about this place. But then, I didn't live around here and it wasn't a part of town I was ever likely to visit.

'Twice a week here at the community centre. Other evenings, we run a soup kitchen in Fordley city centre – under the arches by the railway station. Lots of homeless sleep rough there. We do outreach . . . offer them warm clothes, sleeping bags, that kind of thing. I'm there as often as I can be. But we have other volunteers who work every day. Without them, we couldn't keep going.'

'I'm sorry.'

217

Perceptive blue eyes regarded me above a faint smile. 'Why sorry?'

It was a spontaneous but unaccountable feeling of regret. 'That your services are needed, I suppose. In our city – in this day and age.'

The sinews in his forearms stood out as he wiped his hands again on his apron and came round the table.

'Are you here for an interview with the helpline?' he asked.

'Err, not exactly. But I'm hoping to see the manager?'

'That would be Lexi.'

Lexi Royle. The therapist Ainsley had been assigned.

'She's in today,' he was saying. 'Saw her when we were setting up.' He spoke to the girl serving. 'Can you hold the fort, while I show Dr McCready upstairs?'

He reached behind the table and produced a black walking cane with a silver handle.

'It's OK. I don't want to put you out,' I said. 'If you give me directions, I'll find my own way.'

His gaze followed mine, to the stick held against his left leg. 'Oh this?' He smiled. 'Don't worry about my gammy leg. It hasn't totally given up on me yet. Besides, I could do with stretching it.'

As he walked past the baskets at the end of the table, he picked out some wedges of cake wrapped in cling film and put them in a paper bag – then led the way across the hall.

I fell in step beside him. Concerned about his leg and that I was putting on him.

His eyes followed mine, to his stick. 'A stupid accident with some digging equipment when I was working with the VSO in Africa,' he answered my unspoken question.

'I'm sorry.'

'Don't be.' He smiled. 'It was a long time ago – before I joined the priesthood. In fact – the reflection I did during my rehabilitation, was what prompted me to return to the church.' He lightly tapped his foot with the stick. 'It did me a favour of sorts – so we've made peace with each other . . . my duff leg and I.'

'Does your church fund the soup kitchen?'

'It's cross-denominational – thankfully. Hunger doesn't discriminate between faiths, so neither do we.' His cane tapped hollowly against the polished wooden floor as we went towards a door in the corner – picking our way through rows of tables set out for those wanting to eat inside. 'Saint John's, my church, raises funds, along with other C of E and Methodist churches around the parish. But it tends to be volunteers from my congregation who staff it.'

We'd reached the door to the stairs. He went ahead. By the time we'd climbed two flights, his limp was far more pronounced. My own thigh was aching in sympathy.

He indicated a door down the short corridor. 'Here we are.' There was a sign, which had been done on a printer and laminated, stuck to the door with tape.

SANCTUARY – COMMUNITY HELPLINE.

He pushed the door open and was greeted by wide smiles as people, busy on the phones, looked up and recognised him.

A tall, slim woman, with long brunette hair, was standing behind one of the call handlers, talking quietly over her shoulder. Father Bassett indicated her with his stick.

'The supermodel over there is Lexi Royle. The service manager.'

She looked over and smiled, gesturing with a finger that she would be just one minute.

He held up the paper bag containing the cakes. 'Just going to put these in the kitchen.'

I stood where I'd been left and took in the set-up.

No modern call centre, this. Just a few old office desks, with blue divider screens, offering the person sitting there some privacy. Cheap blue blinds covered the windows, cutting out the glare of the sun on computer screens.

The phones were standard base telephones – with the addition of headsets to allow the volunteers to type notes.

On that Saturday afternoon, there were half a dozen people manning the phones and all of them were engaged on calls.

The young woman finished what she was doing and came over. 'Hi. I'm Lexi, the manager. I'm afraid we don't take walk-in clients.'

'I'm not a client,' I smiled. 'I'm Dr Jo McCready.' We shook hands.

'Oh, are you here for an interview?'

'No. It's you I actually came to see. Is there somewhere we could speak in private?'

Her brow creased in a frown. 'Sure . . . is it about one of our callers?'

'Kind of.' I really didn't want to get into it in front of everyone else. Besides, I wasn't really sure what I needed to ask.

As I followed her to a small, more private office, the priest reappeared.

'Father Luke.' Lexi smiled. 'Did I spot another bag of goodies?'

'Fuel for the troops,' he said, leaning heavily on his stick. 'I'd make you all a brew, but we're in the middle of lunch downstairs.'

'Don't let me stop you, Father.' She patted his shoulder. 'I'll put a donation in the box, for the cakes.'

'Thank you kindly.' He waved at everyone with his cane as he left.

'He's a godsend – pardon the pun,' Lexi said, closing the office door behind us. 'Donations from the church keep us in business . . . and Father Luke keeps us in cakes and coffee. If it wasn't for his fundraising, we wouldn't be here at all.'

She took a seat behind a cluttered desk and gestured me to the chair opposite. 'You're a doctor?'

'Psychologist.' I deliberately omitted the tag 'Forensic' as that would pose too many awkward questions.

She smiled, waiting patiently for me to explain.

'I've been working with a couple of clients who recently used your service.'

Implying Ainsley McKenzie and Vicky had been clients of mine was a bit of a reach. I had 'worked' with them though – after a fashion. I had no problem stretching the point.

'OK.' Her smile was becoming a little thinner as she wondered where this was going.

'They said you really helped them during dark times.'

'Well – that's why we're here.' She ran fingers through her long hair – sweeping it back from her face. 'Not wanting to appear rude – but if they're clients of yours, why did they need to come to us?'

'I wasn't seeing them as a therapist,' I said, thinking fast. 'I work as a mentor at the Fordley DAAT.'

'Oh, I see.'

'The DAAT referred the girlfriend of one of their service users to you, because they can't provide therapy to anyone who's not a client.'

'It often happens that we see the families of addicts. Most of the formal services don't extend to loved ones and it can be as hard on them – if not harder than it is on the service user themselves,' she smiled.

I wasn't sure how to broach the subject of Peter Wearman. Whatever angle I considered, none really worked.

As usual, I decided a direct approach was best.

'One of the other cases I've been involved with lately had the employer of one of your clients calling your service.' I was choosing my words carefully. 'But no one – including your client – seems to know why. If I give you the details, is that something you could give me more information on?'

She was shaking her head before I finished my sentence.

'Client confidentiality applies to us, just as it does in any therapeutic setting.'

'If I can get your client to contact you – giving consent to speak to me?'

She thought about it for a moment. 'They would have to put it in writing. And then there's the employer. They would need to do the same. Even if they didn't engage our services.

'The employer, unfortunately, has recently died.' I registered the shock that flitted across her face for just an instant. 'That's how I became involved . . .'

'Through the police?'

'Home office pathologist, actually.' It wasn't a lie.

'I'll look into the protocols for it.' She was already making a note. 'Can't say it's something I've encountered before.' She glanced up from her note – taking. 'Can you tell me the name of our client?'

'Ainsley McKenzie. She knows I'm here. I'm sure she'll be happy to give her consent.'

'Yes. I know Ainsley.' She smiled, then took a long breath. 'If she puts the request in writing, then, providing there's no objection from anyone I speak to, I suppose it would be OK.' She got up from her desk. 'Sorry, I've just realised, I never offered you a brew. Tea OK?'

'Great – thanks.'

Chapter Forty-Four

Sanctuary Offices – Saturday afternoon

I listened to the chatter coming from the outer office, passing the time by reading the posters on Lexi's office wall. One in particular caught my attention. It was for a local credit union. A kind of community bank. I was still looking at it when Lexi came back with the tea.

'That's interesting.' I nodded to the poster.

She put the cups on her desk. 'Oh, yes. That's a great initiative.' She blew the top of her cup. 'One of Father Luke's suggestions, actually. Some of his parishioners were involved with a loan shark. They called us in various states of distress, but beyond counselling, we couldn't signpost them to any practical help.

'Father Luke had seen a community bank in action at another parish. It's been going for over a year now. Most people on the estate can't get loans from traditional banks. Or they only want small amounts. The credit union can accommodate that. Better than payday loans or worse.'

'Does Father Luke run it . . . the bank, I mean?'

'Oh no. He just came up with the idea. It's run by professionals. A local accountancy firm in Fordley oversees it all.'

'Easy to see why you've become so trusted . . . and needed around here. I'm ashamed to say, I didn't know you existed, until I spoke to Ainsley. How exactly does your service work?'

She sat back in her chair. 'All of our senior call handlers hold either a therapy or a counselling qualification. They volunteer their time. Some have their own clinical practices, or are employed by other services. Others are retired. We also offer placements to psychology students, or recently qualified therapists, who need to get their hours in, as part of their training. Typically, sixty to 100 hours. Obviously, it's unpaid, and they volunteer as and when they can commit the time.'

'Wish there had been somewhere like this when I was training,' I said. Remembering how difficult it had been in the eighties to get real experience of live cases in a clinical setting.

'The therapists take over the calls that require their skills. Then we have "listeners", who are there for more straightforward cases. I train them up, and they spend time shadowing more experienced staff until they're ready to take live calls and go solo. But we always mix the newer volunteers with more experienced people on each shift so they're never without support.'

'What kind of things do listeners deal with?'

'People suffering with stress or anxiety, usually connected to the cost-of-living crisis. They don't require therapy as such – more someone to listen, and then signpost them to services that can help. We have a pathway to refer people to debt management services or the credit union. Welfare advisors who can help them access grants and benefits. Local food banks – that kind of thing.'

'Impressive,' I said and I meant it.

'It all began during the pandemic. People were really struggling with lockdown and bereavement, but couldn't get to see a therapist. My own psychotherapist practice had to shut down, but I couldn't just abandon my patients, so, I set up a telephone service from home and put the word out on social media. It got far bigger than I could handle on my own so I recruited other therapists, willing to give their time for free, working from home and offering phone or Zoom sessions. I never thought it would grow into this. But once we'd started, we couldn't put the genie back in the bottle. People needed us then, and need us probably more now.'

'Do you operate twenty-four hours?'

'We didn't at first – but do now. We ran a recruitment drive last year and have enough core volunteers to man the service round the clock.' She tapped the table in a kind of 'touch wood' gesture.

'Do you offer face-to-face sessions?' Ainsley had already told me they did – but I wanted to hear it from the horse's mouth.

'We can, but not here. We don't have any suitable space. We refer those who want face-to-face to one of our volunteers who run their own private practices and they see the clients there. We have to charge for that, though although we keep the fee to the basic minimum, to cover things like fuel. It takes a volunteer away from the helpline – so most things we deal with over the phone if we can.' She dropped her pen on the blotter. 'Would you like me to show you around?'

I followed her out into the open-plan office. She opened her arms in an expansive gesture. 'This is the empire. Small, but perfectly formed.'

A man, who looked to be in his late forties, ended a call and began entering notes on the computer. Lexi took me to his desk. 'Ted, this is Dr McCready – she's come for a look around.'

I took his offered hand. 'Please, call me Jo.'

Startling green eyes regarded me with a mixture of welcome and curiosity. 'Ted Cornell. Pleased to meet you, Jo. Hope you're joining us? We need all the medical help we can get round here.'

'I'm not that kind of doctor.' I returned his smile. 'Psychologist.'

'Even better,' he grinned. 'We need that kind of help even more.'

'Ted's our most senior therapist,' Lexi said. 'He helps me train listeners and mentors some of the placement students.' She patted his arm. 'Been with us since the beginning.'

'Can't get rid of me now.' His tone was playful.

'Is this your full-time job?' I asked.

225

'No. I do weekends and at least two late nights in the week here, as well as helping with the outreach for the homeless, when I can. The rest of the week, I'm a therapist at the veteran's centre in Fordley. Specialising in PTSD, among other things.'

'How do you fit it all in?'

He shrugged. 'I'm on my own, since the wife ran off with my best friend . . . so nothing to sit at home for.' He was being glib – but there was a pain behind his eyes that belied the lightness.

'I'm sorry,' was all I could say.

'Don't be.' Again, the smile, but more brittle. 'I get to spend more time with the lovely Lexi and this motley crew.'

Lexi indicated a man at another desk.

'This young man is Patrick Swales.' He offered his hand and an uncomfortable half-smile. 'Patrick is in his final year at Fordley University.'

'Studying what?' I directed my question to him.

'Psy . . . Psychology,' he stammered, unable to meet my eyes. He was fidgeting nervously – twisting a pen between his fingers.

'Patrick's training to be a listener. Once he's got his degree, we're hoping he stays with us as a therapist,' Lexi explained. 'As well as proving invaluable on the IT front.' She rested a hand on his shoulder and red blotches immediately stained his cheeks. It was obvious, to me at least, that he didn't like being touched.

'Us oldies are hopeless with the technology, so Patrick does all the stuff that fries our brains.'

He had a stack of index cards by his elbow and it looked like he was entering details onto a database.

He indicated the cards with a nod of his head. 'Dragging them into the twenty-first century.'

'When I started the service,' Lexi explained, 'I kept client details on cards. It was the best I could do when I was working from home. I carried that on when we came here, but eventually realised we would have to transfer it onto computer and store it electronically. Patrick designed the database for us.'

'Got to comply with GDPR – data protection,' Patrick said, again without looking at either of us. And for a second, a micro expression flitted across his face. Irritation? Annoyance?

'Frustrating, isn't it?' I smiled. 'When things aren't done properly.'

He half turned his head to look at me. 'Yes . . . it is . . . very.' He stood abruptly and picked up his mug – heading for the kitchen without another word. Lexi simply raised an eyebrow at me and smiled.

'He can be a bit intense,' she said, sotto voce. 'Suffers from social anxiety.'

I watched Patrick's ramrod straight back as he went into the kitchen. The tension emanating from him was palpable.

People who suffered with their mental health often worked in the field of psychology, in one form or another. Some drawn to the subject as a way to better understand their own condition. Usually, having experienced trauma made them better therapists. But I'd encountered too many who crossed the couch prematurely, before their own issues were fully resolved, using the therapeutic environment as an arena to exorcise their own demons, to the detriment of their clients.

Patrick struck me as one of those. I hoped Lexi would recognise it, before she ever unleashed him on others.

Lexi was going from person to person, making introductions and explaining more about the service. Some of the volunteers were unemployed students, or members of the local community, working as listeners.

Finally, I made to leave.

'If you have a few spare hours,' she said as we shook hands, 'maybe you could volunteer yourself? We're always in need of well-qualified therapists.'

'Another doctor on the books,' Ted piped up, 'might attract some core funding, at our next application. Local council like to see professionals getting involved.'

'Another?' I raised a curious eyebrow.

'Oh, he means the doctor from Parkfield Medical Practice.' Lexi said. 'Volunteers a few hours a week.'

'Who would that be?'

'Dr Stanton. Colin Stanton.'

Chapter Forty-Five

Fordley – Saturday afternoon

I was still digesting that latest piece of the jigsaw as I walked across town to where I'd parked my car.

Dr Stanton volunteered at the helpline. That meant he had a connection to the common denominator that linked Steve Lowry and Peter Wearman. The pieces were finally beginning to drop into place, but I still couldn't see what the final picture would look like.

As I crossed the road, my attention was drawn to a woman walking in the opposite direction, carrying a large cardboard box.

A woman I recognised.

I squinted against the sunlight, to be sure I hadn't made a mistake.

The woman, struggling to keep her arms around the wide box, was Marion Kilpin.

She was a street length away and obviously hadn't seen me.

My first instinct was to call out to her – but something stopped me. On reflection, I wasn't exactly sure what.

Something about the emotional energy she was giving off? Her demeanour? The fact, that she seemed to be in a hurry – a woman with some important but serious business on her mind.

Whatever it was made me step back into the shadow of the building behind me and continue to observe her.

Saturday afternoon meant the city centre was packed. More so, because the weather was glorious. Shoppers and families with young children out enjoying the town. Restaurants and cafés, with tables on the pavements – trying to emulate Parisian street life, but without the same levels of sophistication.

I watched as Marion hurried by, waiting until she was a hundred yards or so in front, with plenty of people between us, before stepping out into the crowds and following her.

It felt wrong, somehow. Like some sordid stalker – but my instincts were telling me that it would pay dividends if I did.

As we walked – together but separately, I thought about why she looked so out of place.

First – she lived in Halifax. That would be her city centre of choice if she was out shopping – though she didn't look like she was. Although Halifax was smaller than Fordley, there wasn't much she couldn't do or get there that she could here.

Second – she was schlepping a box that was obviously a pain for her. I recalled her saying Jordan carried boxes for her to the church, when her husband wouldn't. Why hadn't she brought him along?

I didn't have long to wait for the answer.

We were retracing the route I'd only taken a few minutes before.

Turning the corner, I found myself back on the precinct where the community centre was. There was someone standing outside, by the doors, smoking. As we got nearer, I recognised Ted Cornell from the helpline.

I walked to the end of the row of shops and leant against the corner of In Cod's Name. The lunchtime queue was even longer than before, providing a handy barrier between me and Ted, without blocking my line of sight.

He smiled when he saw Marion, stubbing out his cigarette and walking to meet her.

When she saw him, her whole aura shifted, as if someone had turned up the contrast on a movie image.

Her expression, usually serious, broke into a bright smile – somehow making her look ten years younger.

They met in the middle of the precinct where Ted gallantly took the box. She made a show of rubbing her arms – obviously thanking him as they walked together towards the centre.

At the door, Ted put the box on the ground and I could see it contained coats and blankets. Marion said she'd donated her husband's clothes to charity when he died. It was possible she'd brought his things here. I wondered whether she'd known Ted before – or whether that was how they'd met?

They chatted for a minute and then said their goodbyes. Ted picked up the box and went inside, presumably to deliver it to Father Bassett's outreach.

Marion turned directly towards me.

I walked ahead of her, crossed the road that dissected the precinct and slipped in the doorway of the first shop I came to. But Marion didn't get that far.

She reached the corner of the chip shop and turned right – going along the road I'd just crossed. By the time I came out of the shop and turned into the street she'd vanished.

I stood for a moment in complete confusion.

The street stretched on ahead of me. There were no shops on either side – just the gable ends of buildings. People were walking in both directions, using it as a cut – through. No sign of Marion.

I cautiously followed the route she must have taken and then spotted it.

An alley that ran along the back of In Cod's Name. It was the only place she could have gone.

I leaned against the wall and when the last pedestrian passed and I wasn't being observed – poked my head around the corner and looked along the alley.

It was lined with industrial waste bins and ran the length of the row of shops.

Marion was standing alone halfway down the litter-strewn passage.

There was a clang as a metal door fell back against the wall and Ted appeared from the back door of the community centre.

Whatever I'd expected, it wasn't seeing Marion Kilpin being passionately kissed by the man I'd met just a few minutes before.

This felt uncomfortably like voyeurism. I couldn't watch.

Pulling my head back round the corner, I leaned against the wall, watching the few passers-by. A minute later, I heard the door clang shut again.

Pushing away from the wall, I walked across the road and waited in a shop doorway until Marion reappeared, looking a little dishevelled. She hesitated for just a minute, checking both sides of the street, before walking back the way she'd come.

Keeping a discreet distance, I followed her. Feeling a lot less guilty about it this time.

Marion crossed the precinct and I did the same, letting her get further ahead, but keeping her in sight.

Halfway across, I had the unsettling but certain feeling there were eyes on me.

Adrenalin prickled across my scalp and down the back of my neck.

I swung around, just in time to see a blind on the first-floor window of the helpline office being dropped back into place, by whoever had been watching me.

Chapter Forty-Six

Fordley – Saturday afternoon

Driving out of Fordley, I was still mulling over what I'd seen in the alleyway. And the implications of someone at the helpline watching as I'd followed Marion.

I was driving up the winding lane at the edge of the moors when my thoughts were interrupted by a phone call.

'Jo?' Callum's voice crackled over the speakers. 'Where are you?'

'Driving back to Kingsberry – why?'

'Wanted to bring you up to speed on the latest.' I could hear the shuffling of papers. 'We interviewed Gavney again. Told him we had a witness who saw him going into the block and up the stairs to the flats at the critical time.'

'Didn't tell him it was Billy, did you?' Even as the words left my mouth, I knew it was a stupid thing to say.

'Do I really need to answer that?'

'Sorry,' I said sheepishly. 'So, how did he react?'

'Thought he might tough it out – go "no comment" on us. But for once we got a break.'

'OK.' I was distracted – manoeuvring around a few sheep that had strayed from the moor.

'Changed his story,' Callum was saying. 'To admit he *had* gone into the flats after leaving the newsagents. Said he went to Curtis's place and banged on the door, but there was no answer – so he left.'

'Billy said he didn't see him come back down again.'

'We asked Gavney if there was anyone who could confirm that he'd only been up there a few minutes. Anyone who saw him come back down. He said he didn't pass anyone on the landing and when he got to the entrance there was no one there. So, we only have his word for it.'

My reflection in the rear-view mirror pursed her lips, as I thought about the timings.

'Billy would have been delivering ice cream to his sister then,' I murmured, almost to myself. 'How would Gavney know that, if he was lying?'

'So, why did he lie in the first place?' Callum sounded as frustrated as I guessed he was feeling.

'Maybe he thought it would look bad if he admitted he'd gone up there?'

'Well, he'd be right,' Callum said. 'And it looks even worse now. We've put it before the Crown Prosecution Service. Hopefully what we have now will be enough to cross the charging threshold for murder.'

I was about to tell him about Marion Kilpin when I heard someone come into Callum's office and a muffled conversation.

'Got to go, Jo. I'll catch up later,' was all he said, before hanging up.

No sooner had that call ended than my phone rang again.

'Hi, it's Ainsley.'

'You OK?'

'Fine. Been wondering if you found out why Peter called the helpline? It's been bothering me all day.'

'Actually, you saved me a call.'

I explained that Lexi Royle couldn't tell me anything, unless I got permission in writing.

'No problem,' she agreed. 'I'll call Lexi and then email my consent. Frustrating though . . . I wanted to know.'

'You and me both.'

'Would it help if I got Kaz . . . Karl, to contact them on behalf of Wearman's? To say that the company has no objections either? Seeing as Peter can't consent?'

I thought about it for a moment. 'Can't hurt ... but is Karl the right person? Should probably be the most senior person at the company.'

'Well, that would be Karl ... now.'

'What do you mean?'

'The board of directors appointed Karl to take over as CEO. He's in charge of the company.'

Chapter Forty-Seven

Ferndean House – Sunday

'So, Karl Ronson gets the company now that Wearman's dead?'

Elle looked thoughtful as she sat opposite me at her kitchen table.

I'd been invited over for Sunday lunch and jumped at the chance. Rina's roasts were legendary. Besides, it gave us a good opportunity to catch up on recent developments.

'Not just the company,' I said, over the rim of my teacup. 'I get the feeling Karl and Ainsley are more than "just good friends". She told me Karl offered her her old job back. She's going to work for him.'

Rina spoke over her shoulder as she chopped vegetables at the kitchen counter.

'Sounds like a motive to me.'

I hated to shoot down the theory out of hand, but I wasn't convinced.

'I'm not so sure.'

'Why not?' Rina persisted. 'Wearman's hated by everyone. He dies and popular Karl gets the company *and* the girl. Listening to you two, I know people kill for less.'

'True.' I put my cup down and washed a hand over my eyes – feeling suddenly weary. 'But, for a start, Ainsley wasn't Wearman's girlfriend – so it's not as if Wearman was an obstacle to a relationship between her and Karl. He may not have liked it – especially after Ainsley brought the legal case against him – but he couldn't have stopped them. Besides, I get the feeling it was visiting Ainsley when she was off sick that brought her and Karl closer. If I'm right, it's a recent relationship.'

'Still . . .' Rina was reluctant to let it go.

'I checked on the Companies House website,' I added, 'Wearman's parents were non-executive directors. There are no others.'

'Meaning what?' Rina asked.

'They're not employees – but they hold shares. In this case forty-nine per cent. I suspect they never had anything to do with running the company. Wearman probably structured it that way, so the business was controlled by family.'

'I'm guessing Wearman was the major shareholder?' Elle chipped in.

'Fifty-one per cent. So, he could never be out-voted. On his death, I'll bet his shares reverted to his parents. According to Companies House, Karl's been appointed the CEO and there's a share issue pending, to transfer majority shareholding to him. The parents probably don't want to be involved in the day-to-day – easier to hand it over to someone they trust. Someone they believe their son trusted.'

'Wonder how much he paid for that?' Rina said.

I shrugged. 'No way to know. Unless it gets leaked by the financial press.'

'Overnight, Karl's become a seriously wealthy man.' Elle said thoughtfully.

'So why exactly don't you think that gives him motive to bump Wearman off?' Rina turned, waving a dripping spatula in our direction. 'He hated the way he was treating Ainsley too . . . win-win.'

'Because he couldn't have known he would benefit,' I said simply. 'I doubt Wearman's parents even thought about what they might do in the event of their son's death, seeing as it was so unexpected. Unlikely they'd have discussed such a thing with their son . . . or his colleagues.'

'Jo's right.' Elle backed me up. 'Nice in theory – but too many variables.' She smiled at Rina to soften the blow. 'Life is rarely so neat.'

'And death is messier still,' I said without humour. 'If things come packaged with a ribbon – I get nervous. Chaos is usually normal in these cases.'

'Let's not forget,' Elle said, stretching back in her chair, 'what brought us to this in the first place, was *my* suspicion that a series of so-called accidental deaths weren't accidents at all. I *still* think Wearman, Lowry and Kilpin were murdered.'

'And there's no connection between Karl and Ainsley to Lowry or Kilpin,' I concluded. 'Unless we're not looking at one offender . . . but three separate, unconnected murders.'

That statement rattled around for a moment, until Rina broke the silence. 'Well . . . is that a possibility?'

I took a long breath. 'I bloody well hope not.'

Elle was already shaking her head. 'No, it's not.' She pushed away from the table and started to walk out of the room – calling over her shoulder, 'Which is another reason I invited you over, Jo. There's something I want to show you.'

Rina and I stared at one another, listening to Elle going to her study in the next room. She came back with a manila folder and proceeded to open it at the kitchen table.

'I haven't presented these findings to anyone yet,' she was saying. 'I only found it last night. You're the first to see this.'

Rina wiped her hands on her apron and came over for a closer look.

Elle flicked through a sheaf of photographs and pushed one across the table to me.

'These were taken at the scene of Wearman's death, by the forensic team, before anything was moved.'

I turned the image towards me and studied it.

Wearman was propped in a semi-sitting position against the wall of a dirty alleyway. His once-expensive grey suit trousers were stained a darker grey around his groin and the top of his legs. He was wearing a white shirt, with the left sleeve rolled up, exposing his elbow. His right arm was by his side – the empty syringe still in his hand.

Elle pushed another glossy image to me. It was a close-up of his exposed arm. There was a wide blue latex strip tied just above his elbow, to make a tourniquet.

'The tourniquet's been released slightly,' Elle explained, pointing to it on the image, 'to allow the drug to be injected without bursting the vein – but not enough for it to fall off his arm.' She tapped the photo. 'You can see, on this image, that the loop is still in place.'

'OK . . .' I wasn't sure where we were going with this. But I didn't have long to wait.

Elle sorted through the images and put another picture beside the first.

'This is the photo taken by the crime scene officers at Lowry's scene – again, in-situ, before anything was touched.' She indicated a similar picture of his elbow – tied with an identical band. 'I told you before that it looked like he'd tried to get a vein in his arm, but failed.'

'But he left the tourniquet on,' I said, realising that would be unusual in itself.

'He finally went for the groin.' She showed us the image of the whole scene. Lowry lying on the floor with his trousers pulled down – the needle still in his groin.

'Urgh.' I pushed the picture away. 'Couldn't you have waited until *after* we'd eaten.'

'Sorry,' she smiled, not looking the least bit sorry. 'But do you see?'

Rina leaned over my shoulder, moving the images closer together. 'What am I supposed to be looking at?' she frowned.

'Both blue latex tourniquets?' I ventured.

Elle sat down, opposite me. 'That's one thing of interest,' she said. 'Both are single use, medical-grade tourniquets. The kind you find in medical kits.' She swept her hair back in an artfully tousled look I always envied. 'But if they were getting their paraphernalia from a legitimate service, that's not so unusual.'

I knew that in order to reduce the spread of blood-borne viruses and infections, intravenous drug users were given access to a sterile supply of needles, swabs, and tourniquets, free of charge – through dedicated 'needle exchanges' or pharmacies.

'I only saw it last night. When I was looking at the photos from both scenes . . . side by side. it's the way they're tied.' She indicated the photos.

'So?' Rina sounded frustrated.

'During his post-mortem all I had to do, was pull on this short tail here and the tourniquet released.'

Rina blew her cheeks out. 'At the risk of repeating myself . . . so?'

'Intravenous drug users have to tie a tourniquet with one hand. They usually hold one end between their teeth, or in the hand to be injected, and twist the other end around their arm. Some, less experienced, which Wearman would have been, if we're to believe this was his first time – actually tie a knot – which is really difficult to release.'

'It isn't a knot,' I said, still staring at Wearman's image.

'Medical professionals,' Elle explained, 'don't *tie* a latex tourniquet. They're trained to "tuck" the tails, not twist or tie them. Then they can release it easily with one hand as they draw blood or whatever. Which is the way both Wearman and Lowry's bands were done.'

'Couldn't they have done that themselves?' Rina asked.

'Every phlebotomist or nurse does it slightly differently. Like tying your shoe laces. We all come up with a technique that works best for us, especially if we have to do it quickly and often. But these bands have been applied in *exactly* the same way.'

'Which would be unusual?' I guessed.

Elle nodded. 'There's something else.'

'What?'

'The tails would have been the other way round if they'd tucked it themselves. These were applied by someone else – someone standing, or kneeling in front of them. And whoever it was has medical training . . . and used an identical technique.'

'Two victims,' I murmured. 'One killer.'

Chapter Forty-Eight

Ferndean House – Sunday

As we ate lunch, I told Elle and Rina about my conversation with Ainsley McKenzie and the call logs DS Thompson had shown me, which led to my visiting the helpline.

They listened in silence until I got to the bit about seeing Marion Kilpin and Ted Cornell kissing in the alley.

'Bloody hell,' Rina breathed. 'Wonder how *they* met?'

I pushed my empty plate away. 'Ted said he helped with the outreach scheme in Fordley. Marion is involved in her local church and donates to the homeless street charities. Not a huge leap to assume they met through that, at some point.'

Elle looked thoughtful. 'When we looked at Kilpin's death and you said it was staged, Jo, we both agreed that Marion wasn't capable of manhandling her husband into position behind the bathroom door. But now that we know about Ted . . .' She let the inference hang.

'Seeing Ted gives her another reason for wanting her husband out of the way, too,' Rina said with a certainty I didn't share.

I took a sip of Malbec as I considered it. 'It certainly changes things,' I murmured.

'But?' Elle – perceptive as ever.

'As a standalone case, it fits,' I said thoughtfully. 'Let's assume Marion was having an affair with Ted. She finds out about her husband's abuse of Jordan and they kill her husband.' I twirled the delicate stem of my wine glass. 'Nice and neat. The end.'

'Great!' Rina grinned. 'Job done.'

'But if we look at all three cases you first brought to me,' I went on, about to burst Rina's enthusiastic bubble, 'there's no connection between them.'

'Nothing to tie Marion and Ted to Wearman and Lowry,' Elle finished for me.

'Bugger.' Rina dropped her napkin on the table in disgust.

'Except . . .' I added.

'What?' Rina looked hopeful again.

'The helpline.'

* * *

It was getting late. We'd talked around the three cases from every angle. Each one alone, as Elle had said in the very beginning, had a plausible explanation as an accident. But we'd ruled that out from the start.

The more I looked at them, the more I agreed with my friend's original instincts, that all three had been murdered.

But tying them together – to one lone offender – was proving trickier.

The evidence Elle had produced, about the tourniquets was compelling and defied the laws of random chance. If she said they'd been applied by the same person – that was good enough for me.

Eventually, we'd gone old school. Clearing away the dishes, Elle had produced a large sheet of paper, marker pens and Post-it notes, which we were huddled around at the table.

'Ainsley was getting therapy through the helpline after being bullied and harassed by Wearman.' I ticked each one off with a marker pen, as I went through them. 'So was Vicky, after she'd been assaulted by Lowry. Kilpin's connection to Sanctuary is via Marion's association with Ted.'

243

I circled the thing we'd kept coming back to – right in the centre of our murder mind-map.

'Sanctuary.'

'The only connection to all three,' Elle agreed. 'The *victims* weren't in touch with the helpline – but someone in their life was.'

We all studied the map.

'And someone from that office saw you following Marion – which makes me nervous,' Elle added, grimly.

I shot her a sideways glance. 'Try it from where I'm standing.'

'So, what now?' Rina pushed away from the table and began drying pots draining by the sink.

'I need to go back there.' I glanced at the clock. It was past nine and I was shattered. Not tonight though – tomorrow.

'You can't!' Elle said. 'Not now we know someone's on to you.'

'I said I'd speak to Lexi – the manager. Once she had consent from Ainsley.'

'So, ring her then.' Elle wasn't going to let it go.

I was already shaking my head. 'I want to know who saw me from the window that day and the only way to find out is to walk into that office and see how they all react.'

'Could be dangerous,' Rina said from the sink. 'If we're right, and someone there is a murderer . . . you could be walking into the lion's den.'

'Wouldn't be the first time, would it?'

Elle stood up and stretched her back.

'No. But you can't keep doing it. By the law of averages your luck is bound to run out one of these days.'

There was nothing I could say to that – because she was right.

Chapter Forty-Nine

Fordley – Monday evening

I was trying not to think about Elle's parting words as I walked across the precinct to the community centre.

It was already dusk when I'd parked my car in a side street, about fifteen minutes' walk away.

I'd called Lexi and arranged to see her, but she was working the night shift and didn't start until nine at night.

The air was still warm, with a slight breeze blowing across the square. The area was emptying as the shops were closed now – only a few takeaways still open on this quiet Monday evening as I approached the centre.

As I got nearer, I could hear music coming from the large hall. A sign, taped to the glass doors announced the 'Monday night movers, class'.

Rows of 'movers' in workout gear were dancing with various levels of enthusiasm, whilst being beasted by shouts of encouragement from a woman standing on the stage.

I sidled behind the back row, suddenly feeling overdressed and decidedly unfit, nipping through the door to the stairs.

I paused outside the helpline offices, composing myself before going in. I needed to be ready to catch the spontaneous reactions of whoever was working.

I deliberately didn't knock – just pulled the door open and strode in, my eyes already focused on the space where I knew Ted's desk was.

He glanced up as I entered, momentarily looking surprised, then slightly confused, before managing a slight, far from genuine, smile.

Patrick was sitting at his desk. He glanced in my direction, then quickly looked away. Trying to appear busier than he obviously was.

'Hi.' Ted's greeting sounded a little uncertain. 'Didn't know you were joining us tonight.' He made to get up from his desk, but Lexi called out from her office.

'It's OK, Ted. Dr McCready's here to see me.'

He nodded and sat back down, but I was aware of his eyes following me as I went into the manager's office.

There was already a cup of tea waiting for me on the desk.

'Got you a brew.' Lexi sat down and took a sip from her own cup.

'Thanks. You spoke to Ainsley?'

She nodded, reading from her computer screen. 'She emailed her consent.' She swivelled in her chair and pulled a ream of papers from a tray. 'Karl Ronson also got in touch, to explain about Mr Wearman.' She shook her head. 'So tragic.'

I didn't reply, just watched in silence as she scanned the pages.

'I took the liberty of pulling the files from the dates you wanted to know about, to save us some time.' She ran her finger down a list of dates. 'It appears Peter Wearman called us for the first time on the twelfth of last month.'

I checked my own notebook.

'Who did he speak to?'

'One of our listeners took the initial call but couldn't answer his question so escalated it to me.'

'What was his question?'

She sat back and regarded me for a moment, as if debating whether to tell me. Then sighed. 'He wanted to know who Ainsley's therapist was.'

'Obviously, that was you,' I said evenly. 'Did you confirm it to him?'

She was already shaking her head. 'Of course not. That would violate patient confidentiality. In order to maintain that

I couldn't even confirm or deny that she had contacted our service at all.' She smiled when she looked back at me – but it didn't reach her eyes. 'But you already know the rules, Doctor.'

'What was he like when he spoke to you? Polite? Aggressive?'

'Polite – at first. But when he realised I couldn't – wouldn't – tell him anything, he became ... frustrated. Said he knew she'd contacted us, because we were the only charity helpline in Yorkshire that used qualified therapists.'

Karl Ronson had told him that much. Easy enough for Wearman to narrow it down.

'How did the call end?'

'Pretty much there. I kept it civil. He didn't. Eventually he hung up.'

'Why do you think he wanted to speak to Ainsley's therapist?'

'Ordinarily, I'd say "you'd have to ask him" – but in the circumstances ...' She spread her hands out – palms up, in a gesture of futility.

'You're an experienced therapist,' I persisted. 'Used to working from verbal cues, over the phone. If you had to hazard an educated guess?'

'It wouldn't stand up as evidence.'

'It doesn't need to. This is strictly between us.'

She took a long breath. 'It was obvious to me that Peter Wearman was used to being in control. Also obvious that he was pissed off at Ainsley for the tribunal.'

'She'd told you about that during therapy?'

Lexi nodded. 'The man was a control freak. Type A personality. Direct, forceful, challenging. A narcissist into the bargain. Ainsley told me about him during our sessions. When I spoke to him on the phone he bore out everything she'd said. I'd say he wanted to exert pressure on whoever was working with Ainsley.'

'To drop the case?'

She nodded, taking a sip of tea, before adding. 'We get it a lot. I'm sure when you ran a therapy practice, you had it too.

247

Family members or partners – wanting to influence the outcome. At best, trying to put their side of the story because they worry that they're being character assassinated during therapy. Or at worst, trying to pressure the therapist into steering the client towards a particular course of action.'

She was right. I *had* experienced it.

'He called again, though – even though you didn't tell him anything.'

It wasn't a question – but she took it as one.

'Yes. The following week. On the nineteenth. But he didn't speak to me that time. I wasn't on shift.'

'So, who?'

'Unfortunately, I have no idea. It was during a shift change. The call is logged on the system – so we know he rang. But no record of who he spoke to.'

'But the call *was* answered,' I read from my own notes. 'It lasted three minutes.'

'All calls come through a central number and are answered by whoever is free. It's shown as answered, but not which terminal took the call.'

'So how do you keep track of which clients belong to which therapist?'

'The therapist or listener gets a blank client form or enquiry form up on the screen as soon as they answer. The caller's number is entered automatically by the system. The call handler fills in the remaining fields on the computer record. Name; address; GP details, then their session notes. When they're finished, it's saved to the system and allocated to them.'

'But that didn't happen with Wearman's second call?'

'No. Whoever took the call, never filled in a form.'

'What if he was asking to speak to you? A client form wouldn't be filled in then, would it?'

'No. But an enquiry note would be. They're the equivalent of a Post-it note. Sent to whoever in the office it's meant for, if a someone leaves a message for one of us and we're not available.'

'Do you have a record of who was on shift that night?'

She'd obviously anticipated my question. The staff rota was already among a sheaf of papers on her desk.

'The call came in during a shift change,' she said, passing the list over. 'Early shift packing up and leaving, late shift arriving. People go to the loo – go in the kitchen to make a brew – grab something to eat. There can be a lot of people milling around the office. Anyone could have picked up that call during the crossover.'

I glanced at the list, which showed names from both shifts. Ted and Patrick were both on the late shift.

'Ted's on both lists?' I noted.

She nodded. 'He'd been in earlier to do some training with a couple of new listeners. Then he stayed for his late shift.'

'Does that man ever go home?' I kept my tone light-hearted – to belie any interest.

She laughed. 'Think we *are* his home, to be honest.'

There was a knock on the door and one of the girls from the office stuck her head in. 'Sorry, Lexi,' she smiled apologetically. 'We've got a caller asking for you. Do you want me to say you'll call back?'

'It's OK, Angie. I think we're done here.'

'Would you be able to ask these people whether any of them spoke to Wearman that night?'

She was standing up to go. 'Already have. They all said they didn't. In fact – no one remembers him calling at all.'

Chapter Fifty

Fordley – Monday night

I was still thinking about Wearman's call to the helpline as I walked back to my car.

From what I'd learned of Wearman's character, I doubted that call would be any less heated than his first one. Whoever spoke to him would remember. Yet they all denied taking the call. And whoever took the call failed to log the conversation?

Someone in that office was lying – but why?

I turned the corner into a street on the edge of Little Italy. A part of town named after the Italian immigrants, who had come to the city in the nineteenth century to work in the flourishing woollen industry.

The huge warehouses and mills that had once hummed with the production of textiles were now being converted into offices and city apartments.

But, as yet, the gentrification programme hadn't reached this far.

The streets here were quiet even during the day, the few empty buildings that remained, boarded up and silent. The original cobbled road, only used as a cut through at the edge of town to avoid rush hour traffic, at this time of night, pretty much deserted, making it a sure place to find a parking space, if you didn't mind a walk into town.

I'd left the Roadster here after struggling to find a parking space any nearer to the precinct when I'd driven in earlier.

The sound of my heels rang on the broken paving stones, the solitary sound echoing back from the high walls of surrounding buildings.

It was dark, the few remaining street lights at the far end of the road casting a dim glow that didn't penetrate far enough to make any difference.

I could see my car at the end of the road, parked in front of what had once been a small local theatre. Now secured by perforated steel sheets, which covered its windows and doors, only the ghosts of performers and theatre-goers, now long gone, haunting the once glamorous space.

The black mouth of a ginnel between two buildings, gaped open to my left. Instinctively, I stepped into the empty street, away from the untrustworthy shadows. Picking up the pace – eyes locked onto my car – just a few yards away.

Then something beneath conscious knowing rang an urgent alarm.

The unconscious mind. That sleepless guardian whose only mandate is to keep us alive, sent a rush of adrenalin and cortisol surging through my veins. Lifting the hairs along my arms and tightening my scalp.

In a split second, before I could even register the source of the primeval warning, I began to move – but not fast enough to avoid the blow to the back of my head, that fired sparks across my vision.

'*Stay away.*' A rasping, strange voice from behind. '*Leave it alone.*'

I tried to turn – reaching behind me to grab at something – anything. My fingers closed around soft, padded material. I gripped, hearing it tear, just as another heavy blow sent pain exploding across my shoulders, forcing me to fall forward – sprawling awkwardly into the road.

Over the buzzing in my ears and my own thundering heart-beat, I could hear the sound of pounding feet as my attacker ran away.

I lay still, trying to get my breathing under control and clear my head.

251

The cobbles felt ice-cold and damp against the side of my face.

Slowly, I forced my arm to move. Whatever I'd grabbed had left a small piece of foam padding stuck between my fingers.

I felt in my pocket for my phone. It wasn't there. I groaned at the pain across my shoulders as I rolled onto my back – my boots scraping against the road surface. Gingerly I felt in the other pocket – no phone.

Had my attacker stolen it – is that what this was? A mugging? Then the words came swimming back to me . . .

'Stay away . . .'

Not robbery – a warning.

The pain in my temples throbbed in synchrony with my pulse rate, which had soared off the scale.

I couldn't lie here in the middle of the road, waiting for a lone car to come along and finish the job. Or worse, whoever had attacked me, to decide to do the same.

Slowly, I sat up, and looked around. My vision wobbled worryingly and by the time I got to my feet, the ground was tilting, like the deck of a rolling ship.

I staggered forward a few steps and found myself back on my knees, with no memory of falling.

I stayed there, taking deep breaths – focusing on a spot on the ground until my sight cleared.

Something glinted on the cobbles a few feet away.

My phone.

I crawled on painful knees until I reached it, then sat back against the kerb. My car was just a few yards away, but even as I looked at its tantalising safety, I knew I wasn't fit to drive without risking my life – or worse, someone else's.

I needed help – fast.

My silent prayers were answered when the screen lit up as I unlocked my phone. Then, I paused – staring stupidly at it.

Who could I call? Jen? No – she was at Flamborough Head in a caravan.

So 999? Even as the thought entered my head, I discounted it – hospitals ... ambulances. Although I was hurt, it didn't feel serious enough to take up those kinds of resources. Besides, the pragmatic side of my brain was already listing the practicalities. My car left here all night. Harvey on his own at the house. No.

My thumb hovered over an icon at the top of my screen. A number I'd always had on speed dial. My trusted go-to in any emergency. An icon I hadn't had the heart to remove, even when everything had changed.

Finally, I pressed it.

Chapter Fifty-One

Kingsberry Farm – Early hours Tuesday morning

'You were bloody lucky there was no concussion.'

Callum was sitting next to me on the sofa, his fingers gently exploring the golf-ball sized lump on the back of my head.

Harvey lay on my other side, his large head resting on my knee, as I stroked his silky ears.

After answering my call on the second ring, Callum had made it to Little Italy in record time and, despite my protests, had driven me straight to Fordley Royal Infirmary.

As luck would have it, the doctor in charge of A&E that night was someone Callum knew and I'd been whisked into X-ray with, what seemed to me, indecent speed.

But now I was back home, with Callum refusing to leave me on my own.

'They said you could only be discharged if there was someone with you tonight.'

'I've got Harvey.'

Callum snorted. 'Great as a guard dog, but useless as a nurse.' He fussed Harvey, who lifted his head and nuzzled his hand appreciatively.

I sensed a hesitation, before he asked quietly, 'Why did you call me . . . and not Eduardo?'

My brain wasn't working fast enough to appreciate what was behind his question.

'He's in California,' I replied without thinking.

In the silence that followed I realised he probably took that to mean he was second choice. Before I could say anything to the contrary, he changed the subject.

'What do you want to do about the assault?'

I shrugged. 'I got pushed over in the street – big deal. I'm not badly hurt . . . No robbery. How seriously would it be taken?'

'Not very, if I'm honest. You can't give a description. Male? Female? Even clothing – apart from the fact you grabbed at a jacket and probably tore a piece out of it. Not much to go on. There's no working CCTV in that street – even if we had the resources to go scouring through it for a simple assault. Is anything at all coming back to you?'

I resisted shaking my head in case my brain rattled. 'He came from behind – all too quick.'

'How do you know it was a male?'

I had to think about that one.

'Not sure . . . I just do. The voice. I think they were trying to disguise it – but it sounded male. Then the sound of heavy feet running away.' I gave a light shrug. 'Just an overall impression.'

'You're sure about what was said?'

'Certain. *"Stay away – leave it alone."*'

'Well, at least it's not anyone you know.'

'How can you say that?'

'Because anyone who knows you would know the best way to get you to do anything would be to beat you around the head and tell you to stay out of it.'

I pulled a face. 'Very funny.'

'But true.' His fingers stilled in my hair, but didn't pull away. Cradling my head in his large palm. 'What were you doing down there at that time of night anyway?'

'Visiting Fordley Community Centre.'

'Bums and tums class?' he laughed, ignoring my dig in his ribs.

'The Sanctuary helpline, actually.'

'You volunteering?'

I ignored the obvious sarcasm. 'The helpline seems to be a link between Stephen Lowry, Peter Wearman and Andi Kilpin.'

255

His single, raised eyebrow begged a thousand questions. 'Didn't know you were still looking into those.'

'You told me to "knock myself out" – as long as it didn't cost you anything.'

His fingers absently stroked the throbbing area at the back of my head. 'Didn't mean literally.' His expression was suddenly more serious. 'Is the link a significant one?'

'Could be . . . it's all I've got, right now. Apart from Elle's evidence.'

'That was hardly conclusive. If it had been we'd have followed it up ourselves.'

'I know.' An unexpected wave of weariness flowed over me. The feeling that maybe he was right – perhaps I *was* chasing shadows.

Right now I wasn't sure I had the energy to do this. 'But put everything together and it starts to look convincing.' I sounded more certain than I felt.

Maybe he picked up on my reticence, this man, who knew me better than most. His arm slid down across my shoulders and gave me a squeeze – pulling me closer to him.

'So, tell me,' he said gently.

I told him first about the connection to Parkfield Medical Practice and Dr Stanton.

'But that didn't apply to Wearman, or Kilpin. Then I realised, it wasn't necessarily Stanton but something I'd seen at the medical centre.'

'And it was the helpline?' Callum hooked a stray tendril of hair around my ear.

His touch was distracting. I had to force myself to concentrate.

'There was a leaflet for Sanctuary in the waiting room. Then Ainsley McKenzie – Wearman's PA – gave me a copy. Lowry's girlfriend, Vicky, got referred to them by Tess at the DAAT.' I washed a hand across my tired eyes. 'The only one left was Kilpin. At first, I couldn't see a link to him – and then I did.'

'Which was?'

'Marion,' I said simply.

I explained about my first meeting with Ted Cornell at the helpline office, skipping to the part when I saw Marion's clandestine meeting with him in the alley.

'Could still be coincidence.' But I could hear an element of doubt creeping in to his tone.

'I know. But then tonight happened and I was warned to "stay away". From what – if not the helpline? Makes me more certain than ever, someone there is involved – somehow,' I murmured.

My voice sounded distant, even to me. I was running on empty. Exhausted. The last vestiges of adrenalin and cortisol ebbing out of my system to leave me feeling like a puppet whose strings had been cut. My limbs felt leaden and I was struggling to keep my eyes open.

'Come on, you.' His tone was decisive. 'You're all in. It's nearly two in the morning. We can talk about this tomorrow.'

'Drop the latch on your way out,' I mumbled. 'I'll be fine here.'

'No chance.'

I felt him start to move – and suddenly, I was reluctant to let go of the warmth and familiarity of having him there.

'I'm not leaving you on your own.'

His arms were beneath mine, lifting me off the sofa. 'I'll sleep in the armchair in your room,' he was saying. 'I promised to look after you tonight and it's non-negotiable.'

Chapter Fifty-Two

Kingsberry Farm – Tuesday morning

Harvey's wet nose nuzzled my face. I cranked open one eye to squint at the bedside clock. 6.20 a.m.

I lay on my side with Harvey's face against mine, nudging me to get up, and in that moment I forgot. Until a movement on the bed beside me galvanised my senses.

I rolled over, eyes wide open now and stared at Callum, fast asleep – fully clothed on top of the duvet. His arm flung across my waist as we'd lain, curled into each other, like two pieces of a jigsaw, neatly fitting together.

Early morning sunlight seeped round the edges of my blinds, bringing with it fresh memories of the night before.

His gentleness as he pulled the duvet over me. Going to sit in the armchair in the corner, until I called him back to the bed.

I'd wanted to feel his warmth next to me. His breath on my neck, the weight of his arm around me. Reassuring. Comforting. Just as it had been before everything I'd believed in had changed.

His insistence that he stay fully clothed and on top of the covers.

'Don't want you to think I'm taking advantage of the situation,' he'd murmured, almost asleep as soon as his head hit the pillow.

I'd lain awake for a while. Staring at the shadows shifting across the ceiling. Listening to the even rhythm of his breathing. Remembering how this used to be.

Knowing I was reaching out to something that was broken – that could never be the same – but in the hope it might be. Somehow, in the seclusion of the night, that had been enough.

Now, with the clarity of daylight, I felt suddenly foolish.

An unbidden quote ran like ticker tape across my mind.

'Insanity is doing the same thing over and over and expecting different results.'

Einstein had it right. Evidently, I'd never learn.

I slipped from beneath his arm and slid out of bed, trying to be quiet as I pulled on a dressing gown. As I reached the door, the low rumble of his voice made me turn.

'Hello, you' He smiled – looking unexpectedly boyish in half-sleep.

'Hi.' For some reason I didn't know what to say. 'Coffee?' was the best I could manage.

He nodded and stretched. 'How you feeling?'

'Fine,' I called over my shoulder as I made for the stairs, with Harvey bounding ahead.

* * *

By the time he walked into the kitchen my – rarely used – cafetière was on the table and a fresh pot of tea was brewing on the Aga.

'Smells good.' He leaned against the oven, arms folded as he watched me pottering about. 'Where's the boy?'

I nodded to the open porch door, where Harvey had made a thankful exit as soon as we'd come down. 'Surveying his estate.'

'Thanks for last night,' I said, not able to look at him.

He got mugs out of the cupboard and put them on the table, pulling out a chair for himself.

Our routine. We slipped into this domestic dance so easily. It felt so right and so wrong all at the same time.

'No problem. I wasn't going to leave you – not as soon as you'd been discharged from hospital.' He grinned up at me as I poured his coffee and my tea. 'Anything could have happened in the night.'

259

I ignored the inference. 'Hmm. Well – you didn't have to stay. But thanks anyway. Hope you got some sleep. Must be in short supply lately, with this enquiry running.'

'Maybe not for long.' The faint aroma of his familiar cologne, mingled with the scent of coffee.

I shifted uncomfortably in my chair. 'How come?'

'CPS have given us a decision on Dean Gavney. We're charging him with the murder of Brian Curtis and Stephanie Parks today.'

I frowned. 'You didn't find any gunshot residue on him . . . or any of his clothes?'

'Nope' He stifled a yawn. 'But there were four days between the murders and Gavney being brought in for questioning. Plenty of time for him to destroy the clothes he was wearing and clean any residue off himself.'

'OK.'

'His defence will no doubt argue that lack of residue is crucial, but nothing a good prosecutor can't work around.' He was studying my face in that way he had, which made me feel I was the entire focus of his attention. 'You're not so sure?'

I shrugged, taking a sip of tea. First cup of the day – always the best.

'Gavney just doesn't fit for me. But I can't deny the evidence you have is overwhelming.'

'And we can never rely on a profile alone,' he reminded me – not that he needed to. I appreciated, more than most, that behavioural analysis was just one tool in the toolbox.

'I know . . .'

'But?'

'Given how he reacted when his solicitor told him Stephanie's baby was his? Then there's his behavioural profile. Impulsive. Reckless . . . and drunk on the night of the murder. I don't think he'd have the presence of mind to stage the scene the way we found it.'

260

'He had motive . . . and opportunity.' Callum spoke thoughtfully into his coffee cup. 'He'd threatened Curtis . . . and at the time, he didn't know who the baby belonged to.'

'I can see him being capable of killing Curtis in a fit of rage. It wouldn't be planned – and it would be disorganised' I conceded. 'But not Stephanie. In either case, he just isn't cool – headed enough to stage the scene and for what reason?'

'To throw us off. Make it look as if Curtis and Stephanie had rowed over the baby – and he'd killed her and then himself.' He shrugged. 'Gavney's daft enough to think it would plausible that Curtis would take his own life.' He looked at me with that endearing lopsided smile that had a way of drawing me in. 'He didn't bank on us having you to point out what a load of bollocks that was.'

'I'll take that as a compliment.'

'I'm a cop, Jo. Not a psychologist. I have to go with the evidence. But I've worked with you long enough to value what you do – so I take it on board.'

'But it's not enough to tip the scales,' I added, unhelpfully.

We were interrupted as Harvey skittered in to the kitchen, his huge paws, wet from early morning dew, slipping on the Yorkshire stone tiles. He'd found a tennis ball in the garden, which he dropped at Callum's feet.

'Whoa, big fella.' Callum fussed my dog, unsuccessfully trying to keep wet paws off his trousers. 'Speaking of tipping the scales,' he said, throwing the ball to distract Harvey. 'What were you telling me about last night, about the helpline? Marion Kilpin and this guy Ted Cornell?'

I went over it again, adding the other connecting threads, that ran to Steve Lowry and Peter Wearman. Including Elle's new finding about the disposable latex tourniquets.

'She believes they were applied by the same person . . . Someone who had medical knowledge?' Callum absently stroked Harvey's head.

261

I nodded. 'Lowry and Wearman are linked by the tourniquets *and* by the helpline.' I took another drink. My brain always worked better with tea. 'Kilpin was the outlier – until I saw Marion with Ted.'

'The helpline link again?' Callum still didn't sound convinced.

'It's fragmented, I agree. But what I *do* know is that in all three cases the scenes were staged and the behaviours leading up to their deaths, and the circumstances in which they were found, are odd. *All* of them.' I poured another tea for myself. 'Elle's instincts about that are spot on. What are the chances of these three victims being connected in some way to Sanctuary?'

'It's human nature to look for patterns – you know that better than anyone, Jo. But sometimes, we can see connections that are coincidences and patterns that aren't really there.'

'Apophenia.'

'What?'

'The psychological term for weaving coincidences into an apparent plot. That's how we form conspiracy theories.'

'Or see murder in random deaths.'

For a moment, we both sat in silence. Sipping our drinks.

'I don't scare easily,' I murmured into my tea. 'But this killer . . .' I looked at him, holding his gaze to add weight to my words. 'And there *is* a killer out there, Cal. Whether I can prove it to your satisfaction or not . . . scares me.'

He returned my steady gaze. 'Why?' he asked quietly.

'Because . . . whoever he is, he can do what he does and go unnoticed. He's invisible. How do you catch a killer no one believes exists?'

He nodded slowly, pursing his lips thoughtfully. But said nothing.

'And what's more, if no one is looking for him, he's going to keep on killing.'

Finally, Callum took a breath. 'Look, I agree, there were oddities about all of those cases and I know you value Elle Richardson's instincts as much as I do yours . . .'

'Thanks.' I appreciated that.

'And, I'll admit – you've got me thinking.'

'About what?'

'Gavney,' he said simply. 'I agree – he's no criminal master-mind. And I take your point about it being a stretch that he would stage the scene just to throw us off looking at him.'

'But it won't alter the fact that you're going to charge him with murder?'

He shook his head. 'There's nothing compelling enough to alter that . . . yet.'

'So, what's your point?'

'You're telling me you believe the cases Elle's highlighted, were all murders?'

'Yes.'

'And they were staged?'

I nodded.

'I'm not saying I agree with you. But, after this conversation, I'll take a look into Curtis, Stephanie . . . and Gavney.'

'A look at what?'

'See whether any of them had a connection to Sanctuary.'

I raised my eyebrows in a silent question.

'Could be that I'm suffering from this apophenia, as well. But theirs is another scene that was staged to look like something else too.'

'OK . . .' I said slowly, my mind already going over all the elements of the double – triple – murder in that flat.

'Could be just coincidence. But it's worth checking, if only to eliminate the possibility and put it to rest once and for all.' He stretched then pulled a face at his own armpit. 'God, I stink.'

263

He got up and put his mug in the sink. 'Need to go home and get a shower and a clean shirt before I go back in.'

I watched him shrug on his jacket.

'If you think whoever attacked you last night came from the helpline – do you want me to get uniform to go over there? Ask a few questions?'

I thought about it for a second, then shook my head. 'No. Not yet.'

He stood in front of me – holding my shoulders. Looking down into my face. 'Once I've made a few more enquiries with the Curtis, case, we can talk about it again. Meantime, stay out of it . . . OK?'

I nodded, not meeting his eyes.

He pulled me closer and I breathed in the warm, familiar scent of him.

'I've missed you,' he murmured into my hair.

That was my cue to admit I felt the same. But, somehow, I couldn't bring myself to say it.

This had once seemed so natural. Now, I wasn't sure what to do with it. So, I said nothing as he hugged me, fussed Harvey, and left us both standing in the doorway, watching his car crunch down the gravel drive.

Chapter Fifty-Three

Moorland Road – Tuesday Afternoon

As I was driving into Fordley to meet Elle and Rina for lunch, I put a call in to Lexi Royle.

'What can I do for you?' She sounded hassled.

'Just a quick question.' I kept my tone light – trying to hide the significance of it. 'After I left, last night . . . did anyone else leave the office at about the same time?'

'Err . . .' There was shuffling of paperwork and a muffled conversation with someone in her office. I could picture her holding the phone under her chin, as she multitasked. 'Well, I was almost right behind you. Went to Subway for a sandwich – hadn't managed to eat all day. Why?'

I swerved the question. 'Anyone else?'

'Ted was coming outside for a fag break. Then, as I was coming back, Patrick was leaving, at the end of his shift. That's if you don't count the movers' class. Plenty of them were streaming out of the community centre. The precinct was pretty busy about that time. Why do you ask?'

'It's nothing important,' I said breezily. 'Thanks anyway.' I hung up as she was about to press me for more.

* * *

I'd arranged to meet the girls at The Munch Bunch. A small, cosy café in the heart of Little Italy and a place I knew well.

In a rushed phone call earlier, I'd given Elle the edited highlights of what had happened the night before.

This was the nearest place for both her and Rina, and as neither had the time for a lingering lunch, the café was a simpler option than a restaurant.

Domino, the manager, wiped her hands on her apron, her smile a mile wide as she recognised me.

'Jo.' She beamed. 'To what do we owe the pleasure?'

'Meeting friends for lunch.' I glanced round the empty tables. 'If you can fit us in?'

She came round the counter and gave me a hug. 'You can see how I'm fixed,' she laughed. 'You should have booked.'

I followed her as she wiped down an already spotlessly clean table in a quiet corner. 'Usual lunchtime rush has finished – perfect timing.'

We both turned to the door as the old-fashioned bell above it chimed, announcing Elle and Rina's arrival. They almost burst in, suddenly making the small space seem crowded.

'Sweet pea!' Elle rushed over to me, wrapping me in a tight hug. 'I've been so worried since you rang.' Before I could speak, she'd spun me around and was probing the back of my head with deft fingers. 'Christ – the lump's as big as a duck egg.'

Rina dropped her leather biker jacket over the back of a chair. 'You OK? Elle told me what happened.'

Domino was looking confused. 'Blimey – I miss out on all the drama.'

'I'm fine . . . really.' I brushed away their concerns and took a seat. Domino went to get menus.

'Have you been checked out at hospital?' Elle naturally slipped into doctor mode.

'Yes – and before you ask, there's no concussion or serious injuries . . . except to my pride.'

Rina cut to the chase. 'You think it was someone from the helpline?'

'Who else?'

We paused as Domino took orders for drinks. Tea for me, coffee for Elle and water for Rina.

'Whoever it was,' I picked up the conversation, 'warned me to "Stay away and leave it alone". What else would they be referring to? I'd just left the Sanctuary office.'

Elle agreed. 'Too much of a coincidence. Probably the same person who saw you following Marion Kilpin.'

'You went back there to see if you could work out who that might be?' Rina said. 'So, did you get anywhere? Or was the crack on the head all for nothing?'

I thought about it for a minute. Reflecting on what I'd seen when I walked through the door. 'Ted,' I said simply. 'Although Patrick looked very shifty, as well.'

'Shifty?' Rina grinned. 'Is that a psychological term?'

'It is now,' I smiled. 'He couldn't look at me when I walked in. Whatever is going on – Patrick knows about it.'

Elle raised her eyebrows, spreading her palms out. 'Well go on, why Ted then?'

Domino brought the drinks. We scanned the menu – then all decided we weren't hungry. This was going to be a cheap lunch date.

I thought about the question as I stirred the teapot.

'His demeanour. The micro expression that flitted across his face.' I shrugged. 'Fraction of a second – but I knew when I saw it that he was the one who'd seen me from the window.'

'Which means Marion will know too.' Rina took a sip of water. 'He's bound to have told her. So, she'll be on her guard now. They both will.'

'I also went there to find out why Wearman had called the helpline.'

They listened in silence as I brought them up to speed with what Lexi had told me.

'Think Ted could be the one who took the call and didn't log it?' Elle asked.

'Could be anyone.' I hated to admit we had such a wide parameter to look at – but, convenient as it might be, there was no way to connect Ted to Wearman's call.

'Someone's lying,' Elle stated the obvious. 'And whoever it is could somehow be connected to Wearman's death.'

'Nothing links Wearman to Ted . . . or Marion,' I said. 'Except perhaps that phone call. Neither Ted nor Marion Kilpin know Ainsley McKenzie. So why would they be involved in Wearman's death?'

'What now?' Elle sounded exasperated.

'What we need,' I said slowly, thinking out loud, 'is someone on the inside.'

'A volunteer at the helpline?' Elle asked.

I nodded into my teacup, as if the answers were all in there.

'Someone none of them know,' Elle added.

'With a legitimate reason to be there,' I said. 'A newly qualified therapist . . . building up practice hours, maybe?'

We both looked at Rina. She paused, with the glass halfway to her lips. 'What?'

Chapter Fifty-Four

Kingsberry Farm – Tuesday evening

Rina had agreed to apply as a volunteer at Sanctuary – but unless she got the job, there wasn't a lot more we could do. Even if she *was* accepted, there was no guarantee that she could find anything that would help. But it was the only plan we had.

I was catching up on paperwork in my office when Callum called to say that Dean Gavney had been officially charged with double murder. He was giving me the heads-up before it appeared on the news.

'I know you still have your doubts,' he'd said.

'Gavney's profile just isn't right for this, Cal,' I said again – feeling like a broken record that no one was listening to.

'I know.' His breath gusted down the phone in frustration. 'I don't dispute anything you've said. But the evidence, and a lot of the forensics, puts Gavney at the scene. No one else.'

'Did you check to see if there was any link to Sanctuary?'

'There's nothing.' Even as he said it, I knew it would be a long shot. 'Even checked with Pip Holden, who was the only other person associated with this. She's never even heard of the helpline.'

'No reason for her to,' I said, feeling unaccountably deflated. 'She got her therapy from Doug at the DAAT.'

'Got DS Charlie Thompson to check the phone data, for all the players involved. Sanctuary's number doesn't appear on any of them. Not even the burner phones found on the associates we pulled in after the raid on Curtis's flat.' I could hear him take a drink – presumably the syrupy-thick coffee from the percolator in his office.

'What about Dr Stanton?' I knew I was clutching at straws. 'He volunteers at the helpline ... *And* was in the block at the time of the murders.'

'So were a lot of other people. He's alibied until after 9 p.m. Lots of witnesses can confirm he was in Mrs Cantor's flat until well after the time of the murders.'

'What if the time's wrong?' I persisted. 'Time of death isn't an exact science, Cal. It *can* be unreliable – you know that.'

'Elle narrowed it down to before 21.00.' He sounded weary. 'But it's not just her evidence. We've got neighbours hearing the shots. Then nothing after that. None of the usual comings and goings. Then there's the phone evidence.

'It was business as usual all day. Curtis's typical calls – checking in with dealers and customers. Then Pip Holden saying he suddenly stopped contacting her after 19.30 p.m. The burners we recovered from the flat, showing his runners calling him – but getting no answers. Those were calls he wouldn't have ignored. That was his business – it relied on phone communication. It all stopped, suddenly and unaccountably. Curtis dropped off the planet at 19.36 ... literally. He was dead by then, Jo.'

I listened to him – knowing everything he was saying was right – but still feeling that nagging doubt in my guts.

'Everything we've got points to Gavney, Jo.'

'He doesn't have the imagination to come up with something so elaborate.' I washed a hand across my eyes.

'Maybe not,' he said, taking a long breath. 'It's an anomaly. But unless something else turns up ...'

It wasn't often that we were so at odds in our thinking. But whenever it did happen it was a classic case of 'an irresistible force, meeting the immovable object'. An impasse.

We agreed to disagree.

After he hung up, I decided to call it a day and come out of the office.

When my mind was too full, I turned to one sure way of decompressing. Walking Harvey across the moors – aimlessly and for no particular purpose than to breathe in the warm air, feel the sun on my face and clear my thoughts.

Chapter Fifty-Five

Kingsberry Moors – Tuesday evening

We were out just in time to get the last of the sun, which was beginning to lose its heat as the cloudless sky surrendered to the purple edges of the approaching sunset.

Harvey ran ahead – glad to be out on a long walk – while I followed, lost in my own thoughts. Absently taking in the familiar view. Trying to waken up to it, be less complacent and remind myself how lucky I was to have this on my doorstep.

The moorland was vibrantly coloured with splashes of green and purple heather, humming with bees and the chaotic flight of butterflies.

The tranquillity, along with my thoughts, was shattered by the shrilling of my mobile.

'McCready,' I answered, throwing a stick which Harvey had just dropped at my feet.

'Jo, it's Doug.'

'Hi, Doug.' I was surprised. This was the first time the senior therapist from the DAAT had ever called my personal number. 'What's up?'

'Hope you don't mind my calling – but it's Tess. I'm worried about her and . . . well, thought you might be able to help?'

'Tess?'

'This business with Pat Rodgers, it's getting messy to say the least.'

I sat on a low wall, not wanting to lose the signal by moving, knowing this must be serious.

'Go on.' I launched Harvey's stick for him, again.

'The board of trustees sacked Rodgers for gross misconduct, after an internal disciplinary.'

'I know.'

'That means she can't get a decent reference, beyond confirming the dates she worked for the DAAT.'

'Not sure she deserves that much.' I couldn't raise any sympathy. 'But what's this got to do with Tess?'

'Her statement, along with yours, about that incident with Pip Holden being able to get onto the roof, because Rodgers wasn't on duty, formed a major part of the disciplinary.'

'And?'

'Rodgers is claiming you and Tess cooked up the charges to get her the sack. That the claims were exaggerated.'

'Unbelievable.'

'Doesn't help that, as a result, Tess got Rodgers's job. She's claiming that was the whole reason for you and Tess putting in a formal complaint against her. Get Tess in as manager.'

Harvey had lost interest in the stick and was happily amusing himself sniffing around in the undergrowth.

'The board had been investigating Rodgers for a while,' I said, able to speak freely, now that the disciplinary was over. 'They know the extent of her fraud. Doesn't matter what she says now.'

'She's taken legal advice.' He sounded worried. Unusual for Doug who was always so unfazed by the most dramatic of crises at the DAAT. 'A legal firm wrote to the trustees, putting them on notice that she's taking them to court for unfair dismissal.'

'How do you know all this, anyway?' The board wouldn't have shared this with Doug.

'Tess,' he said simply. 'She's been confiding in me. She's stressed out about it all. She's in a right state. Not eating . . . not sleeping. I'm really worried for her.'

I was confused and said as much. 'This is between the board and Rodgers, surely?'

'Tess told me that Rodgers contacted her directly – more than once. Hassling her to change her statement to the board. Withdraw the complaint.'

I could feel my blood pressure rising as I thought about Pat Rodgers's bullying behaviour, the fact that she was still playing her malicious, manipulating games, even after being given the boot. The woman really was a piece of work.

'Surely Rodgers can't imagine the board will reinstate her?'

I could almost hear him shaking his head. 'I don't think she wants that. Tess says Rodgers needs a good reference to stand any chance of getting another position.' His breath gusted down the phone. 'You know what the third sector's like, Jo. With a gross misconduct charge on her record, she's unemployable.'

'So, she wants the record changing? To say what, exactly?'

'She wants the board to state that she left by mutual agreement. Then to draft an agreed reference. Otherwise, she's going to drag you and Tess through court. She's really putting Tess through the ringer and it's taking its toll on the poor lass.'

I was gritting my teeth as I listened.

Rodgers could take her best shot with me. I was used to being grilled in court by some of the fiercest KCs in the country. Standing in front of an employment lawyer held no fear for me. But to harass Tess like this? I was beyond incensed.

'Does Tess know you're speaking to me?'

'No . . . I'd rather she didn't. I just wanted you to know. Tess trusts you . . . and, well, Rodgers's accusation involves you too. I thought maybe you could speak to the board? Find a way through this mess – take pressure off Tess.'

I took a long breath and slipped off the wall. 'Leave it with me, Doug. I'll see what I can do. And thanks – appreciate the heads-up.'

'No problem.'

I followed Harvey, my mind running through the implications. *That bloody woman!*

I hated bullies. Ever since I'd been a victim at school – until I'd learned to take care of myself. Never ceased to amaze me how a bully in childhood often carried it into adulthood.

In the days when I'd run a private therapy practice, I'd treated more than my fair share of clients suffering from bullying in the workplace, by people like Pat Rodgers.

I was damned if I was going to let Tess be intimidated like this.

'Harvey – come!'

I turned towards the house – much to Harvey's disgust. He followed sluggishly – taking his time, now he knew we were going back.

* * *

Harvey lay on his bed in front of the Aga, his chin slumped on his large paws and was refusing to look at me – even for a treat.

'Sorry, boy.'

I sat down at the kitchen table with a fresh mug of tea and proceeded to go through the pile of post I'd collected from the mailbox when we'd returned.

Two days into Jen's holiday and I was already missing her legendary efficiency. I'd become used to the post appearing, as if by magic, on my desk every day.

Note to self – empty the mailbox, every morning, until she gets back.

'I'll give you an extra-long walk tomorrow.'

Harvey huffed, turning his face towards the warmth of the oven – beginning to snore almost instantly.

I sorted through the pile, until I found the official looking brown envelope bearing the franking mark of the board of trustees.

I knew, as soon as Doug told me what was going on, that they would have written to me when they received Rodgers's legal letter.

I read the neatly typed sheets informing me of the challenge from Pat Rodgers over her dismissal. There was a copy of her solicitor's letter too.

I sipped my tea as I read, every line, pushing my levels of outrage to new heights.

Finally finished, I pulled out my phone. I didn't have Tess's personal number so I called her office at the DAAT and left a voicemail, asking her to get back to me.

Not much else I could do now. Except get something to eat – and try to sleep.

Chapter Fifty-Six

Kinsberry Farm – Wednesday morning

Somehow, July had slipped into August without me even noticing.

The weather outside my office window was glorious, with the temperature already climbing.

I stared out at a group of birds, fighting over the hanging bird feeders around my lawn, and for a moment, lost myself in their antics.

I'd much rather be sitting out there, enjoying a mug of tea, than in here, up to my eyes in paperwork.

I'd just come off the phone to the Head of the board of trustees. She was understandably reticent, as charges of issuing false claims against Pat Rodgers had been levelled at me as well as Tess. But at least I'd had the opportunity to put forward our case.

Rodgers's sacking hadn't been just down to that one incident on the roof. I knew they'd been watching her for a while and evidence of her fiddling expenses and time sheets predated the incident with Pip. It didn't all rest with Tess and I.

I'd been asked to put another statement together, referencing our conversation, and said that, as one of the directors of the DAAT, I would, of course, be kept in the loop with the unfolding drama.

I was so engrossed, typing up the report, that I jumped when my mobile rang.

'Jo, it's Pip.'

'Everything OK?'

'Better than OK, actually.' I could hear the smile in her voice. 'I've found another flat for me and Maisie.'

'Brilliant.' It was nice to have some good news for a change.

'We've got the keys already.' She sounded excited. 'I was wondering if you could do me a favour?'

'Of course – what?'

'I need to go back to the old flat, to collect some of our things. We left with the clothes we were standing up in. I need to collect clothes and Maisie's toys. Few other bits.'

'OK. Forensics have just released the scene.'

'That was one of the things I was going to ask. But, also . . . I don't want to go on my own. It'll feel . . . you know? Going back to where things happened. And them being killed there . . .'

My mind was calculating the time frame. It was probably too early for crime scene cleaners to have gone in there yet. The place would still be covered in the gruesome reminders of recent events.

'Maybe you should leave it?' I suggested. 'Until it's been cleaned . . . I can let you know when it's done?'

'No,' she said, almost too quickly – evidence of how brittle she was. Barely supressed emotions still running high. 'I'd rather get it over with. Besides, I want Maisie to have all her familiar things around her when we get into the new place . . . you know, help her settle in.'

'Why not give me a list of what you need, Pip, and I can arrange to have it collected for you?'

'No. I can't decide what we want until I see it. I'm leaving all the furniture and stuff. I don't want anything they sat on . . . or the beds. It's personal things. I'd rather collect those myself.'

I still wasn't sure. 'There's evidence there, of how they died, Pip. It's not pretty. Honestly, I'd—'

She cut me off. 'I was hoping you'd come with me.' Her voice went up an octave. Buried anxiety, breaking though. 'But if you won't . . . then I'll just have to go on my own.' She sounded on the edge of tears now.

'OK . . . OK.' I caved.

Revisiting the scene of her rape and assault was enough to trigger anyone. Not to mention knowing two people had been brutally killed in what used to be her safe space.

If she was as close to the edge as she sounded, I didn't want her there by herself.

'I'll come with you. When do you want to go?'

'This afternoon?' she said hesitantly.

That was sooner than I expected. I glanced at the grandfather clock in the corner of my office. It was already ten.

'What time?'

'Can you pick me up at the refuge, please . . . about one-ish?'

Even as I agreed, I could hear Callum's warning about not going back to the estate on my own – along with a million other reasons why this wasn't a good idea.

Chapter Fifty-Seven

Kinsberry Farm – Wednesday afternoon

After Pip's call I'd rung the crime scene manager, who'd confirmed that the scene had been released. The door to the flat had been replaced and the new keys booked into the local police station. I'd arranged to collect them, on the way.

My Roadster was too noticeable on the estate. Parking it near the flats, would be like putting an ad in the *Fordley Express* to announce my presence.

I owned an old Land Rover Defender that I kept in the barn behind the house. Usually, it only came out in winter, when the weather up on the moors would make my sports car about as effective as a chocolate teapot.

But today it served another purpose. It was less conspicuous, and it had more room in the back for Pip's boxes.

I parked it on the edge of the green, closer to the block of flats – so we didn't have far to carry everything. Thankfully, we didn't see anyone familiar as we crossed the green and went into the block.

It seemed quiet and empty without Billy kicking his ball in the entrance.

The landing was deserted as we went to the flat, both of us carrying flattened storage boxes.

We paused outside the door.

Pip looked suddenly pale.

'Are you sure, about this?' I asked again. 'I can go in for you?'

She shook her head, her ponytail swishing from side to side, mouth set in a grim line as she stared at the door. As if, by an act of will, she could make this less awful than it was going to be.

'OK.' I slid the key into the lock. 'I'll go in first. If it's too much, just step outside.'

She nodded – still not trusting herself to speak.

I stood in the doorway to the lounge, shielding her from the sight of bloodstains, across the carpet – faded brown now. Holes cut out of the carpet in places where samples had been removed.

She stood in the hallway, looking uncertain, teeth catching her bottom lip. Clutching the flat boxes to her chest – like a shield.

Suddenly she looked like a little girl. Too young to have this crash through her life.

The mother in me wanted to wrap my arms around her and give her a hug. But I knew, instinctively, if I touched her, it would be too much. She'd unravel and never be able to do what she came here for.

'Why don't you start in Maisie's room,' I said gently, knowing it was the one space untouched by the horror.

She nodded and quickly went down the hall.

I turned and reviewed the lounge.

The big toy unicorn stared back at me – blood spattered across his rainbow-coloured horn. I couldn't see any other toys.

I quietly closed the door and went to stand in the doorway to Maisie's room. Pip was busy throwing clothes from the small wardrobe into a box.

'Maisie's unicorn's in the lounge,' I spoke quietly. It felt irreverent somehow, to be loud. Like raising your voice in a chapel. 'But it's not been cleaned.' I chose my words carefully. 'If you want it, I'll wash it in the kitchen?'

She shook her head, without turning round. Still busying herself, folding clothes. 'Nothing that's got ... you know ... stains of anything.'

I nodded, leaning against the door frame. 'Need a hand?'

She indicated the drawers. 'The clothes in there.'

I started emptying drawers. Finally, Pip looked round. Seeming satisfied. Closing the box.

'I'll put this by the door. Then I'll do my room.'

The worst one.

Images of Stephanie's body, curled against the headboard. The blood and skull fragments. The smell.

Pip carried the box out and I nipped quickly down the hall, to her bedroom, gingerly pushing the door open with my foot. I let out the breath I'd been holding.

The room wasn't as bad as I feared. Certainly not as horrific as when I'd first seen it.

The bedding had been removed with Stephanie's body and now, I was relieved to see, the mattress and headboard were missing too. Presumably taken by forensic officers. Only a brown stain remained on the carpet, and an arc of blood spatter across the wall by the head of the bed.

When Pip came back, I stood in front of the bloodstain, trying to hide it. Her eyes flitted over the spot, then looked away and the process of busying herself with bedside cabinets and dressing table drawers began again.

Finally, after what seemed like hours – but was only minutes – we were done.

Pip went out and I followed with the last of the boxes. As I neared the front door, I could hear voices.

'Oh, I'm so sorry, Jean,' Pip was saying.

There were two women on the landing, who looked to be in their sixties. One of them was carrying a small box of her own. She was the one talking to Pip.

'It was a blessing,' she was saying. 'She was ninety-two and in a lot of pain. Although Dr Stanton was very good – he came to see her regularly. Between him and the Macmillan nurses, they kept her comfortable towards the end.'

Pip realised I was there. 'Oh Jean, this is my friend Jo, she's helping me clear the flat.'

Jean juggled the box, which had a large wooden crucifix sticking out of the top, preventing the lid from closing. A framed print of the Sacred Heart of Jesus jostled for space in the box. The same one my mother had above her bed.

She extended her free hand to me. 'We're doing the same,' she said with a trembling smile. 'My mother's just passed away.'

'Mrs Cantor?' I guessed.

'Oh, you knew her?'

I shook my head. 'Sadly, we never met.'

She turned back to Pip. 'We thought she was going to pass a couple of weeks ago. Everyone dashed to her bedside. I thought it was the end. So did Dr Stanton, to be honest. I made sure everything was done, as she would want ... and then she rallied.'

'It often happens like that,' Pip sympathised.

Jean shifted the box to her other arm.

'Is this everything?' Pip nodded to the box.

'Just Mum's personal belongings. The things we want to keep, as reminders.' Jean's chin trembled and her friend squeezed her arm. 'All her clothes and furniture are going to charity.' She sniffed, and pulled a tissue from her coat pocket.

The three of them carried on chatting, but this felt like a private conversation so, I turned and pulled the last of Pip's boxes onto the landing, and busied myself locking the door.

'I'm so sorry you're leaving,' Jean was saying to Pip. 'But understandable after what's happened.'

'Awful,' her friend nodded, expression grim.

'The funeral details will be posted in the *Express*.' Jean said as they walked with us to the lift. 'If you'd like to attend?'

'Your mother was very good to me and Maisie.' Pip sounded emotional. 'I'd like to come – thank you.'

I half listened as they said their goodbyes at the lift. There wasn't enough room for all of us and the boxes – so we let them go first.

I was distracted by a half-heard sound coming from somewhere below us. Maybe the landing . . . or the stairs? It seemed familiar, but I couldn't place it. I tilted my head to listen – trying to block out Pip's conversation with Jean.

Then the door to the stairwell rattled. I turned, expecting someone to appear, but there was no one there.

I gave myself a mental shake, annoyed that I was on hyper alert, watchful, in case Britney Wilson or any of her little girl gang, got wind of the fact we were here.

Callum's warning about my not venturing on to the estate, after my run-in with Britney, had unnerved me.

But they seemed conspicuous by their absence.

Then again – there was no longer a dealer here for them to act as lookouts for. That void would inevitably be filled. Maybe not in this block of flats – but certainly somewhere else on the estate, once the dust had settled and the police presence wasn't as overt.

For now, I was just thankful that – bad as it had been – revisiting such an awful scene, had gone off without any drama.

Chapter Fifty-Eight

Kingberry Farm – Wednesday night

I was enjoying the heat of the sun on my face, sitting on a bench in my garden, nursing a cup of tea, and watching Harvey sniffing the flower beds and hedges.

It wasn't often I took time out like this. To just sit and think and enjoy the space and tranquillity I was blessed to have, up here on the Yorkshire moors.

I was even contemplating swapping my tea for a glass of cold Pinot Grigio and having the evening off.

That's when I obviously jinxed it.

My mobile rang. The caller ID was a number I didn't recognise.

'McCready,' I answered.

'Jo, it's Tess.'

'I was going to call you later. I've had a letter from the board of trustees.' I was keeping Doug's confidence. Easier to let her believe I'd found out by letter.

There was the sound of sheep bleating in the background and wind across the microphone. She was obviously outside somewhere.

'Oh, Jo,' her words caught in a sob.' I didn't know who else to call – what to do . . . Oh my God . . .' She started crying, ragged breathing fragmenting her words.

'Tess – what's happened?' I'd never heard her like this. The raw panic in her voice sent hairs rising on the back of my neck.

'She told me I had to go see her . . . . I didn't want to, Jo . . .'

'Who?' I raised my voice – trying to get her to focus.

'I had no choice . . . I didn't know what else to do . . . I'm sorry.'

'Take a breath . . . talk to me.'

'She knew. She was going to use it against me if I didn't change my statement.'

Statement?

'Pat Rodgers?'

'Jo . . . this is all my fault.'

'What is?'

'Pat . . . she's dead and it's my fault . . . Oh God. Tell the police . . . tell them I'm sorry.'

Listening to such visceral hysteria was gut-wrenching. 'Tess, what's happened? Tess . . . ?' The line went dead – she was gone.

For a moment, I sat staring at the phone in my hand, trying to make sense of what I'd just heard.

Now I had Tess's personal mobile number. At least, I assumed it was hers. I quickly saved it to my contacts – then redialled. It went straight to voicemail.

Before I could decide what to do next, my phone rang again. Caller ID said 'Callum'.

'Hi – I've just—'

'There's been an explosion,' he cut across me.

'What?'

'A narrowboat on the Leeds and Liverpool Canal north of Skipton. Fatalities. At least one body inside. Not much detail – reports only just coming in.'

I swallowed hard – the roof of my mouth had gone dry.

'Oh God.'

'I'm calling you because the boat's registered to Harry Brown.' He said it as if it should mean something to me.

'Don't know him.'

'No – but the woman he was living with on the barge is some-one you *do* know.'

My mind leapt ahead – he was right, I did know. I still needed to hear him say it though – because saying it would make this unfolding nightmare real.

'Who?'

'Pat Rodgers. Looks like she was in the boat at the time. Fire brigade is on scene, but too early to say what caused the explosion.'

I told him about the call I'd just had from Tess.

'You tried ringing her back?'

I nodded – a useless gesture over the phone. 'Straight to voicemail.'

'What time did she call?'

I glanced at my phone log. 'At19.50.'

'Send me her number.' He was all business now. 'If she's connected to this, we need to find her.'

'You can't be certain it's Pat's body in there.' I could hear myself grasping for straws, but I didn't want to believe this – not any of it. The implications for everyone involved were too awful to contemplate.

He let out his breath. 'North Yorkshire police spoke to Harry Brown, the boyfriend. He turned up at the scene – just got back from work. He confirmed she'd been on the boat when he left that morning and he'd spoken to her just before leaving the office tonight. Obviously, they didn't let him near the boat.'

'Obviously.' My mind shied away from the horror of what that would look like.

'But he's pretty certain she would have been on board. The explosion must have happened not long after he'd spoken to her. Poor bastard.'

My instinct was to do something. Anything. I said as much to Callum.

'No.' He was adamant. 'You won't get near to the scene. The towpath is cordoned off in both directions. Nothing you can do there anyway. Forensics will take over. Once we have DNA, dental records or whatever – we can confirm ID of the body.'

'What about Tess?'

'Let me know if she calls you back. If she does – you know the drill. Try to find out where she is. See if she can tell you any more about what happened. Meanwhile, I'll get authorisation for cell site data. See if we can locate her phone and we'll run the index plate for her vehicle. Put a marker on it. If she moves by car, we'll find her. Don't worry, Jo.'

I wasn't sure what worried me most. That they would find her . . . or that they wouldn't.

'The last thing she said] was that I should tell the police she was sorry.'

'Well, now you have, he replied, blunt as ever. As if that should make me feel better. 'Strange thing to say, though, if the explosion was an accident.'

'I can't believe she would have anything to do with this, Cal.'

'I'll keep you posted,' was all he said, before hanging up.

Chapter Fifty-Nine

Kingsberry Farm – Thursday morning

Sleep eluded me. I'd tossed and turned all night, part of me hoping Tess would call but not knowing how I'd feel if she did.

Callum said he'd keep me posted too – so between the two, I'd had one eye on my phone and the clock all night.

By the time dawn crept around the edge of my blinds, I was already in the kitchen, brewing the first pot of tea.

Even Harvey had refused to get off his bed at this early hour, cranking open a curious eye when I'd come downstairs then putting his head back on his paws to carry on snoring.

I took my cup into the garden. The temperature was mild enough for me to sit in my dressing gown sipping tea as I watched the sunrise.

Everything felt messy. Disjointed and illogical. My mind raked over the connections we had and those that were missing.

In the peace of first light – that golden time, that feels somehow stolen because the rest of the world is still sleeping – I reran Tess's phone call for the hundredth time. Analysing every word – every nuance, to squeeze whatever I could from it.

'*She told me I had to go see her . . . I didn't want to . . . She knew. She was going to use it against me if I didn't change my statement.*'

Changing her statement was obviously a reference to Pat Rodgers.

It sounded like Rodgers had summoned Tess to a meeting and if Harry Brown was right about the timing of his call, that meeting would be at the houseboat on the canal.

I made a mental note to check the time of Tess's call to me and the time of the explosion. All of which, the police would have done, so, if Callum was in a sharing mood, he'd be able to confirm the details.

When Tess had called, I could hear sheep and sounds of the outdoors in the background. I got the impression she was walking as she spoke to me.

If Callum had managed to ping the location of her phone when she made that call it could eliminate her from the scene . . . or make things look even more damning.

I took a lungful of clean air and ran my fingers through the tangles in my hair, trying to straighten my thoughts.

Why would she leave the scene of such a devastating accident – if that's what it had been?

Why not call the emergency services – get help?

The Tess I knew would have instinctively done all of those things.

'*She was going to use it against me . . .*'

Rodgers had something on Tess and was using it as leverage.

I could already imagine what Callum would say, when we finally explored that line of enquiry.

'*Bloody good motive for wanting rid of someone . . . blackmail . . .*'

'*Tell the police . . . tell them, I'm sorry.*'

Sorry for being involved in the explosion that had left a person dead?

I took a long breath and rested my head on the back of the bench, watching the dawn paint gold streaks across the sky.

There was nothing I could do until later, when the rest of the world came awake and started its day.

* * *

290

I was in my office later that morning – still gritty-eyed and slug-gish from lack of sleep – when Callum finally called.

'Any ID on the body?' I'd answered, without our customary small-talk.

'Morning to you too.'

'Sorry.' I blew my cheeks out in frustration. 'Been on pins waiting for news. Didn't sleep much.'

'Can imagine. Anyway, in answer to your question – no positive ID yet. We're liaising with North Yorkshire police. Fire fighters pulled the body from the wreckage. All they can say is that it's female . . . probably. But after an explosion like that, there's not a lot left.'

'Jesus.'

'Pat Rodgers's address is officially still in Fordley and the good news is: the Home Office pathologist assigned to the case, is Dr Richardson.'

Elle. That was good. For all kinds of reasons.

'She's the best,' is what I said out loud.

'It's your friend Tess I'm more worried about. I take it she hasn't been in touch?'

'I'd have told you if she had.' That sounded snippier than intended. Worry and lack of sleep had a lot to answer for. If he noticed, he let it pass.

'Fire investigators preliminary report is in. Cause of the explosion was the propane gas bottle under the kitchen sink, used for the cooker. The hose was cracked and it exploded when the gas hob was lit.'

'An accident, then?'

'Was supposed to look like that. But they found accelerant all over the interior of the boat. Fuel, from a can Harry Brown says he kept on board. Suspected arson. If that's confirmed – then it's a murder enquiry.'

'You said you were worried about Tess?'

'She's disappeared.'

'What?'

'Hasn't returned home since her call to you yesterday and didn't turn up for work at the DAAT this morning.'

'What time was the explosion – do we know?'

'Quarter to eight in the evening.'

Five minutes before Tess called me.

'How can you be so precise?'

'The 999 call was made from a guy staying in a narrowboat further along the canal. Poor sod was sitting on the loo – the explosion blew him off the pot.'

I didn't speak for a moment as my mind tumbled over the facts. Callum was way ahead of me. 'Tess called you five minutes *after* that explosion – and now she's missing.'

He didn't need to say – it didn't look good.

'What about her car?'

'Still in the car park of the Anchor Inn at Gargrave where she left it. That's on the side of the canal, on the A65. Few minutes' walk from the boat.'

'Why would she leave her car? Can't get very far on foot – not from there.'

'Might realise it can be tracked by ANPR cameras or CCTV. If she's somehow involved and has done a runner.'

I couldn't imagine Tess thinking like that – not for one minute and I said so.

'She's hardly a criminal, Cal. If she'd just witnessed that explosion, the last thing she'd be thinking about is how the police would track her car on camera.'

'You'd be surprised.' The tone of a cynical cop.

'I'd be friggin' amazed! This is Tess Bailey we're talking about – not some member of an organised crime gang.'

'I don't have all the answers . . . yet. But what we *do* know is that we have her on the pub CCTV leaving her car in the car park. A few minutes later the boat explodes and then she calls you to say Rodgers is dead and it's all her fault. She disappears and her car is still where she left it.'

My mind was racing at a million miles an hour, trying to take all this in.

'OK.' I let out a long breath. 'So, what now?'

'Finding Tess is a priority. I'm calling the team in for a briefing tonight. By then we might have more from forensics. Your mate, Elle, is conducting the post-mortem, this morning. If, by then, you've come up with any suggestions for where Tess might be or how she got there, I'll be all ears.' There was a pause, then he added, 'You're welcome to join the briefing?'

'Thanks,' I said – not sure I wanted to hear any more damning evidence against Tess – or the gruesome details of Pat Rodgers's death.

It felt like I was witnessing a disaster movie unfold in slow motion. Needing to look away – but compelled to watch until the bitter end.

But nothing could prepare me for what was to come.

Chapter Sixty

Kingsberry Farm – Thursday

After speaking to Callum, I'd stayed in my office, trying to be productive but failing miserably. The psych assessment I had to write, for a pending court case, was still sitting on my desk, untouched.

I swivelled my chair to face the window that overlooked the garden, watching the birds on the feeder without really seeing them.

When the office phone rang, I answered, distractedly. 'McCready.'

'Jo, it's Rina.'

I sat up in my chair. 'Everything OK?'

'Was ringing to ask you the same thing.' She sounded hassled.

'Where are you?'

'At work . . . at the DAAT. What the hell's going on, Jo? The police have been here. Is it true . . . about Pat Rodgers?'

I opened my mouth to answer, then hesitated. It was a live investigation and I wasn't sure what information the police were giving out.

'What have they said?' I hedged.

'Not much. Asked us lots of questions about Pat. When had we all seen her last? Had any of us had contact with her since she was sacked? Doug saw the early morning news, about an explosion last night, on a houseboat near Gargrave. He knew Harry Brown had a permanent mooring up there. It doesn't take a genius to put two and two together, does it?'

'Suppose not.' I bit my lower lip, trying to think ahead. But Rina was on a roll.

'Then they asked lots of questions about Tess. She didn't come in to work today and no one's heard from her.'

'It's complicated—'

'No shit.'

'Have you heard from the helpline?'

'What? Oh – yeah, I was going to call you about that today. I've been accepted. Got an induction with Lexi tonight.'

'That's good.'

I was hoping she'd be thrown off track by the change of subject – no such luck.

'So, come on then . . . what's happening?'

'This stays strictly between us.' I still wasn't sure this was a good idea.

'Of course.'

'Not even Doug . . .'

'Jo?' She was losing patience.

So, I told her about my strange call from Tess and the fact that the police suspected the body on the boat was Pat Rodgers.

'Holy shit,' she breathed down the phone as I finished. There was a second of silence as she processed it all, then, 'Tess can't be involved, surely?'

'I agree – but why has she gone off grid?'

'Bloody hell, Jo – what a mess.'

'What she said to me about Pat Rodgers "knowing something" and using it against her . . . got any idea what she meant?'

'Not a scooby.' She expelled a breath down the phone.

'If anything occurs to you, let me know?'

'Sure.'

'Good luck at the helpline – keep me posted on that too.'

We ended the call with an arrangement to get together up at Elle's the next night, so we could all compare notes.

There was nothing to do now, until the evening briefing at Fordley nick.

Chapter Sixty-One

Fordley Police Station – Thursday evening

The incident room was uncharacteristically quiet. None of the usual banter greeted me as I went in. Some of the desks were empty, as officers were out following up lines of enquiry and actions relating to the houseboat death. Other detectives had their heads down – busy with paperwork.

'Preparing the Curtis case for the Crown Prosecution Service,' Beth said as she handed me the obligatory mug of tea. 'Caseload just got bigger with the canal boat death. We just get one major enquiry squared away and another one comes along.'

I thought about Dean Gavney. Still not comfortable with the murder charge against him.

I'd done everything I could. But his behavioural profile was all I had and that was easily outweighed by all the other evidence against him.

Frustratingly, it went that way sometimes. I wished I could be more philosophical about it – but the consequences of an innocent person going to prison didn't bear thinking about. Even if it was a drug dealing scumbag like Dean Gavney.

Beth took a sip from her own mug. 'You knew her?'

'Who? Sorry – miles away.'

'Pat Rodgers.'

I perched on the edge of her desk. 'We weren't friends. Knew her through the DAAT. Tess Bailey *is* a friend though – I'm worried about her.'

Whatever Beth was about to say was cut short as Callum came into the briefing room.

'Right, ladies and gents.' He dropped his notes and iPad on the oval table at the front of the room. 'Let's get started.'

Those members of the team involved in the enquiry took their seats, bringing mugs and notebooks with them.

A whiteboard had already been set up beside the table. I knew it would soon be filled with scrawled notes and scene photographs. Beside it, a map of the area around Skipton and Gargrave had been stuck on the wall.

'You're all familiar with events of last night,' Callum began. 'Houseboat owned by Harry Brown, destroyed by an explosion and subsequent fire. One fatality. Body of a female, believed to be Pat Rodgers. Formerly the manager of Fordley DAAT.' He glanced at me. 'Jo took a call from Tess Bailey, just after the explosion. Jo?'

That was my cue to tell them about the call. Word for word.

'After that,' Callum picked up, 'Tess Bailey disappears.' He looked around the table. 'So, what've we got so far?'

DS Tony Morgan had cued up the pub CCTV. He turned his laptop round so we could all see the screen.

'This is Tess, leaving her Nissan Micra at the pub. Traffic cops from North Yorkshire secured it at the scene last night. It's been taken in for forensic testing. There's no other CCTV between the car park and the boat. Nothing to show where she went after walking down the towpath and out of shot.' He tapped his pen against the screen. 'Along the towpath there are several public footpaths that strike out cross-country. We're gathering CCTV from any houses and businesses around the area to see if we can pick her up, where the footpaths come out into populated areas. So far, nothing.'

Callum nodded. 'OK. Stay on it. What about her phone?'

That was DS Charlie Thompson's area of expertise.

'Taking the time of her call to Jo, we pinged her location.' He went to the map. 'It puts her on the towpath – here.' He pointed to a pin on the map, halfway between the boat and the pub. 'Five minutes after the explosion – which we know was 19.45, because of the witness on the neighbouring boat who called it in.'

'After he'd cleaned the shit out of his hair,' Beth said.

'Gives whole new meaning to the phrase "shit or get off the pot".' DC Shah Akhtar grinned.

A ripple of laughter round the team. Gallows humour – never meant disrespectfully – a coping mechanism for those who have to deal with the darker side of life on a daily basis.

'Tess Bailey didn't make any other calls – certainly not to emergency services. In fact, since calling Jo, looks like her phone was switched off,' Charlie said. 'No social media activity either – which is a departure from her normal behaviour. We're monitoring her phone in case she turns it back on.'

Callum stuck a picture of Tess on the whiteboard – tapping it with his index finger. 'She's in the wind. Not been back to her home or work since the incident. Finding her is a priority. She's a person of interest. At the very least, a witness to what happened on that boat.'

I stared at Tess's photograph. Pale blue eyes looked back at me. The eyes of a friend. Someone I'd known and liked for years. Someone I trusted. It felt bizarre seeing her image on the whiteboard in a police incident room.

Beth shuffled her notes. 'Interviewed Harry Brown and checked his movements. Plenty of witnesses putting him at work when he says he was. His phone shows him calling Pat Rodgers just before he left work. He was in meetings all day – so he's alibied.'

'Officers spoke to staff at the DAAT this morning,' Shah said. 'We're looking into Tess Bailey's life. Currently she's single – but we're checking out old boyfriends. Also looking for places she might lay low. Friends . . . family.'

Callum looked at me in a silent question. I shook my head.

'No idea where she might be,' I said, still struggling with the idea that Tess could be implicated in an offence of any kind.

Callum directed everyone to the report from the fire investigator.

'Still a lot to do, but initial assessment is that the propane gas cylinder in the galley exploded.' He flicked to a page of test results. 'Ordinarily, it would take time for the gas to build up before an explosion. But what makes them suspect arson was the amount of accelerant found inside the cabin. That ignited when the gas hob was lit. Their investigation is ongoing.'

He went to his iPad. 'Pathologist conducted the post-mortem on the body this morning. She can confirm it's a female, aged late forties. Height and build compatible with Miss Rodgers.'

'No formal ID yet though?' Beth asked. 'What about dental records?'

Callum shook his head. 'After an explosion like that – even dental ID is proving difficult. Pathologist won't say officially, but off the record, what she has so far, leads her to believe it's probably Pat Rodgers. But that stays in this room until it's official.' He raked long fingers through his hair. 'Officers collected Rodgers's toothbrush and hairbrush when they went to her home in Fordley. It's being used to compare DNA with the remains. Once those results are back, we'll know for sure.'

'If she's not been seen since the explosion,' Tony said, 'pretty certain it's her.'

'Nothing's certain.' Callum's tone was sharper than he probably intended. I knew him well enough to see that he was stretched thin. Exhausted and strung out after running the Curtis enquiry day and night – and now this. 'No assumptions. And nothing said officially until we have confirmation.'

Everyone around the table nodded silently.

The briefing ran on, but most of it flowed over my head, as Callum went through the process of allocating actions and lines of enquiry. When the meeting ended, I gathered my things and made for the door.

Callum was waiting for me.

'Haven't forgotten about that business with the helpline, Marion Kilpin and your Ted character.' He fell in step beside me as I walked to the lift.

'With everything else you've got on your plate, I'm surprised you remembered.'

He shrugged, leaning against the wall by the lift as we waited. 'Compartmentalising – goes with the territory.' His eyes were studying me in that way he had, that had always drawn me in. Making it feel like there was no one else around us.

'Kilpin's case is officially closed,' he was saying. 'But if any new evidence comes to light we can reopen it. I've spoken to your friend, Elle. She hasn't released his body yet.'

'But surely, with Pat Rodgers's death . . . you won't have the resources.'

The lift arrived and he held the doors open. 'I'll have a word with Charlotte. See what we can do.'

Detective Superintendent Charlotte Warner, Callum's immediate boss.

'Thanks.' I meant it. With his workload and the pressure on the team, I knew what a strain it would put on everyone.

He said nothing – just stood, watching me until the lift doors closed.

300

Chapter Sixty-Two

Kingsberry Farm – Friday

I tried to keep busy but it was difficult to concentrate. The explosion on the boat made the local TV news. But after the initial report, it hadn't appeared since, as police and fire investigators weren't releasing any further information.

Until they had more evidence, there would be no hint to a headline-hungry media that it was anything more than an unfortunate boating accident.

I kept the TV on in the office with the sound muted, so that I could keep on top of any breaking news. I was hoping the team would keep me updated, but I knew from bitter personal experience that in today's fast moving news environment, reporters often broke things first. Especially with social media.

Every member of the public armed with a camera. Independent filmmakers who could upload events as they happened in real time – often catching the police unawares.

Already there were images of the burnt-out boat, that someone had captured from a distance, on their phone, and sold to the media outlets. It wasn't great quality, as they'd obviously zoomed in from the outer edge of the police cordon. But it was enough to see the shell of the houseboat and the white tents erected over the towpath by forensic officers.

I turned back to my computer and looked again at the notes I'd made.

Callum said he would speak to Superintendent Warner about allocating some resources to the Kilpin case – but with a new murder enquiry dropping on his toes, I knew a closed case of accidental death would be about as far down his priority list as it was possible to get.

I glanced across at Jen's empty desk. God, I missed her. Not just her efficiency, but her companionship. To be able to bounce ideas around with, and have her help and support.

She was brilliant, when it came to research, with the patience to trawl through news items and archives that I sadly lacked. But today I was on my own with it. I went back to my search for anything I could find on Ted Cornell, Marion Kilpin and her husband, Andi.

The national register for therapists gave me a biography for Cornell. He'd qualified fifteen years before and, after a few years in general practice for the NHS, had studied for specialist qualifications for the treatment of PTSD. He'd taken up his current post at the veteran's centre in Fordley just two years previously.

I tapped a pencil against my teeth. Interestingly, there was nothing about his life prior to that. Nor did he seem to have any social media presence – which made things even more difficult.

If there was one thing I'd learned, spending time with the techies at West Yorkshire police – it was the scary amount of personal information people put on their social media.

Information easily available to anyone who wanted to find it – or worse, use it for criminal purposes. Unfortunately for me, Ted seemed disinterested in Facebook or Instagram. Or maybe he had other reasons for wanting to keep a low profile?

A quick internet search of census records and electoral register took me down a rabbit hole of Cornells. There were more than I thought – but luckily, not many Theodores. I grabbed a screenshot of the name as it appeared in Liverpool – three years prior. Then began following that particular trail.

Safe to assume I could ignore 'Find a Grave', or the 'Ancestry' sites and any hits for World War Two veterans. Concentrating instead on the living that showed up.

The *Liverpool Echo* gave me the break I was looking for.

His name appeared in an article about a charity run, to raise funds for a proposed needle exchange in the Wirral. A new initiative back then and one that didn't have total support from the local population, worried about drug users coming into their neighbourhoods.

I pondered the fact that nothing had changed much in the intervening years. Proposal for homeless charities or initiatives linked to drug users or probation hostels always managed to get the locals up in arms.

The newspaper had written an article, interviewing the manager of the charity project.

A younger version of Ted Cornell looked back at me from the archived newspaper.

'Gotcha.'

Harvey looked up from his spot on the rug.

'Not you boy. Someone familiar with drug paraphernalia and disposable tourniquets.'

Chapter Sixty-Three

Moorland Road – Friday afternoon

I was driving over to Elle's place with the top down on my convertible, making the most of the glorious weather. Harvey was strapped into the passenger seat with his special car harness, his ears flapping in the breeze and his nose pointed upward, 'wind-surfing'.

It was amusing to see people's reactions when we stopped at traffic lights. The double take as they saw a Boxer dog sitting upright in the passenger seat with an almost human smile on his face.

Elle was walking across the yard from the stables when we pulled along the gravel drive. Harvey could hardly contain his excitement, straining at the harness and barking a noisy greeting.

She waved and waited by the door.

Harvey didn't even wait for me to open his door – just leapt over the edge as soon as I'd unfastened his harness.

'Come on, sweet pea.' Elle hugged me as I got to the door. 'Tea's already brewing.'

It felt good to be wrapped in the warm welcome of friends, in Elle's modern kitchen. Most of my life at Kingsberry Farm was solitary – apart from office hours, when Jen was there. I made a mental note to get some flowers for her desk, when she got back on Monday.

Mug of tea in hand, I was soon out on the back patio, where Rina was sitting on the rattan sofa.

'Where's Harvey?' Rina looked behind me.

'Gone to see Butch and Sundance in the stables,' I said, dropping into the deep chair opposite her.

Elle passed round home-made biscuits and after a few minutes of small talk, we got down to the reason we'd all agreed to meet.

'Update on the helpline,' Rina started, 'induction with Lexi on Thursday went well. I did a supervised shift afterwards, with Patrick. Just inputting index cards to get a feel for the computer system. Then did an evening shift last night, with Ted.'

'Blimey.' I was impressed. 'You don't waste much time.'

'Well, we haven't got it to waste, have we? I'm booked to do a Saturday morning tomorrow, too.'

'They accepted Rina's backstory,' Elle said, dunking her biscuit. 'That she needs a placement just to get her hours in.'

'They don't know you're at the DAAT?' I asked.

Rina shook her head. 'Not that it matters. Most of the qualified therapists have proper jobs, in practices. Just volunteer their time when they can.'

I'd already considered that when we'd suggested Rina apply there.

'Still, think it's better if no one makes the connection to the DAAT,' I said. 'Too many links run back there, from Vicky and Steve Lowry.'

'No worries.' Rina seemed confident. 'I put my last position down as the university. I'm recently qualified so if they contact them, it'll check out.'

The DAAT was Rina's first job and she hadn't been there that long. I supposed, if she left it off her CV, it might not raise too many flags. At least, I hoped not.

'So, what are your first impressions?' I asked, over the rim of my mug.

She pulled a thoughtful face, running a hand across her buzz cut hair. 'No shortage of oddballs working there.'

Elle laughed. 'Pot . . . kettle.'

Rina kicked her playfully. 'Oi.' She sat back into the cushions, half closing her eyes against the sun. 'Anyway, it's obvious Patrick is besotted with Ted.'

'Really?' I hadn't expected that one. 'Is it reciprocated?'

'Nah. Well – not in any romantic way. They're obviously friends. Ted's like a protective big brother to Patrick. Wouldn't want to hurt his feelings or anything. But the young lad follows him around like a lovesick puppy. Bit tragic, really.'

'How's Ted been? Towards you, I mean?'

'Fine.' She took a mouthful of tea and helped herself to a biscuit. 'He's the most experienced therapist after Lexi – so he does initial training for all the newbies. He's also the most unaccountable person there, from what I can see.'

That piqued my interest. 'What do you mean?'

She shrugged. 'He comes and goes pretty much as he pleases. I mean – don't get me wrong – there's no ridged clocking on and off, because everyone's a volunteer. As long as they cover their shift and man the phones for most of it, they can go to the kitchen and make a brew or nip out for something to eat. No formal break times or anything. Ted goes off for a fag break quite often – and pops out to run errands. He goes out to make phone calls on his mobile a lot too. But I suppose, as he virtually lives there, when he's not doing his day job, Lexi can't say anything.'

'Said he worked at the veteran's centre,' Elle recalled.

Rina nodded. 'Specialist in PTSD.'

That was my cue to tell them about my research into his history.

'So, he's got expertise in intravenous drug use,' Elle said, thoughtfully.

I nodded. 'Needle exchange staff are all pretty knowledgeable. Often demonstrate how to use the equipment – encourage users to take sterile kit, rather than reuse old needles and spoons. Managing risky behaviour.'

'He'd know how to tie a tourniquet then,' Rina murmured, almost to herself.

There was a silence as we filed that one away.

Elle leaned into the conversation. 'Rina managed to get a look at some of the records.'

I glanced at the younger woman.

'Yeah,' she said. 'When Patrick was showing me the computer system I helped him input some of those cards and some notes from therapists who didn't have time to update the records before they went off shift.'

'Anything interesting?'

'He left me to input some on my own, once he was happy I wasn't going to blow up the server. So, I had a snoop at the files.'

'And?'

'Had a quick glance at Vicky's record. She wanted help with her anxiety before the court case against Steve Lowry. Also clocked Ainsley McKenzie's notes.'

'Anything jump out?' I asked, hopefully.

She shook her head. 'Apart from how much she hated Wearman . . . almost self-destructive in its vitriol. Karl Ronson was right to be worried about her. Before Lexi started working with her, I reckon, emotionally, she was on a very precarious edge.'

'Anything on Wearman?'

Another shake of the head. 'Lexi was right when she said whoever answered Peter Wearman's second call didn't put it on the system.'

'So, we're no closer on that one,' I said, almost to myself.

'Lots of people come and go in that office all the time,' Rina went on. 'Especially at shift change. If a phone rings, whoever's nearest picks it up and takes a message. If they're on their way home and clocking off they'll either verbally handover to the next person or scribble a Post-it note. It's supposed to be put on a form on the system, but if people have logged off they just handwrite a note and the next person on shift, takes it. Saw it last night, when the priest came in with sandwiches. He picked up a phone that was ringing as he walked past and handed it to Patrick. Anyone could have done that when Wearman called on the nineteenth.'

'Is he in the office a lot?' I asked.

'Who?' Rina frowned.

'Father Bassett.'

Elle laughed. 'Tell me his first name's Bertie?'

I grinned. 'I said that.'

'Takes Allsorts,' Rina quipped.

We both groaned.

Rina put her empty mug on the table. 'He doesn't work on the helpline, if that's what you mean? We're told to signpost people with debt issues to him. From what I can see, he only comes in to the office to bring food left over from the soup kitchen when it's running in the community hall downstairs. The staff get cake and whatever.'

'I'd be the size of a house if I worked there,' Elle grimaced.

'Father Luke says it's calorie free if it's for charity,' Rina smiled. 'Comes in for a chat or a cuppa. He's a nice guy. Seems to know Ted quite well. Think they run the homeless outreach together, down by Fordley train station.'

'When I saw Ted with Marion, she was bringing him a box of clothes,' I said. 'That's probably how she met him.'

Elle leaned forward, her elbows on her knees.

'Well, you're hearing it here first – my update is that the body on the boat is definitely Pat Rodgers. DNA results match the samples I took at post-mortem. Got them back this morning.'

I wasn't sure how that made me feel. I didn't like the woman, but I wouldn't wish a death like that on anyone. I was almost

ashamed that my first thought, wasn't for her – but for Tess –
who *was* my friend.

I told them both about the phone call from her and the fact
that she was missing.

'That doesn't look good, does it?' Rina stated the obvious.

'No,' I agreed. 'It doesn't.'

Chapter Sixty-Four

Moorland Road – Friday evening

The drive back to Kingsberry, from Elle's place at Turnhole Clough, was one I enjoyed. Across the moors, a route that formed part of the Bronte Way, wasn't the quickest way back home, but was definitely the most scenic.

It was just about warm enough to still have the car roof down and Harvey was making the most of it – nose in the air as we drove up onto the high moors.

The solitude was shattered by the ringing of my mobile.

'McCready.'

'Jo?' Callum's voice crackled over the Bluetooth speaker. 'Sounds like you're driving?'

'Just on my way home from Elle's.'

'Has she told you about the ID on the body from the boat?'

'Pat Rodgers.'

'That's one of the things I was ringing about. To bring you up to date. The other thing is, fire investigators have formally confirmed it was arson.'

'Murder investigation now then.'

I knew he was nodding – even though I couldn't see.

'Any news on Tess?' I almost daren't ask.

'No . . .' I sensed his hesitation – as if he were debating telling me more. I used his own technique. Letting the silence stretch out in the hope he'd fill it.

Eventually, he did. 'Something interesting *has* come up though.'

'What?'

'DS Tony Morgan was scouring CCTV and traffic cameras on all the other routes around the canal. See if we could spot Tess.'

'And?'

'He picked up a grey Transit van. Looks like it came from a layby near a public footpath from the canal – then took the A65.'

'Why would that flag up?' He was making me work for this – whatever it was.

'Apart from the fact that it looked as if it'd come from the direction of the incident . . . it's registered to Ted Cornell.'

I didn't know what to say to that, so for a minute I said nothing at all.

He took hold of my silence. 'You still there?'

'Yes. Sorry. Just thinking what that means, exactly.'

'Do you know of any connection between Pat Rodgers or Tess Bailey and Cornell?'

'Not directly.' My thoughts were tumbling.

'Right now I'll take indirectly.'

I was thinking out loud, as I went through the possible links. 'Obviously Tess and Pat are . . . were connected. But I don't know of anything between Cornell and either of them.'

'What about the helpline?' he suggested.

'Tess knows the helpline exists. She referred Vicky to it and Ted works there. But I wasn't aware they knew each other.'

'But it's possible.'

'Anything's possible. What about Rodgers, though?'

'Maybe she knew him through referrals from the DAAT, as well?'

'She was an administrator. Not a therapist. She wouldn't have been involved in making referrals.' I slowed down to avoid a cow that had wandered through a gap in the fence and was happily eating grass at the side of the road. 'But he can tell you himself, when you interview him.'

'That's the other thing I was ringing to tell you.'

I didn't like the sound of this. 'What?'

'He's gone missing.'

'Missing?'

'Officers went round to his home after Tony flagged his van. He wasn't there. Neighbours said they haven't seen him since yesterday.'

Rina saw him last night, at the helpline. I thought. *Do I tell Cal?* That could lead to awkward questions about what Elle and I were doing . . . snooping round on our own. But given this was a murder enquiry I didn't have much choice.

So, I told him the bare minimum. That Rina had volunteered at the helpline, to see if she could find anything out.

'You did say I could look into the three accidental deaths Elle was concerned about.'

'Hmm.'

'And I did tell you about the connection to the helpline . . . Marion Kilpin and her relationship with Ted.' I spoke fast, to head off an outburst.

'And Cornell was training Rina?' He didn't sound as annoyed as I'd feared.

'Yes.'

'Has she seen him since last night?'

'No. Her next shift with him is tomorrow morning.'

'I sent officers to the veteran's centre where he works in Fordley. Manager said Cornell had booked three weeks annual leave. They haven't seen him since last weekend.'

'How long had the leave been planned?'

'That's just it. It wasn't. Manager said Cornell hadn't taken much annual leave in all the time he'd been there – apart from the odd day. No one ever remembers him going away for a holiday. That's why, when he dropped it on them at the last minute, they didn't feel they could refuse him. He also didn't say where he was going.'

'If he's been off since the weekend, that would leave him free to go to the canal boat on Wednesday . . . if that's what he'd done,' I said. 'But it would take some nerve to go there blow up a boat, then turn up for his shift at the helpline the next evening, as if nothing had happened.'

312

'Might look more suspicious if he *hadn't*. If he'd disappeared then. But leave it a day or so and *then* go . . .' He let the inference dangle.

'Possibly.' It wouldn't be the first time a cold-blooded killer had carried on with their usual routines after committing a horrendous crime.

'Don't say anything to Rina or Elle,' Callum was saying. 'We need Rina to go to the helpline as planned. Don't want any deviation in routine scaring Cornell off if he turns up for his shift with her as planned.'

'And then what?' I didn't like the idea of Rina being anywhere near Ted Cornell, if he was our murderer.

'I'll have plain-clothes officers watching the community centre before it opens. If he goes there, we can pick him up.'

'And if he doesn't?'

'Then he's in the wind – along with Tess Bailey.'

* * *

Callum's information about Ted Cornell posed more questions than it answered.

For the rest of the drive home I reflected on some of the things Rina had said – about Ted being good friends with Father Luke Bassett. That they ran the outreach together. Coupled with the fact that Marion Kilpin was involved with Ted, maybe the priest could fill in some of the missing pieces?

I couldn't believe that, if they *were* close, the priest *wouldn't* know about Ted's relationship with Marion. Even if he didn't, he might know where Ted had gone on his unexpected annual leave.

I made a quick stop at the farm to drop Harvey off and then turned around and got back in the car. There were questions I needed to ask and people I urgently needed to see.

Chapter Sixty-Five

Fordley – Friday, late evening

Saint John the Evangelist Catholic Church was situated in a part of Fordley that had once been a place people aspired to live.

A leafy area that, when I was growing up, had been surrounded by farmland and country lanes.

By the time I was in my twenties, most of the farmland had been sold for development and the country lanes morphed into roads that dissected the new housing estates that had sprung up around the old church.

Now, the building looked as if it was perched on an island, with roads running in front and behind it. Flanked on either side by larger houses – built in the sixties as a nod to aspirational living. While the rest of the area was dominated by a large council estate, a few beleaguered shops and a traditional working men's club that was already getting busy.

I parked my car outside the church and walked the familiar path up to the double – arched wooden doors.

Although this hadn't been our parish, being brought up as a Catholic, I had attended services here with my mother. Weddings, Christenings and latterly, the occasional funeral of one or two of Mamma's old friends.

Father Bassett told me when we met at the community centre that his church was Saint John's.

As this was the only Catholic church in Fordley by that name, it was a pretty safe bet I was in the right place, helpfully confirmed by his name on the noticeboard that listed the times of masses and confession.

Inside the gabled porch I automatically dipped my right finger in the stoup of Holy water on the wall and made the sign of the cross.

You can take the girl out of the church . . .

The ingrained habits – triggered by simply entering this building, as unconscious as looking right and left before crossing the road. Even though I was no longer a practicing Catholic it would feel wrong not to do it.

I pulled open the door into the nave and my olfactory senses were immediately hijacked, transporting me back, to my schooldays.

The centuries-old aroma of incense still hung in the air from an earlier mass.

As a kid, I thought heaven must smell like that. The uniquely evocative scent of frankincense and myrrh. Sweet, citrusy, and slightly spicy.

The burning of gum resin, producing an aromatic smoke that curled around the pews, designed to induce an almost hypnotic sense of peace among the faithful. A smell you never encounter anywhere else, or in quite the same way, as in church.

I stood at the back for a moment, taking in the scene.

A few worshippers were scattered randomly among the rows of pews, some sitting, some kneeling in silent prayer, with heads bowed or gazing at the dimly lit altar.

No sign of Father Bassett.

I wasn't sure why I'd expected him to be here. Or maybe, I'd just reasoned it was as good a place as any to start looking for him? If I was honest, I hadn't really thought about it that much as I'd driven into Fordley. Just following a gut instinct that he might have useful information.

The front pews to the right of the nave were the most occupied. Half a dozen people, kneeling on the cushions provided, some clutching rosary beads, lips moving silently as they recited their prayers of penance.

Then the door of one of the confession boxes opened and an elderly man came out and joined those on the front benches.

This evening was obviously a scheduled time for confessions and Father Bassett was probably the one hearing them.

Sometimes, when it feels like you're pushing water uphill, fate has a way of giving you an unexpected break. Or maybe, as I was in church, it was God and not fate that presented me with an unforeseen development?

As I was about to go check the noticeboard, to see what time confession would finish – someone caught my attention.

I recognised the blond hair and sculpted profile of the young man sitting on the front pew.

Jordan Kilpin was so deep in thought that he didn't realise I was there until I sat next to him.

'Oh.' He glanced up. 'Hello . . . what're you doing here?' His voice was hushed.

'Could ask you the same question,' I whispered, nodding towards the confessional box. 'Are you here for confession?'

It would be unusual. Non-Catholics weren't allowed to take the sacrament.

'I can't . . . unless I convert,' he said.

I thought I caught the hint of a blush across his cheeks before he dropped his head, looking intently at the hands clasped in his lap. 'You won't tell Aunt Marion, will you?'

'Of course not,' I whispered back. 'Why would I do that?'

He shrugged, still not looking up. 'Think she might be a bit upset . . . you know, being as she's Protestant.'

I was always surprised that things like that mattered these days, with the country seemingly more secular. But I knew that it did to some people – especially in families.

I took a long breath of perfumed air. 'Does it matter . . . to her, I mean?'

Another light shrug. 'Maybe not . . . but I wouldn't want to take the chance, not yet anyway.'

Not yet . . . That begged a few questions.

'Then . . . when?'

I wasn't even sure what question I was asking. But his words had opened a door to his psyche. Just a chink . . . but well worth pursuing.

He stared ahead to the life-size cross above the altar bearing the plaster-cast figure of Christ, crucified.

'When I'm ready to tell her.' He looked at me then, with a slight smile.

I realised I hadn't seen him smile before. Not genuinely.

'Tell her what?'

'I'm thinking of converting.'

'Really?'

Whatever I'd been expecting, it wasn't that. Not the kind of thing most fifteen-year-old boys spent their time thinking about.

Before I could ask any more, he cut in. 'So, why are *you* here?'

'Came looking for Father Bassett.'

'Me too. We'd arranged to meet here – you know – to talk about everything. He was going to lend me some books and stuff. But he's not here.' He couldn't hide his disappointment. 'Another priest is taking confession.'

'Do you know where I might find him?'

He shook his head. 'Been called away to see a bereaved family, apparently.'

'Shhh!' the old man behind us hissed, even though we'd been doing our best to whisper.

I touched Jordan's arm. 'Shall we go somewhere we can talk?'

At the end of the pew, we both genuflected to the altar, then he followed me back to the porch.

Jordan perched on the edge of a table scattered with leaflets and hymn books.

'How do you know Father Bassett?' he asked.

'Met him at the community centre.' I leaned against the exposed red-brick wall.

'He's great, isn't he?'

My smile was non-committal. Letting him talk, I got the impression he'd been bursting to confide in someone.

'He's had such an interesting life,' he went on, enthusiastically, 'I mean, all the places in the world he's seen – all his travels. I'd like to do that.'

He absently flicked through a hymn book as he spoke. 'First saw him about a year ago, when I was helping Aunt Marion set up a church fete, but not to talk to or anything. Then, when I was helping her bring stuff here, for the homeless outreach – met Father Bassett and Ted Cornell.' He looked up and his blonde fringe flopped across his forehead, making him look somehow vulnerable. 'I just loved this place . . . so peaceful. I liked spending time here.'

'Do you know Ted well?'

'Not very.'

'But you've obviously had some pretty deep conversations with Father Bassett? I mean, if you're thinking of converting.'

'He didn't suggest it,' he said quickly. 'In fact – when I asked about it – he tried to dissuade me. Said I should take time to think about it . . . do more studying.'

'So, how long have you been thinking about it?' I was curious.

Again a shrug. 'Only since Christmas, really. Aunt Marion brought me. We helped Father Luke and Ted with a Christmas meal for the homeless before midnight mass.' An almost wistful expression settled on his young face. 'I'd never seen anything like that. The whole service just . . . blew me away.'

'I was blown away by a lot of things, when I was fifteen,' I said with a gentle smile. 'But can't say mass ever did it for me.'

'You're a Catholic?' he asked and I realised there was no reason he should have known that.

I nodded. 'I suppose, when you're born into it – maybe you don't appreciate it in quite the same way.'

'You're lucky. I mean, to have been christened into it.' He picked up a leaflet and put it down again – displacement activity for a youthful energy that had nowhere to go.

He looked up into the oak-vaulted ceiling. 'I find it so calm here. Like the chatter just stops in my head and I have time to think . . . clearly. Not all jumbled up. No pressure.' He gave me a self-conscious smile. 'Like time stands still or something. Nothing exists outside of the prayers. I sort of lose myself listening to it.'

'I know what you mean.'

'Not sure how Aunt Marion will be about it.' He frowned, scuffing the toe of his trainer against the stone floor.

'She knows Father Bassett,' I said reassuringly, 'and obviously has connections with the church here – I'm sure she'll be OK. Probably pleased. I mean – at your age, there's a lot more dodgy things you could be getting involved with.'

He smiled. It lit up his whole demeanour, not just his face. 'I think I'd like to work with charities.' He was becoming more animated.

This young boy, who'd suffered so much, wanting to turn that into something good. An experience he could use to help other people.

'The homeless, or addicts,' he went on. 'Maybe train as a counsellor – like Ted.'

'I'm sure you'd be great,' I said, warmed by the thought of his healing helping others. That's why most of us were drawn to the job in the first place.

'Do you have any idea where I might find Ted? Could he be at the outreach at Fordley train station?'

He shook his head. 'It's not there tonight.'

'Is your aunt around?'

Maybe Marion would know where Ted was.

319

For a fleeting moment, I considered asking Jordan whether he knew about his aunt's relationship with Ted Cornell. But dismissed it almost as soon as it entered my head. Not least, because if Ted was somehow involved in Pat Rodgers's death, I didn't want to reveal anything about an ongoing investigation.

If Jordan wasn't aware of his aunt's relationship – I didn't want to be the one to let the cat out of the bag. Especially if their affair had a connection to his uncle's death.

'No. She's gone away. I came by bus. Leanne's picking me up later. She's been really cool about me coming here for study sessions.'

My mind scrolled through all the questions he'd thrown up, just in that one sentence.

'What do you mean, Marion's gone away? Where to?'

'Dunno. Said she needed a break after everything that'd happened. You know . . . my uncle. Then the police stuff.'

I searched his tone for any hint of blame towards me in that statement. Surprisingly, there wasn't any.

'I feel guilty, though,' he was saying.

'About what?'

'That she needs to go away . . . because of the stress of everything to do with the police.'

'That's not your fault, Jordan.'

'That what Aunt Marion says.'

'Then let that one go. You weren't to blame for any of it.'

'Thanks.' He gave me a thin smile.

I hesitated to broach my next question, gauging his body language before I took the plunge. 'Have you confided in Father Luke . . . about what happened with your uncle?'

His eyes held mine for a moment, before sliding away as he gave a slight shake of his head. 'No . . .'

He'd just lied to me.

Then, as if he realised that I'd read the falsehood, he looked back at me and added, 'Not everything . . . you know, not all of it.' He blushed.

In the heavy silence that followed, I almost read his mind, through the signals leaking through his porous body language.

I nodded a silent understanding. 'Big thing to carry – all on your own,' I said quietly.

He nodded again – staring intently at the floor.

Time to change the subject. I'd already learned what I needed to.

'Did your Aunt Marion say where she was going?'

He took a relieved breath – happy that I wasn't pursuing the uncomfortable subject any longer.

'Just that she'd be gone a couple of weeks. Something about staying with a friend who had a villa somewhere.'

I wanted to push for more but had to tread carefully. This needed to feel like a conversation, not an interrogation.

'Leanne's looking after you then?' was what I actually said.

'Yeah.'

'And she doesn't know where your aunt's gone either?'

His eyes narrowed then – a trickle of suspicion creeping in, as my tone tipped the conversation just a little too far away from casual.

'Why is it so important?' he asked, cautiously.

My turn to shrug. 'It's not.' I smiled. 'Just want to make sure you're OK, you know? That you're being taken care of . . . after everything that's happened. You're too young to be left in that huge house on your own.'

His shoulders dropped as he relaxed. 'Well, I am OK. Leanne's great. Said she'd talk to Aunt Marion when she gets back. If I decide to convert.'

I smiled. 'Sounds to me like you've already made your mind up.'

Again, that boyish grin. 'Yeah, pretty much. But Father Luke's making me take it slow.'

'Very wise.'

The door to the nave opened and people began walking out. Confession was obviously over and so was our conversation.

As I left the church a theory was beginning to form. But before I could be certain, I had phone calls to make.

Chapter Sixty-Six

Kingsberry Farm – Friday night

'Cal – it's me.'

He'd answered almost immediately. 'Was just about to ring you. What's up?'

'I spoke to Jordan Kilpin this evening. Marion's gone away.'

'Where?'

'That's just it, he doesn't know.'

There was a pause and I could hear office noises in the background. He was obviously still at work. But then, where else? During a murder enquiry – or in this case, more than one – the team would be putting in the hard yards. That meant no breaks, early mornings and very late nights.

'That's saved me a job. I was going to get officers round to her place – see if Cornell was there.'

'He's not. Jordan said Leanne, Marion's daughter, was looking after him. Just the two of them there. He had no reason to lie to me about that.'

'What else did he say?'

'He's met Ted Cornell, through the outreach program.'

'Another connection to Sanctuary,' he muttered, more to himself than to me. 'We spoke to Lexi Royle – told her not to say anything to the staff. She confirmed Cornell's still rostered for an early shift in the morning with Rina.'

'You planning to have officers there waiting for him?'

'That's the idea. We've kept surveillance on his home, but he hasn't returned there and there's no sign of his van since we picked it up by the canal.' I could hear him taking a drink – no doubt coffee, to keep him going.

'Any news on Tess?' I was almost afraid to ask.

'Nothing. She hasn't been in touch with you, I take it?'

'You know I'd say if she had.' I was almost offended, but now wasn't the time. 'Anyway – what were you going to call me about?'

'Can't take the credit for this one. DS Charlie Thompson, you know he was seconded to the team, to take on some of the extra legwork?'

'What about him?'

'He did some digging, in his own time, into your assault.'

'Oh – good of him.'

'He's got a bit more time as he's not part of the main enquiry. Anyway, he scoured CCTV from buildings on the periphery of Little Italy, around the time of your attack. Got a hit.'

'Really?'

'Male, running from the direction of Little Italy – then slowing down and walking the rest of the route. Stood out because he had a scarf pulled over his face and hood up – unusual in the summer. Also, the jacket he was wearing, had a tear on the right sleeve. Consistent with you grabbing your assailant's arm and ripping a chunk out of the fabric.'

'Could he track where he went?'

'Onto the precinct – which is when he dropped the hood and pulled the scarf away. Charlie got a good look at his face from a camera on one of the shops.'

'Any ID?'

'He's not in our system, but we know who it is because of where he went.'

'Where?'

'The community centre.'

He was deliberately stringing this out.

'Don't keep me in suspense – who?'

'Patrick Swales.'

'Patrick – from the helpline?'

324

If I'd had to guess, I wouldn't have picked the nervous young man, with social anxiety. 'Bloody hell.'

'Like I said at the time, wouldn't have had the resources, ordinarily. But Charlie did it in his own time . . . plus the fact it was you who got attacked. Think he's got a soft spot for you.'

'I'm flattered . . .'

'Like a big sister.' I could hear the grin in his voice. 'Or an older aunt.'

'Oi – steady. Anyway, tell him thanks. I'll buy him a pint.' I was still trying to get my head around the fact that young Patrick was my attacker.

'Any idea why Swales might have wanted to warn you to stay away?' Callum was saying.

'Same ideas you've probably come up with,' I said, making a note on my pad. 'In the cases I'm looking at, all roads lead to the helpline. Also – he's besotted with Ted Cornell—'

'How did you know that?'

I was thinking out loud, more than conversing. 'Not a huge leap to think Patrick might somehow be involved in all this, through Ted, is it? He could have been warning me to stay away from the helpline . . . or Ted.'

'Charlie only brought this to me today. As we've got officers down at the precinct tomorrow – we'll kill two birds. I'll have Swales brought in for the assault.'

'OK . . .' I said slowly, unsure how I felt about that.

'Meantime, if anything else turns up, I'll call you.'

I thought about the hunch I'd had earlier. Something – maybe nothing. Certainly not concrete enough yet. But, in the absence of Jen – my dependable sounding board – I wanted to bounce the theory off someone I trusted.

'I've had some thoughts . . .' I started tentatively. 'But need to work through them tonight – see if I can make sense of any of this.'

'OK. If anything occurs to you – call me. Sorry – got to go.'

I stared at the phone in my hand after he'd hung up. So much for a sounding board.

It felt as though I was looking at a tapestry from the back and all I could see were random threads running all over the place. Tangled and twisted into knots.

If I could only turn the tapestry over, all those threads would finally make sense and I'd see the completed image.

One thing I *was* certain of – the picture we were looking for had one central focal point.

Sanctuary helpline.

Chapter Sixty-Seven

Kingsberry Farm – Late Friday night

Leaning back in my office chair, I squinted at the computer. I was so tired I could barely focus on the notes that glared back at me from a screen that felt painfully bright.

The mellow ticking of my old grandfather clock and the glow of the table lamps was having a relaxing effect that was eating away at what little concentration I had left.

I glanced at my notepad and ran down the list of facts I'd gathered, from what Jen would have called, a 'deep dive into our persons of interest'.

As well as the usual searches, available to anyone, we had subscriptions to the electoral roll, Companies House and advanced contact registers, that could often provide a starting point.

In addition, because of the nature of the work we did and the organisations we were involved with, Jen had built up a network of contacts, which included the FBI Behavioural Sciences unit in Quantico and other overseas agencies.

There was nothing significant about Marion Kilpin that I could find on any of them. Fundraiser, churchgoing Christian and generally all-round upstanding member of the community. If it hadn't been for the fact that her husband had been found hanging, naked and surrounded by gay porn in the family home, her life would have seemed singularly unremarkable.

The same applied to her daughter. Nothing of note. But then, if there had been, Callum's team would have picked up on it when they first looked at the case.

It was a fact that, usually, somewhere in the way a person lived, there were clues to how or why they died. If investigators were lucky, in a suspicious death, maybe even clues that pointed to the 'who' as well as the 'why' dunnit.

Certainly, since the initial police investigation, Elle and I had turned up information about Andi Kilpin's private life that would point to more than one potential motive for his murder – which I knew, beyond doubt, is what we were dealing with.

His hidden life also gave us more than one suspect who could be involved in his death. But suspecting it – no matter how certain we might be – was very different to proving it.

If Callum was going to persuade Superintendent Charlotte Warner to reopen the investigation – he needed the elusive 'new and compelling' evidence.

Eventually, I turned my attention to Pat Rodgers's death. Unsurprisingly, there was nothing on Tess Bailey. No hidden past or dodgy history. I hadn't expected there to be, but it was a relief all the same.

Her boyfriend, Harry Brown, was also squeaky clean. Besides, he had an alibi for the time of her death and no motive that I could see.

I still had a couple of people on my list who hadn't formed part of the police investigation. I was compiling some queries to send to a contact who might be able to help when my train of thought was derailed by a WhatsApp message.

I glanced at my mobile.

ELLE: Fancy coming to ours for lunch tomorrow – catch up then?

They'd hosted me so much lately, it was beginning to feel decidedly one-sided. I tapped out a quick reply.

Time I returned the favour. You both come to Kingsberry Farm instead. I'll cook. One o'clock?

A heart and a thumbs up came back almost immediately. Hasty emojis – telltale signs that Elle was working late too.

When I turned back to my computer I'd lost the fragile thread of concentration I'd already been struggling to follow. I'd had enough and needed to sleep.

I sent one last email, to a contact I had overseas, who – due to the time difference – would be awake just as I was going to bed, then switched off the lamps.

I'd think about it all again in the morning.

Chapter Sixty-Eight

Kingsberry Farm – Saturday, late morning

I'd probably have slept far later had I not been chased from a disturbed sleep by the shrieking of my phone.

'Huh,' was all I could manage.

'Sorry – have I woken you?' Callum didn't sound in the least bit sorry.

'No,' I mumbled.

'Liar.' I could hear his grin. 'Anyway if I'm awake, you should be too. I'm ringing with an update.'

I sat up and leaned against the headboard, pushing the hair out of my eyes.

'OK,' I yawned.

'Ted Cornell didn't turn up at the helpline this morning.'

'Predictable, really.' I wasn't surprised.

'Hmm. He left a voicemail on Lexi Royle's office landline, saying he's taken indefinite annual leave. He called late last night.'

'Any good news?'

'We arrested Patrick Swales for your assault. He's in custody, here at Fordley nick.'

'Has he said anything?'

'Apart from crying when he got arrested?'

'Oh, don't.' That made me feel irrationally guilty.

'Said he's never been in trouble with the police before and his mum's going to kill him when she finds out.'

'Stop,' I groaned, washing a hand over my face. 'Did he say why he did it?'

'No. He seems to have slipped into a shocked silence. We're waiting for a duty solicitor to arrive.'

'Why do I feel like the baddie here?'

'Don't,' he said firmly. 'He wasn't thinking of you when he laid you out in the street, was he?'

'I know, but . . .'

'But nothing. If he's big enough and ugly enough to commit the crime he can do the time. No good crying for his mum now, is it?'

'Suppose not.' But I still couldn't help feeling bad for him.

'The only other thing he said when we asked him, was that he doesn't know where Cornell is. That he was expecting him in this morning, like everyone else. But we got a hit on an ANPR camera for Cornell's van on the outskirts of Fordley – early hours. Traffic went to the location, but couldn't find the van. So, we know that he was still in the city then at least. I've got cars flooding the area – see if we can pick it up again.'

I wanted to talk more but it was obvious he'd just snatched a brief moment to give me a call. He needed to get back, so I let him go.

I needed to check my emails anyway. See if anything had come back from the searches I'd put in motion the night before.

Besides, I needed tea to get my brain working.

* * *

I'd barely taken my first sip of the day, when my mobile rang. Caller ID said it was Rina.

'Morning,' I answered.

'Barely. Don't tell me you've just got up?'

'Of course not.' I lied, taking another mouthful of tea – willing the caffeine to start firing some synapses.

'Eventful morning at the helpline.' She sounded excited.

'I heard. Callum just called.'

'Ted Cornell dropped his unexpected leave on Lexi. She's not happy.'

331

'If he's involved in Pat Rodgers's death – or what happened to Andi Kilpin – she's got more misery to come.' I murmured into my teacup.

'Add the drama of Patrick getting arrested for assault. Didn't think he had it in him.'

'People can surprise you,' I muttered, feeling decidedly jaded at the thought.

'Anyway – no point in staying at the helpline, this morning,' Rina went on, hurriedly.' No one to supervise me, with Ted not there. Lexi had to help out on the phones. She sent me home.'

'OK.'

'I'm going into the DAAT instead.'

'It's not open today – Saturday.' I frowned.

'I know. Which is why I'm going. Have a snoop around.'

'For what?' I knew I was being slow on the uptake. A broken night's sleep had a lot to answer for.

Her breath came down the phone in a loud gust and I could imagine her rubbing a hand over her shaved head. 'Pat Rodgers kept records of everything. Wrote things down – she was anal about it.'

'Unless it was her own timesheets,' I pointed out.

She ignored the sarcasm. 'We know she had something on Tess. Something she was holding over her . . .'

'Think blackmail is the word you're looking for.'

'I want to go through her files and stuff in the archives. Have a look at her computer – while the place is empty. See if I can find anything that gives us a clue.'

'How are you going to access her computer?' I could hear myself trying to come up with obstacles before she got too carried away.

'Tess had to get into it when she took over as manager.' She couldn't keep the triumph out of her voice. 'Techies at the trust gave her a temporary password, after they managed to get access. But it was just a string of numbers and Tess couldn't remember it . . . so, she wrote it down. It's on a Post-It note on her desk.'

'She would have changed it to something she could remember by now.'

'Nope. Too busy. Hasn't got round to it.'

I was running out of obstacles.

'Bit of a long shot.' Was the best I could come up with.

'Agreed – but can't hurt, can it? And if I do find something, it might help Tess out of this mess she's in with the police.'

'Or make things worse.'

I hated sounding like the eternal pessimist in this conversation – but there was the distinct possibility that Rina might find more than she bargained for.

'If Rodgers had something bad enough to use as blackmail.' I pointed out. 'It's not going to exactly cover Tess in glory – whatever it is.'

'What's worse than murder?'

'I can think of one or two things,' I said without humour. 'Look, Rina – I know you want to help. You're a fixer . . . that's why you wanted to get into this profession – I get that. But what if you find something that incriminates Tess? Could you turn a blind eye? Just bury it and forget about it?'

There was a silence as she processed that.

'Don't know,' she said quietly. 'Suppose that would depend on what it was?'

'Really?' I doubted Rina's morals were so flexible. 'Making the tough decisions, is also part of this profession. It's not black and white. Not always easy for us to do the right thing . . . and bloody hard to live with sometimes, even when we do.'

I was speaking from bitter personal experience.

There had been times when I'd pushed the moral boundaries and sailed close to the edge of legal ones. Not something I was proud of. It kept me awake some nights. Especially as I couldn't share my secrets with the people I cared about.

I certainly couldn't ever let Callum find out.

Much as I hated Elle's derogatory nickname for him – the Boy Scout – she was right. He was a cop – first and foremost – and if he knew what I'd done, to save the people I cared about in the past, he wouldn't hesitate to let the law take its course with me.

'I know,' Rina was saying. 'But I still think it's worth a chance.' She wasn't going to be dissuaded. 'If anyone finds out I'll just say I was doing some overtime. Catching up on case files. No rules to say we can't go in the office after hours.'

'True.'

'I've got my swipe card for the door . . . but I need the alarm code.'

'That's the reason you're ringing me?'

'Err – yes. Have you got it?'

I could have lied and said I didn't. But there was the tantalising chance Rina might just find something useful.

I took a breath and another mouthful of tea – before giving her the code.

'Call me if you find anything.'

'I'll try – but you know how shit the phone signal is in that place unless you're in the right spot.'

It was true. The old warehouse building had stone walls, three feet thick. You had to be near a router to get any kind of decent signal.

'Call from Rodgers's office – it's good in there – and for God's sake, be careful.'

'It's an office, not a minefield,' she laughed, before hanging up. 'What's to be careful about?'

If only we'd known – a minefield would have been safer.

Chapter Sixty-Nine

Kingsberry Farm – Saturday

After speaking to Rina, I went to the office and checked my emails from the night before. My contact had come back with information on most of the people on my list.

I read through the pages – each one solidifying, what had previously been a nagging suspicion.

The information sent me down a frantic rabbit hole of further research. There were so many lives hanging on this, so many serious consequences if I got this wrong, that I found myself checking and double-checking the facts.

I was so deep in thought, I jumped when my mobile vibrated across the desk with an incoming WhatsApp message.

ELLE: Is Rina with you? She was supposed to pick me up from work after her shift, to come to yours for lunch. Tried calling – just get voicemail.

I'd been so distracted I'd totally forgotten I was supposed to be cooking lunch for us all.

It was obvious Rina hadn't told Elle she was going to the DAAT.

I composed a reply, feeling like the worst kind of friend.

Rina gone to the DAAT. Will explain later. Sorry, forgot about lunch.
Don't worry, I'll stay here. Snowed under anyway. If you get hold of Rina – let her know.

I was about to call the DAAT when my phone rang from the office number there.

'Jo.' Rina sounded excited. 'I've found it.'

'Elle's been trying to get hold of you—'

'Never mind that,' she cut across me. 'I know what Rodgers had on Tess.'

'Go on.'

I went through Pat's computer. She wasn't very tech savvy . . .'

'Know that feeling.'

'She's tried to be cute and hide some files. Probably thought they were locked. Obviously didn't know how to create a secure folder with password protection. There's a "hide files" option under the "view" tab on folders. I asked it to "unhide" all files and there it was.'

'Didn't think it'd be that easy,' I admitted.

'Me neither – but like I say, she wasn't good with techie stuff. Besides, she didn't expect to get escorted from the premises on the day she was sacked. Didn't have chance to get to her computer and delete the files.'

'What's in them?'

'Captured footage from a camera in one of the therapy rooms. Rodgers sent the file to her private email account, then must have saved them here too.'

'There are no cameras in any of those rooms,' I frowned.

The only part of the DAAT allowed to be covered by CCTV, was the car park. People attending drug rehab could be very nervous about being on camera. All the treatment rooms were strictly private to protect client confidentiality.

'That's just it. This footage is from a hidden camera in room two. It was obvious from the footage which room it was. So, I went to look for it.' She was breathless with adrenalin. 'There's a pinhole camera hidden in an ornament on the bookshelf. Rodgers must have put it there when she suspected what was going on with Tess - to catch her out.'

'Catch her out doing what?'

'Shagging a client on the sofa in there – after hours.'

'Steve Lowry?' I guessed.

'You knew?' Rina couldn't help sounding deflated.

I felt guilty about stealing her thunder.

'Not for sure. I started to suspect when I spoke to Tess about Lowry and his girlfriend, Vicky.'

'What did she say that tipped you off?'

'It was everything she *didn't* say.' I ran a hand across my eyes. Suddenly weary from a mixture of sadness and disappointment.

After all the years of doing this job, I was used to the deceptions people perpetrated. If it wasn't for that frailty of human nature, I wouldn't have a job at all. But when it was those I knew personally. Friends . . . lovers . . . it hurt at a much deeper level.

Rina expelled a breath. 'Remind me never to play poker with you.'

'I hate card games.'

'Las Vegas must thank God for that, every day.'

'Suspecting Tess was closer to Lowry than she was admitting was one thing,' I said. 'But we wouldn't have been able to prove it without this. Well done you.'

'What do you think Rodgers was going to do with it?'

'Maybe nothing – until she needed it.' I shook my head. 'The cold calculation of just having dirt on someone tucked away in her back pocket in case she needed it – shows how low that woman really was.'

A thought occurred to Rina. 'Bloody hell – do you think she had cameras in *all* the therapy rooms . . . watching *all* of us?'

'It's a distinct possibility,' I had to admit, though it was a creepy thought. 'We'll check later.'

'What good is it to Rodgers, though? I mean, Tess was single, she wasn't doing anything wrong. Vicky wouldn't have been pleased to know Steve was shagging someone else – but it's hardly earth-shattering.'

'Going to Vicky with it wasn't enough to worry Tess. But professional misconduct *is*, for all the same reasons Rodgers would struggle to get another job with a gross misconduct mark against her. If she'd made it known to the trustees that Tess was in an intimate relationship with a client, she'd have lost her job and found it almost impossible to get another one in this business. She was breaking all the rules of therapeutic practice. She's worked in the third sector since she left school. It means everything to her. Given what Tess said when she called me from the canal towpath, it looks like Rodgers was using it to get her to withdraw her statement to the trustees. Get the charge of gross misconduct dropped.'

'You don't think Tess could have been responsible for the explosion on the boat, do you?'

'No. But the police do and the fact that Tess has gone missing doesn't help her case either.'

'So, what now?'

'Can you email those files to me? I'll get them to Callum and the team.'

'OK,'

'Then go home and let Elle know where you are. She's stayed at work because she couldn't find you.'

'Will do.'

A minute after ending our call, my email pinged with the incoming files from Rina.

I scanned through the footage, just to be sure it was as damning as she'd said. Unfortunately, it was.

My next call was to Callum – but I got voicemail. I called the incident room.

'The boss is in a briefing with the Super.' DS Tony Morgan had picked up. 'Anything I can do?'

I briefly told him about my call from Rina and the files she'd found.

'Can you email them here and I'll make sure the boss sees them?' he said, over the hubbub of noise in the office.

'No problem.' I was already typing the email as I spoke.

* * *

I lost myself in work for the rest of the day, until my attention was drawn to the TV in the corner of the office. The twenty-four-hour news was on, with the sound muted.

The ticker tape running across the bottom had the 'Breaking News', that Dean Gavney had appeared in Fordley Magistrates Court – only to confirm his name and address.

He'd been remanded in custody and the case referred to Crown Court. His trial, for the murder of Brian Curtis and Stephanie Parks, would be set at a later date.

I watched the silent running of images. Photographs of Curtis and his girlfriend. Then news cameras catching Dean Gavney being driven to court from his prison cell, photographers jumping up at the blackened windows of the prison van, cameras flashing in an attempt to get a lucky shot.

It all felt suddenly depressing and I wanted to get some fresh air.

The porch door was open and Harvey was in the garden, amusing himself chasing butterflies.

I poured a brew and went to sit on the bench, watching him leaping at his delicate tormentors, his jowls making a whomping sound as he snapped at frustratingly empty air.

The late sun was warm on my face. Not even the whisper of a breeze.

I tilted my head back and closed my eyes, breathing in the smell of lavender. The heavy scent reminding me of the incense in the church.

It would have been so tempting to sleep.

The night before, I'd tossed and turned. Twisting in dreams, woven with a collage of random scenes.

Jordan Kilpin's youthful face – alive with excitement . . . the scent of incense and wood polish from the church pews. Plaster reliefs along the walls, depicting stations of the cross. Pip talking to the old ladies on the landing at the flats . . . a toy unicorn splashed with blood . . . walking across the polished floor of the community centre hall . . . sounds . . . scents . . . Dean Gavney being led into a police van . . . Brian Curtis, lying face down on the floor of the flat . . . the door to the stairwell rattling when no one was there . . . sounds . . .

My eyes flew open.

Harvey stopped playing when he saw me run back towards the house. Thinking this was a much better game, he pounded down the gravel path and followed me through the kitchen and into the office.

I snatched up the phone and made a call to Fordley Social Services.

By the time I put the phone down, I knew who had killed Brian Curtis and his girlfriend . . . and it wasn't Dean Gavney.

Chapter Seventy

Kingsberry Farm – Saturday evening

This wasn't something I could do over the phone. Besides, I already knew Callum was incommunicado and I didn't want to leave a message with one of the team.

Running out of the house, I got in the car and headed for Fordley. I wanted to be in the incident room with Callum when I presented my theory. Convinced now that I could prove it was more than conjecture.

In my file on the passenger seat I had printouts of the background information, on our 'persons of interest'. Information that proved someone had lied to me, about something seemingly insignificant.

Why would they do that? Unless it wasn't inconsequential at all.

Unless it was the key to everything.

My mind had been processing the kaleidoscope of information. Like shards of coloured glass that seemed to create meaningless patterns – until that last piece of the puzzle made them all fall into place.

It was no coincidence that the police had been faced with another staged crime scene when Brian Curtis and Stephanie Parks had died.

I knew now – they'd been killed by the same person who murdered Steve Lowry, Peter Wearman and Andi Kilpin.

A callous killer who made murder look like an accident.

A shiver ran through me as I contemplated how long this predator could have continued to kill and get away with it if Elle hadn't followed her instincts.

She'd been right – and now I could prove it. But the clock was ticking and if I was right, we'd have to move fast, or other people would die.

* * *

As I reached the outskirts of Fordley, my phone rang. The caller ID was the last person I expected to hear from . . .

'Tess!'

I was so surprised; I stopped in the middle of the road.

'Jo . . .' Her voice caught in a sob. 'I'm so sorry . . .'

'Where are you?'

'I need to see you.'

'Just tell me where you are.'

There was a pause. She was struggling to speak.

The driver behind me leaned on his horn, getting me to move my car. I pulled in to the kerb, on double yellow lines, as traffic streamed passed.

'I know the police are looking for me.' Her voice shook so badly, she could barely speak.

'Don't worry about that now, Tess. We can sort it.'

'I can't live with this.' She was almost whispering. I had to strain to hear her over the traffic.

'With what?'

'I did it . . . I killed Pat – on the boat . . .'

'Oh Tess—'

'It was an accident,' she said quickly, her words tumbling. 'I never meant it to happen – it just got out of hand. You have to believe me, Jo . . . you of all people. I need you to believe me.'

There was something in her tone, that jarred.

Tension – yes. But different, than I would expect in a conversation like this.

I closed my eyes, to concentrate on the verbal clues – the only ones I had to go on.

'How?' I asked, keeping my tone measured – non-judgemental. 'What happened on the boat?'

Another pause. It dragged on that long I thought she'd hung up. Just as I was about to speak she broke the silence. 'I . . . I'll tell you everything. But not over the phone.'

There it was again. That quality to her voice that was sending me flashing red lights.

If I hadn't recognised the voice of my friend I would have doubted this could be her speaking. But I knew with a sickening dread that it was.

'This isn't like you, Tess,' I said.

'I don't know what else to do, Jo.' More monotone now – flat. As if the emotion was simply draining out of her and she was running on autopilot.

'What do you mean?' An ice-cold vice gripped my stomach.

'You have to promise me, you won't bring the police with you . . .'

'OK,' I said, not exactly promising anything.

'Don't call them . . . or Callum . . . please, Jo.' The pain was back in her voice. Raw . . . visceral. A terror I could hear. 'I need a chance to talk to you. Just us . . . so I can explain everything.'

'And then you'll let me help you?'

'I need . . . I can't . . .'

'Talk to me, Tess.' I could sense where this was going and it filled me with horror.

'I can't go to prison, Jo . . . I can't.'

'However bad you think this is now . . . there's always something we can do.'

A wave of déjà vu washed over me. Uttering these same reassurances to another desperate woman, just a few short weeks ago.

'If you tell anyone . . . call the police . . . I'll do it, I swear.'

I took a ragged breath, eyes still closed – nipping the bridge of my nose as I fought the urge to scream 'NO!'.

'What are you thinking of doing, Tess ... talk to me ... please?'

'I can't go to prison ...' She said again, as if that explained everything.

In a way, I knew that it did.

I understood her fear and her pain. The hopelessness she felt right at this moment.

'You said it wasn't intended,' I said gently. 'At the boat ... Pat's death was an accident. So, you won't go to prison, Tess. I can help you. We can work through this together. There's always hope. Please don't give up, Tess.'

'Promise me,' she said quietly. 'That you won't call anyone ... that you'll let us talk, just the two of us.'

'I promise ... tell me where you are.'

'The DAAT,' she said, before abruptly ending the call.

Chapter Seventy-One

Fordley – Saturday

As soon as I finished the call with Tess I pulled back out into the traffic and broke every speed limit on the way into Fordley.

On the way, I kept glancing at my phone, desperate to call Callum. But I'd made a promise to a friend that I wouldn't.

If Tess was as despairing as she sounded, breaking that promise might be the final straw. A betrayal of trust at a time when those things could mean the difference between life and death.

The first thing I saw as I drove into the car park of the DAAT was Rina's motorbike, standing alone at the far end.

She should have left hours ago.

This wasn't good.

I pulled up next to her bike and sat, for just a moment, scanning my surroundings. My mind running through all the possible reasons Rina would still be here.

My instincts were screaming that this scenario wasn't all it appeared to be.

There was no doubting the genuine fear and desperation in Tess's voice and I couldn't dismiss that without risking her life.

Her call had brought me to the edge of town, in an area that quickly became deserted by early evening. No shops or cafés around here. No trendy wine bars. Just old mills and warehouses. Some converted into offices that lay silent at the weekend. Others boarded up – giving the place a depressing, desolate feel.

As if to match the occasion, the sky had begun to dim, bruise-black clouds gathering overhead, turning the early evening darker than usual.

I glanced at the file on the seat next to me. The one that held my notes – explaining everything I'd discovered. The file I'd been going to deliver to the enquiry team before Tess's call had diverted me here.

Notes that now included the identity of our serial murderer.

A prickle of apprehension trickled down my spine. I took a breath and thought about what was in that file. The revelations I'd been about to make.

Information that changed everything.

If Tess was as desolate as I believed her to be, I had to go to her. But if I was right about the other players in this deadly game, I could be walking into something far more dangerous.

I locked my car and walked to the DAAT as the first splashes of rain plopped heavily onto the dusty surface of the car park.

The heavy doors were unlocked. I pushed them open and walked into reception.

The building was eerily silent,

It was dark – the only light coming from the corridor that led to the offices.

I stood – allowing my eyes to adjust for a second.

'Tess,' I called out. My voice sounded shockingly loud in the silence that followed.

No reply.

'Rina.'

Nothing.

I went to the corridor and stopped to listen. The only sound, a distant rumble of thunder.

Pat Rodgers's office was the first door on the left. The door was ajar. I pushed it open with my foot.

A desk lamp cast a golden pool of light over scattered files and paperwork. The computer screen was still on – the screensaver scrolling the DAAT logo on an annoying loop.

I went in and touched the mouse, causing the screen to jump into life. It looked as though Rina had simply got up and walked away, the files and notes just where she left them.

I slowly went down the corridor, checking the therapy rooms and offices, hoping to find Rina or Tess.

Every door presenting the tantalising possibility they would be sitting there – chatting and drinking tea – safe and well. But I was left disappointed.

Back in the reception area, I could see something dark on the carpet at the foot of the stairs. I walked over and crouched down to get a better look.

The stain glinted in the light from the landing window. I touched it – then looked at my finger – stained red with fresh blood.

There were more splashes further up the stairs and some on the banister.

Avoiding the handrail, I went up, the sound of my shoes ringing in the echoing stairwell. When I reached the first landing, I flicked on the lights.

The landing overlooked a small, secure courtyard at the rear of the building. Hemmed in by high walls and protected by a metal gate, it was only visible from this vantage point.

I glanced down as I passed the window, then stopped.

Used for deliveries and storing the bins, there was ordinarily nothing of interest down there.

I stared at the roof of a grey Transit van parked in the courtyard. The same colour and make as Ted Cornell's vehicle.

I paused, with my foot on the step, staring at the Transit as if it was about to give me all the answers.

That's why the police hadn't picked it up on any cameras. It's been hidden here.

Ted Cornell.

My eyes followed the stairs to the top. There were more, smaller, droplets of blood all the way to the steel door that led onto the roof.

Slowly I climbed the last flight, then paused, with my hand on the fire door push-bar.

If my suspicions were right, when I went out on to that roof, everything was going to change. Maybe forever.

Taking a long breath, I braced myself and pushed open the door.

Chapter Seventy-Two

Light from the stairwell spilled across the gravel on the roof. I stood in the doorway, feeling the weight of the steel door against my shoulder.

Ahead of me and to my right, a hunched figure was sitting on the parapet wall. Just on the periphery of the runway of light . . . too far for me to make out who it was.

Ironically, the same spot Pip had chosen – not too many weeks ago.

The sky overhead, was solid black, fading to silver as it touched the glowing skyline, illumination from high-rise buildings in the city piercing the darkness like fairy lights.

The heavy door creaked in protest as I pushed it as far as it would go – making sure it wouldn't slam shut and plunge us into blackness.

The gravel crunched as I took my first, tentative steps towards the figure on the ledge.

I could see now it was a woman. Head down, staring into the void beneath her feet.

'Tess?' I spoke quietly.

The figure didn't move. Head still down, but as I got nearer, I could see the slight shaking of her shoulders. Silent sobs, wracking her ridged body.

'Tess,' I said again – certain now that it *was* her. 'Look at me.' My tone was gentle.

Slowly, she turned her face towards me. Her nose was bloody . . . explaining the drips on the stairs.

Her tear-streaked cheeks, sunken since I'd last seen her. Eyes hollowed out with exhaustion and something else – fear.

She didn't speak – just stared, as though she was seeing me for the first time.

Shrinking inside herself – as if something was dying, leaving only an empty shell.

I'd seen this look before. The emotional pallor of the hopeless whose pain and fear were too overwhelming to contain. Someone who knew, with dreadful certainty, that their life was over.

And I knew why.

'I'm not going any closer to her.' I raised my voice – beyond Tess – into the shadows. 'I won't let this play out the way you want, so, you're going to have to come out and face me.'

Chapter Seventy-Three

'Don't, Jo.' Tess's voice was ragged. 'He'll shoot us both.'

I held her gaze with my own – injecting as much quiet reassurance into the look as I could.

'No, he won't.' My voice sounded surprisingly calm. 'Because, if he did, it wouldn't look like suicide, or an accident . . . would it, Luke?'

The air seemed to shift behind me – raising the hairs along the back of my neck.

I knew, even before I turned to face him – what I was going to see.

The priest, stepped into the arena of light. His walking cane, like a British Army drill instructor's pace-stick, tucked under his left arm. In his right hand, he held a pistol.

His eyes followed mine to the blood on the heavy silver handle of the cane.

'I didn't want to hurt her,' he said it matter-of-factly.

'Rina?' Panic gripped me by the throat, as images of what he might have done to her spooled through my head.

'She's been safely taken care of.'

The volatile alchemy of ice-cold fear and white-hot fury, made me take an unthinking step towards him. Quickly halted as he jerked the pistol in my direction.

'Don't,' he said.

'What have you done to her?' I forced the words out – though I couldn't bear to hear the answer.

'That's of no concern now.' He wasn't answering the question. 'The blood isn't Rina's.' He indicated Tess and her damaged nose. 'She refused to make that call to you. I needed to exert some pressure.'

'Is that what you used to hit Brian Curtis on the temple?' I asked – willing my pulse rate to descend, so I could think. 'Rendering him unconscious before putting his own gun in his hand and shooting him in the head?'

He stayed silent – probably calculating just how much I'd worked out.

I didn't want to listen to denials; we'd all come too far for that, so I gestured to the gun in his hand.

'A 9mm Baikal. Twin to the one Brian Curtis always carried. The one you stole from his flat after you killed him and Stephanie Parks.'

'I was afraid you'd work it out.'

'Did you know she was pregnant?'

His eyes widened in genuine surprise. 'No . . . I . . . I'm sorry.'

'Sorry? For who? Stephanie? Her unborn baby . . . an innocent child? There aren't enough apologies in the world to cover that.'

He remained expressionless – his voice unnervingly calm. 'Sometimes, the innocent have to be sacrificed to punish the guilty.'

'I've heard the skewed logic of some twisted bastards in my time,' I said through clenched teeth, still thinking about Rina, 'but you're one of the coldest.'

'When I saw you talking to Pip and Mrs Cantor's daughter, Jean, at the flats, I knew it wouldn't be long before you made the connection to Curtis.' He waved the gun to indicate our surroundings. 'That's, unfortunately, why we're here.'

The stairwell door rattling, when no one appeared . . .

'It took me a while to realise what I'd heard that day . . . in the stairwell.' I nodded to the cane under his arm. 'The tapping of that stick. The one you use for effect . . . you don't really need it that badly, do you? But it adds to the image of the anodyne priest, the avuncular Good Samaritan, doesn't it, Luke?'

'*Father* Luke,' he corrected me.

'I think you forfeit any right to a religious title when you start killing . . . don't you?'

He glanced at the stick under his arm, as if it offended him.

'Was that it?' he sounded surprised. 'The sound of my stick. That's what gave away the fact that I'd killed Curtis?'

'Not entirely,' I admitted. 'But speaking with Jean. The crucifix and religious pictures in the box . . . Catholic items.'

I thought about the file in my car. Glad that, whatever happened here, it would be found and the police would know the sequence of events.

'On the night Jean thought her mother was dying,' I said. 'The same night Brian Curtis and his girlfriend were murdered . . . everyone rushed to Mrs Cantor's bedside and Jean said she made sure "*everything was done as her mother would wish*".' I matched his half-smile . . . it didn't reach my eyes either. 'It didn't occur to me until later, what she meant by that. Until I thought about the fact that they were a Catholic family. Then it made sense.'

An image of my mother – an Italian Catholic – making me promise that when her time came – I'd make sure 'everything was done properly'. Even though she only attended church on high days and holidays.

'It was the last rites, wasn't it? You were there, along with Mrs Cantor's friends from church. A person no one thought to mention – the priest at his dying parishioner's bedside, administering the final sacrament.'

The grey man – like a waiter in a restaurant. There to serve, but unremarkable and almost unnoticed in the bigger drama of death and doctors and paramedics. Especially as he'd probably been a regular visitor during the old lady's illness.

My earlier call, before I left Kingsberry, to social services, was to get a message to Billy Wilson. To ask him directly whether he'd seen Father Bassett that fateful Thursday night.

The answer was yes. Along with the other 'God botherers' who'd been visiting Mrs Cantor.

'Easy for you, when everyone was leaving that night, to take the lift down two flights and knock on Curtis's door. He wouldn't have anything to fear from a priest. He'd let you in . . . turn his back on you as he went inside. What reason did you give for being there?'

He said nothing – so I pressed on.

'Pip?' A micro expression flitted across his face, for just a second, but enough for me to know I was right.

'You told Curtis you were there because you'd been in touch with her. He was desperate to know where she was. That would be enough for him to let you in.'

'But you,' his tone was ominously calm. 'How did *you* know I'd spoken to her?'

'She told me . . . up here on the roof.' I nodded to where Tess was sitting on the ledge. 'She'd gone to confession on her way here. Poured it all out to a priest – to save her soul, before she took her own life. I checked. Between her daughter's nursery and here. Only one Catholic church – St John the Evangelist – *your* church.'

He still said nothing, so I carried on, frantically trying to delay whatever he had in mind, until I could come up with something . . . anything.

'I checked the board when I went there last night. Monday morning is when you run the early confession. 7.30 to 8.30 a.m. That's when she told you about what Curtis had done to her. The confession of a desperate young girl. Not over the helpline, like all the others . . . but in the sanctity of your confessional.'

'You can't possibly understand,' he said, sharply.

'Oh, I think I do. You see, the roots of a person's behaviour are embedded in their background.'

'Rather a cliché, don't you think?' The tension in his body was almost palpable.

354

'It was the same with Jordan, wasn't—'

'He's never taken confession,' he cut across me.

'He had no connection to the helpline, but he confided in you, during his discussions about converting. About his uncle. The abuse he was suffering. He couldn't talk to his aunt, but he *could* confide in you . . . and maybe Ted Cornell too?' I looked around the roof, over Bassett's shoulder, suddenly remembering the van in the courtyard.

'Where *is* Cornell?'

The priest frowned – a genuine and spontaneous expression of confusion that was impossible to fake. 'Ted's not here.'

My turn to look confused.

He read my face and jumped ahead of me. 'Ahhh, the van. Yes, it belongs to Ted, but he lets me use it for the outreach. I collected it from him on Wednesday – then gave him a lift into Fordley last night, before he left with Marion.'

Left with Marion . . .

'You haven't got *all* the answers, have you, Doctor?'

'Where have they gone?'

He shrugged. 'He didn't say – just that he was taking her away, a break, after everything she's gone through.'

'Everything *you* put her through.' The way he could dissociate himself from the fallout of his killing was truly shocking.

'To free Jordan from a monster,' he shouted.

'Making a widow out of Marion Kilpin, robbing Leanne of a father!' I shouted back.

'Making sure the insurance company paid out,' he said simply. 'Setting Marion up to be financially secure and allowing her to be with someone she loves.' He slowly shook his head in a gesture of disappointment. 'Apart from meeting Marion and having an affair, Ted isn't involved in any of this . . . it's not his cause—'

'Cause?' I couldn't hide my incredulity. 'Is that how you see this?'

'Helping others is my purpose . . . to do good . . .'

'By *killing*?'

'The people I killed didn't deserve to live.'

'You're NOT God, Bassett.' I couldn't stomach using his first name anymore. 'You don't have the right to decide who lives and dies.'

'I made people's lives better!' His eyes flashed sparks of a manic anger, barely contained beneath the surface. 'Everyone I saved, who called the helpline in desperation.'

'Like Ainsley McKenzie?' I pressed. 'You read her therapy notes, didn't you? You were the one who answered Peter Wearman's call to the helpline that night – that's why it was never logged.'

'He'd pushed her to the depths of despair!' Bassett shouted, spittle flying from the corner of his mouth. 'If I hadn't intervened when I did, that man would have driven her to suicide.'

'You had no right!' I snapped back.

'No right?' Bassett spat the words. 'I saved her life!' His eyes flashed an anger he could no longer supress. 'That I should be the one to pick up the phone that night, you can call it fate or serendipity . . . I call it God's hand.'

'Is that going to be your defence?' I gave a short laugh. 'That God told you to do it? You talk to *me* about clichés – that's the most overused of them all.'

'He was delivered into my hands, the night he rang.'

'What did you say, when you picked up his call? Tell him you were Ainsley's therapist?'

'We arranged to meet.' He didn't even try to deny it. 'I followed him when he left the nightclub. He went down the alley to relieve himself . . .'

'And you decided that's where he should die?'

'Easy to incapacitate someone with that much alcohol in them.' There was almost a note of pride in his voice. 'Then a syringe in his arm and he's just another junkie in an alley. Almost poetic, when appearance and status were everything to a man like him.'

And then it made sense – one question that had bothered me.

'Is that why you chose to stage Andi Kilpin's death in the way you did? To humiliate him?'

'To show the world what he really was,' he sneered. 'Expose him . . . literally.'

It would have been easy to gain entry into Kilpin's house. With Marion's connections to the church. Andi Kilpin would think nothing of a priest coming to the door.

That same priest was staring at me intently, like a snake eyeing up a field mouse.

'Then the drugs, like GHB,' I said. 'Drugs you can easily get hold of from the client base you work with – addicts, the homeless?'

'I made a difference!' He spat the words like broken glass. 'Solved people's problems, when they were truly desperate. I saved their lives by taking the lives of their tormentors. No amount of therapy could do that.'

'And there it is.' There was no triumph in my voice. 'That "saviour complex". The pathological altruism that tips the need to help others into something darker . . . or in your case, something deadly.'

'No!' he shouted.

'Or would you prefer a different psychological term for the way you're wired, Bassett? "White Knight Syndrome" – does that sound more palatable?'

He was silently shaking his head – trying to deny, inside himself, the things I was saying.

I was on a roll – ever mindful that while he was focused on me, he wasn't watching Tess.

'Vulnerability attracts people like you. That compulsive need to "save" others. The thing that drove you to work for the VSO,

357

then enter the priesthood when a bullet wound ended your military career.'

Whatever he'd expected me to say, it hadn't been that. It had thrown him off his stride – which was exactly what I wanted to do.

Something flickered behind his eyes, like an emotional flinch, and I knew I'd hit the sensitive bullseye I'd been looking for.

'It didn't take much to track your record.' I pressed the advantage. 'I've got contacts in the military – people who can access your records. You *did* work for the VSO – but there was no accident. I had to ask myself why you would lie about something like that? So, I did more digging. You left the VSO to join the Royal Army Medical Corp as a combat medic.'

'A past life.' He waved his hand dismissively – but he was rattled.

'One you didn't want people to know about . . . because they might make the connection between your medical and military training and the knowledge our killer had.'

While he processed what I'd said I took the chance to shift another step to the right, then half-turned, so I could see them both. Tess on my right. Bassett on my left.

'That day, in Helmand Province,' I kept talking, in an effort to distract him from Tess. 'You were shot in the leg because you were reckless. You were ordered out – but you stayed . . . longer than you should.'

'No.' The word – almost whispered.

I watched his eyes – knowing he was reliving that moment – a moment that changed his life forever.

'Driven by that same compulsive, masochistic need to over-extend yourself.'

He'd heard enough. Snapping out of it – coming back to the task at hand.

'You're wasting time.' Gone was the tone of the amiable priest. He waved the pistol, indicating I should move aside.

I slowly shook my head. 'Come off the ledge,' I urged Tess.

He stepped to one side, to have her in his sight again. 'Stay put!' he barked, making her jump.

'Come away from the edge,' I said again – more firmly this time.

Her frightened eyes darted between Bassett and me. Like a rabbit caught in the headlights. Frozen by fear and indecision.

'I . . . I can't.'

'We were both supposed to go over that ledge tonight, weren't we?' I directed myself to Bassett. 'A tragedy . . . while I was trying to talk my suicidal friend down. Did you tell her to take me down with her?' I glanced at Tess. 'He got you to write a note, didn't he, confessing to the murder of Pat Rodgers?'

She gave a slight nod, her eyes fixed on the priest.

'Where is it?'

She reached inside her jacket pocket and pulled out a crumpled envelope, then lowered her head, sobbing quietly.

'Why her, Bassett?' I asked through barely gritted teeth. 'Surely not just to get me up here?'

Although, as ploys went – I had to admit, it worked.

'She saw me,' he said simply. 'On the canal towpath.'

I hazarded a not-so-wild-guess. 'After you killed Pat Rodgers and blew up the boat?'

'Oh God,' Tess wailed, softly.

Bassett made a move towards her, but I stepped between them again.

'You had nothing to do with Pat's death – did you, Tess?'

'I'd gone to see Pat about the videos she had,' Tess was babbling. 'The boat blew up before I reached it. I was running towards it when I saw Father Luke.'

I rounded on him. 'And you couldn't let her go after that, could you?'

The Transit van the police identified by the canal.

'You'd borrowed Ted Cornell's van, to go there?'

He didn't reply.

Tess wiped her sleeve across her bloodied nose. 'He . . . he threw me in the van. Kept me in the basement under the vestry at the church . . . until today.'

I thought about my visit to St John's – the night I'd seen Jordan. Chilled to think that she had been there all along.

'Why didn't you kill Tess, then?' I asked him, knowing the question was brutal but needing to know.

'It has to look like an accident,' he replied, as if we were talking about the weather.

'Of course it does.' I couldn't hide my contempt. 'No one looks too deeply when it's an accident, or suicide, do they?

The invisible dead.

'The police delivered it to you on a plate when they issued statements saying they were looking for Tess in connection with the explosion on the boat. The idea of her taking her own life would be so plausible. Poor girl, wracked with guilt. So, you held on to her until today, when you knew this place would be deserted. Tess has the keys . . . and you could get rid of the one witness who'd realised *you* were the killer.'

'I did it for *her*.' Bassett jerked the gun towards Tess. 'She talked to me about Rodgers. About what that woman was doing to her . . . blackmailing her. The woman was evil.'

It never ceased to amaze me how people like Bassett, only saw evil in others . . . never in themselves.

'Why him, Tess – why did you tell him of all people?'

'I made referrals to him for the community bank. We spoke all the time on the phone,' she said, wearily. 'I needed to talk to someone . . . safe.' She gave a humourless laugh at the irony. 'Someone not connected to the DAAT. I couldn't tell Doug – or you. He's a priest . . .' Her words caught in a choking sob.

'If she hadn't been on the towpath . . .' he said. 'Hadn't seen me that night – she would have been all right.'

'She doesn't deserve this, Bassett.'

I could see in his eyes; it was a hopeless plea. 'She knows. Like you.' He shrugged.

A crackle of lightning, forked across the sky, feeling unnervingly close to the roof – though it probably wasn't.

Tess's nerves were stretched so tight she yelped as a clap of thunder followed.

'Tess, for Christ's sake, get off the edge!' I shouted.

She stared at me – her tear-stained cheeks tight with fear, but she still couldn't move.

Bassett took another step closer to Tess – his right arm raised as he levelled the gun.

'Enough talking.' His voice was flat – unemotional – and I knew we were fast approaching the end of the game.

Tess was spent. Emotionally and spiritually broken, too terrified to move away from the edge and I was too far away to reach her.

I knew, in that moment, if Bassett commanded her to jump, she would.

More terrifyingly, I could see he knew it too.

'Then what?' I asked, frantically playing for time.

My words held him, for just a second, as he was about to go towards Tess.

He looked at me, as though seeing me for the first time. Knowing exactly what I meant.

Tess wasn't going to present him with any challenge.

'And then . . . you,' he replied.

Tess sobbed, looking from me to the priest. Thankfully, not understanding this coded communication. Not realising he was talking about the order in which he intended us to die.

My brain scrambled for something – anything – that would delay him. Give us a few more seconds. Prolong what looked to be inevitable.

361

'You think I'll just step onto the ledge for you?' My voice sounded remarkably calm.

'Encouraged by this.' He looked pointedly at the gun in his steady right hand. 'Most people will do as they're told . . . just to get a few more precious moments of life.'

'I'm not most people,' I said, the fury I'd held back until now breaking the surface.

'And she *never* does as she's told!' an unexpected voice said, from the darkness to my right, making us both turn.

Chapter Seventy-Four

We both froze – listening to the gravel crunching underfoot as whoever was there walked slowly towards us.

'Callum . . .' I breathed, as he stepped into the shaft of light from the open door.

His eyes were fixed on the priest. 'It's over, Bassett.' He continued to walk slowly towards us, his right hand held out towards the gun. 'If this was to get rid of witnesses, so you can carry on killing – it's pointless now.'

The priest kept the gun raised, but his arm swung away from Tess – towards Callum. 'Stop,' was all he said.

'OK.' Callum stayed where he was – just a few feet to my right, closer to Tess than I was.

I looked beyond him, wondering how he'd got on to the roof without using the stairs. Realising there must be a fire escape from the courtyard at the back of the building.

'I'm DCI Callum Ferguson . . .'

'I know who you are.' Bassett seemed unphased, though I knew his mind would be working overtime – computing his options.

'It's over,' Callum repeated. 'I didn't come here alone. I've got officers in the building. There's nowhere to go.'

Bassett side-stepped, like a crab, towards the parapet on his left – never taking his eyes off Callum. Quickly, he risked a glance over the edge into the quiet streets below.

'You're lying.' He looked back. 'There are no police vehicles down there.'

Callum gave a half-smile. 'No blues and twos in a situation like this . . . didn't want to risk alerting you.' He glanced at Tess's back. 'Or scare anyone into doing anything dangerous.'

He took a few steps closer to Tess, ignoring the jerk of the pistol in Bassett's hand. 'Let Tess go, Luke,' he said calmly. 'There's no point in hurting her now, is there?'

'He's right,' I said quietly, trying to gauge how many steps I was away from Bassett. 'This was all because she saw you. The police know – what's the use of hurting her?'

Bassett's arm moved imperceptibly towards me, then back to Callum as he took another step towards Tess.

Callum was only an arm's length from her now. 'Tess,' he said, gently. 'Reach out your arm to me . . . please.'

All of my attention was on Bassett. His arm . . . his hand. The finger inside the trigger guard of the pistol. Calibrating every nuance of his body language.

I had to do whatever I could to distract him from Tess and Callum.

'Luke.' I reverted to his first name – trying to inject as much calmness into my voice as I could. 'He's right. You can let Tess go. Hurting her won't change anything now.'

His arm seemed to waver, just a fraction. 'It might.'

'How?' My eyes still fixed on the gun, which had moved to point directly at Callum's chest as he leaned nearer to Tess – still holding his hand out to take hers.

'I think you're lying, Ferguson,' he said. 'You're alone.'

Callum was within touching distance of Tess. I held my breath, as she half turned her body – reaching a hand back towards him.

'Let him help her, Luke,' I pleaded softly. 'What she saw – what she knows, doesn't matter now.'

'It's not about witnesses now,' Bassett said, to no one in particular. 'It's about not going to prison.'

Callum took his eyes from Tess, for just an instant – sending me a look, with an almost imperceptible shake of his head.

He knew what I was thinking, even before I'd decided myself. But I couldn't let it make a difference.

'I know,' I said. 'But you still have me.' Callum froze – staring at me as if, by force of will, he could erase my words. 'Let him help Tess . . . please.'

I exhaled a slow breath, as the priest slowly nodded. 'I never wanted to hurt her in the first place,' he said it almost reluctantly.

Tess leaned back as Callum clasped her hand. She half slid, half fell off the ledge onto the flat surface of the roof.

She began to cry, softly, as Callum helped her to her feet and began walking her to the door with his arm around her shoulders.

Bassett jerked the pistol towards him. 'Just her,' he snapped. 'She can leave on her own – you stay.'

Bassett waved towards the door, sending Tess stumbling towards it, a hand clasped over her mouth as she tried to stifle her sobs.

Then he turned the gun towards Callum – just a few feet in front of him. Bassett was against the parapet. He risked another quick glance over, then smiled at Callum.

'There's no cavalry in sight, Chief Inspector.' He made an exaggerated show of peering around at the darkened rooftops. 'No police marksmen . . . no heavy boots rushing up the stairs. Just you to arrest me.'

'We know everything.' Callum sounded calmer than he had any right to. 'Even if you don't surrender to me – your identity is circulating as wanted.'

Bassett's short laugh was humourless. 'Surrender? No . . . I don't think so. I have no intention of going to prison.'

'There's nowhere to go. Ports, airports, are all being watched.'

'Right now, I don't have to worry about leaving the country – just leaving here.'

Bassett was pointing the gun squarely at Callum's chest. The muscles in his extended arm and shoulder tensed and I watched, in horror, as his trigger finger began to pale as he applied pressure.

Whether Callum saw anything to alert him, I'd never know, but he began to move at the same moment I rushed at Bassett.

My outstretched hands knocked the priest's arm, just as the ear-splitting sound of a gunshot ricocheted from the walls.

To my right, Callum fell. His scream of agony combining with the gunshot into a sickening cacophony that echoed in my skull, blotting out everything else.

'No!' I screamed, throwing my full weight against Bassett, holding on to his right arm with both hands.

I was dimly aware of his left hip hitting the edge of the parapet with a sickening crack. His left hand reached for me as he began to topple sideways.

He dropped the gun – both hands, grasping fresh air – until his right hand tangled in my hair.

He pulled, desperate to retain his balance, but my own momentum added to his and we began to fall.

I tried to jerk my head back but his grasp was too strong. Literally holding on for his life.

As he went over the edge, his face was inches from my own. He tightened his grip on me, deliberately pulling me over with him. He pushed away from the wall with both feet, intent on taking me with him. Purposefully propelling us away from the building into terrifying nothingness and in that last, desperate, second – he smiled at me.

I grabbed for the edge of the parapet, feeling my fingernails tear uselessly on the rough stone as I left it behind.

The only thing my hands found to hold onto – the shoulders of the man dragging me into the hollow abyss.

I dug my fingers into the fabric of his jacket with the insane thought that somehow it would stop our descent – but nothing could.

Bassett let me go – flinging his arms wide. Falling below me.

His eyes, piercing points of light, locked on to mine as he disappeared into the vastness below us.

My body – weightless – twisting in the dark, until I'm looking back up at the roof.

My brain, racing in its final thoughts, made time slow to a crawl.

I'm dying.

Oh God – this is how it's going to end.

The wind whips long hair around my face as I fall backwards. Fatal gravity pulling me down.

Alex – my son. I'm so sorry.

Why did I do it?

I know why, as I look at the shocked face staring over the edge of the roof. Callum – his expression one of utter horror. Watching me fall. Helpless to stop it. Mouth open, screaming last words I can't hear through the wind whistling past my ears. The thundering of my heartbeat.

I see him reaching out towards me. Futile now as I'm dropping fast.

At least he's alive – thank God, he's alive.

I did it for him.

So much to say.

Too late now.

I brace myself for the ground.

The last time I'll touch the earth.

Chapter Seventy-Five

Fordley Royal Infirmary

Everything was all consuming pain. Crawling through a nightmare of disjointed sights and sounds. Until, eventually – slowly – a semblance of reality returned.

Bright light at first felt like needles in my eyeballs and they'd kept the blinds down. But today the morning sun was streaming into my room.

Still feeling like needles – but blunter ones.

'Linear skull fracture.' Elle was saying, as she popped another grape into her mouth. 'No surgery needed. You were lucky.'

'Remind me to buy a lottery ticket,' I smiled, but even that hurt.

'If it hadn't been for that window cleaner's cradle,' Elle reminded me, 'you'd be suffering more than multiple fractures, sweet pea.'

Apparently, after we'd fallen, I'd been 'lucky' enough to land on the broken cradle, three floors below, while Bassett had gone the full distance – cracking the concrete car park with *his* skull.

'He was so desperate to kill me,' I said, to no one in particular. 'He killed himself instead.'

Elle frowned. 'How do you make that out?'

I tried to shrug, but my body reminded me that movement had consequences. 'I only hit that cradle because he pushed us out ... further away from the building. If he hadn't, he might have been the one to land on it instead.'

'The evil bastard did us all a favour then,' Rina said.

Thankfully, I didn't remember anything after hitting the solid surface – but I'd been told by Rina that half of Fordley centre had been closed off as the fire brigade extracted me from my precarious position.

Over the next two days, as I lay oblivious, my mother and Jen had taken it in turns to sit by my bedside, only leaving the previous day to get some much-needed rest when I'd finally regained consciousness.

I looked at my surgically repaired left wrist, held together with pins and in a plaster cast, along with my broken right ankle.

Elle was right. I had been lucky.

Rina leaned over me, her cool fingers gently touching the bruises on my face. Yellow and black skin, stark against the white bandage on my head.

'I'll ask the nurse for something for your poor torn lip,' she said gently. 'It splits every time you smile.'

I stroked her face with my uninjured right hand. 'God, I'm so glad you're OK.' Just saying those words overwhelmed me – hot tears spilled down my cheeks.

My emotions were so raw lately, I seemed to cry at anything and everything.

Rina wiped the tears away with her thumb, then held my hand in both hers.

'I feel like a proper fraud,' she smiled. 'Getting locked in the basement at the DAAT while all hell broke loose on the roof.'

Rina had been in the archives when Bassett had arrived with Tess. Expecting the building to be empty, he'd realised someone was there when the door was unlocked and the office light was on.

'Didn't even know I'd been locked in until I tried to leave.' Rina carried on.

'With no signal down there,' Elle said. 'I was going out of my mind – not able to get hold of you.'

'If Bassett's plan had worked,' I said wearily, 'he would have left after dispatching me and Tess from the roof and you'd have been found in the basement by first responders. They'd probably assume Tess locked you in.'

'Never thought I'd say it,' Elle popped another grape, 'but thank God for the Boy Scout.'

'You know he slept in that chair next to your bed, when you were first brought in here?' Rina sounded impressed. 'Wouldn't leave until he knew you were out of the woods.'

'Your mum and Jen kept telling him to go home,' Elle added. 'But he refused to budge.'

I felt those embarrassing unbidden tears again.

'When the gun went off and I saw him go down, I thought he was dead,' I murmured.

My mind automatically replayed the images that had haunted my nightmares ever since.

'I don't kill that easily.' A low voice from the doorway made us all turn, to see Callum, leaning against the wall. 'Bit like you,' he grinned.

I drank in the sight of him. Something I never thought I'd see again.

'Hi,' was all I could manage to say.

'Good job you landed on your head,' he was saying. 'Otherwise, it could have been serious.'

I pulled a face – which hurt my lip again.

'Right.' Elle sprang up from the chair beside my bed. 'Time we were off.' She leaned over and kissed my cheek. 'Come on, you.' She nudged Rina. 'You're making dinner tonight, remember?'

'Oh, yeah . . .' Rina hastily grabbed her backpack to follow her girlfriend, stopping at the door when she reached Callum. 'If you upset her,' she said, flashing him her sweetest smile, 'I'll rip your head off and crap in the hole.'

'Now there's an image,' he grinned down at her.

'Don't you forget it, Boy Scout,' she called as she went down the corridor.

In the silence that followed, Callum stayed where he was, watching me from the doorway.

'Hey,' he said finally.

'Not coming in?'

He glanced after my friends. 'Do you think it's safe? Wouldn't want to upset your protector.'

'You'll be OK. As long as you don't upset me.'

He came to sit in the chair Elle had vacated.

'Doesn't look very comfortable,' I remarked.

'What?'

'For sleeping. Heard you stayed there a couple of nights.'

'Couldn't leave you on your own, could I? Look what happened last time.'

I gave a tired smile. 'How's the arm?'

He carefully shrugged off his jacket, revealing a heavily bandaged left bicep. 'Thanks to you the bullet just grazed it.'

I held on to those penetrating blue eyes with my own. 'When the gun went off, I thought . . .' My voice cracked, the words sticking in my throat.

His warm hand covered mine. 'Shhh. It's OK . . . I know what you thought.'

His smile was as weary as mine. Both of us running on emotional empty. Both strung out on overdoses of adrenalin and stress.

He looked down, studying the floor. Speaking so quietly I had to strain to hear him. 'Same thing I thought, when Bassett took you over the edge.'

When he looked back at me – his eyes were moist. 'Christ, Jo . . .'

For a moment, neither of us could speak. Both thinking the same thing. Both still in shock over the odds we'd beaten that night.

My whole body ached and I knew, without looking at the clock, that I was due more pain relief. The heaviness of a fatigue

I'd learned not to fight was overtaking me – but there were still things I needed to ask.

'How did you know where to find us?'

'Tess's phone. We'd been monitoring it since it'd been switched off, after the explosion on the boat. When it came back on – when she made that call to you – Charlie pinged the location.' He smiled. 'I've asked for him to be permanently attached to the team.'

'Why?' I raised an eyebrow. 'Because he helped save his elderly aunt.'

'Don't flatter yourself.' Though he couldn't supress a smile. 'Because he's good at what he does . . . besides, I think he sees you more as a big sister.'

'I'll take that.'

'As soon as I knew where Tess was and that she'd called you. I wanted to get down there.' His fingers gingerly touched the bandage on my forehead. 'She was a suspect in Rodgers's murder, but I knew you'd go to her if that's what her call was about. Like I say . . . can't leave you on your own for a minute without you getting yourself in trouble.'

I took a slow, shallow breath, wincing at the sharp pain under my ribs. 'You shouldn't have come to the DAAT alone.'

His eyes held an intensity I hadn't seen before as he studied me for a moment. 'I called in the cavalry. I knew they'd be on their way – but I wasn't about to wait for response units to catch up. If I had – it would have been too late for Tess . . . and maybe you too.'

'Thank you,' I said quietly.

He stared at me for a moment, then drew a ragged breath, getting the topic back on less emotional ground. 'We found out more in this last week.'

'About?'

'Bassett – how he probably operated.'

'Like what?'

'The overnight shelter for the homeless – it's run by the church.'

'And?'

'Before rough sleepers can stay, they have to hand over any banned items. It's a house rule.'

'Drugs?'

He nodded. 'There's no judgement, and they get their things back when they leave, but they hand over paraphernalia ... drugs ... pornography. Anything the hostel deems inappropriate.'

'You think that's how Bassett got access to the heroin he used to kill Lowry and Wearman?' I guessed.

Callum nodded. 'And the GHB.' He rolled his shoulders to ease the knots. 'Staff at the hostel say that some residents are high when they check in and can't always remember how much stuff they handed over. It would be an easy matter to skim some stuff, here and there.'

'I'll bet that's where the old porn magazines came from that you found at Kilpin's scene,' I said, forcing my brain to crawl through the facts. I was feeling so bone-weary. Even talking was feeling like too much effort.

'We've interviewed Tess,' he was saying.

'How is she?'

'Shaken up.'

'I can imagine.'

'She was able to tell us everything that happened before I got up to the roof. Said you'd uncovered Bassett's backstory.'

I nodded and winced as the pain shot behind my eyes. 'He'd joined a seminary after university – wanted to be a priest from the beginning.'

Callum leaned back in the chair. 'We found that out – unfortunately he was dead by the time we started researching his background.'

'But they "persuaded" him, maybe the time wasn't right.' I quoted directly from the psychologist who had assessed all candidates prior to ordination. 'So, he left and joined the VSO. Was with them for a year and then went into the Army Medical Corp.'

'We've requested all his records,' Callum said. 'They haven't arrived yet.'

'Well, the psychologist from the seminary couldn't say too much – client confidentiality. But as a professional courtesy, he *did* tell me that they felt Bassett had certain psychological issues that needed to be resolved before they could accept him fully into the priesthood.'

'Which means what, exactly?'

I shrugged and winced again. 'Pretty much what I worked out. That he was driven to help others – to a degree that was pathological.'

'This "saviour complex"?'

'After he was invalided out of the army, he went back to the church,' I said. 'He'd learned how to mask it by then and after a military career like that . . . older, more mature – the hero wounded in action while helping other casualties. They welcomed him back with open arms. Probably believed his issues had been resolved to an acceptable level.'

'Acceptable to who?' Callum shuddered.

We were interrupted as a nurse came in with a small plastic cup containing two tablets. My pain relief.

When she left, Callum made a show of plumping up my pillows then settled back down in the chair.

'Was he a lunatic?' he asked finally.

'Bassett?' I shook my head. 'White knight syndrome . . . whatever – isn't listed as a mental illness. By definition, he wasn't insane.'

'If what he did wasn't insane . . . what the hell is?'

I smiled, wearily. 'Welcome to my world.'

'No thanks.'

We fell into a companionable silence for a few minutes. Callum broke it, bringing us back to business.

'Tess filled in a few gaps for us.'

'Oh?'

'Steve Lowry. His girlfriend, Vicky, was being treated for anxiety, through the helpline.'

I nodded, keeping my eyes closed. 'Tess referred her there.'

'Bassett knew about her case through the helpline – decided to make her anxiety go away . . . permanently. But Tess didn't know Bassett had killed Lowry – until we told her.'

'Poor Tess.' I couldn't imagine how she would be feeling – knowing that Bassett had killed Rodgers because of what she'd told him. And then to think he'd killed Lowry too.

'The team picked Ted Cornell and Marion Kilpin up at Manchester airport on Saturday night. While we were on our way to the hospital.'

'Are they involved . . . in any of it?' I asked as my brain began to slow to a crawl.'

'Not that we can see. No crime in taking a holiday.'

'So, Bassett was telling the truth? About them just getting away together?'

I felt him nod. 'Timing was shit, though. Making themselves look guilty, by disappearing.' He reached over and pinched a grape. 'That's what your attack was all about.'

'Attack?'

'In Little Italy,' he reminded me. 'Your first crack on the head.'

'Oh, yes.' Fatigue and strong painkillers were taking their toll.

'Young Patrick Swales told us everything once his duty solicitor arrived.'

'Which was what?'

'He knew about Ted Cornell's affair with Marion Kilpin. Ted confided in him that Marion had been questioned again by the police, because of you, over her husband's death and what

Andi Kilpin had been doing to young Jordan.' He slowly shook his head. 'Patrick thought he was being a hero – taking it upon himself to warn you away from the star-crossed lovers.'

'So, nothing to do with Bassett, or what was going on at the helpline?'

'Not as far as we can see – no one there knew what Bassett was doing.'

'Well, that's something I suppose.'

It was a relief to know Patrick wasn't involved with Bassett's 'cause'. That no one else had been tainted by his delusions.

As fatigue began to draw my eyes closed, I said as much to Callum.

I felt him take hold of my uninjured hand.

'Jen told me she's contacted Alex.' He was saying – but his voice was coming to me from the end of a long tunnel. 'He was abroad when she reached him. He should be here tonight.'

The sound of my son's name caused tears to well up behind my closed eyelids. I felt them spill from under my lashes.

'That's good. I need to see him.'

My words sounded thick with fatigue. The drugs were taking effect and my limbs felt leaden.

The sun, streaming through the window, felt warm against my skin. I turned my face towards it as I felt Callum lean over and kiss my forehead.

Finally, I gave myself up to sleep.

Acknowledgements

As always, my thanks go to everyone at RCW Literary Agency. In particular, my agent Jon Wood for all his support and much needed reassurances. He has far more faith in me than I have in myself.

Thanks also to the brilliant team at Zaffre, who have looked after me so well, especially my editor, Ben Willis. I'm so excited that Jo is continuing her story with Zaffre and I can't wait to see what the future holds for both of us.

Writing, itself, is a solitary process, but no book comes into the world without the help and support of a lot of other people. I'm eternally grateful for the help given to me by the experts I consult, in an attempt to get things right.

For this book, Lotte Stringer, founder and former CEO of a suicide prevention charity, was a priceless source of advice around the sensitive subject of suicide. Her experience, running the crisis helpline for those who find themselves in such desperate situations, was invaluable. She is one of those wonderful people, who gives selflessly to others, both in her work and her private life. I owe a debt of gratitude, for sharing her time and experiences with me.

Former Detective Superintendent Stu Spencer gives help and advice on the police procedural aspects of the book. Sometimes I have to forfeit accuracy for the sake of the story, so any errors in that regard are entirely mine.

My good friend and fellow author, Sharon Birch – known to many as Effie (another story) – generously shared her extensive knowledge and real-life experiences on safeguarding issues for this book. Thank you, my friend, the gin is on me.

My friends, Alex Royle and Ainsley McKenzie, I promised to put you in a book one day. Here it is – I hope you like the result.

There are a few people I share my words with, before I dare show them to the rest of the world. Sharon Beddoes, Alison Barnes, Katie Brayzier and Maria Sigley. Your kind and gentle feedback is very much appreciated.

I am eternally grateful to my family, who support me along the way. Especially my sons, Adam and Kyle, who are always on hand to help with the technical stuff and even, occasionally, contribute ideas for plot lines. Although some of their suggestions are far too dark – even for me.

Massive thanks must go to my best friend and long-suffering partner, Ian, who gives me time, space and endless cups of Yorkshire Tea, to fuel this crazy pursuit. Your love and encouragement are priceless. I simply couldn't achieve any of this without you.

Finally, some of the issues covered in this book are, unfortunately, a dark reality for many people.

If you, or anyone you know is struggling, please, break the silence. Talking about feelings can really help and there is always someone available to listen, twenty-four hours a day, seven days a week.

You are never alone. Whatever you're going through, there is someone to face it with you, without judgement or pressure. Pick up the phone and call your local services. Your GP can often help – or you can reach the Samaritans by calling 116 123 – FREE from any phone, anytime night or day.